The Prince's Ultimate Deception
by Emilie Rose

ᴆᴥᴈᴥᴆ

"I have been waiting for this."

Damon emphasised his words by running his hands up Madeline's arms. The heat of his palm warmed her skin. Electricity raced through her.

Judging from the quick flare of his nostrils, she wasn't the only one feeling the sparks.

He lowered his head and briefly sipped from her lips.

She didn't want to talk, didn't want to do anything to lessen the intoxicating effect of his lips and hands on her. She wound her arms around his neck and sifted his soft hair through her fingertips.

The waiting was over.

The Billionaire's Baby Negotiation
by Day Leclaire

ᘓᕲᎆᕲᘗ

To: Joc Arnaud
From: Rosalyn Oakley
Re: *Our* Potential Baby

Joc,

As you know, the results of my pregnancy test will appear shortly. You have your list of demands, should a pink line appear. I have mine:

1: The baby will be an Oakley and have *my* name. Oakleys have deep roots in these parts. Roots are important to *me*.

2: The baby will grow up on *my* ranch – which by the way, I will never sell to you! – not your gated palace.

3: You will not tell me what to do.

Sincerely,

Rosalyn OAKLEY

The Billionaire's
Baby Negotiation
DAY LECLAIRE

The Prince's
Ultimate Deception
EMILIE ROSE

MILLS & BOON®

Pure reading pleasure

*First published in Great Britain 2008
by Harlequin Mills & Boon Limited,
Eton House, 18-24 Paradise Road, Richmond, Surrey TW9 1SR*

The publisher acknowledges the copyright holders of the
individual works as follows:

The Billionaire's Baby Negotiation © Day Totton Smith 2007
The Prince's Ultimate Deception
© Emilie Rose Cunningham 2007

ISBN: 978 0 263 85904 1

51-0608

*Printed and bound in Spain
by Litografia Rosés S.A., Barcelona*

THE BILLIONAIRE'S
BABY NEGOTIATION

by
Day Leclaire

Dear Reader,

You met Joc Arnaud as a minor character in *The Prince's Mistress*, where he "negotiated" a marriage contract between his sister, Ana, and Prince Lander Montgomery. Lander warned Joc that the time would come when Joc would find himself in a similar situation. "Someday you'll find yourself boxed into a corner like this. Remember me when that happens, Arnaud. Remember, and know that you brought it on yourself when you forced this agreement on the one woman you should have protected, and the one man who will do whatever it takes to see that you pay for your arrogance."

Well, that time has come and Joc is thrust into the negotiation of his life.

I love stories that put characters into tight spots and force them to make tough decisions. It strips them down to the bare essence of who they are and what they want – and what lengths they'll go to obtain that ultimate desire. Stories like those make me wonder…what's most important in our lives? And what extremes will we go to gain what we want most?

For more information about my latest releases, please visit me at my website: www.dayleclaire.com. I love hearing from readers!

Best,

Day

DAY LECLAIRE

is a multi-award-winning author of nearly forty novels. Her passionate books offer a unique combination of humour, emotion and unforgettable characters, which have won Day tremendous worldwide popularity, as well as numerous publishing honours. She is a three-time winner of both the Colorado Award of Excellence and the Golden Quill Award. She's won *Romantic Times BOOKreviews* magazine's Career Achievement, and Love and Laughter Awards, a Holt Medallion, a Booksellers Best Award, and she has received an impressive ten nominations for the prestigious Romance Writers of America RITA® Award.

Day's romances touch the heart and make you care about her characters as much as she does. In Day's own words, "I adore writing romances and can't think of a better way to spend each day."

To Hazen F Totton. Thanks, Mom!
You're always there when I need you most.

One

Enough was enough! One way or another all this nonsense ended today.

Rosalyn Oakley approached the pair of gigantic double wooden doors leading to Joc Arnaud's inner sanctum and paused to gather her self-control. She wiped her damp palms on the seat of her jeans. *Steady*. She could do this. She just needed to remember how much was at stake. Security wouldn't have let her get this far if Arnaud hadn't approved it. A humorless smile touched her mouth. Maybe he was as curious to meet the one woman who refused to cave to his demands, as she was to meet the one man who never gave up.

The thought helped fortify her, and she thrust open the doors and stepped into Arnaud's conference room and into another world. An endless sweep of tinted glass surrounded her, offering a dazzling panoramic view of the city of Dallas. Heat and humidity shimmered on the far side of the windows, while inside all remained cool and quiet and rich.

Rich in possessions. Rich in design. Rich with people.

An inlaid conference table stretched before her, the strips of wood that made up the surface a kaleidoscope of type and color. The craftsman had employed every variety of wood imaginable from a deep masculine mahogany to the blush white of red oak to the plummy tones of cherry. She sensed a design present, but didn't have the opportunity to examine the table, not with the several dozen people seated around the circumference, their papers littering the surface.

At her advent, all eyes swiveled to clash with hers and she took a moment to sweep her gaze over each person in an attempt to identify which was Arnaud. For an instant she keyed in on the person seated at the head of the table before dismissing him. And then she noticed the man standing to one side of the room, leaning against a sideboard, steaming coffee cup in hand. She focused her attention on him.

Business Executive was written all over him, from the tips of his Gucci shoes to the black Armani suit stretched across impressive, broad shoulders. He topped her by a full nine or ten inches, every one of his sculpted inches packed with lean, solid muscle. She tilted her head back and peered out from beneath the brim of her Stetson. His height forced her to look a long way up to meet his gaze, and put her at an instant disadvantage.

Deep-set obsidian eyes stared at her from one of the

most striking faces she'd ever seen. Lean and golden, with high, sharp cheekbones, the blood of his Native American ancestors had left an indelible stamp on that impressive bone structure. His hair was black and longer than conventional, which surprised her considering this had to be Joc Arnaud—the top honcho.

He returned her look with an open once-over that felt less offensive than something more discreet. He lifted a sooty eyebrow. "Lost your way?"

"On the contrary. I just found it." She approached him. "Do you know who I am?"

"Rosalyn Oakley," he answered promptly. "Age, twenty-eight. Born April 5. One hundred eighteen pounds. Sole heir to Longhorn Ranch." A hard smile flitted across his mouth. "Which, I believe, is where I come in. You own the ranch. I want it."

His swift summation of the facts threw her off stride, no doubt the purpose of his little recital. She recovered with all due speed, getting straight to the point. "Your two henchmen just paid me a visit. I'm returning the favor." She spared a glance at the suits-and-ties grouped around the conference table, who were listening with avid curiosity. She jerked her head in their direction. "You want to do this in public? Or would you rather we settle our differences in private?"

Without taking his gaze from her, he issued a single word, "Out."

There was a dignified scramble after that, one that would have left Rosalyn laughing if the circumstances had been different. The instant the door closed behind the final underling, she squared off against him. She'd spent the entire trip into Dallas planning what she'd say and she gave him chapter and verse in a single, direct volley.

"You've approached me—or rather your employees have approached me—about selling my ranch to you. And I've been civil with them each time they've turned up on my doorstep. I've told them no as clearly and politely as I know how. But it's gotten to the point where I can't turn around without tripping over them. It's going to stop and you're going to make it stop."

To her dismay, the only change in his expression was a deepening intensity in the way he watched her, and a slight smile that added immense appeal to an all-too attractive face. The distraction cost her. It took her a split second to remember where she'd left off in her script and get back on point.

"Anyway," she continued doggedly, "I've come to tell you in person that I'm not selling, in the hopes that you'll finally get the message and leave me alone. I don't care what you do, I don't care how many thugs you send, I'm not leaving my land."

At the end of her recital, he returned his coffee cup to the sideboard and faced her. She could tell from his expression she wouldn't like his response. Before he could speak, a discreet buzz emanated from a nearby phone. With a brief apology, he took the call. "No interruptions," he said without preamble. He listened for an instant before grimacing, then glanced at Rosalyn and said, "This will only take a minute."

"Do you want me to wait outside?" She hated making the offer, but common courtesy had been bred into her bones.

He shook his head, before addressing the caller. "Hello, MacKenzie. What can I do for my least favorite sister?"

Rosalyn could hear the furious blast from clear across the room and winced. Someone wasn't happy.

"Sorry. Half sister. Is that better?" Apparently it wasn't, because the angry diatribe continued until he cut it off. "Unless I'm mistaken, you've called to ask me a favor. Instead of bringing up old history, I suggest you get to it."

He listened at length and Rosalyn shivered at the cold bitterness of his expression. Is that how he really felt toward his sister? She didn't understand it. So what if they were half siblings? Family was family was family. Something hideous must have happened between them to cause this serious a rift.

"I'm not selling it, MacKenzie, and that's final. Your mother sold the property to me, and if you're not happy with Meredith's decision, I suggest you take it up with her." A wintry smile swept across his face. "At least you and my brothers—excuse me, half brothers—can comfort yourselves knowing it's still in the family, even if it's the illegitimate branch."

With that he hung up. Though he appeared calm and collected on the surface, she observed a raw quality gnawing at the edges of his restraint, a ferocity struggling for expression. He focused his inky gaze on her and she met it head-on. Slowly the anger eased and when he spoke it was with impressive composure. "Why don't we start over and do this the right way?" He held out his hand. "Joc Arnaud."

She hesitated a brief second. Unable to help herself, she offered her hand in return. "Rosalyn Oakley."

He captured her in his grasp and suddenly the spacious conference room became a suffocating box. Everything about him overwhelmed her. His grip. The dichotomy of callused fingers and palm attached to the hand of a white-collar exec. His size. His innate power. Even the crisp, masculine scent that clung to him invaded her senses and threatened to rob her of her will.

It became hard to breathe, let alone think, especially when he stood so close. She shouldn't have this sort of physical reaction to a complete stranger, especially when that stranger was her worst nightmare. Unfortunately he'd just proven beyond all doubt that she had no control whatsoever over her visceral response to him. Maybe it would have been easier if he weren't so drop-dead gorgeous. And even though she'd handled gorgeous on occasion in the past, one small problem tripped her up when it came to this man.

The face.

This particular face was organized into a masculine toughness, the sort that had most men maintaining a wary distance while women stumbled over themselves to get closer. It also happened to be the most attractive— not to mention dangerous—of all the faces she'd ever encountered. Worse, underpinning his toughness was a blatant appraisal, almost sexual in nature, that challenged her on some instinctive level.

What had she been told about this man? Black eyes, black hair, black heart. Why, oh why, hadn't anyone warned her about the equally black desire he could arouse with one simple touch?

He continued to hold her hand in his. "Let's start

from the top," he suggested. "I want to buy Longhorn Ranch. What will it take to make that to happen?"

That one question freed her from his spell and had her tugging her hand from his grasp. She managed to resist the urge to wipe her palm against her jeans—just—and took a swift step backward to give herself some breathing room. She didn't care if her retreat gave him a slight edge in whatever game he'd set in motion. Distance was more important right now than gaining a negotiating advantage.

"I'll make this easy for you, Arnaud. I won't sell."

He swept her claim aside as though it were inconsequential. Maybe in his book it was. "I don't think you understand. I win. Always. No matter what it takes."

A chill shot up her spine and she fought to keep the apprehension from showing in her expression. "Not this time."

"Every time." He folded his arms across his chest. "Now explain it to me. Why are you being so stubborn? I've offered you a generous price, haven't I?"

She stared at him in disbelief. Whipping off her hat in a "getting down to business" gesture, she tossed it toward the empty conference table where it landed with a soft thud. "This isn't about money! That land has been in my family since before Texas became a state. The only way I leave it is in a box." She tilted her head to one side. "Is that how you plan to steal it away from me, Arnaud? Do your goons take matters that far, or are they limited to simple threats and warnings?"

"I've never resorted to physical violence." A frown crept across his face. "Have they touched you? Harmed you in any way?"

"Neither of them has actually touched me, but—" She shrugged, remembering the implied threat in both word and look. "Men like that say a lot without saying a lot, if you understand what I mean."

"I'll take care of it. Violence is never necessary. Why would it be? Everyone has a price." His expression grew knowing. "What's yours?"

"There is no price," she insisted.

A hint of amusement gleamed in the rich darkness of his eyes. "Of course there is. You just don't realize it, yet. But I'll find your weakness. And when I do, you'll sell."

He shot her a smile and she froze. How was it that with one simple smile he could melt all that was most feminine in her, while at the same time turning her blood to ice? It was like confronting a grizzly. One was awed by the power and beauty of the animal, wanting to somehow embrace such magnificence, while at the same time knowing that one did so at their own peril. One swipe of his paw, and the bear could end your existence.

She swallowed. Hard. "And if I don't sell? What then?"

"I up the ante until you do."

"And if that doesn't work?"

Anxiety had her voice growing soft and unsteady. Damn it! She couldn't afford to show this man any hint of weakness. Based on his expression, she'd done precisely that. Great. Just great. Now that he'd picked up on her vulnerability, he'd never back down.

His smile flashed again, unnerving her. "There's always a way to get what I want if I'm patient. It's a matter of finding which option will work best. I keep trying different ones until I find the right lever." He took a step in her direction, that single stride bringing him to within a foot of where she stood. "I don't suppose you'd care to tell me which lever would work best with you?"

He was too close. Far too close. More than anything, she wanted to fall back another pace. Instead she dug in her heels. "I'd rather not." She folded her arms across her chest. "So you're not going to call off your goons? You're going to keep harassing me?"

"I'll call them off. They won't bother you again, I promise. As for harassing you…" He dismissed the suggestion with a shake of his head. "That's such a negative word. I prefer to think of it as getting better acquainted."

She blinked at that. "Why would you want to get better acquainted? Why would I, for that matter?"

He appeared surprised by the question. "So you'll be in a better position to negotiate, of course."

Enough was enough. "I'm not interested in getting to know you any better than I'd want to become better acquainted with a rattlesnake. I don't negotiate with them any more than I would with you."

He lifted an eyebrow, clearly intrigued. "Off with their heads?"

"If that's what it takes. As for you, well… Everyone has a price." She parroted his own words back to him. "Even you. You just don't realize it, yet. But I'll find your weakness. And when I do, you'll go away. Permanently."

She'd said all she needed to. Coming here had been pointless. It was clear Arnaud wouldn't give up on trying to buy her land. That didn't mean she had to sell. He seemed to think he had something she wanted. He didn't.

There was nothing she wanted or needed that she didn't already have. The sooner he realized that, the better.

She spun on her heel and marched toward the door. Her gaze shifted to the table as she passed it and what she saw almost had her breaking stride. Without all the papers to clutter the surface she could make out the design of the inlaid wood—a huge, magnificent wolf.

Her analogy had been dead wrong. Arnaud wasn't a grizzly, but a timber wolf. She'd seen one once, had been riveted by the keen intelligence glittering in its golden eyes. A loner. A predator. Proud and protective. She could understand why the animal had been deified by various cultures over the millennia. She didn't dare look back at Arnaud. But an acute awareness filled her.

She'd just pitted herself against the legendary Big Bad, himself. And unlike in fairy tales, this particular wolf didn't lose.

Joc watched Rosalyn cross to the far side of the room, her stride long and loose. It spoke of a woman comfortable in her own skin. He also saw her glance at the table and the hitch in her step when she caught a glimpse of the wolf motif. He smiled at that telling reaction, amused all the more by the fact that his table had intimidated her more than he had.

She reached the exit and stood there for a split second as she opened the door, captured by the morning sunlight filtering in through the windows. It embraced her with its heavy rays and set her hair on fire. The view held him spellbound. Well, hell. He'd roped himself a redhead, the red so deep and rich he hadn't noticed it until the sun had betrayed her secret. The instant she left the room, he pushed a button in the console by his chair.

"Yes, Mr. Arnaud?"

"Lock down the elevators."

"Right away, Mr. Arnaud."

Joc crossed to the end of the table and picked up the hat Rosalyn had forgotten to retrieve on her way out the door, no doubt because she'd been knocked off-kilter by the wolf design. The Stetson had seen serious wear. It was the hat of a working rancher, not an accessory to demonstrate state pride or as a fashion statement, but for vital protection against the elements. It told him a lot about its owner…and how he might handle her.

He left the conference room and started toward the elevators. His executive assistant's desk was on the way and he paused long enough to give Maggie a list of instructions and have her release the elevators. That done, he tracked down Rosalyn.

He found her stabbing at the button for the elevator. Joc slowed, taking the time to study her. He'd had the impression of height when they'd talked, a false impression he realized now. Maybe it had been her subtle perfume that had distracted him, or the striking shade of her Texas Bluebonnet eyes, but he could see now that she was a compact package, not nearly as long and lanky as he'd first thought. She'd also committed a serious crime against mankind by scraping her hair back into a tight little knot at the base of her neck. No wonder he hadn't noticed the true color. He itched to release that knot and run his fingers through the silken mass. To feel the texture and see the vivid color fanned across her pale shoulders.

Years of hard ranch work had honed her body into lean, tempered strength and contributed to the appealing curve of her legs and backside. She'd also been blessed with ideal-sized breasts, neither too small nor too large, but the sort that filled a man's palms to perfection. When it came to her face, though, nature had gifted her with true beauty.

She had the type of bone structure that would accentuate her loveliness even at ninety, with the pale, creamy complexion of a true redhead. The winged eyebrows, soaring cheekbones and full lush mouth, would have made her features too flawless for his taste if it weren't for the redeeming crook in her otherwise straight nose. He almost grinned. Now how had that happened?

The elevator pinged behind her and she whipped around with an exclamation of relief and swept into the car. Joc followed her in, sparking an interesting combination of reactions—alarm, wariness and a feminine awareness that roused an intense, masculine urge to pursue. The door closed and they began their descent.

"I believe you forgot something." He held out her Stetson.

He'd disconcerted her, breaking through the barriers she'd been swift to erect. "Thanks," she murmured. She took the hat from him and crammed it down on her head, hiding every scrap of hair.

"You're welcome." He reached around her and pushed a button that brought the elevator to a smooth halt.

"What are you doing?" He could hear the hint of

trepidation in her voice and the breathless awareness of his proximity. "Why did you stop the elevator?"

"I'd like to make you another offer."

She cut him off with a graceful sweep of her hand. "Please, don't. I've heard your offers and I'm not interested."

"You haven't heard this one."

She jerked her head in his direction and then away again, fixing her stare on the control panel. If he were a betting man, which he was, he'd be willing to wager a cool million that it took every ounce of self-control in her possession to keep from jabbing at the buttons in order to get the elevator moving again. Her hand inched toward the control panel before she dropped her arms to her sides in clear surrender.

"How many ways do I have to say I'm not interested?" she asked with quiet dignity. "I wasn't interested in any of your previous offers. I won't be interested in this one, either."

"I thought I'd give you the chance to convince me of your disinterest over dinner."

That caught her attention and she turned to confront him. "Dinner?"

"Right. That's the meal that comes after lunch and before bedtime."

Instead of laughing, a hint of a frown crept across her brow. "Why would you want to take me to dinner? You know I'm not going to agree to any offer you might make."

He flicked his thumb against the brim of her hat. It knocked the battered felt toward the back of her head and gave him an unobstructed view of her face. So much character, he marveled. So much strength and determination. And the passion. She smoldered with it, thickening the air with ripe feminine power. What would it be like to ignite all that? To kindle those banked flames into a raging wildfire? He wanted to find out. Needed to. But, first things first.

"How do you know I won't be persuaded to change my mind about buying your ranch? Think about it. You'll have all evening to argue with me. Uninterrupted time where you'll have my full attention. Hours in which you can explain why I should just go away and leave you alone."

"Tempting." She studied him and he saw a wild animal's wariness in her gaze. "What's the catch?"

"What makes you think there's a catch?" he countered.

"Because you're Joc Arnaud and you want something from me."

Smart woman. "You'll have to figure that out for yourself."

"And if it's something I can't give?"

"You say no." He gave her a verbal shove. "You do know the word, don't you?"

She surprised him by absorbing his comment with equanimity, confining herself to a single comeback. "Be careful or you'll find out how well I know it." She took a minute to consider. "Dinner and talk. That's it?"

"That's it."

Unless more happened. Because this wasn't just about business, anymore. There was more between them, something elemental running beneath the surface. It was that something that had Joc coming to an instant decision. Her ranch was of secondary concern, mainly because he'd have that before long, whether she acquiesced to his demands or he wrestled it away with her fighting him over every inch of land. Right now other needs were of far greater urgency. No matter what, he'd have this woman in his bed. Have her until he was sated, regardless of how short or long the taking…or how much she resisted.

"Okay, I agree," she said at last.

"I thought you might," he murmured. He reached around her and released the elevator, allowing it to continue its downward plummet.

No doubt it was taking them both straight to hell.

Rosalyn stared at the elevator doors and fought to regain her self-control. Joc had knocked her Stetson to the back of her head and now she crushed it low on her brow. Okay, so she was hiding her expression from him. So, what? That didn't matter anywhere near as much as the fact that he had her acting like a total idiot. A rock dumb, bat blind, total idiot.

Arnaud had already warned her that he always won. This give and take between them was nothing more than a game to him, an avenue toward another check in the win column of his playbook. For her, the stakes were far higher. Her ranch was her life, keeping its legacy safe for future Oakleys her sole ambition. She'd promised to do just that, a deathbed vow that left no maneuvering room for negotiation or personal preferences.

Granted, Arnaud didn't care about her reasons for

resisting his business proposition. Still… What if she could explain that sort of emotion to him in language he could understand? What if she could talk him into going away and leaving her alone? It wouldn't solve all her problems, but it would solve her most immediate one.

She spared him a swift glance from beneath her lashes. He was staring at her, his lazy grin warning he knew what she'd been thinking. Not that it mattered what counteragenda he might be working on the sly. She'd committed herself to going out to dinner with him and she would. She'd even try to change his mind about buying her out, though she doubted she'd succeed.

Nevertheless, he was right about one thing: spending a little time with him would give her a better handle on his strategy and what her chances were of winning— though at a guess that would be somewhere in the neighborhood of zero to none. She weighed that against the feminine intuition that warned that he wanted far more from her than her property. It filled her with the urge to change her mind and run home to safety, the protective instinct for flight eclipsing the desire to fight. She opened her mouth to give instinct a voice.

"You can't." His voice came from just behind and above.

How had he gotten so close without her noticing? "I can't what?"

"You agreed to dinner and you can't change your mind."

"How did you know—" She closed her mouth with a snap and glared at the elevator doors. "Okay, I get it now."

"Get what?" Laughter. Arnaud was laughing at her!

"I understand why you're so successful. You can read minds."

"Only when the thoughts are strong. Or the emotions," he added.

She winced. Was that his subtle way of telling her he'd picked up on her reaction to him? She needed to get off the ranch more. Date. Get a better grip on the male psyche and how to handle men like Arnaud. Because Mr. Big Bad had quite the grip on the female end of things, which put her at a distinct disadvantage.

"I promised I'd go to dinner with you, and I will." If she sounded reluctant, that couldn't be helped. He'd boxed her in and she didn't like it. "When I give my word, I stick to it."

"As do I."

She turned and studied his expression. Not that it helped much. He had "inscrutable" down to a science. "You'll give me a fair shot at changing your mind?" she asked.

"Yes."

She wanted to pin him down further but didn't have a clue how to do it. They were so mismatched, it was downright pathetic. Still, she'd try her best. What other choice did she have? "Are you open to changing your mind?"

"In my business it pays to be flexible." His expression hardened. "It also pays to go after what you want with every strength, skill and asset at your disposal."

"Thanks for the suggestion. I'll do just that." An idea occurred to her, one that might put her in a better bargaining position. "And I'd like to start by adding an addendum to our agreement."

He lifted an eyebrow. "A negotiation?" he asked, intrigued. "My favorite pastime. What's your addendum?"

"You come to my place for dinner."

He nodded in complete understanding. "You want to negotiate on your own turf. Good move."

He leaned in and it took all her concentration just to inhale and exhale in a normal fashion. His deep-set eyes were the most intense she'd ever seen, the black so absolute she couldn't tell pupil from iris. But it was his mouth that drew her, that stirred something she hadn't felt in years. For such a hard man, his mouth was broad and full and sensual and she couldn't help but wonder what those incredible lips could do to her. Her own lips softened in anticipation. How would it feel to sink into them, to lose herself in their heat? Did he kiss as well as he made money? Chances were excellent he did, which made her all the more curious to find out.

"My turf or yours, it doesn't matter," he was saying. "I don't play softball, Red. My pitch is low, fast and inside. If you don't watch out, it'll put you in the dirt."

It took her a moment to register his comment. Once she did, she took a hasty step away from him. What was wrong with her? She'd been daydreaming about kissing the man, while he'd been figuring out how to steal her land out from under her. "Why are you telling me this?"

"Because you're out of your league."

She didn't know whether to feel outraged or apprehensive. "You're offering me pity advice?"

"Stow your pride and take it," he suggested. "It's the only help you're going to get. From now on, you're on your own."

No question about that. But maybe, just maybe, by having him on her home turf it would give her just enough of an advantage to uncover his weakness. A tantalizing thought occurred, one that opened all sorts of fascinating possibilities.

What if his weakness was *her?*

Two

Normally, Joc would have used his car and driver for the trip to Longhorn Ranch so he could utilize the time to work. On this occasion, he refrained. Somehow, he didn't think showing up in a limousine would go over well, so he drove himself, arriving at the ranch precisely on time.

He was greeted at the door by an elderly woman who wore a sour expression he'd lay odds she'd spent most of her life cultivating. She gave him the once-over before reluctantly admitting him. "You must be Arnaud."

He offered his hand. "Joc Arnaud."

She gave him a firm handshake in return. "Rosalyn's in the kitchen putting the final touches on your meal. She should have been working on bookkeeping. But since she invited you, she felt obligated to do the cooking. I'm Claire, by the way, the Oakley housekeeper."

He gave her the wine he'd brought. "My contribution to dinner."

She eyed it with suspicion. "This the kind that needs to breathe?"

"After nearly twenty years of being corked, I'm sure it'll be grateful for the opportunity," he answered gravely.

She gave a snort of laughter. "Come on, then. I'll show you the way."

He looked around with interest as she escorted him to the back of the ranch house. It was a beautiful place, with polished wooden floors, beamed ceilings and generously sized rooms in an open floor plan. The kitchen proved equally impressive, with a brick hearth and cast-iron stove from a different era mingling with modern-day appliances. Rosalyn stood at a butcher block chopping vegetables with practiced ease.

"I'll finish up here," Claire said in a tone that clearly stated that this was her domain and she wanted all invaders out of it. "Dinner will be ready in thirty minutes."

Rosalyn shot Joc a look of amusement before crossing to the sink and washing her hands. "Thanks, Claire. I appreciate your help."

"I gather she doesn't like feeding the enemy?" Joc inquired as soon as they were out of earshot.

"Mostly she just doesn't like people in her kitchen." Rosalyn opened the door to a snug parlor, complete with a love seat in front of a hickory-scented fire and decanters of liquor arranged on a silver tray. "But she also considers this meeting a mistake."

"She could be right."

In more ways than one. When Rosalyn had first approached him, they'd been in an office setting, both wearing work attire, even if hers had been a battered Stetson, faded jeans, scarred boots and a flannel shirt. But here, in a more intimate setting, the barriers between them had slipped, blurring the line between business and pleasure.

This go-round, she wore her hair loose, the rich waterfall sweeping past her shoulders in a cape of auburn silk. She'd traded in her ranch gear for tawny slacks and a simple ivory blouse, while a plain gold necklace drew attention to the pale length of her throat and the hint of cleavage that peeked from the shadows of her neckline. A touch of makeup emphasized the startling shade of her violet-blue eyes and made her lips appear fuller and softer. Kissable.

She lifted an eyebrow. "If you think this is a mistake, then why did you suggest dinner in the first place?"

He fought his way back to reality, struggling to regain his focus. He was here on business. That he had to remind himself of that fact didn't bode well for the rest of the evening. "I hoped we could come to an agreement in a more relaxed setting."

"Speaking of which…" She gestured toward the sideboard. "Would you like a drink?"

"Single malt, if you have it."

"Oh, we have it."

Something in her tone snagged his attention. "You don't care for whiskey?"

"On the contrary." She poured them both a drink and joined him by the fire, handing him one of the glasses. "I indulge on rare occasions."

They sat next to each other on the love seat. To his amusement Rosalyn buried her hip against one end of the narrow couch in an attempt to keep as much distance between them as possible. "What occasions do you feel warrant a drink?" he asked, genuinely interested.

"Anniversaries." She flinched from some memory, and the firelight flickered across the elegant planes of her face, revealing a heartbreaking vulnerability. "And when I'm working on the ranch accounts."

What anniversaries? Judging by her drawn expression they weren't celebratory ones. He'd have to recheck her dossier and dig into her past a bit more in order to discover what had caused such a deep hurt. He deliberately kept his response light. "I assume bookkeeping isn't your favorite task?"

"As far as I'm concerned, it requires serious fortification." Her gaze grew pointed. "Sort of like when dealing with you."

"I know a few people like that."

"There are actually people out there who drive you to drink, Arnaud?" His comment had distracted her and some of the pain and tension ebbed. She also relaxed into the cushions so they almost touched. "Sounds like my kind."

"It's my sister. And she is your kind."

"MacKenzie?"

He shook his head. "MacKenzie is my half sister. Same father, different mothers. She drives me to drink, but for different reasons. And I sure as hell wouldn't waste a good single malt on her. No, I'm talking about my full sister, Ana, as well as her husband." He sipped his whiskey. "Or should I say His Highness, Prince Lander Montgomery of Verdonia."

Rosalyn buried her nose in the glass. "Not my kind, after all."

He stretched his legs out toward the fire and smiled. His sister was also a fiery redhead, while his brother-in-law was one of the most protective and honorable men Joc had ever met. Lander had initially become engaged to his sister in an attempt to protect her reputation. He'd even given up a shot at the throne of Verdonia for the good of the country.

"They're both very much your kind. Direct. Down-to-earth. Protective. And they both enjoy flaying a strip or two off my hide whenever the mood takes them. We've had some interesting run-ins."

"Huh. I'd have said your hide was too tough to flay." She swiveled to inspect him, causing a strand of hair to drift across her face. She gave him a swift, searching glance that made him want to pull her into his arms and discover if she tasted as good as she looked. "Maybe I should call them for suggestions."

"I think you're managing just fine on your own."

The strands of hair continued to cling to her face and he reached out without conscious design, intent only on brushing it aside. It was a simple contact, the tips of his fingers barely grazing the fine-boned curve of her cheek in order to sweep the spill of hair away from her eyes. And yet, his instantaneous reaction caught him off guard. Heat poured through him, as though he'd fallen headlong into the popping flames just a few feet away.

The slight hitch in Rosalyn's breath told him he

wasn't the only one affected. She stared at him, her eyes startled. He'd thrown her. Badly. He felt it rippling through her and saw it reflected in the tautness of her features. Her eyes darkened to a shade of blue the sky took on somewhere between dusk and nightfall. And her mouth—that plump, ripe mouth—trembled in a way that tempted him almost beyond endurance and made him want to kiss away her apprehension.

One touch. It had been one casual, thoughtless touch, a touch that never would have happened if it hadn't been for that rich red hair and those glorious eyes. But the instant he'd run his fingers across her creamy skin, he'd lost it. If they'd been anywhere else, he'd have tumbled her to the floor and taken her, and to hell with the consequences.

What was it about the woman that reduced him to his most basic and primitive instincts? He was a man who prided himself on his self-control, who used that control, along with his innate intelligence and ability to see the big picture and get what he wanted. How was it possible to lose all that with a single touch? It had never happened before, not once in all his thirty-four years, nor with a single one of the women he'd taken to his bed.

He tossed back the last of his whiskey before shooting her a hard look. "We're in trouble. You realize that, don't you?"

Rosalyn shuddered. With that one single touch, wanton desire spilled across her skin in a wave as hot and humid and gripping as Dallas in August. With the heat came the sizzle, a buzz of sensation that went from her cheek straight to the pit of her stomach. She was barely aware of what he said after releasing her. Damn it! She was in deep trouble.

She shot to her feet to give herself some breathing room. Her hand tightened around her glass and she tossed back her whiskey in a single, disjointed movement before returning his look with a hard one of her own. "That can't happen again."

"How are you going to stop it?" he asked, genuinely curious.

"Distance would be a good start."

Her frankness made him smile. He stood as well, throwing a question over his shoulder as he returned his glass to the sideboard. "Is it any better now that I'm across the room?"

"Yes." She thrust a hand through her hair. "No."

"I agree."

She regarded him warily. "So what do we do now?"

A knock sounded at the door and Claire's voice boomed through the heavy wood. "Dinner's on. Shake a leg in there."

Joc crossed the room until they stood toe to toe. Somehow she managed to stand there without giving away the wash of emotions cascading through her. But she couldn't hide the truth from herself, no matter how hard she tried. She wanted him to touch her again, wanted it with a passion that almost had her quivering.

"I suggest we eat," he said in reply to a question she'd already forgotten. "What happens after that is up to you."

"Nothing is going to happen," she stated without

hesitation. "Nothing other than you climbing into your fancy car and returning to Dallas."

"Then neither of us has anything to worry about." He inclined his head toward the door. "Shall we go?"

She hesitated, anxious to recover some of the ground she'd lost and remind them both of why she'd agreed to dine with him. "You promised that I'd have your full and undivided attention. That you'd give me a fair shot at changing your mind about buying my ranch."

"I gave you my word and I'll keep it."

She'd have to be satisfied with that. Together they crossed to the dining room. With every step Rosalyn ran through her game plan. She was a cards-on-the-table type of woman, and she didn't intend to change that with Arnaud. So she'd be blunt with him about why she refused to sell out. But she'd also attempt to unearth any weakness he might possess and exploit it. After all, she wasn't a total fool, not when it came to the safety and security of her ranch. So far, the only weakness she'd discovered involved her and a bed. And as much as that appealed, she'd be an idiot to use it. With her luck he'd walk away with everything she held most dear. No, she needed to spend the next hour or two getting a better handle on him and how she might win this war that had erupted between them.

"Nice," he complimented as they entered the dining room.

Despite his comment, she couldn't help but see her home through his eyes and the sight left her flinching. This was a man accustomed to the best life had to offer, a man worth billions. How plain and countrified her home must appear to him, with its simple wood table decorated with her grandmother's best linen and her great-grandmother's rose-patterned china. Rosalyn had even had the unmitigated nerve to think her meal of pot roast and home-grown vegetables would appeal to a palate fine-tuned to five-star gourmet cuisine.

"It's not fancy."

He must have caught the defensive edge in her voice, and he turned to face her. "Are you apologizing for your lifestyle? Because if you don't like it, I can fix that for you."

It was precisely what she'd been doing and the knowledge hit hard. Her hands balled into fists. She had nothing to apologize for. Absolutely nothing. "No, thanks. I like what I have."

He offered the smile that never failed to sink into her bones and slip through her veins like quicksilver. "I thought I had you for a minute there."

"Not a chance."

They took a seat at the dining room table, she at the head, he on her right. She left him to eat his first course in peace—the salad she'd been preparing when he'd arrived. Most of the vegetables were ones growing just outside the kitchen door, where similar household crops had been tended and cultivated by the women of the house for as long as the homestead had stood.

It wasn't until they'd finished their main course that he turned their conversation to business. "Shall we negotiate our differences or would you rather table it for the evening?" he asked.

"Since this is my only opportunity to change your mind, I think we'll negotiate." She shoved her plate to one side. "Let's start with something easy. Why do you want my ranch?"

"It sits at the heart of land I own," he answered promptly.

"Land you purchased within the last year."

"It only became available this past year." He lifted an eyebrow. "Does it matter when I purchased the property?"

She shook her head. "No. What matters is that you've wasted your time and money since there's no chance of acquiring my ranch."

To her frustration, he simply shrugged. "Time will tell."

Claire appeared with their dessert and Rosalyn stewed over his calm certainty that she'd ever consider selling her home. Unable to stand it another minute, she said, "Explain it to me, Arnaud. Why are you buying up this particular section of Texas? What could you possibly want with it when you could have any other place in the world for the asking?" Her hair drifted into her face again, and she swept it behind one ear, aware that he followed the movement with far too much interest. "Is it the history attached to my place? Is that it? Are you after roots? A heritage? What?"

She asked the exact wrong series of questions. His expression closed over into a sterner mask than she'd ever seen before. "Why would I want those?"

"Don't play ignorant with me." She fought to contain her anger with only limited success. "You know what I'm asking. For you, this land is a possession. You want, therefore you take. For me, it's something far more personal." She leaned forward, her voice ripe with passion. "It's a part of me. A part of my heritage. A part of who I am and where I come from."

He gave her a hard, unwavering look. "That's a lie handed down through generations of Oakleys. You are not the land. You live on it for a brief period in the grand scheme of things. A hundred years from now, two hundred, what happens here tonight won't matter. No one will even remember it. We will have come and gone. Only the land will remain." He paused long enough for that to sink in before summing it up with characteristic succinctness. "It's dirt, Red. Nothing more than acres of dirt."

"You can't honestly believe that?"

"I promised I'd tell you the truth and I am." He opened a door she suspected he kept shut tight in the normal course of things. "I assume you know I'm illegitimate, so I suppose it's only natural you'd think I want your ranch because of the history behind it, or the roots or heritage it represents."

She allowed her doubt to show. "Are you sure that's not it?"

"Not even a little. How long has your family owned this land? A hundred years? Two hundred? If I wanted roots and heritage I could have gone to Europe and married into lineages far more impressive than what anyone in the States can claim. It wouldn't have been difficult. When I was visiting my sister in Verdonia, there were plenty of opportunities. Family that stretched back close to a millennium. Estates that could have given me a title and roots and prestige, if that's what I wanted." He spoke with a stunning disdain, his comment edged with a bitter chill. "I don't."

"You must recognize that it's important to others,"

she argued. "You bought your own family's homestead.
I heard you discussing it with MacKenzie. Keeping the
Hollister land intact must have some meaning for you
to have purchased it and now refuse to sell."

"I haven't stepped foot on that land, and I never will."

Shock held her silent for a long moment. "You don't
want it for yourself, but you also won't allow the Hollisters to buy it back?"

"I have my reasons." Something in his eyes warned
that she'd opened a door that should have remained
locked. "I recognize that some people allow the owner-
ship of property to define who they are. But it's an
illusion. You're the last of the Oakley line, Red. When
you marry and have children, they won't be Oakleys.
They won't bear the Oakley name. And what if you
sold the ranch...or lost it? Does living on Oakley land
define who you are? Are you no longer that person
when you leave it?"

She swept the question aside. "It's my land," she
retorted. "You can't force me to give that up or to sell
it if I don't want to."

"True. But at some point I'll hit on something you
want more than your land, just like Meredith Hollister.
And that's when you'll sell."

"I won't." She made the words as adamant and un-
compromising as possible. "It was shortsighted of you
to buy the surrounding property without knowing for
certain whether or not I'd sell. That's just plain bad
business—a first in the career of the great Joc Arnaud."

He surprised her by inclining his head in acknowledgment. "The land around yours suddenly

became available and I had to act fast. I was told you were not only willing to sell, but eager, or I wouldn't have gone through with the deal."

Understanding dawned. "Those two employees of yours, the two who've been after me this past year... They lied to you?" She shook her head. "That was brave of them."

She shivered at the darkness that settled over his expression and turned his eyes to black agates. "More stupid than brave. And my *former* employees won't be troubling you anymore. I've taken over the job of persuading you to sell, personally."

Heaven help her. "Just out of curiosity, if I did sell Longhorn to you, what would you put here in place of my ranch?"

He hesitated, refreshing their wineglasses, before responding. "This isn't for public consumption, yet, but it's only fair you know. I'm building a complex for the various Arnaud corporations and business interests."

She stared in dismay. "What sort of complex?"

"A huge one," he admitted. "In addition to the actual office buildings, there will also be day-care centers, spas, medical facilities, gyms, a sports complex, cafeterias. Even a movie theater or two. I also plan to build apartments and condos for employees who want to live within walking distance of their job."

Stunned, she grabbed her wineglass and took a long sip of the rich, floral-scented pinot noir. It sounded like he intended to build a miniature city. She'd read about computer companies and Internet corporations doing something similar, and been impressed by the breadth and scope of their endeavor. But those were built at a safe distance, not in her own backyard. Hell, not *on* her backyard. A slight tremor betrayed her alarm and she carefully returned her wineglass to the table.

"That's quite an undertaking." And must have been under consideration for years, she realized in dismay. If so, she'd have an impossible time changing his mind. "No wonder you need your own corner of Texas."

"And why I'll do anything to get it." He leaned back in his chair, his expression relaxing into a smile that never failed to distract her. "Now that you know what I plan to do and how committed I am to purchasing your property, you're in a unique position. Not many can claim that when it comes to negotiating with me. Name your price. Any price you want, Red, and I'll pay it."

"You still don't get it, do you?" She gestured toward his plate. "Are you finished eating?" At his nod, she shoved back from the table. "Come with me. I want to show you something."

She escaped the table and promptly caught her boot heel in the loose hallway runner just outside the dining room. If Joc hadn't caught her at the last second, she'd have taken a nasty fall down the stone steps leading to the sunken living room.

"Are you okay?" he asked.

They were touching again, something she'd sworn wouldn't happen. She felt the tension vibrating through him, a mirror image of her own. "I keep meaning to have one of the boys tack that down," she replied in a breathless voice. "But I keep forgetting."

"I suggest you move it up on your priority list. Next time I might not be here to catch you."

Her mouth curved into a reluctant smile. "Actually…that's the whole idea. I'm trying to get rid of you, remember?"

Pulling free of his grasp, she led the way outside to where her Jeep stood parked beneath an overhang attached to the barn. She made a beeline for it. He followed, climbing into the passenger seat while she hopped behind the wheel and cranked over the ignition.

The engine started with a roar and she wrestled the gearshift into reverse. It was a cantankerous old vehicle, but she had a fondness for it because it was the first car she'd ever driven. It could also access almost every part of Longhorn Ranch. She eased off the clutch and the Jeep bucked with all the affront of a saddle-shy bronco. Then it stalled, quivering beneath the fading sunlight. Refiring the engine, she fishtailed through the mud from the previous night's deluge before the wheels found purchase. The instant they did, she punched the gas.

She took the rut-filled path deeper into Oakley land, between pastures filled with cattle, one of them showcasing the longhorn for which the ranch had been named. She guided the Jeep toward the old homestead, to where it had all begun, in the hopes that seeing it would provide a more eloquent explanation of what this land meant to her, and succeed where mere words had failed. She downshifted as she tackled the final rise leading to the heart of her property. The storm had turned the dirt road into a sea of mud and she fought to keep the vehicle from bogging down. The path curved sharply and she hit the muddy bend in a flat-out skid.

The Jeep let out a gasp of relief at having made the steep grade and died not far from an ancient single-room cabin. Rosalyn sat silently for a moment, allowing Joc to look his fill. "It's the original Oakley homestead. My ancestors constructed it from riverrock."

He shook his head. "Can you imagine starting your life in this wilderness, with only those four walls protecting you from the elements?" He glanced at her, allowing his admiration to show. "Brave people."

"That's what I come from, Joc. People who carved a home from nothing. Who faced not only the elements, but dealt with all the war and strife the past couple hundred years have thrown at them."

The fading sun painted the stones in deceptively gentle shades of pink and mauve, and even managed to make the picket fence delineating the weed-choked yard appear whimsical rather than ramshackle. She exited the Jeep and circled the cabin. Joc followed silently as she led him to a small cemetery not far from the original homestead.

Close to two hundred years of Oakleys were tucked beneath the protective embrace of a towering stand of cottonwoods. He took his time wandering among the gravestones. The most poignant were the ones he approached last, the recent ones. Five sites were huddled close together. Four of them—Rosalyn's grandfather, her parents and a five-year-old brother—had died a full decade ago, all on the same day. The other, her grandmother, just a year ago.

"The anniversaries," he murmured somberly. "These are the anniversaries you toast with a glass of whiskey."

"Yes."

"What happened to them?"

She crouched beside the gravesites, clearing them of the few weeds that had cropped up since her last visit a few days before. "Small-plane crash my senior year in high school."

"And you?" She couldn't detect a single scrap of emotion in the question, and yet she could feel it. It crashed outward from him in waves of concern, a concern that took her by surprise. "Were you onboard?"

"No. I was sick that day. Nanna stayed home with me. Otherwise…" She shrugged. "We wouldn't be in our current predicament. The ranch would have been sold long ago."

"God, Red. I'm so sorry. And I thought my formative years were bad."

She rocked back on her heels and gazed up at him. "You need to understand something, Joc. When my family died, I lost a huge part of myself. All I had left to fill that hole was this ranch and my grandmother. I quickly realized that I could give up or carry on."

"You carried on."

She nodded and swept a hand in a wide arc. "All this you see around me? It's my legacy. My responsibility. It's as much a part of me as my blood and bones. It's part of my flesh. Part of who and what I am. I promised my grandmother on her deathbed that I'd do everything within my power to protect that legacy, and I will." She stood, rubbing the bits of grass and dirt from her hands. "You want my land, Joc. Well, I'm part and parcel of this land. You can't separate me from it or pull my roots loose any more than you can break the connection that joins me to every single soul in this cemetery. I won't sell, and that's final."

The sun hovered on the horizon, a burning ball of red, throwing its dying rays outward in a final blazing explosion. Joc stood within its burning embrace, sculpted in harsh contours of light and shadow, the embodiment of his Native American ancestry. A determined expression settled over his face, one that left her shivering.

"I guess there's nothing left to discuss," he limited himself to saying.

"Then you'll leave me alone?"

He simply stared at her for a long, silent moment. "You're asking too much. I won't leave you alone. I can't."

"How can you think I'll ever sell? How can you believe for even one minute—"

"I'm not talking about your ranch. It's you I can't leave alone."

He came for her then, eating up the ground in a half dozen long strides. The instant he reached her, he caught her in his arms. "Don't fight me. Not on this front." And then he consumed her.

She'd always found a first kiss to be tentative. A slow sampling, oftentimes awkward, as lips fought to discover the right angle and pressure. But with Joc that awkwardness didn't exist. His kiss was everything she'd anticipated and then some. Their lips mated with an ease and certainty that should have taken dozens of kisses to achieve.

Everything about him epitomized power and strength, and she found that true of his kiss, as well. He combined those qualities with a ruthless demand that stunned both body and mind. His mouth slid across hers in blatant hunger, stifling any thought of protest. She hesitated, aware that she should pull away, but wanting just another second or two of this incredible bliss. In that moment of indecision, he slid his hand down the length of her spine to the hollow just above her backside and urged her closer, locking her in place between his thighs.

Their bodies melded, the fit sheer perfection. He had a hard, muscular frame, lean and well-sculpted. It surprised her since it seemed more suited to a fellow rancher than a man who made his living behind a desk. Unable to resist, she measured the breadth of his shoulders, shocked to discover her fingers trembled. He did that to her, coaxing to the surface emotions she wanted to deny, but couldn't.

He cupped her face and teased the corners of her mouth with his thumbs until her lips parted. The instant she relaxed, he deepened the kiss, dipping inward. She should fight her way free of their embrace, and put an end to this farce. But she didn't want to. To her eternal shame, she kissed him back, allowing him to forge a connection between them that wouldn't easily be severed, regardless of her preference in the matter.

She needed this moment, needed tonight. If she were honest, she'd admit that she secretly yearned for Joc's possession. But a tiny rational part of her clung to reason and shouted a warning about all she stood to lose if she gave herself to this man. The price would prove high if she weren't careful, destroying everything she'd worked so hard to build.

Even knowing that, she couldn't bring herself to put an end to their embrace. It wasn't until she heard the small growl of triumph that rumbled through his chest that she came to her senses. With an exclamation of horror, she yanked free of his arms and retreated several stumbling steps. She touched her mouth with fingers that shook, stunned by how he'd managed to turn her world from reason to insanity with a single kiss.

"Tell me how we're supposed to go our separate ways now," he demanded.

"I can't... I won't—" She shook her head. "You're not going to romance my ranch out from under me."

"This has nothing to do with your ranch," he insisted impatiently. "This is strictly between the two of us."

"There is no *us*. This is nothing more than—" She broke off, hoping the gathering shadows hid her discomfort.

"Sex?" he offered with a humorous smile.

"Fine. Yes. It's nothing more than sex. And I won't let you use it to take my ranch."

He laughed, the sound dark and dangerous, penetrating deep inside her. "You don't get it, Red. I've changed my mind." Two swift steps had him within touching range again. "It isn't just your ranch I want anymore."

He stroked her cheek, just as he had before dinner. And she reacted every bit as strongly, swaying helplessly toward him, before locking her knees in place and resisting with every ounce of determination she possessed.

She knew. On some deep, purely feminine level, she knew the answer before she even asked the question. "What do you want now?"

"You."

Three

"Forget it. My ranch isn't for sale, no matter what you offer." Naked passion shot through Rosalyn's words and was reflected in her face. "And neither am I."

"I know you're not for sale, and I'd never insult you by suggesting such a thing. But you want me every bit as much as I want you. Deny it, if it makes you feel better. Fight if you want. But in the end neither of us is going to be able to resist." Joc stepped back, giving her some much needed breathing space. "I have a suggestion, one that might take care of our little problem."

"You're going away and leaving me alone?"

He didn't take the hint. "Too late, Red. You walked through my door of your own volition. Don't blame me if I refuse to let you go."

"I can say no." She shook her head, as though to clear it. "I will say no."

He couldn't help smiling at her confusion. "I hope to God you do. It would make things easier." Then he grew serious. "One night, Red. One night together and we should be able to satisfy whatever this is between us."

Her eyes widened in disbelief. "What are you talking about?"

"I'm taking a short trip tomorrow. Come with me. No ranch talk. No negotiating. No contention. Just you and me and a single night of romance."

Her breath caught before escaping in a rush. "You can't be serious."

He offered a fleeting smile. "Well…if you insist on negotiating the sale of your ranch, I won't refuse. But I'd rather focus on pleasure and save business for some other time. What do you say?"

"That this is insane."

His smile grew at her bluntness. "Granted. But so what? Let's be insane together. Come with me, Rosalyn. You won't regret it, I promise."

She was tempted, so very tempted. She forced herself to take another step backward, when what she wanted more than anything was to throw herself into his arms and surrender to madness. *She was his weakness,* she realized, the earlier suspicion easing toward fact. But it didn't bring her any satisfaction since she refused to use that to gain an advantage. If she were so foolish as to take him up on his offer, she'd do it because she wanted to be in his bed and not for any other reason.

"I can't." She forced herself to be honest. "I won't."

"You've never done a one-night stand before, have you?"

"No." She couldn't help laughing. "Nor do I think it would be wise to start with you."

He tilted his head to one side, his eyes shrewd and watchful. "Is there anything I can say or do that might change your mind? Drop my attempt to buy your ranch, for instance?"

Her humor faded. "Not cool, Arnaud. I don't handle business that way and I never will."

He appeared pleased by her answer. "I was hoping you'd say that."

She didn't like the direction he'd taken the discussion. Time to put an end to it. "It's getting dark. We should go."

Spinning on her heel, she headed back to her Jeep, not caring if Joc followed or not. He arrived at the driver-side door at the same instant she did and reached around her to open it. His voice slid through the gathering dusk, low and filled with regret.

"I've offended you and I'm sorry. I'm accustomed to a world where people have agendas, most of which are hidden. I can't trust what I see on the surface. I have to constantly look beneath in order to discover their true motives."

"I'm not like that," she retorted without turning around. "What you see is what you get."

"I don't trust easily."

This time she did turn, practically finding herself in his arms. "You're wrong, Joc. It's not that you don't trust easily. You don't trust at all."

"Maybe I could with you."

She shook her head. "I doubt it. You'd always wonder if our relationship wasn't my way of protecting my ranch. You'd always suspect everything I said or did because of Longhorn. That's why you're offering a one-night stand. You're hoping we'll get each other out of our systems, so that we can put our relationship back on a business footing."

He gazed down at her, impressed. "Honey, you're wasted on a ranch. You should come work for me."

"No, thanks." Retreating, she slid behind the steering wheel. "Let's go, Arnaud. We've had our fun. It's time to be enemies again."

They returned to the ranch in silence and she parked the Jeep in its space beside the barn. One of her hands, Duff, approached as they crossed the yard toward Joc's vehicle. "Excuse me, Miss Rosalyn. I'll be heading into town tomorrow on a mail run and wondered if you had anything you needed me to do while I was there."

"I have a list. I'll also be doing accounts tonight so if you'd stop by the house first thing in the morning, you can pick up the list, as well as the bills and get them posted. And make sure that mortgage payment is the first one into the mailbox."

"Sure thing." He tipped his hat to both of them and then headed for the bunkhouse.

"I gather from your expression there's another glass of single malt in your immediate future," Joc said once Duff was out of earshot.

"It's entirely possible. The spring calving has put me seriously behind on everything except getting the bills paid." She grimaced. "I can't remember the last time I balanced my accounts."

"Take it from someone who knows… That's not a good idea."

"Thanks for the tip."

He smiled at the reluctant concession. "And thank you for dinner. If you change your mind about tomorrow, I'll send a car for you at eight sharp."

"Tempting, but I'll pass."

He started to reach for her, but after sparing a swift glance in the direction of the bunkhouse, changed his mind. "You don't need to bring anything with you. Just come. I'll take care of all the rest. You've worked hard all your life, Rosalyn. Let me give you one night of pleasure."

Almost. She almost caved, but subdued the helpless agreement at the last possible instant. "Please go."

He lowered his head until his mouth practically brushed hers. "Please come." The words blew across her lips like a warm, tropical breeze, filled with exotic scents and tastes.

She'd like to, more than anything. But she didn't dare say it aloud.

He read her mind, anyway. "Do it. My car's going to show up here at eight tomorrow no matter what you say right now. But if you decide to join me, I promise you won't regret it. We'll spend a night together that neither of us will forget."

And then he was gone, leaving her standing there in the gathering darkness, dreaming of what it would be like to share a single night of incredible bliss with Joc Arnaud.

* * *

Promptly at eight the next morning Rosalyn found herself climbing into the back of Joc's limo onto butter-soft leather seats. All the while she called herself every type of fool. After the intensity of the harsh morning sunlight, the interior seemed dim and cool, probably because the windows were darkened for privacy and the AC ran at full-blast. It was also quiet. Too quiet. And rich. If money had a special blended perfume, this place would reek of it.

Why was she doing this? Clearly she'd lost her mind. During the forty minutes it took to rendezvous with Joc, she forced herself to sit without fidgeting, deliberately holding the full weight of her foolishness at bay by keeping her mind a blank.

"First time?" Joc asked the minute he joined her.

She jumped. "What? Oh, in a limo? Yes."

"I didn't expect you to come." He tilted his head to one side. "How long did that decision take?"

"From the time you left right up until I found myself walking out to your limo and getting in." Before then she'd had every intention of sending the car on its way. Now all she could do was silently curse her impulsive stupidity. She stared at Joc in a combination of dawning horror and disbelief. "I just told Claire goodbye and that I'd see her tomorrow and to hold down the fort while I was gone."

He chuckled in genuine amusement. "I gather you left before she had time to bar the doors and tie you to the nearest chair."

"Pretty much."

"And now you're having second thoughts."

"Was it the shaking that gave it away, or the hyper-ventilating?"

"Don't worry. I'll be gentle."

"I think that's what the Big Bad Wolf said right before he ate Little Red Riding Hood," she muttered in reply.

That won her another laugh. He leaned forward and removed her hat, tossing it onto the seat across from them. Without the protective shade from the brim, she felt far too exposed and folded her hands in her lap with a grip so tight her knuckles blanched. She frowned at the dichotomy of battered Stetson resting on pristine cream leather.

"Now there's a sight I never thought to see. Not a comfortable fit, is it?"

"You might be surprised at how comfortable the fit becomes, given time." He tilted his head to one side, assessing her reaction to his comment. "I could prove how comfortable it would be, but it might take more than a single night."

Even she could read between those lines. "I'll pass."

Twenty minutes later they arrived at a private airport. The limo was waved onto the tarmac and pulled to a halt not far from a corporate jet. In no time they were up the steps, aboard the plane and buckled into the spacious seats. She stared at Joc, struggling for something innocuous to say, something that had nothing to do with their plans for the next twenty-four hours.

"So, where are we going?" she asked.

He accepted her nervous volley with equanimity. "A small island between the Gulf and the Caribbean called Isla de los Deseos."

The information left her shifting in her seat. "I didn't realize we'd be going so far."

He signaled the flight attendant and held up two fingers. The next instant they were each presented a cup of coffee before their server made herself scarce. "I promised you a romantic evening, and I guarantee it'll be one. This particular jet was built for speed. It'll only take a few hours to reach Deseos. In the meantime, relax. There's a selection of movies you can watch and we have a full library of books and magazines. When's the last time you had a break from work?"

She stared at him without speaking, which was answer enough.

"I gather you don't believe in vacations?" he probed.

"I own a ranch," she replied, as though that single statement said it all. And maybe it did.

"You have employees. Or isn't the word 'delegation' part of your vocabulary."

"It's in there somewhere. I just can't—" She broke off and sipped her coffee.

He knew what she'd been about to say. She couldn't afford to delegate. A wave of protectiveness caught him by surprise. She shouldn't have to work so hard. If he took the ranch off her hands, maybe she wouldn't have to. His mouth twisted at the thought. How altruistic of him.

"Put your chair back and relax. I have an hour or so of work to do before we land."

To his surprise, she did as he suggested. When he next looked up it was to find her fast asleep. Her hair had slipped over one shoulder like a silken flow of lava, just skimming the upper curve of her breast. She'd turned her face toward him at some point and sleep eased the contours, making her appear young and innocent. The upper few snaps of her shirt had come undone and he caught a glimpse of fragile bone structure and the soft curve of rounded flesh before it vanished into the confines of a utilitarian white bra.

He forced his attention back to his work, examining the final details of the partnership he'd be dismantling early the next morning. But through it all he could see that combination of creamy white alongside deep auburn. Could feel the tug and hear the whisper that urged him to wake Red with a kiss.

And he wanted. Wanted with a growing passion that defied all attempts to control and threatened all he hoped to achieve.

Rosalyn woke with a start only moments after they'd landed and Joc watched her struggle to bring her brain online. In those first few moments he suspected she didn't know where she was, whether it was night or day, or how she'd gotten wherever she'd ended up. He knew the feeling well enough to recognize it in her expression. It also allowed him to see her with her guard down, at her most open and vulnerable.

She turned her head and he sat there, watching her with an intensity that warned he found her more interesting than any woman in memory. The instant she caught him staring, her barriers slammed into place, shutting him out of the one place he most wanted to be.

"We just landed on Isla de los Deseos," he said. "We got here by corporate jet. It's one in the afternoon,

Thursday. That's Dallas time, not local. You agreed to spend the night with me, something I'm sure you're now regretting."

She straightened in her seat. "Thanks. That fills in the gaps beautifully." She spoke with a hint of formality, and yet her voice slid through him, warm and deep and sleep-roughened.

"You must have been tired." He stood, though that meant ducking a bit to fit his six-foot-three-inch frame beneath the five-and-a-half-foot ceiling. "You work too hard."

"How would you know?" She waved the question aside. "Never mind. Knowing you, you've had me investigated up one side and down the other."

He didn't bother confirming it, since it was the truth. "Hungry?" he asked.

"Starving."

"Then I'll show you to our room and we'll grab a bite to eat."

She followed him off the plane, exiting into heat and humidity only a little less intense than Dallas, although the quality of the air felt far different here. He wondered if she'd notice. For some reason, the dampness had a lighter, mistier quality to it, a soft stroke across the skin instead of a thick blanket. She took a deep breath and he acknowledged her soft exclamation of delight with a nod of agreement.

"Different, isn't it?"

"Sweet. And…and exotic. Is it the flowers?"

"The flowers. The salt air. The spices. It gets to you after a while. Forces you to relax."

After a short drive from the airport, they arrived at a resort complex. A bellman escorted them directly to a large cabaña tucked off to one side of the main hotel. It rambled across a lush, fern-covered rise with a breathtaking view of the ocean on one side and verdant rain forest on the other. Inside, large airy rooms flowed one into the other. Terra cotta slate composed the entranceway, while the rest of the rooms featured hand-scraped bamboo flooring covered with woven area rugs. All of the rooms had been decorated with refreshing accents in exotic shades of mango, kiwi and pineapple. Overhead, a soft breeze stirred from the wicker ceiling fans. It was a welcoming haven, a place where they both could relax and give in to fantasy.

"I arranged for a picnic lunch. I thought we'd eat it down by the lagoon." He gestured toward one of the main corridors. "You'll find everything you need in the bedroom at the end of the hall. It's stocked with all the basic amenities. There should be a bathing suit that'll fit you. Go ahead and change and we'll head out."

It didn't take her long. Just as he'd finished tossing ice cold bottled water into the lunch basket, she reappeared wearing an emerald-green maillot with a matching floral print wrap tied at her waist. She'd replaced her Stetson with a wide-brimmed straw hat and a pair of oversize sunglasses were perched on the end of her nose. She held a bottle of sunscreen in one hand.

"I managed to get everywhere but my back. Do you mind? I burn like crazy, otherwise."

He suspected she wouldn't appreciate it if he turned

dousing her with lotion into foreplay. And judging by her expression she expected him to do just that. Instead he drizzled the cream onto her back and rubbed it in with brisk efficiency. She relaxed when it became clear that he didn't plan to jump her, which told him he'd elected the perfect tack. Rosalyn might have chosen to come on this little jaunt, but the more rational part of her still dealt with the potential fallout from that decision.

He could tell she wanted him. And that simple fact had thrown her completely off-kilter.

"Is this one of the hotel suites?" she asked as they exited the cabaña and headed for a gorgeous curve of beach.

"Owner's residence."

She shot him a wry smile. "I should have known." She turned her attention toward the water and nodded in approval. "It's stunning."

Pristine-white sand flowed toward a protected lagoon, stumbling over the occasional coconut husk before sliding beneath crystalline aquamarine waves. A row of palms fenced off the area, bravely defending their line to prevent the spill of jungle forest from encroaching onto the powdery sand. To his amusement, a few wayward palms had abandoned their post and congregated halfway between wave and woodland. Most tempting of all, some truly brilliant individual had strung a pair of hammocks between the palms.

Rosalyn appropriated one of them, flipping her hat and sunglasses onto it, along with her wrap. Tossing a quick grin over her shoulder, she made a beeline for the crystalline water and struck out across the lagoon with long, swift strokes. He shook his head in amusement.

He had to hand it to her—the woman worked hard at relaxing, swimming with utter focus and intensity. He joined her, matching his tempo to hers.

Twenty minutes later, she paused in her exertions. "I can't swim another minute. I need food."

"Now that I can provide."

He caught her hand in his and dragged her from the water. Her skin was the pale, milky alabaster of a true redhead and he didn't bother to hide his admiration. "For someone who spends her days out of doors, you have very little tan."

"I inherited my complexion from my mother." She paused at the ocean's edge to wring out her hair before tossing it over her shoulder. It tumbled in a heavy, wet curtain halfway down her back, the sun splintering the deep auburn into shades that ranged from autumn russet to red-gold. "She and my grandmother drummed the importance of good skin care into me practically from the time I was born."

"Savvy women."

A hint of sorrow shadowed her expression. "Yes, they were."

"I'm sorry," he said, instantly contrite. "I wanted today to be romantic, not sad."

"That's okay. I'll survive it." She crossed the sand toward the hammock and flopped onto it with impressive dexterity. Wriggling into a comfortable position, she stretched like a cat. The emerald-green bathing suit pulled taut across boyish hips and decidedly unboyish breasts, the wet material leaving little to the imagination. She was quite simply glorious, her figure sculpted into a lean musculature, no doubt the result of years of intensive ranch work.

"Okay, Arnaud. Feed me before I pass out from hunger."

He flipped open the lunch basket. "I think I have just the perfect thing to satisfy both of our appetites."

All through lunch he kept the conversation light and casual, using the opportunity to study her. She was one of the most beautiful and intriguing women he'd ever met—a temptation he found irresistible. Unfortunately that temptation created something of a dilemma.

He frowned. Time to face facts. There was a ranch war coming, one he hadn't anticipated, granted. But it was a war he intended to win. Not that winning would prove easy or decisive. Nor would it come without a carefully executed plan of action. He allowed himself one last, long minute to study his battleground as she swayed delicately in the breeze, savoring a variety of fruit wedges.

Oh, yeah. There was definitely a war coming. And he knew, without doubt or hesitation, where that final, deciding skirmish would take place.

He and his lovely rancher would pitch that final battle in bed.

The afternoon proved to be one of the best Rosalyn could ever remember. Joc went out of his way to offer her every pleasure—food, drink, amusing company and an ocean of gentle waves and warm caresses.

Eventually she abandoned her hammock in favor of his. Or rather, he forced her to abandon it when he picked her up and tumbled with her into his. They stayed there for an endless time, quietly talking as they watched the sun work its way toward the horizon. As the afternoon waned, the sky took on a palette of colors so breathtaking, it brought tears to her eyes.

It was then that she realized that most of the conversation had revolved around her and how she'd handled the management of her ranch after the death of her parents. She hadn't learned anything about Joc or his background. She settled herself more comfortably into his arms. Time to change all that. "You said you had a traumatic childhood. Do you mind my asking what happened?"

He dismissed the question with a shrug. "I doubt there's anything new I can tell you that hasn't already been reported in newspapers or magazines."

"If you don't want to tell me, I can understand. I don't often talk about my parents' death." She fought to speak through the thickness in her throat. "Or my brother's."

"Ana and I don't share the sort of relationship with the Hollisters that you had with your family." A thread of weariness underscored his comment. "They despise our existence as much as I despise theirs."

Her brows pulled together. "It wasn't their fault, Joc, any more than it was yours and your sister's. There's only one person to blame for this tragedy."

"I'm well aware my father is responsible for the accident of my birth."

There was a bite to his words that should have had her backing off. But for now, she'd follow her instincts. "I'm not sure any of you do realize it. Otherwise there wouldn't be such animosity between all of you." She allowed her fingertips to drift across the hard contours of his bare chest. "What was your father like?"

He caught her hand in his and lifted it to his mouth, kissing each fingertip. "Boss was…charming. Arrogant. Brilliant."

"Sounds familiar."

He released a short, harsh laugh. "You aren't the first to make the comparison. It doesn't help that I look just like him, too."

"And you hate that."

There was an endless pause, and then his voice came out of the silence, low and full of old pain. "I hate most how similar my personality is to his. How close I came to being him. He died in prison, you know. At one point, I thought I might end up there. Die there."

She lifted onto one elbow and stared at him in dismay. "What do you mean? How did you almost end up like him?"

He fell silent for a long moment and then he said, "I was ten when I found out that my father had two families. I saw a news report about him on the television. He stood there posing for the camera, his arm around his wife and his four adorable children lined up in front of him."

"You didn't know before that?" she asked, shocked. "Your mother never told you?"

"She walked into the room just as MacKenzie was answering some question about school. We were in the same grade, and I couldn't understand how that was possible. My mother turned off the set and sat me down and tried to explain. But what could she say? She was the mistress of a married man and nothing was going to change that." He combed his fingers through her hair in a restless movement, though she doubted he even realized he was doing it. "I went a little crazy after that. I started hanging with a bad crowd. There were six of us, including me. Mick, Joey, Peter…and a couple others. Eventually we decided to form a little business partnership."

She shook her head in confusion. "I don't under-stand. What did that have to do with your father?"

"I decided I'd prove I was every bit the businessman he was. I tried to emulate him, for a while." His voice dropped another notch, the words sounding as if they'd been pulled from some deep, dark place. "Over time, I became him. Shadier, in fact. It was all about the bottom line, financially. All about what I could get away with. All about wheeling and dealing. Nothing else mattered. Not who I ran over to reach my goal. Not the better good. Not finding a balance. The win was everything."

She couldn't help stiffening, remembering some-thing he'd said when they'd first met. *I win. Always. No matter what it takes.* "What's changed since then?"

He understood what she was asking and shrugged. "A lot. I do it aboveboard and I don't cheat. If you sell your ranch it's because I've offered you something you want more than Longhorn."

She took a moment to absorb that. "What convinced you to transform yourself?"

"Not a what, but a who. My sister, Ana. I was a cocky twenty-year-old and she was all of twelve. I bragged to her about this great deal I'd pulled off with Mick and the boys—a scam, really—and she burst into tears. By that time my father's illegal activities had already surfaced, as well as the existence of my mother, and Ana and me. Boss had died in jail the previous year. Ana was terrified that I'd be arrested like our father and she'd be left all alone."

"What about your mother?"

"She was gone, as well. I always felt she'd been hounded to death by the press after the scandal about my father broke." He scrubbed a hand across his jaw. "I guess I felt that since everyone expected me to be my father's son, I would be. Ana made me look—really look—at my life. I made some hard decisions that day."

"What did you do?"

"I ended my association with Mick and the others. From then on, I went out of my way to make sure that every single business deal was scrupulously honest. I went back to school. Eventually I got into Harvard. And I made money. A lot of it."

"And your father's other family? The Hollisters?"

"MacKenzie's mother, Meredith, is a socialite who had the money and the name to match my father's. My mother was a dirt-poor farmgirl from the wrong side of the tracks. He married the one and made a mistress of the other."

"And his children paid the ultimate price."

"Yes." He sat up abruptly, setting the hammock swaying, his face a mask of pain. "I intend to make damn certain history doesn't repeat itself."

"How are you going to do that?" she asked apprehensively.

"It's simple." His eyes turned winter-cold. "I won't have any children. That way I can't screw up their lives."

Four

Joc's remark put a swift end to their interlude on the beach. After they collected their possessions, they returned to the cabaña. Darkness descended, filling the air with new night-blooming scents that were even more intoxicating than those Rosalyn had picked up on during the day. But the mood between her and Joc had changed and she followed him inside without pausing to wallow in the unique fragrances.

"I have nine o'clock reservations at Ambrosia. It's one of the newer hotel restaurants," Joc said. "I suspect you'll be more comfortable using the spare bedroom to freshen up. So take your time getting ready."

She appreciated his consideration in not forcing an unnatural intimacy. She loitered in the shower, and afterward exited into the attached bedroom. To her surprise, a box rested on the bed with her name scrawled on the tag. She examined it with equal parts curiosity and trepidation. Ripping apart the outer wrapping, she tore off the lid of the box and stared at the contents. To call it a dress didn't do it justice. She eased it from its nest of tissue and shook her head in amazement.

The floor-length gown would have been lighter than a feather if it hadn't been for the beadwork. Of course, if it hadn't been for the beadwork, the wearer would have been arrested for public indecency. The black gown was as sheer as a negligee, swirls of beads in the shape of exotic flowers fanning the bodice and curling across the pelvis and buttocks. Two spaghetti straps claimed to hold the gown in place, but Rosalyn suspected they lied.

She gave the gown a light shake and a scrap of paper floated to the ground. It landed faceup on the carpet and she picked it up. *I hope you'll wear this for dinner tonight. No other woman could do it justice.* It was a pretty lie, one she chose to believe for a few, sweet moments. Then she examined the gown again, her brow creasing in a frown.

There were reasons she couldn't wear his gift, even if she were willing to accept such an expensive present, reasons Joc couldn't have possibly guessed. The gown was going back right now. Wistfully she ran a hand across the delicate beadwork. It was so beautiful, so feminine, so…so daring. She shook her head. Not that it mattered. Back it went. The instant, the very moment, the exact second after she tried it on.

Giving in to temptation, she tossed aside the robe

she'd donned after her shower and eased the gown over her head. One quick shimmy had it dropping into place and two cautious steps had her in front of the full-length mirror affixed to the bedroom wall. She shook her head in disbelief. The mundane rancher had been transformed into something…glamorous.

The gown fit as though painted on, clinging to every sleek curve. From the front it had the unmitigated gall to appear modest, the bodice only hinting at cleavage. She suspected the same couldn't be said for the back. Rotating, she examined herself over her shoulder. Holy mother! The gown plunged endlessly, screeching to a halt a scant half inch above the curve of her buttocks. Coiling flower stems outlined in flashing red snaked along the edges of the deep U, drawing the eye on a helpless journey down her spine before arriving at the sassy collection of beads that cupped her bottom.

No way. No way would she wear this gorgeous, out-rageous, elegant gown in public, especially since it risked revealing things she'd rather keep concealed. She stepped closer to the mirror, eyeing her abdomen through the beads before turning to check whether anything could be seen along her right hip. To her delight, nothing was visible. As with the one-piece maillot she'd worn to the beach, not a single flaw showed. Oh, dear. It truly was the perfect gown.

Before she could wiggle out of it a knock sounded at the door, and she crossed the room to answer it. From knee to floor, the gown fluttered as she walked, belling outward in flirty wisps. She gave an experimental skip, feeling the most feminine she had in ages—maybe ever.

Of course, it was hard to feel feminine when your typical mode of dress was a sweat-soaked plaid shirt, boots and a pair of worn jeans stained with elements best left unidentified.

She opened the door a scant inch and peeked through the narrow opening. Joc stood there. "I want you to wear it," he said without preliminary.

She gave a short laugh. "One of the saddest aspects of life is that we don't always get what we want."

"What will it take for you to agree?"

She lifted an eyebrow. "Another negotiation?" she asked. "I thought we weren't negotiating on this trip."

"If that's what's necessary to get you into that gown, that's what we'll do."

"Before you try to get me out of it?"

His chuckle was one of agreement, the soft, intimate sound sending an unwanted shaft of desire arrowing through her. "You can't hang a man for dreaming, Red."

"Condemn him, maybe."

"Only if I manage to turn that dream into reality."

She flashed on an image of his powerful hands on her shoulders, snapping the thin straps of the gown. Rapt masculine eyes watching as the weight of the beads sent the dress plummeting to the floor in a glittering pool of black, edged with flaming red. The vulnerability of nudity mixed with a painful, unremitting want. His reaching for her. Her retreat toward the bed. His pursuit. The endless tumble to the waiting mattress. Helpless desire growing with each touch before the inevitable mating of body and soul—

She dismissed that possibility without hesitation,

though something hot and heavy settled deep in the pit of her stomach, something that had the beads of the gown shuddering in agitation. "That's not going to happen," she managed to tell him. Or were her words meant for herself?

"Time will tell. So, are you going to wear it?"

She couldn't resist sneaking another peek over her shoulder, the mirror reflecting an image she'd never seen before. Common sense warred with an irrational, wholly feminine craving. For the past decade, she'd always put the interests of Longhorn ahead of her own. Always. For the first time ever, she wanted to be tempted. Wanted to surrender to the forbidden. To the fantasy in which she found herself.

She spoke before common sense won out, giving way to the baser of her two choices. "I either dine in this or the jeans I wore to fly out here."

"Actually, it's that or your bathrobe since your other clothes are being laundered." His eyes gleamed with laughter at having boxed her in so neatly. "So, will you wear it?"

"I guess I don't have any other choice."

"Not a one," he agreed.

"I do have a request, however."

"Name it."

She glanced down at her toes poking out from beneath the hem of the gown. "I think I'll need more than just this dress. I'm guessing Ambrosia has a policy against dining in bare feet. Unless you want me to wear my boots?"

"Check the box. You'll find shoes and underwear."

Her brows tugged together. "Underwear?"

"Dig around. There are a couple of beads strung together with dental floss that you're supposed to wear under the dress. I'm not surprised you missed it."

She'd been so focused on the gown, she hadn't noticed the shoes, let alone the underwear. She stirred uneasily. "Listen… Just so we're clear. There aren't any strings attached to your gift, right?"

"Only the ones that hold the beads in place." He checked his watch. "If you'll excuse me, I have a brief appointment I can't avoid. Why don't I meet you at Ambrosia at nine?"

"I'll be there."

But even as the words escaped, a part of her warned that she was a fool, allowing herself to be seduced by Joc and his fantasy world. Come tomorrow she'd be back to reality and that transition would come fast and hard…and no doubt as painful as a fall from a bucking stallion.

At precisely nine o'clock, Joc had the intense pleasure of watching Rosalyn stride through Ambrosia toward him. He wasn't the only one watching. Of course, the gown she wore might have played a part in the attention she received. It provided a dramatic contrast to her wine-red hair, pale complexion and spectacular physique. But it was more than the dress. It was the strength of her personality that held everyone's attention—the life force that caused the very air to shimmer around her.

His smile deepened. She truly was glorious. In four-inch heels she appeared downright statuesque. The subdued lighting flashed off the beading of her gown like a series of warning beacons as she cut through the collection of tables blocking her path with a lazy, long-legged grace. Conversation halted briefly at her approach before swelling with her passage. Not that she noticed. Nor did she notice the maître d' scurrying in her wake, outraged that she'd invaded his domain without permission, escort, or so much as a by-your-leave.

Joc stood at her approach, their gazes locking. Eyes as stunning a blue as a deepening sunset regarded him warily. "You look beautiful," he offered.

"Thanks." Her mouth curved to one side as she gave his suit the once-over. "So do you."

Her frankness filled him with a fierce satisfaction. Whatever mysterious quirk of nature had sparked the attraction between them, it was definitely mutual. As hard as she might resist that attraction, what would happen between them had been determined long ago. She could fight the inevitable—no doubt would fight—but ultimately, there'd be no turning from it.

He waited while the maître d' held her chair before taking the seat across from her. She finally became aware of the beleaguered man's presence and flashed him a generous smile that earned her instant forgiveness. Joc concealed his amusement at how sublimely oblivious she was to the undercurrents swirling around her.

Perhaps it was her intense focus on the path she forged through life that kept her from noticing such subtleties. Or perhaps the people who crossed her path sensed what he had when he'd first met her—that she was someone special. Whatever the root cause, the outcome remained the same. Rosalyn left an indelible mark wherever she went, attracting people with effortless ease.

The sommelier arrived just then to discuss the extensive wine list, followed by the waiter, who took several minutes to describe the various dishes and house specials. The instant they'd placed their order, she glanced at him and Joc suddenly realized that she was down-to-the-bones nervous, the emotion implicit in every aspect of her appearance from the flash of flame-red hair and black beads, to the ripple of tension across shoulders and arms that her gown so beautifully revealed.

"What's wrong?" he asked quietly.

She didn't bother dissembling. "I'm just not sure why I'm here."

"You can leave at any time. I told you there weren't any strings involved in our night together and I meant it."

She gave him a direct look. "I can change my mind and you wouldn't be upset?"

Blunt and to the point. He liked that about her. "Disappointed, but not upset." He reached for her hand, pausing just short of touching her in order to make his point. His fingers were splayed so close above hers, that she could feel the warmth, feel the current of attraction that flowed between them. It forged a connection, one she couldn't ignore. "But you won't change your mind."

He caught the slight tremble of her fingers before she steadied them. She was strong-willed, he'd give her that. And tenacious. But no matter how hard she fought to put rationality before emotion, her body betrayed her. All it took was that almost-touch and the heat flared between them. Carefully she slid her hand out from beneath his and rubbed her palm across her thigh, as though attempting to erase her response to him. He doubted she was even aware of her actions. In fact, he knew she wasn't.

As she struggled to regain her equilibrium, a demi-sec Vouvray arrived at their table, along with their appetizer. The platter contained a selection of bite-size delicacies. Ice-cold prawns vied with spiced calamari. Delicate slivers of sautéed scallops were artfully arranged on *galettes au fromage*. And clam-shaped pastry puffs were guarded by stalks of marinated asparagus.

He transferred the most succulent of the selections to her plate while she sampled the wine. Plucking a prawn from her plate, Rosalyn dipped it in the chef's specialty cocktail sauce and took a bite. She closed her eyes and sighed with pleasure. His teeth clamped together at the expression on her face. He wanted her to look at him like that, to lie in his bed with moonlight gilding her nudity and look at him in just that way as he slid inside her. He made a decision there and then. He didn't care what it took. He didn't care what he had to promise. He wanted this woman. And before the night ended, he'd have her.

"Good?" To his relief, she didn't seem to hear the primitive male aggression ripping apart that single word. But she was no one's fool. If he didn't get himself under control—and fast—she'd figure it out. And chances were excellent, she'd flee. If she were smart, she would.

"This is outstanding." She looked at him then, her eyes heavy-lidded and drunk on sensory pleasure. "The best I've ever had were some tiger prawns in New Orleans, but I think there's a new winner in town."

She helped herself to some of the calamari. "So, did you take care of your business?"

He shook his head. "I won't be able to do that until tomorrow morning. My appointment this evening was with my lawyer. Preliminary work before I meet with the other owners of Deseos."

"Huh. It didn't occur to me that you might have partners. I just assumed you were the sole owner of the island." She offered a swift, self-deprecating smile. "Silly, huh?"

"Not at all. As a matter of fact, by the end of tomorrow I *will* be the sole owner."

That stopped her. She returned the scallops she'd been about to sample to her plate. "That sounds ominous."

He shrugged. "The partnership didn't work out. I should have known, based on our past history."

Her eyes narrowed as she worked her way through his deliberately oblique comment, dissecting it bit by bit. "By any chance are we talking about Mick and your other school friends?"

She was quick, he'd give her that. "The very same."

"Why would you—" She broke off. "I'm sorry. That's none of my business."

"No, it's not, but I'll answer, anyway." He couldn't keep the hard quality from infiltrating his voice. "Mick and the others came to me, all of them together like the band of brothers we'd once been. They claimed they'd fallen on hard times. Made bad choices in their lives. They said they'd finally come around, just as I had all those years ago, and were ready to change. All they needed was a helping hand. Of course, that wasn't what they were after."

"What were they after?" she asked softly.

"Deseos, of course." He bit off the end of a bread-stick and crushed it between his back teeth. "And the opportunity to screw me over because I'd left them behind all those years ago. Left them behind and made my fortune without them."

Noting her shock, he abandoned the subject and moved the conversation to more neutral topics. He wanted the night to revolve around romance, not dissention. To entice her, not scare her off. The rest of the evening passed with surprising ease, the discussion flowing from one topic to the next. He found Rosalyn an intriguing companion, sharp, witty and one of the most confident women he'd ever met. He couldn't remember the last time he'd met someone so comfortable in her own skin, so aware of who she was and where she came from.

After they'd finished their dinner, Joc suggested a walk on the pier, an offer Rosalyn accepted with alacrity. They wandered through the hotel garden and he mated his stride to hers, not quite touching, but close enough to catch her unique fragrance and feel the warmth of her body.

They reached the pier and she struggled to deal with the uneven planking in the ridiculous shoes he'd bought for her. She only stumbled once, but it was enough to elicit a hiss of annoyance from him. He cut in front of her. The instant she checked up, he crouched at her feet.

"Hang on a sec. You're going to break an ankle in those things and I'll be to blame. Let me get them off you."

Encircling her ankle, he lifted her foot across his thigh. His fingers were warm and careful, caressing the sensitive skin around her ankle with a feather-light touch. Rosalyn held herself rigidly erect, feeling like the world's most awkward stork. Teetering, she doubled over and clamped onto his shoulders. He shot out a hand to steady her, cupping her hip. His fingers splayed across the curve of her backside, his thumb following the line of the single elastic thread—dental floss, he'd called it—that held her thong in place. He lingered, stroking for a brief, delicious instant.

The sizzle from that stolen caress burned through the thin material of her gown, igniting a shock wave that caused every bead on her dress to glitter in distress. He lifted his head, his face only inches from hers. She could hear the rasp of his breath, fast and rough. Feel his desire. Practically taste the urgency that flowed between them. It was wrong, wrong in every possible way. Even knowing that, her hold on him gentled, eased from grip to embrace. She wanted to fall into him. Consume him. Battle toward the sweetest of surrenders. His name escaped of its own volition, hovering in the air between them.

He responded by reaching out and stroking her bottom lip with his thumb. "Soon," he murmured.

The promise broke whatever spell she'd been under and she eased back, suddenly self-conscious. "There's no rush."

"So I've been telling myself. Based on our reaction to each other, I'm not convinced that's true." He finished removing her shoe before following suit with the second, his touch more impersonal, as though that moment of desperate awareness had never happened. Standing, he hooked the heels over the lip of his pocket. "Ready?" he asked.

She snatched a quick, steadying breath and nodded. "I can walk, if that's what you mean." Barely.

Get a grip! she ordered herself as she headed toward the end of the pier. What was wrong with her that the instant he came too close she lost every intelligent thought she possessed? Did she want him to kiss her? Did she hope to use that kiss as an excuse? An excuse to what? Fall mindlessly into his arms? To have a one-night stand with him and be done with it? She couldn't say for certain, which only served to alarm her all the more. She was losing control, something she couldn't afford to do.

Once she left fantasyland she had a ranch to consider—and a man with the drive to win at all costs intent on wrestling it away from her. She couldn't afford to lose herself in a sexual haze while he busied himself working out a plan for circumventing her and achieving his goal.

She had to remember it was her duty to protect her land at all costs. It was part of her heritage, part of the Oakley legacy that had been passed from generation to generation for nearly a hundred and eighty years. Maybe if she focused on that, on her need to protect her ranch by uncovering Joc's weaknesses, she'd find a way to get through the rest of the evening.

Small groups pocketed the lighted boardwalk, some fishing, some wrapped in an embrace, others just gazing out at the ocean. She walked in silence until they could go no farther. No one else had ventured quite this far, and she paused beneath the circle of light cast from a wrought-iron lamp.

"What's wrong?" he asked.

She didn't bother prevaricating. "I'm just wondering why I agreed to come here with you." She swept a hand downward to indicate her gown. "What am I doing here, dressed like this, intent on having a one-night stand with you?"

"Have you changed your mind?"

She glanced at him. "Have you?"

"Not even a little."

"I want you," she admitted with devastating honesty. "But I'm not sure how smart it is to give in to that want when it might put my ranch in jeopardy."

"You don't trust me."

She shook her head. "No more than you trust me. Or your old friends. Or the Hollisters." She fixed him with an unflinching stare. "So, why am I here, Joc? What do you really want? Is this your way of romancing the ranch out from under me?"

"Damn it, Red." Ripe frustration underscored his words. "You know what I want, and right now it has nothing to do with your ranch. I want you in my bed. I want to make love to you until neither of us can think straight."

An image of them together flashed through her mind. It came easily. Too easily. The sounds, the scents, the feel of him over and around and inside of her. The breeze tugged at her hair, kicking free a silken strand. It danced around her face, highlighting her agitation. "And afterward?"

He fought to clamp down on his emotions, and she marveled at his struggle. It was an impressive one. "Afterward, we're back where we started," he admitted through gritted teeth. He approached, halting a scant foot away. Without her heels, he towered over her. For the first time in more years than she could recall, she felt small and vulnerable and unsure of herself. "Does that even matter? If we both agree that whatever happens tonight has nothing to do with our business association—"

She cut him off without hesitation. "We don't have a business association."

"I repeat. Then where's the problem? You want me. I want you. Your ranch has nothing to do with what's happening between us. All we have to do is return to the cabaña. Agree, and we can both have what we want most."

Stepping outside of the circle of lamplight, she tried to separate desire from practicality. Not that she succeeded. Right now she didn't care about the consequences, despite knowing that though this felt right, it was guaranteed to go wrong. "I don't know, Joc. I need to think."

He followed her into the shadows, allowing the darkness to swallow them both. He dropped his hands onto her shoulders. "You chose to come with me. There's only one reason you'd have done that."

Her gaze never left his face. He was right. There was only one reason. More than anything, she wanted this one night in his bed. He must have read her answer in her eyes. He cupped her shoulders and drew her against him. Then he lowered his head and took her mouth with his.

A desperate need raced through her, just as it had when he'd kissed her by the old homestead. The feeling bit just as urgently now as then. Heady desire stole every thought from her head, and drove her to wrap her arms around his neck and pull him closer yet. Her lips parted beneath the insistent pressure of his and his tongue swept inward to duel with hers. He tasted of wine and passion, deliciously warm and moist, gifting her with an intense pleasure unlike anything she'd ever experienced before.

His hands slid from her shoulders downward, tracing her back where her gown bared her. She shuddered beneath the teasing caress. Unable to help herself, she pressed closer, feeling the unyielding ridge of his arousal. She needed to touch him, to forge a more intimate contact. She found him with her hands, cupping him through the trousers of his suit. He groaned, the sound rough and primal, and she made her decision.

"Please take me back to the cabaña," she whispered against his mouth.

Without a word, he took her hand in his and retraced their steps. The walk to the owner's suite seemed endless. She didn't dare pause to admire the scenery. She simply focused on putting one bare foot in front of the other and moving forward with all due diligence and speed until they found themselves standing in the foyer of Joc's cabaña.

He didn't say a word. He didn't have to. His eyes said it all. He stared down at her for an endless moment with a gaze that reflected moon-drenched nights filled with unforgettable passion. Reality faded beneath that look, tempting her to indulge in pure physical pleasure.

But she couldn't, not entirely. She was too pragmatic

for fantasy and had faced too many painful endings to believe that a single night of desire could lead anywhere but to another painful ending. Even knowing all that, she still couldn't resist the inevitable, though she'd do her best to make that ending a little less painful.

She moistened her lips. "If we…if we—"

"Make love."

"It's not making love. It's sex," she insisted, before plowing onward. "If we have sex, I need you to understand that it has nothing to do with the ranch or our negotiations."

"I know."

"I don't use sex as a tool. I never have and I never will."

He dropped her shoes and tipped her face up to his. "Listen to what I'm saying, Red." His hands sank deep into her hair. "I know you don't. That you wouldn't."

"I just needed to make that clear." She snatched a quick breath and forced herself to admit the truth, more for her own benefit than for his. "I want you. Physically. And then I want to walk away and never see you again."

He shook his head. "That's not going to happen."

"Those are the only rules I can live with. One time," she negotiated desperately. "Then never again."

"You're about to discover that I'm a man who breaks all the rules." He feathered a kiss across her mouth, eliciting a helpless moan. "Our first time will be tender and slow and as prolonged as I can make it."

She moaned again. "You just want to make me suffer."

"I plan to do my very best. And it won't be one time. It'll be all night long. By the time we're through, we'll be so intertwined we won't be able to tell where one of us begins and the other ends."

If he hadn't been holding her up, she would have melted into a puddle at his feet. "And then we walk away." Assuming they could still walk. "After we get untwined, we go our separate ways, right?" She had to win one concession in this devil's bargain, because she'd fast come to realize that, like it or not, they were in the middle of an intense negotiation.

"That might be a little difficult considering we're on an island. We still have to fly home together tomorrow."

"But after that. Never again. We part company. Otherwise…otherwise no sex." Who was she kidding?

His grin flashed in the darkness. "I guess there's not much I can do about it, if that's what you want."

"That's what I want. One night and after that we're through with each other." And after they returned to Dallas, she'd never see him again. Never allow him to touch her again. Never be held in his arms again or shudder in anticipation of what would happen over the coming hours. Her arms tightened around his neck. But that was tomorrow. She still had tonight. "Make love to me, Joc. Quick. Before I change my mind."

Five

Joc lifted Rosalyn with an easy strength. Instead of carrying her to either of the two bedrooms, he headed for the lanai. It was more humid here, but nighttime cool. Lush, delicious scents filled the air, scents that the air-conditioning hadn't scrubbed clean.

He lowered Rosalyn to her feet and she crossed to the screen door and stared out toward the lagoon. Shadows covered much of the view, but she could see the moonlight gleaming on the white-tipped waves as they curled toward shore, and could hear the muted crash as the water pounded the sand, followed by the soft hiss of retreat.

Tonight she intended to be selfish. Tonight was hers. Just this one night, with moonlight drenching them and the stars raining down. Just one night of greed, to take what was offered. To use and be used until she couldn't see or think straight. To have every last problem blown straight out of her head. To have a few hours to herself without worrying about finances, or a broken fence line or sick livestock or promises she was honor bound to keep.

Joc wrapped his arms around her. "Where have you gone, Red?"

She turned in his arms and blew out a sigh. "I'm an idiot."

"Second thoughts?"

She dropped her head to his shoulder. "It's not that." She started to laugh, hoping he didn't hear the heartbreak that hid behind her amusement. "This—" She gestured to encompass the room and the island and him. "It's supposed to be a night off. A night of fantasy."

"An escape from reality."

"Yes."

He lifted her chin and grimaced at her expression. "Started thinking, did you?"

"I did." He surprised her by smoothing the furrows from her brow and she relaxed against him. "I don't suppose there's something you can do about that?"

"I'll give it my best shot."

He kissed her. Not with the desperate passion of earlier. Not with a blistering stamp of possession. This was an exploration, a delving into something new and fascinating. Something not to be rushed. Her breathing quickened, as did her want. It rose like the tide, building and curling, a wave of need rushing toward shore. She reached for him as it broke, wrapping her arms tight, tight, tight around his neck. His tongue dueled with hers, teasing, taunting, mating. She couldn't get enough. Not close enough, not hard enough, not…just not enough.

He edged her away from the screen door and deeper into the lanai, deeper into the shadows and the blessed darkness. She felt his hands in her hair. Felt the quick tugs as he plucked free the pins holding her hair in place.

"I've wanted to do this all night." Her hair slid downward and he filled his hands with the weighty mass. "Why would you keep something this beautiful hidden away?"

She stared in bewilderment. "It wasn't hidden."

"First that stupid hat."

"It keeps the sun off my face."

"Then tonight."

"I was going for sophisticated. I thought it matched the dress."

His gaze lowered. "Yes. The dress. Let's see what we can do about that."

He slid the spaghetti straps from her shoulders before finding the zip and lowering it. The weight of the beads sent the bodice of the gown dropping. It didn't stop there. It slid all the way to her hips and clung for a brief instant before gravity sent it plummeting to the floor with a nervous chatter of beads.

She stood before him in nothing more than a wispy thong and acres of pale naked skin. Suddenly self-conscious, she shifted so she remained clear of the moonlight, hoping the cloak of shadows hid most of her flaws. "You still have all your clothes on," she said. "That strikes me as patently unfair."

He couldn't take his eyes off her. "I'm forced to

disagree." He cupped her breast and stroked his thumb across the tip. "You're as perfect as I'd anticipated."

She shivered at the agonizing tightening of her nipple, the sensation piercing straight to her core. How could she be wound so tight that every nerve felt on the verge of exploding, while at the same time that single touch had her entire body loosening and softening?

"You didn't have to anticipate too hard." She fought to speak through a haze of desire. "That dress didn't leave much to the imagination."

"Which is why I chose it with you in mind." His voice deepened. "And then, with you out of it in mind."

His fingernail scraped again and she lost it. She yanked at the tie moored at his neck until she'd managed to rip it loose. The buttons of his shirt came next, the studs that held it closed hitting the wooden floor with soft pings as they scattered. She worked her way past his shirt until she reached hot, hard flesh. There she paused, reveling in the feel of him, in the strength and power of endless muscle and sinew. God, he was in incredible shape. She covered him with kisses as she removed each article of clothing.

When he was as naked as she, he backed them toward one end of the lanai to a love seat which he flattened into a daybed. She tumbled backward onto the thick cushions. They were soft and cool against her back and his weight had her sinking into them, the dichotomy of searing and inflexible above, and light and downy beneath, making her head swim.

"Joc!" His name escaped in a desperate rush, pleading for something she couldn't seem to express any other way.

Determination cut across his face and he touched her, soothing without saying a word. His mouth found hers, the joining of lips and tongue filled with a tenderness at odds with the fierceness of his personality. There was a newness to their kiss, as though they'd discovered some fresh and unexpected delicacy and were intent on savoring every moment. She'd never experienced anything like it—lustful, yet sensitive. Passionate, yet poignant.

He cupped her breasts, teasing the peaks before this attention drifted downward. Before she could stop him, his hands swept across her abdomen and he froze. Instantly she blocked his view with her arm, an instinctive attempt at self-preservation.

"No, honey, don't." He interlaced her fingers with his. "You don't have to hide from me."

Rearing back, he shifted her arm to one side so silvered moonlight spilled across her torso, merciless in what it exposed. She stared at the ceiling and the pounding of her heartbeat filled her ears as she waited for his reaction, waited to see if he accepted or rejected her. Then he touched her again, tracing the jagged scar from where it started, just beneath her left breast. Inch by excruciating inch he followed its path across her abdomen to where it terminated, high on her right hip.

She shivered beneath the intimate touch. Other than the physicians who'd treated her, only one other person had ever seen that scar. At the end of their affair, he'd told her he'd made love to her despite it, even though it sickened him to look at it, or to accidentally touch it. But Joc seemed determined to examine every aspect. Just when she was on the verge of erupting off the love seat, he spoke.

"How, Red?" He sounded vaguely outraged. "How did this happen?"

She fought to speak in a normal voice. "It was an accident."

"I'm relieved to hear it wasn't on purpose. But…that must have been some accident."

"It was."

"Aw, hell. This happened when you took over running Longhorn after your parents' death, didn't it? That's when you were scarred."

She nodded. "My first week on the job. I was eighteen and in way over my head. The bull knew it and explained the facts of life to me."

He bit out a curse. "You were gored?"

"Yes. I've carried that scar as a reminder ever since."

"A reminder of what?"

"Of what I owe the legacy I've been given, and the toll that legacy sometimes exacts."

"You're self-conscious about it, aren't you?"

In response, she threw an arm across her face. Her withdrawal stirred an instantaneous reaction. He lowered his head and his ebony hair caressed her belly, his breath warming her chilled skin. And then his mouth closed over the scar. A shudder erupted from deep inside, directly beneath his lips, spreading outward in surges of liquid heat.

"I hate that this happened to you," he murmured. "But what I hate worse is that it's stolen your self-confidence and made you uncertain at a moment when you should be at your most powerful. When you should be the most secure in your femininity."

His words slipped deep into her soul, thawing something that had long been frozen. Tears filled her eyes and tracked a silent path along her temples and into her hair. "I thought it might repulse you."

He looked at her, a look that allowed her to see deep inside, to know that when he spoke it was with absolute honesty and sincerity. "This is a mark of survival. How could it repulse me?"

She didn't know how long she lay there, absorbing the shock of his words. All she knew was that he'd stripped her bare, uncovering the one place she was most vulnerable. He was her enemy, and she'd exposed her wounded underbelly. But instead of taking advantage of her defenselessness, instead of ripping her to shreds, he'd given her back her strength. She reached for him, determined to match strength for strength, to give as he had.

She cupped his face and tugged him back into her arms. He kissed her, his mouth warm and demanding, welcoming her inward. She wrapped herself around him, staking a claim.

"Please, Joc." She lifted her hips in a suggestive swirl. "I want you."

When he refused to take their embrace further, she seized the initiative. She gently scored his chest with her nails before trailing her fingertips across his rippled abs. And then she dipped lower still, cupping the very source of his desire. His breath escaped in a harsh gasp.

"Are you trying to kill me, woman?" The question burst from between clenched teeth.

"Not kill you. Not quite." She peeked up at him with a teasing grin. "Do you like it?"

"Oh, yeah." He caught hold of her wrists and pulled them above her head, anchoring them there with one hand. "Now let's see how you like it."

He cupped the moist delta between her legs, dipping inward in slow, teasing strokes. He didn't stop until she was arching beneath his touch, pleading for his possession. Not that it helped. She could feel herself losing control, her muscles clenching and fluttering on the verge of climax. She lay beneath him, open and wanting. As though sensing how close to the edge she hovered, he slipped between her legs.

"This was inevitable from the beginning," he told her, as he reached for protection. "From the moment I first saw you, I knew it could only end one way."

"Then let it end," she begged.

There was no more talking after that. He joined them, sheathing himself in her heat with a single powerful stroke. What came next was a primal dance as old as time.

She rode the moment, wishing it could last forever. But she was too close to the edge for that to happen. The fluttering began again, rippling and fisting. Joc threw back his head, his throat moving convulsively as he drove home. And then the rapture came, overwhelming in its intensity.

Rosalyn had thought this night would be a simple sexual act. But in that timeless instant, where two became one, in that moment of perfect union, what she felt grew into something far deeper. Something that bonded her to him. Something that forever changed her.

Far worse, it became something she knew with absolute certainty she'd never be able to walk away from.

* * *

Joc watched, once again, as Rosalyn slowly woke. As before on the plane, her sleepy expression held a heart-wrenching vulnerability, one that cut him to the quick. All of her secrets were exposed to his scrutiny—the helpless passion he'd roused in her. The physical scar she'd hidden from him so self-consciously. The emotional scars she protected with even greater care. And worst of all, the events that had transpired just a few short hours ago. It was all there in the nervous caution with which she regarded him.

"Morning," he greeted her, the word taking on a gruff quality.

She eased upward, pulling the sheet to her chin. "Morning." She closed her eyes and released a cha-grined laugh. "Listen to us. Considering what happened last night—"

"Not to mention this morning."

Her gaze clashed with his at the reminder. "Not to mention this morning," she confirmed with impressive calm. "After all that you'd think we'd be more comfort-able with each other."

"Speaking of this morning…" He watched the color come and go in her cheeks. "I seem to recall we were un-fortunate enough to have a slight equipment malfunction."

"You mean—"

He didn't temper his words. "I mean, the condom broke. Are you on the pill?"

She shook her head. "There's never been any need."

"Then we have a problem."

The sophisticated woman from the night before

vanished beneath the unrelenting tropical light of day. She sank deeper into the pillows, shadows darkening her eyes, and pulled her legs tight against her chest. "There's every chance it isn't a problem," she insisted. But he could hear the note of uncertainty coloring her declaration.

He forced himself to use a calm, reassuring tone of voice, the one that had always brought him the most success during tense negotiations. "I assume we won't know for a few weeks."

Her confession barely topped a whisper. "No."

"Are you in the middle of your cycle or toward one end?"

"Middle."

He scrubbed his hand across his face. "Okay. There's nothing we can do about it at this point, but I'd like to make a simple request."

"I'm almost afraid to ask… What's your request and how simple is it?"

"I'd like you to promise to call me one way or the other as soon as you know. Will you do that?" He watched her closely, searching for any hint of prevarication. To his relief he saw none.

"Absolutely."

A phone rang deep within the cabaña and with a swift apology, he went to answer it, dealing with details for the upcoming meeting with impatient efficiency. By the time he returned to the lanai, Rosalyn was gone, having used the interruption as an opportunity to escape. Not that he blamed her. No doubt she felt the less said on the subject, the better, as though ignoring it would make it go away.

He stood for a long moment in silent contemplation. A baby. She could be pregnant with his child. He'd always sworn he'd never have children, not after what he and Ana had gone through. But he couldn't get the image of Rosalyn out of his mind. He could see her as clearly as though she were standing there. Strong. Lean. Forthright.

And ripe with his child.

Once again he wanted. Wanted with a passion that defied all attempts at control and threatened all he hoped to achieve.

Rosalyn took her time in the bathroom, scrubbing every inch of herself. But it didn't change anything. Her skin still glowed from Joc's possession, her body forever branded by his touch. She could even smell him, his unique scent lingering on her lips and saturating her senses.

How could she have thought that a single night with him would be sufficient? Last night had been unlike anything she'd ever experienced before, and if she were honest, she'd admit that she wanted more. She'd been a fool to think they'd be able to indulge in a one-night stand and then walk away without consequences, both emotional and…

Her hand slid downward to splay across the flatness of her abdomen. Was it possible? Could she be pregnant? It had only been one slip-up, a slight tear in the "equipment" as Joc referred to it. What were the odds that a baby could result? The probability had to be low. Still… What if it had happened?

She closed her eyes, allowing the hot spray to

cascade over her head. Joc had already made his position perfectly clear. Not only wasn't he interested in having children, but he'd stated in no uncertain terms that he refused to have them. Period. So where did that leave her? Between the proverbial rock and hard place, that's where.

It didn't matter, she decided. If potential became reality, she wouldn't ask Joc for anything. She'd raise the baby on her own. He or she would be an Oakley, with a heritage the child could embrace with pride. The Oakley legacy would continue for another generation. Nothing would make her happier than that.

The water cooled and she hastened to turn it off. She'd wasted enough time. It wasn't in her nature to hide and she wouldn't start now. She'd made a choice last night and she'd face it without flinching. She spared a few minutes to dry her hair and touch up her face with the cosmetics that had been left for her use. She found her clothes from the previous day freshly laundered and folded on the bed. Even her Stetson had been cleaned and blocked. Five minutes later she emerged from the bedroom, ready to face Joc and anything he threw her way.

She found him nursing a cup of coffee, papers spread out on the table in front of him. He stood at her appearance and poured a second cup for her. "How do you take it?"

She gave him the standard Longhorn response. "Black as tar and thick as mud."

That won her a smile. "I have the tar part down, but I'm afraid you'll have to skip the mud and settle for thirty-weight oil."

She returned his smile with one of her own, pleased they were back on a more casual footing. "Not quite as thick, but I'll make do."

"I'm about to head over to the office complex for my meeting." He passed her the coffee. "I'd appreciate it if you'd join me."

His offer caught her off guard. Despite the nonchalant manner in which he'd made the suggestion, she sensed a deeper purpose behind the invitation. She eyed him warily as she downed her coffee. "Just out of curiosity, why would you want me there?"

"I think you'll find it…educational."

She tilted her head to one side, a spark of annoyance flickering to life. "You think I'm in need of an education?"

"When it comes to this particular arena, it wouldn't hurt." He checked his watch. "We'll be leaving for Dallas immediately after I've dissolved the partnership. I should have you home by midafternoon."

Well, what had she expected? That he'd declare his undying love and fix all that had gone wrong in her life? It was a ridiculous dream, particularly when he'd been the one to cause most of her current problems. Besides, she'd been handling endless trials and tribulations for a full decade now. She didn't need a man to rescue her when she was perfectly capable of taking care of herself.

He continued to wait for her response and she gave a brisk nod of her head, hoping she sounded relaxed and easygoing instead of utterly out of her depth. "Fine. I'm always open to new experiences." Not that they'd ever compare to what she'd experienced last night. "I'd find it interesting to sit in on one of your meetings."

As soon as they finished breakfast, they headed over to another rambling building almost identical to the cabaña on the outside, but which bore the undeniable stamp of a business complex once they stepped across the threshold. A secretary ushered them to the conference room, one that didn't share any of the features or characteristics of its counterpart in Dallas.

Light and airy, it reflected the colors and qualities of the island. A plush white carpet the exact shade of the local sand stretched beneath her feet, while the walls were a rich aquamarine that perfectly matched the crystalline water of the lagoon she'd enjoyed the previous day. Instead of a long, rectangular conference table, this one was round, appealing and convivial. It was a room meant to soothe, to allay worry and concern and instill warmth and camaraderie. Or so she thought, right up until she saw the mosaic wolf motif that decorated the surface of the table.

Memories of her first confrontation with Joc came storming back. It made for a harsh transition from the lovemaking they'd shared the previous night to the hard, cold business venue of today. She'd had her romantic interlude. It was over. Bringing her here told her more clearly than words that they were back on a business footing. The time had come to switch gears. Fast.

She glanced around the room, noticing for the first time a group of five suits-and-ties. They stood bunched on one side of the room, helping themselves to coffee and pastries. They chatted in perfect accord, their ease with one another speaking of long acquaintance. So this was Joc's childhood gang. Next to him, they looked normal, average even. They didn't resonate with Joc's unique power or brilliance. Or sexual chemistry. She wondered which one was Mick. She'd find out soon enough, considering he'd probably take the lead opposing Joc during the meeting.

Reluctantly her gaze switched to Joc and she tensed. He'd taken up a stance on the opposite side of the room. He leaned against a sideboard, his full attention focused on the men, while his eyes gleamed with hungry intent. Oh, man. They were clueless. Utterly clueless to their impending doom. They might as well have "Free Rabbit Meat, Bite Here" stamped on their backsides. And though Joc's posture remained relaxed, she could see him gathering himself in preparation for the takedown. Even his features appeared different, the skin taut across his cheekbones, his mouth and jaw set at an angle that shouted a warning to those astute enough to listen.

Then Joc turned to look at her. To her consternation she realized the predator remained. Only now it prowled in her direction. His black eyes glittered with the intensity of it. A memory of the last time they'd made love dwelt there, an acknowledgment of how it had changed them, as well as a promise that soon—very soon—he'd deal with her, too. Where had her lover gone? she wondered in dismay. Or had that man been no more than an illusion?

He caught her stare and indicated a chair apart from the table. "Why don't you sit there?"

"Out of the line of fire?"

He smiled at the dry tone. "Something like that."

As soon as he had her settled, he crossed to the table

and took a seat. The men took their time joining him. From their quick, sidelong glances Rosalyn knew it was a deliberate maneuver. What benefit they thought it gained—other than to tick Joc off—she couldn't imagine. Or maybe that was the point. A subtle power move. "We may be on your turf," they seemed to be saying, "but we're in charge." They had a lot to learn.

One by one they gathered at the table, still conversing among themselves. Next, they took their time arranging their papers. When they were through, a small stack rested before each man, while the expanse of table in front of Joc remained pristine.

"Well, Arnaud," the leader of the group began. Mick, no doubt. "I think this may be the first time you've ever lost. If it makes you feel any better, at least it'll be some of your oldest friends who take you down."

Rosalyn flinched. Was that how she'd sounded when she'd confronted Joc? Was this how she'd appeared, like these foolish rabbits, intent on tweaking the nose of Mr. Big Bad? Heaven help them. And heaven help her.

Joc leaned back in his chair. "What exactly is it I'm about to lose, Mick?" he asked, confirming his opponent's identity.

The men exchanged quick grins. "Isla de los Deseos," Mick said. "We've voted and it's unanimous. We've cut you a check for your share of the partnership. It's nowhere near the value the island will have once we're done developing it, but it is what the agreement calls for."

To Rosalyn's amazement, Joc didn't appear upset by the news. If anything, he seemed…amused. "I assume this is because I wouldn't agree to your plans?"

"We've tried to explain countless times," Mick said. "This place is a gold mine. All we have to do is mine it."

"You mean cover it from end to end with resorts."

"Exactly." A hint of resentment crept into Mick's voice. "You have all the money you could ever want. What's wrong with some of your old gang getting our fair share? It's just one island."

"And the indigenous life?"

"There are other islands. Let them find one of those."

"We've known each other since we were kids, Mick."

Rosalyn caught an odd quality in Joc's voice. A containment that she recognized because she used that same tone whenever she tried to hide her own pain. It took every ounce of self-possession to remain seated and keep her emotions in check when what she really wanted to do was leap from her chair and rush to Joc's side. To throw her arms around him and offer some form of comfort.

"You'd end our friendship over money?" Joc continued. "Or should I say, over more money?"

Mick stared at Joc as though he'd lost his mind. "Hell, yes. Since we need a unanimous vote to develop the island any further, and we can't get a unanimous vote without ousting you…" He tapped the stack of papers in front of him. "You see our dilemma."

"This partnership deal was supposed to help you get back on your feet. All of you."

Mick's hands collapsed into fists. "And now that we're on our feet, we want more. You should understand that. That need for more is what's driven you all these years. You can't deny that."

Joc didn't argue the point. "You do realize I crafted our partnership deal with great care," he said instead.

Mick shook his head. "Not enough care, Joc. You left a clause in there where we could buy you out." He shrugged. "Guess you were feeling altruistic since we were all friends."

"I wouldn't call it altruistic, or even generous. It was more along the lines of…curiosity."

Rosalyn closed her eyes. She had a sneaking suspicion she knew where Joc was going with this. From everything he'd said, he'd been taught at an early age to distrust, even those closest to him. How must it feel to have that distrust confirmed, and all because of money?

Mick leaned back in his chair, attempting to school his face to patience. "What were you curious about?" He didn't really care about Joc's answer, that much was clear. "What could make you so curious you'd be willing to go into a partnership deal with us, particularly one that gave us the upper hand?"

"I was curious to see if you'd screw me over. And you've answered that question."

A hint of red crept into Mick's face. "Glad to help," he growled. "Now let's get this over with."

"Yes, let's. I've arranged for the five of you to leave the island within the hour."

"You don't own the island anymore, Arnaud." Apprehension bled into Mick's fury, giving it a strident edge. "We voted. You're out."

"Read the partnership agreement more carefully.

Hire a lawyer." Joc's gaze shifted down the line of men to the smallest one at the far end. "A real lawyer who specializes in corporate law and partnership agreements rather than hit-and-run cases. He'll be able to point out this small clause I buried in our contract. One you'll find impossible to break. If you vote to remove me as a partner and it's unanimous, I reserve the right to buy out your shares." He checked his watch. "I have better things to do with my time than find where the lawyers put it, but it's there somewhere. Now, if we're through here?"

All four turned to confront the man at the end, the one Rosalyn assumed was the lawyer who specialized in hit-and-run cases. He shrank in his seat. "I didn't see anything," he mumbled. "MacKenzie never said—"

It was as though the air had been sucked from the room. "MacKenzie?" Joc repeated sharply. "She's involved in this? How?"

No one said a word. The men's gazes dropped to the papers in front of them and stayed there. Rosalyn watched Joc struggle with his fury, gather it up and tuck it away behind a growing wall of disillusionment. Once he'd regained his self-control, he addressed the five.

"One more thing," he said, his voice barely above a whisper. "I wasn't going to enforce the second half of that clause I inserted in our contract. But now that I know that MacKenzie's involved in what you're trying to pull, and that you betrayed me by going along with her plan, I've changed my mind. Not only do I have the right to buy out your shares, but it's at the original buy-in price. None of you will see one dime of profit from this place."

"What the hell—"

Joc shoved back his chair and stood. "Trying to stage a coup out of greed is one thing. I can almost understand that," he bit out. "But you brought a Hollister into this. You allowed her to get to me through all of you. No one does that and profits from it."

All hell broke loose after that. It took a full hour for the shouting to die down. The team of lawyers who swept in and gave an explanation of page, line and verse of the buried clause helped bring the disastrous meeting to a close. When it was over, there were no winners as far as Rosalyn could tell. The partners had lost their bid to take over Deseos. But Joc had lost something far more valuable—his friends. Worse, he'd lost the ability to trust, if he'd ever possessed that quality. She suspected he never had or he wouldn't have buried that clause in the partnership agreement.

She realized something else. She'd been invited to witness that scene for a reason. It was Joc's version of a warning. Cross me at your own risk. He didn't lose. Nor did it matter who he took down—friend or foe, it was all the same to him. She'd been the one to insist the previous night remain outside the scope of their business relationship. Today, he proved that wouldn't be a problem.

At least, not for him.

Six

The minute the meeting ended, Joc escorted her straight to the jet. She waited until they were aboard and in their seat with their seat belts fastened before speaking.

"I'm sorry, Joc," she said.

"For what?" But he knew. She could see the bleakness of that knowledge gathering in his eyes.

"Is there anyone in your life you can trust?"

He hesitated before shrugging. "My sister, Ana."

"Ana. The one who lives in Verdonia. How often do you get to see her?"

His expression remained impassive, but she caught the flicker of pain before it vanished behind a facade of indifference. "Whenever I feel like flying out there."

Her heart went out to him. "You're all alone now, aren't you? Instead of having Ana in your corner, she's moved thousands of miles away. She's married to a prince and has a fabulous life. One you aren't part of. It isn't the two of you against the world, anymore, is it?"

"Don't."

He spoke just that one word, but it told her more about him than anything he'd said until this point. Anguish bled through his voice, as well as an immeasurable loneliness. He had no one. He'd cut himself off from personal connections, all because he couldn't trust. She grieved for him, grieved for all he lacked in his life. He'd chosen that path of solitude, whereas it had been thrust on her. Even so, she had friends and neighbors and ranch hands, not to mention Claire. Until last year she'd also had her grandmother. But the main difference between them was that she trusted each and every one of those she'd included in her life. They were as close to her as family.

"We have a problem, Joc. And I don't see an easy solution to it."

He fixed her with his dark gaze, throwing up barriers so high and dense that she didn't have a hope of penetrating them. "What problem?"

"If I'm pregnant, you're going to have to let me in. And if not me, you'll need to open yourself up to our child. Otherwise, how will his relationship with you be any different than your relationship with Boss?"

There was nothing left to say after that and Rosalyn closed her eyes and pretended to sleep. She wished she could nod off. She hadn't slept much last night and she'd have to hit the ground running the instant she arrived in Dallas. She didn't want to think about all the work that had accumulated while she'd been busy playing the role of billionaire's mistress.

To her surprise she did nod off at some point, waking with a soft moan to Joc's distinctive touch. She wanted to blame the way she responded to him on being in that helpless realm between dreams and reality. But in truth, she leaned into him, softened against him, lifted her mouth for his possession for one reason and one reason only.

She wanted him still.

She wanted him on the most visceral level possible, a level that ignored logic and common sense. A primitive, physical level that demanded a taking she could no longer have.

"Wake up, Red." A gentleness slid through his words that confused her since she knew he wasn't a gentle man. "We need to talk."

Catching back another moan, she forced her eyes open. He crouched beside her seat, leaning in so close that all she had to do was bridge that scant inch gap and her mouth would meld with his. She moistened her lips and watched the darkness in his eyes ignite.

"Are we there?" she asked. The words had a sleep-roughened edge, one that seemed to affect him all the more. "I can't believe I slept again."

"We just landed." A swift smile softened the harsh contours of his face, an intimate, revealing smile. Then the mask slammed back into place and he was the Joc from the boardroom once more. "We need to talk," he repeated.

She levered her seat upright, forcing him to shift back. To her relief, it gave her more breathing room. "What do we need to talk about?" she asked. As if she didn't know.

"I'm going to leave instructions with Maggie, my personal assistant, to put you through anytime you call. Don't hesitate to make that call if you need me. For anything."

"Including an unexpected pregnancy?"

His mouth kicked to one side. "Especially that."

There wasn't time to speak after that. The plane door opened to glaring Dallas sunshine and sweltering humidity. Nearby two vehicles sat idling, a familiar-looking limo and a private car. Five minutes later found Rosalyn settled in the car, battered Stetson in hand. Joc leaned in, his smoldering gaze resting first on her face before sliding pointedly to her abdomen. And then he shocked her by taking her mouth in a kiss as hungry and passionate as any she'd received during their night together.

"I'll be expecting your call," he said. And then he left her and crossed to his limo.

Tears pricked Rosalyn's eyes as she watched him drive away. What was wrong with her? She should be delighted to have him out of her life. She didn't need the complications he represented. And she sure as hell didn't need any more on her plate—such as the unplanned advent of a child.

But that didn't stop her from dreaming. Dreaming of a life that had Joc smiling at her the way he had right before he'd taken her in his arms. It didn't stop her from dreaming of holding a baby in her arms, his tiny head thick with hair as black as his father's and eyes the same rich ebony. To have a home that didn't echo with painful memories, but one filled with the laughter and joy of a husband and children. To have the legacy continue. To watch the roots she'd sunk deep in Texan soil grow and expand and shoot toward the sun with endless branches peopled with endless future generations.

Picking up her hat, she dropped it on her head at an angle that had the brim covering her face. Then, leaning back against the plush seat, she allowed the tears to come.

Joc crossed to his limo and climbed into the back, forcing himself not to watch as the car carrying Rosalyn swept off the tarmac and headed away from Dallas toward her ranch. What the hell was wrong with him? He should be grateful to have her out of his life. He didn't need the complications she wrought. And he certainly didn't need the possibility of her carrying his child.

But that didn't stop him from imagining. Imagining a life that had Rosalyn smiling up at him in bed. It didn't stop him from imagining a baby in his arms, her tiny head thick with hair as red as her mother's. To finally know a home of joy and laughter…his wife and children eager to greet him each night. To have the legacy that had always been beyond his reach.

He'd been denied that possibility his entire life. And he'd convinced himself he didn't want it. But now… The limo slowed as it approached Arnaud's, the glass and chrome building stabbing skyward like a finger raised in defiance. Cold, haughty, a safe and remote citadel.

That's what he wanted. Not a worn-down ranch run by a far too discerning redhead. He wanted power and control. But perhaps he'd find a way to have Rosalyn, too.

* * *

Rosalyn stood in the bathroom and read the directions to the home pregnancy test for the third time, determined not to make any mistakes. It appeared straightforward enough. Take the test and a few minutes later the little window would either give her a plus sign if her interlude with Joc three weeks ago had borne fruit, or a negative sign if she was just running unusually late. She followed the instructions to the letter and stood impatiently, her stomach in knots as she waited to learn her fate.

The uncertainty left her feeling like her life was spinning out of control. She longed for stability. For security. To not constantly be teetering on the knife's edge of disaster. The past three weeks had been the most difficult of her life. There hadn't been ten minutes straight over all those days where thoughts of Joc hadn't slipped into her head and left her staring into space, gripped by a longing she couldn't escape.

The small timer she'd set to warn her when the results of the pregnancy test were ready to be read gave off a strident ping. She picked up the plastic stick. A large plus sign showed in the window and she sagged against the sink. Dear God, she was pregnant. She should be horrified. She should be terrified. In a panic. Her brows drew together. Why wasn't she in a panic?

Her hand stole across her abdomen. Her baby grew here, nestled deep within her womb. Hers and Joc's. She wasn't panicked, she realized, any more than she was horrified or terrified. Rather, wonder filled her. A child. Dear heaven, she'd been given a child. She'd been given the chance to have a family again. The tears came then, but to her amazement, she discovered they weren't tears of despair or fear.

They were tears of gratitude.

"Rosalyn!" Claire's shout echoed up the steps, filled with a rare alarm. "Get down here. Fast!"

Escaping the bathroom, Rosalyn pelted down the stairs. She hit the hallway outside the dining room and stumbled on the loose carpet runner, almost taking a nosedive into the sunken living room. The close call scared her, and she pressed a hand to her belly. Time to get that stupid thing tacked down. It wasn't just her neck at risk anymore. She had a baby to consider now.

Claire joined her in the hallway. "What happened?" Rosalyn demanded. "What's wrong? Are you hurt?"

"The barn," Claire gasped. "The barn's on fire."

The next several hours were the worst in recent memory. Thanks to the fast reaction of her employees, they were able to save the horses stabled there. But they weren't able to save the structure, despite a near heroic attempt. Exhausted, choking on smoke and covered with soot, they all grouped together in grim exhaustion. Her foreman pulled her to one side while Claire served cooling draughts of water and platters of sandwiches.

"I think you need to call someone."

Exhaustion had her frowning in bewilderment. "What are you talking about? Call who?"

"When we lost those cows, I wrote it off as bad luck. Downed lines, it happens. Calves gone missing, questionable but not necessarily criminal activity. But there's no question anymore, Rosalyn. That fire was set. Deliberate. Somebody's sending you a message. I suggest you find out who and do something about it."

She stared, stunned. "No. You must be mistaken."

"There's no mistake. The place reeked of gasoline." The foreman wiped his face with the sleeve of his shirt, smearing a trail of soot across his forehead. "We're lucky we saved the livestock. Next time we might not be so lucky."

"Who would do such a thing?"

"Only one person I know who wants to get his hands on this place."

She shook her head, refusing to believe it. "No. It couldn't be Joc."

Granted, he wanted her property. Even so, he'd never stoop to something like this. Not the man who'd held her in his arms and made love to her all through the night. That man wouldn't treat her with such ruthless disregard. And he sure as hell wouldn't put her in danger—or the child he knew she might be carrying.

But maybe he could help her find out who was responsible. "I'll deal with it."

"Soon?"

"Right now," she promised.

She started toward her Jeep, only to realize that she'd parked it in its usual spot beneath the barn overhang. It stood amidst the smoldering ruins, gutted by the fire. That hurt almost as much as losing the barn. Her father had used that Jeep to teach her to drive. It had been a connection to him over the years, his memory with her each time she bumped and ground her way across Oakley land. Setting her jaw, she spun in her tracks and crossed to the pickup Duff used for his mail runs.

Time to face the man who'd turned her life upside down and who'd crept into her heart and mind and soul. A man she longed to have in her life for more than a single night. To find out if he were the man she remembered from Deseos…or the man who put business ahead of every other consideration.

Time to face the father of her baby.

Joc stood at the window of his office and stared out at the sprawling metropolis before him. Heat shimmered beyond the tinted glass, giving the air a heavy fluidness, as though he rested underwater rather than high above the earth.

Damn it! How was it possible that out of all the women he'd ever known, Rosalyn was the only one capable of tying him up in knots? Granted, she was beautiful. Dynamic, and then some. Opinionated. Bullheaded. Glorious. Radiant. And the most passionate of any woman he'd ever held in his arms. He'd never been so distracted by a woman—never allowed a woman to distract him. But this one… What was it about this one?

He couldn't count the number of times he'd picked up the phone, intent on calling her, on demanding she come to him. Nor could he count the number of times he'd instructed his driver to take him out to the Oakley homestead, only to rescind the order an instant later. As if she, alone, weren't distraction enough, a strong possibility existed that she carried his child. Otherwise, why hadn't she called to tell him they were in the clear?

If she was pregnant, there'd be only one resolution to the situation. Only one resolution he'd allow, regardless of Rosalyn's opinion on the matter.

"Joc?"

He stiffened at the sound of his assistant's voice. Hell. He hadn't even heard her enter, which told him how bad the problem had become. Gathering his self-control like a cloak, he turned to face her. "Yes, Maggie? What is it?"

"I was about to go to lunch when security called. They're detaining a woman who's insisting on seeing you immediately. I had them send her up. It's…it's Rosalyn Oakley."

A hungry grin slashed across Joc's face. "Thank you, Maggie. I'll handle it. You can go to lunch."

Red had returned. And this time he wouldn't be so foolish as to let her go. Before the day ended, he'd have her back where she belonged. In his bed. He wanted her. She wanted him. What could be easier? They'd work through whatever peculiar chemical reaction had them panting after one another. Clearly it needed longer than a single night to excise from their systems. Now that he'd had time to consider the matter, he doubted anything short of a full-blown affair would be sufficient. And if there was a baby?

They'd find a way to deal with that, too.

The door into the office opened. And there she was in all her glory. She must have been in a hurry coming here because she hadn't dressed for the occasion, as most women confronting a former lover would have. Not a scrap of makeup touched the porcelain surface of her face. He frowned. In fact, it looked like she'd fallen headfirst into a coal mine. Her hair escaped its customary knot, drifting untidily to her shoulders. Just as she had the first time they'd met, she'd dressed in utilitarian ranch gear, jeans and a plaid shirt. But she must have been in a serious hurry, since she'd snapped her shirt together wrong and her clothes were smudged with soot.

Soot!

"What happened?" he asked sharply.

She answered with typical bluntness, giving it to him straight. "My barn burned down."

For most of his life Joc had been described as a brilliant tactician, a man who never allowed emotion to cloud his judgment. He'd always maintained impeccable control and timing. But in the space of two seconds flat Rosalyn Oakley managed to vanquish every ounce of his control and timing as his emotions streaked out of control.

He crossed the room in a half dozen swift steps and grasped her arms, sweeping her with an all-encompassing look. "Are you injured? Were you hurt?"

She shook her head. "I'm fine. Tired. Dirty. But fine."

"Your men? Your animals?"

"All safe." She gazed up at him, her violet-blue eyes reflecting a worrying combination of anger and fear. "Someone burned it down, Joc. On purpose. And there've been other problems, as well. Cut fence lines. Cows taking sick. Calves gone missing. But it wasn't until today that my foreman was certain that it was deliberate."

He froze, suspicion crashing over him. Did she think he was involved? Was that why she'd approached him after three weeks of silence? "And you came here because…?"

She stiffened ever so slightly. "You said to contact you if I needed you. For anything. Were you just saying that, or did you mean it?"

"I meant it."

Relief spread across her face and she swayed toward him before catching herself. Extracting herself from his hold, she paced across his office. The maneuver betrayed her, shouted her physical awareness of him, a fact that gave him an intense masculine satisfaction. It also roused the predator lurking within, filling him with the overwhelming urge to give chase.

She spun to face him. "You have no idea how difficult this is for me to say, and to you of all people. But I need your help."

"You have it."

Her chin trembled for a brief instant before she managed to firm it, anger coloring her words. "Could you find out who's doing this so I can stop them?"

He clamped down on the surge of relief. "I need to ask you a question first."

"Anything."

"How do you know that I'm not behind the incidents?"

Her anger drained away, leaving her eyes huge in a face gone stark-white. He heard the hitch to her breath and saw alarm bleed the vitality from her. "Oh God, Joc," she whispered. She took a swift step in his direction and lifted a hand in appeal. "Do you think I'm here because I suspect you?"

He was careful to keep his voice dispassionate. "Do

you? After all, I showed you who and what I am when I took down my partners at Deseos."

She dismissed that with a jerk of her shoulders. "You took down partners who were intent on stealing the island out from under you after you'd lent them a helping hand. I may not have known you for long, but it's been long enough to learn that you don't do business by burning barns or rustling cattle."

It was the oddest thing. It felt as though he'd been captured in a moment frozen by time. He could see Rosalyn staring up at him with total and utter faith. It seemed as though he had endless moments to search her expression, to look inward and assess the strength and veracity of that level of trust. To know that it existed. That she didn't have a single doubt about the honesty of his assertion. Just complete confidence and acceptance that his word was the absolute truth.

He couldn't take his eyes off her. Sunlight poured over her, setting her hair on fire around a face as pale and beautiful and compassionate as an angel's. "No one has ever trusted me." The words were ripped from him. "I've had to prove my honor again and again. Prove that I'm not the crook my father was."

A line formed between her brows. "I'm so sorry, Joc. That must have been difficult for you."

"No. You don't understand." He tried again. "You didn't demand proof that I wasn't involved. You didn't question my veracity. You accepted my word without a minute's hesitation or doubt."

"Oh." She thought about that for a second, before asking gravely, "Shouldn't I have?"

"Are you poking fun at me?" he asked in disbelief.

"Just a little bit." She pinched two fingers together. "A very little bit. You're sort of an easy target when it comes to that particular issue."

"Give me a straight answer, Red. Do you trust me, or not?"

She didn't hesitate this time, either. "Yes. I trust you."

"Now I have an even more important question for you." He decided to be as blunt as she'd been. "Are you pregnant?"

He knew the answer before she even opened her mouth, saw the mixture of wonder and nervousness that turned her eyes a brilliant shade of blue. "Yes, I'm pregnant. I found out right before the barn went up in flames."

As much as she trusted him, he still found it difficult to return the favor. "Were you going to tell me? If the barn hadn't burned, I mean?"

"Of course! This isn't something I'd keep from you. I promised."

There was no mistaking her sincerity. "Fair enough. I'll arrange for a doctor's visit as soon as we get to my place."

She held up her hands and took a swift step backward. "Whoa. Slow down, Arnaud. What do you mean…when we get to your place?"

"Do I have to spell it out for you, Red?" He crossed the room to confront her. "You're pregnant. Someone is destroying your property, and according to you it's escalating. It's not safe for you to stay at Longhorn." He invaded her space. "And just to be clear? This isn't open to negotiation."

She opened her mouth to argue. One look at his expression had her closing it again. After stewing for a few seconds, she asked, "What about my employees and animals? If I'm not safe, they aren't, either."

"I'll make arrangements to safeguard them all."

She brightened at that. "If you're going to safeguard my men and property, then there's no reason I can't return home."

"Only one."

"Which is?"

"I won't allow it."

Joc didn't give her an opportunity to come up with a response. Instead he did what he'd longed to since she'd first walked into his office and took her in his arms. His mouth locked over hers, the fit even more perfect than he remembered. She melted against him, as though their three-week separation had never been, responding with a fervent eagerness that made him wish they were back on Deseos with it's tropical breezes and sultry nights. Where a bed was only steps away and they were guaranteed endless days and nights of privacy to take their embrace to the ultimate conclusion. Instead he accepted what he could get in the here and now, and submerged himself in her unstinting warmth.

He knew this woman on a visceral level, recognized her scent and touch and taste. Most of all, he recognized the generosity with which she responded to him. He'd been a fool to think that a single night would satisfy either of them. He'd never be satisfied with just that one encounter. Not one embrace. Not one kiss. Not one night of lovemaking. What had started as a business encounter had become something reckless and passionate and infinitely dangerous. The softest of moans escaped as she opened to him, welcoming him home. Her hands crept beneath his suit jacket and splayed across his back, tugging him close. She sank into his kiss, her body moving helplessly against his.

He forked his hands into her hair and tilted her head so he'd have better access to her mouth. Then he drank, giving, taking, on the bare edge of control, showing her without words how much he'd missed her. A hunger filled him, a craving far worse than anything he'd experienced with any other woman. He wanted her. Here. Now. Any way he could have her. And even that wouldn't be enough. This craving was too intense to easily be sated. He might never have his fill of her or grow tired of having her in his arms.

She ended the kiss with unmistakable reluctance, snatching a final taste before pulling free. "That wasn't fair," she complained. She fought to bring some order to her hair and shirt. Glancing down, she groaned when she discovered that half her snaps had come undone. She fumbled to close them without much success. "And kissing me isn't going to make me forget our earlier discussion. You still haven't told me why I can't return to Longhorn if you're going to put safeguards in place. You can't just say you won't allow it and expect me to accept it."

"Then let me put it another way." He gathered her close and cupped her abdomen, warming her belly through the layers of denim and cotton. "I'll do anything and everything within my power to protect you and my child."

Seven

She shouldn't be surprised. She knew Joc was the take-charge type. So, finding herself bundled into his car and whisked off to the mansion he called a home shouldn't come as any surprise. What did surprise her was how he treated her in the next few days.

Initially he handled her as though she were made of fine crystal, as though the least word or touch risked shattering her. He didn't broach the subject of the baby, other than to arrange for a visit to the doctor so she could confirm both her pregnancy, as well as her overall health and well-being. She didn't expect his reticence to last long, not once he decided how he wanted to handle this latest development. Until then, he was playing his cards close to his chest.

As the days built toward a week, she discovered that

she didn't object to staying with Joc as much as she'd anticipated, though she did find what she privately dubbed his "quasi-palace" somewhat intimidating. It wasn't the size as much as the interior design. It struck her as uncomfortably formal, the pieces rich and elegant and reluctant to be touched. Not what she'd have called a home. As the first week passed and she became more integrated into his daily life, the differences between them became more and more apparent—and made her more and more uncomfortable.

How would she handle those differences now that she knew she was pregnant with his child? Would he expect their baby to live in his world? A frown touched her brow. How would that work? And of even greater concern, how did he expect her to fit in? The thought filled her with a panic that followed in her wake like an approaching storm front.

The guest rooms he offered for her use were the most sumptuous she'd ever seen. But she rattled around inside, lonely and uncomfortable while she waited to return to Longhorn. She'd spent most of the twenty-eight years of her life working from sunup until sundown. A life of leisure didn't suit her. Nor did feeling like she was a kept woman. She remained painfully aware that she wouldn't be here if it weren't for her pregnancy.

Joc's daily routine also caused problems. They met each morning at breakfast where an earnest young man would give Joc a report that encompassed everything from urgent news that had occurred during the night, to his schedule for the day, to calls, e-mails, and messages that could only be handled by the top man, himself.

Eventually Joc added another person to the mix—an earnest young woman who gave Rosalyn a similar report about the condition of her ranch, the investigation into the fire and other problems that had occurred on Longhorn since her return from Deseos. At the end of her first week with Joc, Rosalyn had had enough.

In the middle of the dual reports, she shoved back her chair. Picking up her plate and cup of coffee, she escaped the formal dining room for the lighter, friendlier sunroom that connected off the kitchen. It reminded her of the lanai on Deseos. Best of all, gentle morning light filled the spacious area and floor-to-ceiling windows offered a wide-ranging view of the garden. She deposited her breakfast and coffee on a small glass-and-wrought-iron café table and settled onto a thickly cushioned chair. She stretched, releasing a deep sigh of pleasure. Better. Much better.

"I gather you don't care for our morning briefing." Joc's voice came from the doorway behind her.

She didn't bother to turn around. "Not really."

"I thought it would help you to hear what efforts I'm making to find whoever's responsible for the problems at Longhorn. At least we know that it wasn't the men I fired for harassing you."

This time she did swivel to face him. "It does help to know that. Seriously, Joc. I appreciate everything you've done very much."

His mouth tugged to one side in a wry smile. "You just don't appreciate it over breakfast."

She shrugged. "I work every bit as hard as you—or I used to. But I don't spend every minute at it. And I surely don't allow it to interfere with my digestion."

His smile grew and he crossed to join her at the table. "We'll find the people responsible for your problems. I promise. In the meantime…" He dropped into the chair next to hers and took a swallow of the coffee he'd brought with him. "This is nice."

She sat quietly for several minutes while she polished off her breakfast. "As long as we're talking about changes to our routine, there's another one I'd like to make."

His voice took on a hard tone. "So long as it doesn't have anything to do with your return to Longhorn, you can have anything you want."

That had her eyebrows shooting upward. "You aren't going to ask what it is before you agree? That's not like you."

"Is this particular change open to negotiation?" A wicked gleam crept into his dark eyes. "I'm always happy to enter into a negotiation with you."

She shook her head. "Refuse and I'm out of here."

"That's what I figured." He leaned back in his chair and stretched out his long legs, hooking one ankle over the other. "Since that's the case, name it, Red, and it's yours," he offered expansively.

"Okay, fine. I don't like the bedroom you assigned me."

He frowned. "What's wrong with it? Whatever it is, I'll have it fixed by the end of day."

"Excellent." She took a final swallow of decaf coffee and shoved back her chair. "I'll move my stuff into your bedroom right away."

His cup crashed against the glass table. "What did you say?"

"You heard me." She met his gaze with as much composure as she could muster. "The baby's fine. I'm healthy. You don't have to treat me like I'll break. I thought after a few days, you'd get over it. But this is getting ridiculous."

He stared at her for an endless moment before exploding into action. One minute she was sitting at the table and the next he was propelling her through the mansion to his suite of rooms. The instant the door closed behind him, he wrapped his arms around her.

"Are you sure this is what you want?" he asked. "Be very certain, Red, because once I have you back in my bed, I'm not letting you out again."

"I'm positive."

Joc cupped her face and kissed her. With a low moan, she opened to him, holding nothing back. The bed rose up to meet her and he followed her down. The next few minutes passed in a breathless wrestling match as they both stripped off their clothes with frantic speed. When there was no more between them but heated flesh, they stilled, the encounter slowing, stretching, quieting as they cautiously opened one to the other.

Over the past few days Rosalyn had sat beneath the stars in Joc's formal garden and contemplated her feelings for him and for the baby he'd given her. Had looked up and absorbed some of the magic and mystery of those shards of hope sparkling above her. But in that moment, she realized there couldn't be a more magical or insightful moment than this.

Joc must have felt the same. With an incoherent exclamation, he lowered his head and kissed his way from her mouth to the beaded tips of breasts already showing the early changes her pregnancy wrought, to the still-flat expanse of her abdomen. And there he lingered, whispering a secret message to the child cradled deep beneath his lips.

Rosalyn closed her eyes against an unexpected wave of tears. She found this man endlessly fascinating, a creature of shadow and light, pain and grace. A hard man. A lonely man. A man who'd seen the worst and chosen to pursue the best. He offered their child its first kiss, explaining without words the emotions he fought so hard to deny. Each touch of his hand spoke of longing, of the need to connect, to belong. Didn't he see? Didn't he understand the importance of roots? Somehow, someway, she'd show him how vital they were. She slid her fingers deep into his hair and drew him to her, offering the only gift she could freely give.

Herself.

He came to her without words, finding his way home. Slipping between her thighs, he drove straight to the core of her with a single unerring stroke. She could feel the pain that filled him, that had haunted him for most of his life. She wrapped herself around him in response, absorbing the pain and replacing it with everything she had to give.

When she'd lost her family, she thought that feeling had been lost to her, as well. But she'd found it again. Found it within the arms of this man. With their joining, hope had returned.

And together, bound and tangled as one, they tumbled.

Hours later, Joc lifted onto an elbow and feathered a series of kisses from the curve of her jaw to the curve of her breast. "I have a charity gala toward the end of this month that I can't avoid." He lifted a shoulder in a half shrug. "Maybe that's because I'm the host. I'd appreciate it if you'd attend with me. And before you use the excuse that you have nothing to wear, I still have that beaded gown you wore on Deseos."

She started to refuse, but hesitated at the last moment, curiosity getting the better of her. "Why do you want me there?"

"Because I'd enjoy your company." He traced the path his mouth had taken with his fingertips, eliciting a helpless shiver. "I won't even try to negotiate with you about it. It's a no-strings-attached invitation."

"I wouldn't fit in," she demurred.

"Your family is one of the oldest in Texas." There was a vague brusqueness underscoring his comment, one she didn't comprehend until he added, "Trust me, you fit in better than I do."

"Oh." She caught her lower lip between her teeth as a possibility occurred to her. The Hollister name was also one of the oldest in Texas. "Will they be there?"

He didn't pretend to misunderstand. "Probably. My Hollister relatives attend most of the local charitable affairs. Since I'm hosting the event, we may get lucky and be spared their presence."

"How do they react when you all meet?"

"It depends on what they need from me. It runs the gamut from smoldering glares to demands for excessive donations to looking at me as though I were something unpleasant they'd accidentally stepped in."

That simple explanation said so much, revealed so much of what he'd gone through over the years. Her heart went out to him. "I'm sorry."

"Don't let it bother you. I don't."

Did he really believe that? Or was that how he managed to get past the pain they inflicted? She couldn't bear the idea of him facing MacKenzie on his own, not after what she'd pulled with Joc's partners on Deseos. "Yes, I'll go with you."

He traced a delicious circle around the tip of her breast. "A pity date, Red?"

She shivered beneath the teasing caress. "You think I pity the great Joc Arnaud?" she managed to scoff. "Not even a little. Besides…" She slanted him a teasing look. "Do you want to see me in that beaded dress again or not?"

"Hell, yes."

"Then where's the problem?"

"The problem is that I'm going to want to strip you out of that dress as soon as I see you in it." His voice dropped to a husky whisper, one filled with tender amusement. "But at least now I know that you're going to let me."

"So, what's the point of tonight's affair?" she asked several weeks later on the drive to the gala. "Or is there a point?"

"Charity. We're raising funds for the National Marrow Donor Program."

"Excellent. I hope you're also twisting a few arms so that people do more than contribute money. Let's hope they also join the registry."

His smile flashed white in the darkness. "That's why I find you so fascinating, Red. You don't care about the odds. You're always on your feet, ready to battle for the underdog."

"I have to admit, right now I feel like one of those underdogs." At his quizzical glance, she clarified, "I'm a bit out of my element this evening."

"You'll get used to it."

She shot him a look of alarm. "What does that mean?"

"Just what I said. In time, you'll get used to these black-tie events and it won't bother you anymore."

She shifted in her seat to face him. "Listen to me, Joc. I have no intention of getting used to this or any other part of your lifestyle. I don't belong here. I belong on a ranch, dressed in a pair of jeans that are so old and worn that they know to wrap themselves around a horse's belly without even being asked. I don't belong in this latest getup that makes me feel like I'm…I'm—"

She couldn't bring herself to say "a kept woman," which might be just as well considering the way Joc tensed. He didn't say a word, which made her all the more apprehensive. Shadows burrowed into the rough-cut angles of his face, making his appearance more austere than usual. Only his eyes glittered, the color as black and hard as obsidian.

"You will tell me if anyone so much as suggests such a thing about you."

"And you'll do what?" she asked, genuinely curious. "Give them hell? Threaten them? Destroy them for daring to speak the truth?"

She struggled to ignore his crisp, masculine scent, to forget how protected she felt when he held her in those powerful arms. Or how delicate and feminine she was when he swept her against the hard, broad expanse of his chest. But how could she? From the moment they'd met they'd been unable to keep their hands off each other. And from that desire, a desire unlike anything she'd ever experienced before, a miracle had been created. She struggled to gather up her emotions so that she could continue without betraying her inner turmoil.

"Don't you get it? I walked into our relationship with my eyes wide-open. I wanted to sleep with you, to cut loose for once in my life. So, I did. But it came with consequences, and I'll pay the price. But don't expect me to be happy about it."

He stiffened. "You consider our baby a price you have to pay?" The question cracked like a whip. "Is that how you think of him?"

Her breath caught in dismay. "No, of course not. I didn't mean the baby, I meant tonight. Being in this getup is the price I have to pay."

He seemed torn between laughter and anger. "Most women wouldn't consider tonight some sort of punishment."

"Yeah, well. I'm not most women," she muttered.

"No, you're not." He reached for her and drew his thumb along the curve of her cheek to her mouth, tracing the full sweep of her lower lip. "I don't want you to be anyone other than yourself. I've had my fill of women trying to conform themselves to my expectations. Or to what they perceive as my expectations. I'm not interested in them. I'm interested in you."

"For the sake of my ranch. For the sake of the child I'm carrying."

"I'm interested in you because of what you do to me anytime I come near you. I thought that one night would take care of it. But it hasn't. Nor have the past several weeks, or what we were doing right before we left the house. If anything, I want you more than ever."

"It won't work, Joc. We come from different worlds, with too many issues between us to think anything can come out of whatever this is between us. My priorities have to be my baby and my ranch—a ranch you're still thinking of taking from me."

The limo drew to a halt just then and light poured into the back, cutting across his face with sharp precision. What she saw revealed there had her catching her breath in dismay. She'd hurt him. She wouldn't have thought it possible. But for that one instant, she saw the wound that blanked his eyes and spasmed across his expression.

"Joc—"

He cut her off without compunction. "Don't. I know on an intellectual level you don't trust me because I still intend to purchase Longhorn."

"I do trust you."

He shook his head. "Not yet. Not completely. Not when it comes to our baby or your ranch. But there have been other occasions when you haven't had time to think, when you've had to go with your gut instinct. Those are the times that count. Because each and every one of those times, you've trusted me. You went with me to Deseos. You allowed me to make love to you. You believed me when I said I wasn't responsible for the problems on your ranch. You've believed me based on no more than my word, alone." He tilted his head to one side. "Have you ever wondered why?"

And with that he exited the limousine, leaving her to

sit in stunned silence. It was an excellent question. It was also one she didn't dare answer…because that answer threatened to tear her world apart.

From the moment they entered the charity gala, Joc played the role of gallant escort and affable patron to the hilt. No one was more charming. Or gracious. Or witty.

Rosalyn watched his performance with growing dismay. She hadn't realized until that moment how completely Joc had let down his guard around her. She didn't know this man, though she suspected most everyone else here did. Worse, she disliked this caricature of the man she loved with tear-provoking intensity. They were emotions wrought from hormonal imbalance, she tried to tell herself, partially from the baby and partially from having surrendered to her need to be with Joc. But deep down she recognized the lie for what it was.

With every ounce of passion she possessed, she longed for the man who'd swept her off to Deseos. And she accepted the fact that she'd helped nail in place the facade he now wielded with such skill. She wanted her wolf back. Elemental. Keen-eyed. Ruthless.

Loving.

Rosalyn found herself so focused on Joc and how he'd changed that she didn't at first notice people's reaction to her. She was surprised to discover that those Joc introduced her to were friendly, for the most part, though she couldn't have said why she expected anything different. Some were speculative, and a select few were assessing, as though seeing a new playing piece on a game board and wondering how best to maneuver it to their advantage. Well, they'd soon discover that her particular game piece wielded no power and held no advantage. Maybe she should make it easy for them and stamp Pawn across her forehead.

Halfway through the evening, she realized she was actually having a good time. At least she was right up until a woman approached them, a woman who could have passed for Joc's twin. Familiar deep-set black eyes glittered within a striking face accentuated by high, elegant cheekbones and a wide, sensuous mouth—a mouth curved into a cold smile.

Joc inclined his head. "MacKenzie," he greeted the woman, confirming her identity. "Hope you're enjoying the gala. I believe the buffet table has a generous helping of sour grapes I ordered for your personal enjoyment."

"You think you won?" She laughed. "Deseos was just my first volley in our little war."

"A volley you lost."

Her amusement faded and she shrugged. "True. But I won't lose the next round. Of course, if you sell the Hollister homestead to me, there won't be another round."

He shook his head before she'd even finished speaking. "That's not going to happen, MacKenzie. You couldn't afford it even if I were willing to sell."

Anger glittered in her dark eyes. "What did you do to her all those years ago?" she demanded in a low voice. "How did you manage to steal that property away from my mother? What hold do you have over her that she neglected to tell us she sold our home to you a full decade ago? Tell me, Joc! What dirty little secret did you uncover that forced her to sell out to you?"

He simply shook his head, his expression giving nothing away. "I suggest you ask your mother those questions."

She balled her hands into fists, frustration implicit in every line of her body. "I have. She won't tell me. I've been asking ever since I found out—a full year ago."

"Because there's nothing to tell." He made the comment with surprising gentleness. "Maybe the land holds bad memories for her. It would be understandable, all things considered. Boss's activities couldn't have been easy for Meredith, any more than they were for the rest of us."

She cut him off with a swipe of her hand. "I don't want your pity. Just because you've made it big by swindling widows out of their life's savings doesn't mean that people actually respect or like you. They just want your money. Or didn't that little incident on Deseos prove how little regard your friends have for you?" Her gaze shifted to Rosalyn and narrowed. "You're making a mistake being with him. You will regret it, I promise."

"Don't." Joc's voice cut sharper than she'd ever heard it. "You want to come after me, fine. But you leave Rosalyn out of it."

"If you don't want her in the line of fire, don't put her there." With that MacKenzie turned on her designer-clad heel and stalked away.

Joc immediately grasped Rosalyn's hand and swung her onto the dance floor. "Relax. You don't want her to see that she got to you."

"I don't have the practice you do at concealing my feelings." She did her best to smooth the signs of distress from her face. "Just out of curiosity… Why won't you sell the Hollister homestead to her?"

"She can't afford it, for one thing."

Rosalyn shot him a sharp look. "Don't lie to me, Joc. If you don't want to tell me, fine. But it's not the money that's stopping you. If you wanted her to have the property, you'd be generous enough to price it at something she can afford." When he didn't reply, she tried again. "You know, holding on to the Hollister homestead is inconsistent with what you told me about your attitude toward family and connections. Are you sure this particular land isn't more than mere dirt to you? Maybe you don't want to sell because it gives you a connection with your own roots."

"It's an interesting theory, but wrong." His hand left her waist to cup her chin and force her to look at him. "Let's make a pact, you and I."

She tensed within his hold and stared up at him with undisguised wariness. "What sort of pact?"

"For the next ten minutes let's agree that everything we say to each other will be the absolute, dead-honest truth. Agreed?" At her nod, he said, "I despise what my father did to all of us. The Hollisters. My mother. My sister and me. I won't go into the reasons I bought the land, but trust me. It has nothing whatsoever to do with unresolved daddy issues."

"Then what?"

"No way, Red. Now it's my turn." His pinned her in place as they drifted across the dance floor. "First question. When you walked into the conference room, you were attracted to me, weren't you?"

Okay, she could answer that one with reasonable honesty. "Yes, I was attracted to you, which confused me no end."

"I can imagine."

The corner of her mouth kicked upward. "I was furious at you for siccing your goons on me. I actually hated you for your unremitting attempts to try to force me to sell my ranch. And I assumed that hate would grow by leaps and bounds when I confronted you in the boardroom." Her smile turned bittersweet. What a fool she'd been. "It didn't."

Held within his arms, she could feel his gathering tension. "You're joking."

"No." The admission came hard, almost as hard as when she'd first realized the truth. "It's not something I'm happy about, you understand."

"I can imagine." He waited a beat, before pressing on. "And when we shook hands? Do you remember that?"

Rosalyn froze. She understood then, understood his plan and what he hoped to accomplish with his questions. He wanted her to remember. Remember how she'd responded to him. Felt. Ached. Hungered. He wanted her to confront the truth head-on and experience those same reactions all over again. She wanted to lie. Badly. But she'd agreed to answer his question truthfully, and come hell or high water, she would—even if doing so stripped a few protective layers off her hide.

A combination of pain and regret washed through her. "I wish I could forget that moment." More, she wished it hadn't changed something vital inside her—all because Joc had come into her world and turned it upside down.

"But you can't, any more than I can."

When she didn't respond right away, his hand drifted from her face to her shoulders, generating a path of fire. The song ended and he urged her from the dance floor and through a bank of doors that opened onto a huge garden. Dusk had settled in and the heady scent of evening primroses heralded the approach of night. Soft lighting illuminated the pathways, allowing them to wander at will.

"You haven't answered me, Red," Joc prompted. "What did you feel when we first touched?"

Her movements slowed as they followed one of the deserted walkways. What she'd felt then was no different from how she felt now. "It was just a casual contact," she whispered. "Two strangers shaking hands."

"But it generated instant heat."

"Made an instant connection." She paused in a small alcove formed by a stand of lilacs and closed her eyes in a vain attempt to block him out. To her distress, it only intensified her awareness, sharpening her other senses. Heaven help her, but she wanted him. "I was attracted to you," she admitted. "More attracted than I've ever been to anyone before."

The words hung in the air for an endless second. Joc pulled her closer, mating their bodies, locking them together in a fit that could only be described as sheer perfection. "And when we were at Longhorn? When I brushed the hair out of your eyes. Do you remember how you reacted to me then?"

She clamped her teeth together and turned her head away. "What does it matter?"

"Did you feel it? Did you feel the heat? The connection?"

"Of course I felt it." She opened her eyes, her gaze drawn to him like a moth to flame. "It was all hot connection and broken circuits with a bit of lust thrown in for good measure."

"That's how strong the chemistry was before that night on Deseos. Before we made love. How it's been from the start. Nothing has changed, has it? In fact, it's only grown stronger. Every time we touch. Every time we kiss. From the moment we made love. It caused whatever this is between us to become more powerful. Isn't that the truth?"

"Yes, it's true." And the truth made her want to weep. "I can't keep my hands off you. I don't want to keep my hands off you."

She couldn't resist looking at him again. And that was all it took. It happened again, just like the first time. The instant heat, the desperate want, the sizzle and burn that came whenever they were within touching distance. He must have read the admission on her face, felt it in the helpless give of her body, because he acknowledged it with a knowing smile.

And then he kissed her. She'd anticipated a kiss of possession, a hard and passionate storming, designed to breach her defenses. And it did breach them, just not through strength. He slipped beneath her guard with a gentle taking, the passion a light, joyous exchange. Worse, he offered no more than a prelude, a reminder of how it had been and what it could become once more. He tantalized her with a single taste before setting her free. But that one taste wasn't enough. Could never be enough. All it did was intensify the craving without offering any satisfaction.

"Why are you doing this?" she asked unsteadily. "What do you want?"

"You're pregnant with my baby, Red. I want you to marry me."

Eight

"She turned me down flat, Ana." Joc paced his study, as he waited impatiently for his sister's response.

"Let me guess. You proposed a business merger instead of a marriage."

"I'm not that stupid," he retorted, stung.

"Oh, really? This is Joc Arnaud, right?" She tapped the receiver with her fingernail. "Hello? Hello? Who are you, and what have you done with my big brother?"

"Damn it, Ana—"

She cut him off without compunction. "No way, Joc. You don't get off that easily. Allow me to refresh your memory, brother dear. Are you, or are you not the same man who signed a contract with Prince Lander Montgomery and made marriage to me a clause in said contract?"

"Rosalyn's pregnant with my child."

Dead silence greeted his statement. "I'd ask how that happened," she said at length, "but I'm forced to assume it was in the usual way. I'm surprised. Check that. I'm not surprised, I'm flat-out shocked. You're normally so scrupulous about those things."

He spoke between clenched teeth. "Could we stay on topic? It happened. Now she won't marry me."

"I don't suppose you proposed to her once you found out she was pregnant?"

"Of course I did. What other choice was there?"

"Oh, Joc. For such a brilliant man, there are times you can be as thick and brainless as the proverbial brick. Hang on a sec. Lander just walked in." A brief, muffled conversation followed, and then Ana came back on the line. "My husband wants me to give you a message."

Joc thrust a hand through his hair. "Hell."

"He said he warned you that one day you'd find yourself boxed into the sort of corner you boxed him in. And that you were supposed to remember him when that day came." Her tone grew dry. "I think that's Verdonian for 'I told you so.'"

"I called you for advice, Ana," Joc snarled. "Not so you and Prince Not-So-Charming could rub my nose in my mistakes."

"Fine. Here's my advice. Women want to be married for love. It's that simple."

He opened his mouth and closed it again. Love. Damn. Why did it have to be love? He could negotiate his way around any number of troublesome issues. But not that one. He drew the line at making claims he couldn't back up with hard evidence, especially not when it came to something that serious. He cared for Rosalyn. He wanted her with a passion that defied understanding. But love? He shook his head. He'd never trust a woman that far or expose himself to that sort of vulnerability.

"There must be an alternative. What other choices do I have?" he demanded.

"Well, you can always follow in Lander's footsteps and simply announce your engagement to the press. But I wouldn't recommend it. I doubt Rosalyn will take it any better than I did."

"Thanks, Ana. I'll think about it."

"So, when's the baby due?"

"Mid-February," he replied absently.

Maybe if he offered to end his negotiations to buy Longhorn she'd reconsider his proposal. With any other person, that would undoubtedly work. Any other person would be downright grateful. But somehow he had the feeling that gratitude would be way down on the list of Rosalyn's reactions. Like, maybe dead last.

"That's fantastic," Ana was saying. "The two cousins will share a birthday."

It took a minute for that to sink in. Once it had, it stopped him dead in his tracks. "*What?* Ana, are you pregnant?"

"Wow. Score one for the financial genius," she said with a laugh. "Maybe you aren't so brainless, after all. I'll talk to you later, Joc. Good luck with Rosalyn. Let me know what happens." And with that she cut the connection.

Joc tossed the phone aside and leaned against the desk in his study. He scrubbed his hands across his face.

There had to be a way around his predicament. Something that Rosalyn wanted enough to agree to marriage. Analyzing the problem from a business standpoint filled him with a calm determination. He just had to find the right lever that would win her agreement. Because he wouldn't claim to love her when he didn't. And he sure as hell didn't love her. That decided, he went to find his woman and start the negotiations.

It was well past midnight before Rosalyn slipped into the room she shared with Joc. The instant they arrived home from the charity gala, she raided the kitchen, desperate for a light snack, while Joc excused himself to make a phone call. She didn't know how long he'd be, but she suspected he would want to return to the subject of marriage, something she'd managed to avoid during those final few hours of the night's affair. She'd seen it in the determination burning in his gaze each time he looked at her, as well as the hard set of his mouth.

Tension built across her shoulders at the thought of another confrontation. More than anything she wanted to strip away her evening finery and crawl into something plain and comfortable and, above all else, cotton. Somehow she didn't think she owned any cotton anymore, and probably wouldn't as long as she lived under Joc's roof. Kicking off her heels, she reached behind her to ease down the zip. Her fingers collided with Joc's.

"Let me help," he murmured.

Her heart picked up a beat. "I didn't hear you come in."

"No, you were lost in thought."

He helped her strip off the gown, along with the ridiculous thong, before dropping a nightgown over her head that felt remarkably like cotton. She gathered it up, her tension draining away. "It *is* cotton," she said in delight. "Where did this come from?"

"From me. I noticed over the past few weeks that you weren't comfortable wearing the other nightgowns I purchased for you."

She shrugged awkwardly. "They were all silk and I'm used to something a bit plainer." She ran her hand over the fabric, realizing as she did so that the cotton she wore at home held little similarity to what was clearly an Egyptian blend with a thread count in the trillions. It amazed her what such a small change made to her overall well-being. It felt good to be back to normal. Or almost normal. "Thank you."

He crossed the room, stripping off his tux as he went. She eyed him apprehensively. They were interrupted right after she'd refused his proposal and there hadn't been an opportunity to discuss it further. She suspected that wouldn't be the case for much longer and she had to admit, she didn't have a clue how to handle the conversation.

Giving herself time to think, she bent her head and spread her hand low across her abdomen, marveling that a life grew there. Dear God, a baby. She still hadn't absorbed the full meaning of the event. A moment later, Joc crouched in front of her, his hand joining hers over the life growing in her womb.

"We need to protect this little one," he said.

His simple statement had her slipping from his grasp and retreating across the room. She gathered the last remaining vestiges of her fading energy. Time to deal with his proposal once and for all. "And marriage will do that?"

"You had to know this particular negotiation was coming." He pursued her, his intonation remaining calm and cool. Painfully businesslike. "You had to at least suspect that I wouldn't allow a child of mine to come into this world a bastard. Been there, done that. And it's not happening to my baby."

"He or she will be an Oakley, not a bastard. And that's not open to negotiation."

He'd boxed her in so she couldn't retreat any farther. "Wrong, Red. He's going to be an Arnaud. I won't compromise on that point. I'm willing to make concessions on any other stipulations you'd care to name. But not that one." His face settled into inflexible lines. "I told you about my childhood. I told you how my sister and I suffered. Are you willing to inflict that on our baby?"

"What I'll be inflicting on our baby is Oakley roots," she corrected. "The Oakley line will continue. This isn't the way I planned to do it, but since it's happened and there's no changing it, I want our child to sink his roots as deeply into Texan soil as I have. Those roots may mean nothing to you, but they mean everything to me."

"Don't you get it?" The question held an edge of impatience. "His roots may be planted in your world, but he'll have to live in mine."

She released her breath in a rough sigh. "Face facts, Joc. I don't fit in your world. I'll never fit in your world."

"You will. And so will our child."

How could he say that? "Because you say so?"

"Yes."

Simple and direct. She groaned. And probably true. When Joc Arnaud spoke, everyone else jumped. Well, not her. "Look—"

He cut her off. "No, you look. This baby will be under a microscope from the minute he's born. I will do whatever necessary to protect him from that onslaught, to raise him—" He broke off and lowered his head, reminding her of a wounded animal gathering himself for a final, desperate attack. "To raise him with honor and integrity and…and love."

"Oh, Joc," she whispered.

"Listen to me, Red." A hint of strain colored his words, as though he were fighting a pitched battle. And maybe he was. It occurred to her that this was probably the most important negotiation of his life. "We can make this work. I know we can. There's something there between us. Something that binds us. Something more than the baby."

She fought to keep every scrap of hope from her voice. "Are you saying you love me?"

"I don't know how to love. That's the God's honest truth." His jaw worked for a moment. "But I'm willing to try."

"Marrying you won't change my need for roots. Having your baby won't either. If anything it sends those roots that much deeper." Unable to help herself, she cupped his face in her hands. "You have to know what you're letting yourself in for."

"I have a fair idea."

She shook her head. "It isn't just me, Joc. You'll also have to deal with those roots you dread. That connection

you deny. Our son or daughter will grow strong and tall."
She feathered a kiss across his mouth, encouraged by his
instant response, a response that came without hesitation
or forethought. "And it will be at Longhorn. That's where
he or she will learn to appreciate the land and the importance of emotional integrity over materialistic excess. I
want my child raised there, not out of some corporate
headquarters or quasi-palace. And if they are raised there,
they'll put down more roots, roots you won't be able to
yank free any more than you could mine."

"And if I don't agree?"

"Then I won't marry you and there's nothing you can
do to force me into it." She released him and stepped
away, allowing cool air to replace the warmth of her
embrace. An odd smile tugged at the corners of her
mouth. "For some reason I've been having these bizarre
dreams about trees. I don't know, maybe it's the change
in hormones. Whatever the cause, it made me realize
something. Some trees can't reproduce without being
grafted, one onto another."

He tilted his head to one side, considering. "Is that what
we've done, Red? Have we grafted onto each other?"

Her smile grew. "I haven't heard what we were doing
that night on Deseos described quite that way before.
But however you want to put it, the graft took. Our tree
is definitely reproducing."

"True enough." He gave her offer some serious
thought. "I'm beginning to understand why Hades
forced Persephone to live in the Underworld with him
each winter. At least that way he had her in his world
for part of each year."

"Is that what you want to negotiate next? You want me to play Persephone to your Hades?"

He shook his head. "I couldn't do that." He dropped his head and considered for a moment. "If I agree that our son or daughter—all of our sons and daughters— will be raised at Longhorn, will you marry me?"

Tears filled her eyes. "Yes, Joc. I'll marry you. And I'm hoping, really hoping, that Longhorn will be as much your home as it's been mine."

"Then we have an agreement."

She released her breath in an exasperated sigh. "Why do I feel as though we should be shaking hands?"

"There's only one way to seal a bargain with you." He approached, his movements filled with a lazy grace. He slid his hand beneath her hair along her nape and eased her up to meet his kiss. He took his time, the kiss slow and thorough and filled with unmistakable hunger. When he finally released her, he said, "There's a seventy-two-hour waiting period before we can marry. Or we can fly to Vegas and get it done in the morning."

She continued to stare at him, trying to see past the barriers straight to his heart and soul. "You and I, we're Texans, Joc. This is where we should marry."

He nodded in agreement. "What do you say we apply for that license first thing in the morning?"

"I'd like that."

His voice lowered, roughened. "I swear I won't let you down."

And that was all it took. She fell into his arms and allowed herself to believe, to believe that somehow it would all work out and that this marriage they contemplated had a real shot at success. To believe that one day he'd fall in love with her.

Because somehow, at some point, Little Red Riding Hood had fallen in love with the Big, Bad Wolf.

Perhaps it was the silence that woke him, that hushed moment where night gave over to day. That particular instant when the creatures that serenaded the night fell silent and those that welcomed the day slept. Or maybe it was the absolute rightness of having Rosalyn back in his arms, tucked so close that Joc couldn't distinguish between her heartbeat and his own.

He'd never before experienced such contentment. Never known such pleasure and satisfaction. It was the baby, he tried to tell himself. That explained the connection he felt to Rosalyn. She was pregnant and he was the man responsible. He'd have felt the same no matter who carried his child.

An image of other women and other occasions flickered in and out of his head, offering a swift reminiscence of time and place and romantic encounter. And one by one he dismissed them, dismissed them all without so much as a moment's hesitation. They were wrong, each and every one of them. Worse, it felt wrong thinking about them with Rosalyn sound asleep in his arms.

The time had come to face facts.

This woman was different. He'd known it from the moment he'd first set eyes on her. Everything within him urged him to take her. To keep her. To protect her with every ounce of power, money and skill at his disposal.

He closed his eyes, facing the unpalatable truth. And even that wouldn't be sufficient. Rosalyn didn't want his power or his money or his skill. She only wanted one thing, whether she recognized the truth or not. She wanted his heart—a heart he wasn't sure he possessed.

Because loving meant trusting. Loving meant surrender. Loving meant loss, or the risk of loss. It was fine to demand those things from others so long as he remained protected from the threat they posed. How long had he worked to ensure just that? A lifetime. Somehow Rosalyn had changed all that. She'd stormed into his life and altered him in some indelible way. He couldn't go back to the man he was. Nor could he allow this current opportunity to slip away.

"Joc?"

He smiled at the way his name escaped her throat—half moan, or was it more of a groan? "I'm here, Red."

Her eyes remained shut, her voice faint and wistful. "I had a dream. We planted the most incredible tree, the biggest tree in the entire world. And it grew into a giant forest filled with all these magical creatures. I wish we could go there."

He brushed her mouth with a kiss. "Did I help you plant the tree?"

"Of course. Joc?"

"I'm still here."

"Let's go plant a tree tomorrow."

He closed his eyes, filled with a contentment unlike any he'd felt before. "I'd like that."

Even more he'd like to be around to watch it grow and

spread its branches, to fill up the sky and seed an entire forest. Somehow that appealed far more than any project currently resting on his desk. For that matter, it appealed far more than any project that had ever crossed his desk.

And in that hushed moment where night gave over to day, that peculiar instant when the creatures that serenaded the night fell silent and those that welcomed the day slept, Joc surrendered to the inevitable. His hand slipped around her waist and cupped his future, warming it within his palm.

No, not his future. Their future.

They woke the next morning to disaster. A call from Claire had them driving out to Longhorn as quickly as the speed limit allowed. Off in the distance, rain-laden thunderheads piled up, tumbling closer with each mile they covered.

"I don't understand," Rosalyn fussed. "Why wouldn't she tell us what's wrong?"

"She'll explain when we get there," Joc tried to assure her.

Rosalyn felt the color bleed from her face. "There's been another fire. Someone's burned down the ranch house."

"We wouldn't be meeting Claire there if that were the case. Stay calm, Red. Whatever it is, we'll deal with it. Together."

And with that, she had to be satisfied. To her relief, the homestead still stood, and her heart quickened at the sight. Until they'd pulled into the long, gravel driveway, she hadn't realized how much she missed being home.

She could see Claire standing on the porch, tension vibrating off her motherly frame.

Rosalyn jumped out of the car the instant Joc pulled to a stop. "What's the problem?" she demanded.

"I'll give it to you straight. Some townie sashayed in here and insisted to see you. I tried to run her off, but she wouldn't budge. Said she'd wait until you got home. Rosalyn…" Claire twisted her hands together. "She's claiming she owns the place."

"What?" Rosalyn tried to laugh, but for some reason her throat had gone bone-dry. She shoved open the front door and stepped into the foyer, just as the skies opened. Rain slapped against the glass panels on either side of the front door with an urgent staccato. "Where is she?"

"I put her in the living room."

Joc stepped forward. "Red—"

She spun to confront him. "Do you know anything about this?"

There was a long, hideous pause. Then he asked, "Are you asking if I've somehow found a way to steal your ranch from you?"

She should have been warned by the extreme calm with which he spoke, or the way his eyes went flat and cold. But suspicion had taken hold and nothing would shake it. "Have you found a way?"

"So much for trust."

She could hear a small voice, deep inside, screaming at her to take the words back. But another voice, just as insistent, reminded her that Joc was the sort of man who wanted it all—her, their child and her ranch. And if an opportunity presented itself to seize control and gain leverage over the situation, he'd take it. Especially if it gave him everything he wanted.

"Let's find out what's going on," she said, ignoring his comment.

She turned on her heel and hastened down the flagstone steps into the living room. She caught her first glimpse of their visitor and nearly gasped in shock. Behind her, she heard Joc swear. Then, "MacKenzie, what the hell are you doing here?"

"I'm checking out my latest acquisition." She leaned back in the chair she'd commandeered and crossed her legs. "What are you doing here, brother dear?"

The wind kicked up, rattling the shutters while the rain began clawing at the windowpanes. "I belong here, which is more than I can say for you."

"Not anymore. You and your..." She lifted an eyebrow. "Friend?"

"Fiancée."

MacKenzie laughed. "That's rich."

"Stop it, both of you!" Rosalyn burst out. "I want to know what's going on."

MacKenzie swung her foot back and forth in a leisurely rhythm. "It's really very simple. You're a pawn, my dear. My brother wanted your land, which means so do I. In the normal course of things, he'd have found a business angle to use in order to get it. I would have then countered. And in the end, one of us would have won and the other lost." She glanced in Joc's direction. "Isn't that how the game's played?"

"This isn't a game," he answered.

"Of course it is. You've just changed the rules a bit.

Instead of paying for your pleasure, you've decided to romance it away from the poor, gullible rancher." MacKenzie switched her gaze back to Rosalyn. "That's you, in case you didn't realize. Only, he's too late. As soon as I learned he wanted this property, I purchased the note. I then made…oh, let's call them certain arrangements with a gentleman named Duff. Did you know your ranch hand has a gambling problem?"

Beside her Joc swore and Rosalyn fought to speak without her voice trembling. "You bribed him?"

MacKenzie lifted a shoulder in a casual shrug. "I can't be held responsible if your employee kept forgetting to mail the mortgage. Nor can I be held responsible if you never caught the omission. A piece of advice. You really should balance your bank accounts more often. I'd have thought Joc would have taught you that much, if nothing else."

Rosalyn shook her head. "No. That can't be right."

"It's right." A hint of sympathy touched the other woman's face. "You'll find that when it comes to cutthroat business deals, I'm as good as my brother."

"What do you want, MacKenzie?" Joc broke in.

She offered him a sunny smile. "Not a thing. I have what I came for. You're just annoyed because I got here ahead of you and managed to block whatever development deal you have going. I guess that land you purchased all around the Oakley place was a waste of good money." She tisked in mock sympathy. "What a shame."

"This has nothing to do with Rosalyn. Don't put her in the middle."

"I didn't. You did," his sister shot back. "I warned

you about that last night, but as usual the all powerful Joc Arnaud thought he held the winning cards. Well, you don't."

"You're the one who's caused all the problems around here," Rosalyn accused. "The one who burned down my barn."

MacKenzie frowned. "I most certainly did not. I merely asked Duff to keep you busy so you wouldn't have time to realize I was foreclosing on you. I can't be responsible if he was a trifle overzealous."

Rosalyn's hands balled into fists. "You're treating this like it's some sort of game. Or a joke. It's not! This is my life. This is my home."

"Not anymore." MacKenzie swept to her feet. "You have until the end of the week to clear out."

"MacKenzie," Joc growled. "Don't do this. She's an innocent bystander in our little feud."

A cold, bitter anger settled over his half sister's features. Overhead thunder boomed as the storm closed in. "Allow me to make myself clear to both of you. Nothing you say or do will change my mind."

Rosalyn drop-kicked her pride. "I'll make up the payments," she pleaded.

Joc dropped a heavy hand on her shoulder. "Red—"

She shook him off and continued to address Mac-Kenzie. "I have the money. I'll pay whatever penalty you require. I should have balanced my accounts, I admit that. Please don't take my home."

"I suggest if you want to blame someone for this mess, blame Joc. He's the one who refuses to sell me the Hollister homestead." She collected her purse and crossed to the steps leading to the hallway. "Just so we're clear, I won't be changing my mind. I suggest you start packing. Because if you're not out by the end of the week, I'll send the law out here to forcibly remove you. First thing Monday morning I'm bringing in the bulldozers and I intend to raze every last structure on this land."

Rosalyn fought to breathe. No. She couldn't mean it. She looked at Joc and that's when she knew. Not only did MacKenzie mean it, but she intended to do it. And there wasn't a chance in the world that Joc or anyone else could stop her.

Without a word, Rosalyn shoved past MacKenzie, intent on escape. She raced up the steps and hit the loosened carpet just outside the living room at a dead-run. Too late she remembered that she'd never had it tacked down. She hooked it with her boot heel and started to trip. She pinwheeled in a desperate effort to save herself. For a split second, she thought she'd be able to, that her foolishness wouldn't meet with disaster. But then she pitched backward toward the stairs. Two thoughts haunted her in those few precious seconds before she hit.

She'd never told Joc she loved him.

But far worse, her thoughtlessness had killed her baby.

Nine

"Red? Oh God. Talk to me, Red."

Joc dropped to her side and carefully lifted the sideboard that had tipped onto her when she'd clipped it falling down the steps. She didn't move. Yanking out his cell phone, he placed an emergency call. The connection phased in and out because of the storm, making it difficult for him to relay the necessary information. It soon became clear that it would be impossible to send in a Life Flight helicopter given the current weather conditions.

During the endless minutes that followed, she didn't stir. More frightened than he could ever remember being, he checked for a pulse. When he found it, he could have bawled like a baby. He spared MacKenzie a deadly glare. "Get out," he ordered. He didn't bother watching to see if she obeyed, instead returning to the call. Demanding. Pleading. Swearing.

The next half hour, as he waited for the EMTs to arrive, proved the longest of his life, driving him to the very brink of despair. If Claire hadn't been there, her steady, reassuring voice a comforting balm, he'd have totally lost it. He crouched above Rosalyn, more helpless than he'd ever been before in his life. The great Joc Arnaud couldn't buy or bargain or bribe his way out of this disaster. There was only one thing he could do, something he didn't remember ever having tried before.

He prayed.

Once the emergency personnel arrived, they stabilized Rosalyn before whisking her out to the ambulance. He lost count of the number of times he told them she was pregnant. Or how many times he told them they were supposed to marry in less than seventy-two hours. He offered everything he could think of in exchange for their help in saving her. None of it did any good. The events of that night leaked through his fingers on a course all their own, beyond his ability to direct or control.

It wasn't until the paramedics had loaded Rosalyn into the ambulance that he faced a truth he'd been dodging for weeks. He loved her. He loved her more than life itself. How could he have not recognized it sooner? Maybe because he'd never experienced such depth of emotion before, not that it mattered now. During the endless ride to the hospital, he made up for that lapse. He didn't know whether she heard. He could only hope that somehow, someway, his words slipped through to that realm of oblivion where she hid from him.

He'd been blind not to have recognized his feelings sooner, to have believed that what he felt for her could be anything less than love. The first chance he got, he'd correct that oversight. He just needed one more chance. That was all. Just one.

He couldn't disguise his relief when they arrived at the hospital. He glanced down at Rosalyn. She lay on a bed of white, her skin and face almost as pale. Only her flame-bright hair provided any color. He took her hand in his as they barreled through the ER doors. It didn't occur to him that he wouldn't be able to stay with her, that they'd take her from him. But they did, overriding his furious protests with the ease of long practice.

And in that moment, standing all alone in the middle of an antiseptic waiting room, Joc learned the true meaning of helplessness.

Over the space of the next two hours, Joc paced every inch of the waiting room. By the end of the first sixty minutes he'd memorized each stain on the rug and all twenty-three nicks, holes and blemishes on the walls. By the end of the second, he could have named every cookie, candy and drink item offered for sale in the vending machines. And he could have done it blindfolded.

Still no one came to give him an update on Rosalyn's status. Finally he'd had enough. He didn't care if he had to buy the damn hospital, someone was going to give him the information he needed. He started toward the door when Rosalyn's doctor appeared in the doorway.

"How is she?" Joc demanded. "Is she all right?"

"Does Ms. Oakley have any family?"

"I'm her family." He struggled to keep from shouting at the man, fought to keep his tone level. "Please. How is she?"

"She'll live. Cuts, bruises and abrasions. The concussion has us a little worried, but all the scans are clear."

"And the baby?"

The doctor checked his chart. "I gather she's very early in her pregnancy?"

"Six weeks."

"She hasn't miscarried. But there's still that risk," the doctor warned. He gestured to the nurse standing behind him. "You can see her now, if you'd like. The next few days should tell the story."

When Rosalyn came to this time, the pain wasn't anywhere near as bad as the other half dozen occasions she'd regained consciousness. This time she took note of her surroundings, realizing she lay in a hospital bed. The air smelled sharp and cold with the acrid scent of disinfectant and whatever medicines the doctors had dripping into her arm. Somewhere nearby machines beeped softly.

She struggled to focus, fighting the splitting headache that blurred her vision and made her want to retreat into oblivion. Someone had turned down the lights to dim the room, making it difficult to see clearly. But even so she could make out a familiar form holding up one of the walls of her room.

"Joc?"

He straightened at her whispered call and crossed to the bed. Muted midday sunshine filtered in from a shaded window and gilded the hospital room with the faintest golden glow, a glow that flowed over and around him like a halo and gave him the appearance of a fallen angel.

"I'm here, Red."

She asked the same question she'd asked every other time she'd awakened. "The baby? Did I lose our baby?"

And he gave her the exact same answer. "Our baby's safe."

Tears tracked down her cheeks. "I'm sorry. I was so upset and so angry. I forgot about the loose carpet. I've been meaning to have it fixed for months now. If I had, none of this would have happened."

He leaned down, feathering a gentle kiss across her mouth. "You don't need to worry about that now."

"But I could have killed our baby." She scrubbed at her tears with the heels of her palms, flinching when she inadvertently hit bruised skin.

He caught her hands in his and drew them away from her cheeks. "Let me take care of that for you. You're a bit banged up. When you tripped, you fell against a sideboard and it tipped over onto you. You've got the mother of all shiners."

"I don't remember. I don't remember anything after I tripped." He dampened a washcloth with cool water and cleaned her face with such exquisite care that tears flooded her eyes all over again.

"Hey, cut off the waterworks, Red," he teased with a tenderness that stole her breath. "You're leaking faster than I can mop up."

"Joc—" She moistened her dry lips. "What happened with MacKenzie?"

The question caused a mask to drop over his face, one she found impossible to penetrate. "I kicked her out of the house after you were injured."

It wasn't what she meant and she suspected he knew it, knew it and was avoiding her question—which could only mean one thing. Her heart sank. "For how long?" At his silence, her desperation grew. "Does she really own Longhorn?"

"I don't know." He kept his response light, but she could see the truth in the bleakness of his gaze. "I'll have my lawyers look into it first thing tomorrow. If we can get Duff to admit that he disposed of the mortgage payments instead of mailing them and that MacKenzie paid him to do it, there's a chance we can get this turned around."

She shifted restlessly. "I can't lose my ranch. I can't."

"Right now you need to relax and give yourself time to heal." He splayed his hand across her abdomen, his touch feather-light. "Your recovery is more important than anything else."

He was right. Her health and that of their baby's came before everything else. She nodded, feeling exhaustion tugging at her again. She reached for his hand and squeezed it in acknowledgment, too tired to do more. Her eyes fluttered, then closed. "Think I'll rest now," she mumbled.

"Red?" She heard Joc's voice from a great distance. "Sweetheart? I need to tell you something. I need you to know…"

She tried to hold on, struggled to fight against the relentless drag of sleep and listen to what he was telling her. But she lost the battle and slid into a soft, gentle darkness where nothing could harm her or her baby. Where she still owned Longhorn and the man she loved stood strong and proud at her side while they raised their baby together.

Joc sat slumped in the chair beside Rosalyn's bed, shifting in a vain attempt to find a more comfortable position. Not possible, of course, not that that kept him from trying. He checked to see whether she still slept, reassured when he saw the slow, easy give in and take of her breath. It was a far more natural sleep than earlier, and a hint of color tinted the unbruised portions of her cheeks a healthy pink.

Had she heard him earlier? Had she heard him declare his love? He thought her lashes had flickered in response to the words, but he couldn't be certain. His jaw firmed. Next time she woke, they'd be the first words out of his mouth. He'd make sure of that. Restless, he pushed himself to his feet only to discover MacKenzie standing in the doorway staring at Rosalyn.

"What the hell are you doing here?" he demanded in a harsh undertone.

She was perceptive enough not to advance any farther into the room. "I had to come," she explained in a rush. "I'm so sorry, Joc. I know I'm partially responsible for the accident. How is she?"

"How is she?"

Pain howled through him and he lost it. Completely, thoroughly lost it. It was as though his brain disengaged from his body and all his senses went off-line. One minute he was in perfect control and the next he was streaking toward her, running off pure instinct and adrenaline. Maybe he would have been able to maintain some semblance of restraint if he hadn't been so exhausted or so terrified of losing everything that mattered most to him. When he came to himself, he had MacKenzie up against the wall, his hands fisted around the lapels of her blouse.

"If anything happens to her or our child, I swear to you I'll take you apart, piece by piece." His voice escaped low and guttural and filled with bone-chilling intensity. "You got me?"

"Child!" MacKenzie shook her head in stunned disbelief. "No, no. Oh God, Joc. She's pregnant? Have they said how the baby is? Is it safe?"

"So far." His jaw worked and the breath shuddered in and out of his lungs. It took endless seconds before he could gather up his self-control once again. "I'll make you pay, MacKenzie. If anything happens to Rosalyn, I swear I'll take you down."

She stiffened within his hold. "How dare you threaten me? You started this, Arnaud. You had to take the Hollister homestead. You couldn't get it through legitimate means, so you stole it away from my mother. Well, I've got news for you. You can take my home, but it still won't make you one of us."

He flinched, amazed that he still had the capacity to feel hurt after all this time. He suddenly realized he continued to hold her pinned against the wall, and with great care, opened his hands and released her. "I've kept my distance in the past out of respect for your mother." He fought to keep his voice to a mere whisper so they wouldn't disturb Rosalyn. He backed away from

MacKenzie, putting some much needed breathing distance between them. "But that ends after today. So we're clear? The gloves come off. As far as I'm concerned, we're no longer family. Hell, you never wanted to be, anyway."

"Do your worst, Joc, but it won't get you Rosalyn's ranch." She yanked at her blouse and straightened the crushed collar. "Only I can give you what you want."

That gave him pause. "Don't play games with me. Are you willing to sell Longhorn to me, or not?"

"Oh, I'm willing."

Now for the vital question. "How much do you want for it?" As far as he was concerned, everything and anything was on the table so long as it didn't adversely impact Rosalyn and their baby.

She stared at him with eyes that had haunted him all his life, eyes he wanted to hate. His father's eyes. But the pain that filled MacKenzie's were far different from any expression he'd ever seen in Boss Hollister's. The expression he read there was one he'd seen all too often, and always in the same place.

In his own mirror.

"I don't want your money." Her mouth quivered for an instant before she firmed it. "I want the Hollister homestead. I'll trade it for Longhorn."

He swore beneath his breath. He should have seen it coming. Maybe if he hadn't been so distracted by Rosalyn and the baby he would have. MacKenzie's offer left him wanting to howl in fury. "That's the one thing I can't give you. Name anything else, MacKenzie. I'll pay any amount you want."

Tears of fury glistened in her eyes and she trembled visibly in an effort to control them. "I don't want money, damn you! I want my home."

"I can't."

"Fine. Don't make the deal. I'll leave you to explain to your fiancée—" Her glance flickered in Rosalyn's direction. "Or maybe that's now your ex-fiancée—why you refused to save her home from my bulldozers. Something tells me you're not going to have much success."

Joc spun around. Rosalyn lay there, her eyes a violent blue and filled with heart-breaking disillusionment.

"Why?" Rosalyn asked. She couldn't believe what she'd overheard. "You have it within your power to save Longhorn and you won't do it. Why?"

He held his position on the far side of the room, distancing himself from her. The instant he realized she was awake and had overheard his conversation with MacKenzie, his face had fallen into impenetrable lines, giving nothing away. "I'm sorry, Red. I can't do it, and I can't explain why."

"Can't...or won't?"

"Take your pick."

She didn't understand it. Didn't understand his attitude. Didn't understand his remoteness. This man bore no resemblance to the one she'd fallen in love with, the one she could have sworn had declared his love for her. She tried again, desperate to break through the barriers he'd thrown up. "You told me that your father's land held no importance to you. That you weren't trying to reconnect with him through his homestead."

"I'm not."

"Then why—"

He simply shook his head.

She believed him, at least on that front. He'd been too adamant on that subject. If he'd been lying to her, or even to himself, she'd have picked up on that by now. She scrambled for another explanation. "Is it revenge? Is that it? Is this your way of hitting back at the Hollisters? Is getting even for what Boss did to you still so important after all these years?"

"Would you believe me if I said no?"

She shook her head, wincing at the pain pounding between her temples. "I don't know what to believe anymore. And you won't explain. What am I supposed to think?"

He approached then, sliding a hip onto the edge of her bed. "I need you to trust me, Red."

"You've asked that of me again and again. And each time I have." She swept tears from her cheeks, the jarring contact with her bruises making her flinch. "But you have the ability to save my property and you refuse to do it. Is hanging on to your father's land that important to you?"

"All I can tell you is that I have a good reason for my actions."

Another possibility occurred to her, one that broke her heart. "Was MacKenzie right? Is this all a game to the two of you?"

He hesitated. "Until now, I suppose it has been some sort of game."

"Well, this isn't a game to me. It's my life!"

"Listen to me, Red. MacKenzie despises my existence. It doesn't matter that I had nothing to do with the circumstances surrounding my birth, or that Ana and I are as much a victim of Boss's callousness as MacKenzie and her brothers. She's intent on besting me. And she doesn't care who gets in the way or how badly they're hurt, so long as she wins."

"But you can put an end to it. It's within your power." She couldn't keep the desperation from her voice. "All you have to do is give her what she wants. Or is the win as important to you as it is to her?"

He replied with painful gentleness. "I'll tell you what I told her. Ask me for anything else, anything at all, and it's yours. Despite what you think, this is the one thing it's not in my power to give you." He searched her expression and his mouth compressed. "You won't be able to forgive me if I don't make the trade, will you? It will always stand between us."

She wanted to deny it, wished she could be generous enough to shrug off the loss and move on with her life. But she'd been the sole protector of Longhorn for too many years to do that. It was her only connection with her parents and the generations of Oakleys before them. Her chin quivered, her silence condemning her.

He stood. "I'll be back tomorrow. We'll talk more then."

"Don't come," she whispered. "There's nothing left to be said."

He hesitated, then inclined his head. Without another word, he walked out of the room.

The instant Joc left, Rosalyn leaned back against her pillows and closed her eyes, fighting a resurgence of tears. Something was terribly wrong. She didn't know what, but every instinct warned of it. She had a horrible feeling the problem extended beyond the situation with her ranch and the Hollister homestead. But for the life of her she couldn't figure it out. And unless Joc trusted her enough to tell her the truth, she doubted she ever would.

Her hand stole across her belly. What would have happened between them if she'd miscarried the baby? Or if she hadn't trusted Duff with mailing her loan payments and still owned the ranch? Would Joc still be insisting on marriage?

How could she make a rational decision from this point forward if he wouldn't talk to her about whatever secret he was keeping? How could they have a successful marriage if he shut her out?

Or if he was marrying her for all the wrong reasons?

The door to her room thrust open and for a split second she thought it might be Joc. That he'd returned to tell her he'd made a terrible mistake and that he'd do whatever necessary to save Longhorn. Instead a nurse entered to check on Rosalyn's vital statistics.

Why hadn't he been willing to trade Longhorn for MacKenzie's old home? The question nagged at her. The only reason she could think of was the one reason she most wanted to deny. He hadn't been willing to make the trade because doing so would force her and their baby to live in his world instead of on the ranch. That it would give him the control he'd lose by agreeing to her stipulation about marriage. Could he be that ruthless? She rubbed her aching head. Who was she kidding?

Joc had invented the word.

* * *

It was past midnight when Joc placed the call. A sleepy voice answered on the fifth ring.

"It's Arnaud," he announced. "We have a problem."

"Do you realize what time it is?"

"I'm well aware of the time." His hand bunched into a fist. "I need your help, Meredith."

There was a long moment of silence. "I would have thought I'd helped you quite enough."

He let that slide. "MacKenzie managed to get her hands on Rosalyn's ranch. She's going to raze it if I don't trade your old place for Longhorn. You need to stop her."

"Oh God. I'll speak to her, but I doubt it'll do any good."

He fought to remain calm. Never before had self-control been an issue. But it was an issue tonight. "You can do more than speak to her," he insisted.

There was a moment of silence, then, "We've had this conversation before. You made a promise to me and I expect you to keep your word."

He closed his eyes. "Do you doubt I will?"

"You made a commitment to Ana that you'd change your life when you were a twenty-year-old hoodlum. To the best of my knowledge, you haven't broken your word since then. I assume you're not going to start now?"

"No."

Relief bled through her words. "I'll do what I can, but MacKenzie can be as stubborn as you when it comes to certain issues."

"I can't lose her, Meredith," he whispered. "Not Rosalyn. Anything but her."

"You love her?" she asked, shocked. "You, Joc?"

"More than anything. That ranch means everything to her." He fought to speak through the thickness clogging his throat. "Even more than me."

"Okay, I'll do what I can."

Ten

Thirty-six hours later, Rosalyn checked herself out of the hospital. Her doctors weren't happy, particularly when they learned that Joc wouldn't be picking her up. But then, how could he when she'd neglected to call him? Since both she and the baby were fully recovered, they reluctantly agreed to discharge her.

Exiting through the front doors, she took a deep breath. She might be inhaling city air rather than air sweetened with the grass and flowers and ripening grains of home, but at least it was better than a hospital room scented with the harsh odor of bleach and illness. Now she just had to decide where to go next.

Joc's place was out. She needed time to deal with all that had happened between them before confronting him again. She could return to Longhorn—it was hers for a few days more at least. But did she want to go back there? Before she could decide what her next move would be, a sleek black car drove into the entry circle and pulled to a stop in front of her.

The passenger door swung open and a woman called out to her. "Ms. Oakley…Rosalyn? I arranged with your housekeeper, Claire, to pick you up."

Rosalyn blinked in surprise, cautiously approaching the car. "I'm sorry. Do I know you?"

"Indirectly, my dear. I'm Meredith Hollister. I think we need to talk."

Rosalyn made a snap decision and slid into the car, studying Meredith with interest. The woman appeared to be in her forties, despite the fact that basic math put her somewhere in her fifties. She was also every bit as striking as her daughter, although their appearances couldn't be more disparate. Where MacKenzie shared her half brother's height, and eye-catching, dark looks, Meredith was a small, sleek package with a cap of streaked blond curls and a lovely, fine-boned face.

"How did you know I was being discharged at this moment?" Rosalyn asked, genuinely curious. "Joc didn't even know."

Meredith dismissed that with a wave of her manicured hand. To Rosalyn's surprise her fingernails were simple, polished ovals. Practical rather than flashy. "I bribed one of your nurses to give me the heads-up. Then I called your housekeeper and offered to take you where you needed to go."

"I'm not sure what we have to talk about." Rosalyn snapped her seat belt in place, wincing at the protest of still-tender muscles. "But I appreciate the ride."

"I thought we could talk about Joc."

The comment was so unexpected Rosalyn didn't know what to say. "You want to talk to me about Joc?" she offered hesitantly. "That can't be good."

Meredith shot her a sparkling look, one filled with good humor. "Why would you think that? I admire Joc immensely." She pulled away from the hospital. "Where can I take you?"

"I guess I'll settle for home. Unfortunately it won't be mine for much longer," Rosalyn answered, hoping she didn't sound too pathetic.

"Ah. You're referring to MacKenzie. My daughter doesn't play fair."

That provoked a spurt of temper. "She bribed one of my hands to tear up my mortgage payments. Since she held the loan on my place, it allowed her to foreclose on it. So, you're right. She doesn't play fair."

"She wants her home back. She thought Joc would trade."

"I don't hold that against her. I understand all about roots. What I object to is how she went about getting her way, and that she used me to get at Joc."

Meredith frowned in concern. "You're getting worked up about it. That can't be healthy. Why don't you put your seat back and rest? I expect the drive to take a while."

"I'm not really tired—"

"You left the hospital before they wanted to release you. Consider the health of your baby, if nothing else."

Every last protest vanished beneath the logic of that one statement. When it came to pushing buttons, this woman was good. Grumbling beneath her breath, Rosalyn reclined the seat and closed her eyes. She didn't actually nod off. Instead she lay in that dreamy world somewhere between consciousness and sleep. It wasn't until the car slowed that she sat up again. They turned onto a long, sweeping driveway, one that was all-too familiar. Rosalyn stared in dismay as they approached Joc's mansion.

"What are you doing? I didn't want to come here."

"Didn't you? Oops. My mistake. I thought you said you wanted to go home."

"This isn't my home."

"Huh. I thought it was." Meredith pulled to a stop at the base of the broad, shallow staircase that led to Joc's massive front entryway. "Would you mind if I offer you some advice?"

"I'd rather you didn't," Rosalyn answered truthfully.

"I understand. But I think I will, anyway." Fine lines spiked outward from the older woman's mouth and eyes, lines that spoke of an old, bitter pain. "I've learned the hard way that when we lose the things that are most important to us, we can become angry and cynical. Or we can find a way to take what we have left and make the best of it. You're facing that choice now. Joc loves you, you know."

"That's not true—"

Meredith cut her off. "It is true, just as it's true that you love him. You have a choice, Rosalyn. You can either put the past behind you and create a new life with the man you love, or you can use what's happened as an excuse to shut yourself off from happiness. When I was faced with a similar dilemma, I made the wrong choice. So has most of my family." She held Rosalyn with a gaze both pleading and commanding. "Don't do that to Joc. He deserves better."

Rosalyn stared in disbelief. "How can you defend him? He's taken everything from you."

"You're wrong. Boss did, not Joc." Her chin firmed and she nodded as though in response to some private decision. "Do me a favor, won't you? Tell Joc I'm releasing him from his promise. He'll know what I mean."

Rosalyn remained where she was for several long minutes, before releasing her breath in a sigh. "You're going to sit here until I get out, aren't you?"

"'Fraid so." She wiggled her fingers in the direction of the front door. "Off you go, my dear. And don't forget to give Joc my message."

Rosalyn thrust open the door and exited into a blanket of stifling humidity. Without a backward look, she trotted up the steps and entered Joc's home. She walked into blessed coolness, her advent startling one of the maids who greeted her with a smile of delight.

"Ms. Rosalyn, welcome home."

"Thanks, Lynn. Do you know where Joc is?"

"In his study."

Rosalyn's stomach knotted. She didn't want to confront Joc again, not after how they'd last parted. But she didn't have any choice. Meredith had seen to that.

The door to the study was closed and she paused outside, her fist raised to knock. Meredith's words continued to haunt her, and her arm fell to her side as she took a moment to gather up her self-control.

Meredith was right. She did have a decision to make before she saw Joc again. She could hate him for refusing MacKenzie's offer, could spend the rest of her life resenting what had happened. Or she could accept responsibility for her part in the disaster and move on. If she'd kept her bank accounts reconciled she might have realized in time that her mortgage checks weren't being cashed and put an end to MacKenzie's scheme before it had a chance to get off the ground.

More to the point, Joc had no obligation to use his assets to save Longhorn. A hard realization struck. Good Lord! If he had bailed her out, he'd own the property, not her. And he'd be within his rights to build the complex he wanted, rather than keep her ranch intact. Why hadn't that occurred to her before? Perhaps it had been the knock to her head or the medications she'd been given. Whatever the cause, she hadn't been thinking straight.

She pressed a hand to her abdomen. Boss had caused so much strife and turmoil, putting his own selfish desires before his wife and children, not to mention Joc's mother. It would be such an easy path for her to take, as well, a path of bitterness and emotional dearth. Or she could trust Joc, trust that he'd do everything within his power to care for her and their child. And maybe in time, Meredith's claim that Joc loved her might come true.

Closing her eyes, Rosalyn made her peace with the

past and with all she'd lost. From now on, she'd focus on the future and on the life she wanted to create for her child. It was time to provide a new legacy for the next generation. From this point forward, she'd put down new roots. She straightened and knocked on the heavy oak.

"I told you I didn't want to be interrupted!"

She thrust open the door. "Too bad, Arnaud. I'm here and you're going to have to deal with me."

"Red!" He shot to his feet, his drink sloshing over the rim of his tumbler. "Are you all right? The baby?"

"Mother and baby are both fine, thanks."

She studied him, secretly shocked by his condition. Though it had only been days since she'd last seen him, he looked as though he hadn't slept in a month. Deep lines bracketed his mouth. But it was his eyes that held her, eyes that were bottomless wells of pain.

"I was told you wouldn't be released until tomorrow." He circled the desk. He started to reach for her, his arms dropping to his sides at the last instant, as though he were afraid to touch her. "Why didn't you call me? I would have come and picked you up."

"I didn't want to see you."

He stiffened at that. "Then why are you here?"

"Not out of choice, at least not at first. Meredith drove me out here."

His face darkened. "How did she know to pick you up?"

"Apparently bribery and deception run in the Hollister family. Meredith paid one of the nurses to alert her when I left the hospital." She stepped past him and

wandered deeper into the study, before spinning to face
him once again. "She had a message for you, by the way."

Every scrap of expression vanished from his face.
"What message?"

Interesting reaction. She studied him more closely.
"She said she releases you from your promise. You're
supposed to know what that means."

"That's all she told you?"

"Yes." She'd wasted enough time on the Hollisters.
"Could we talk? I mean, really talk."

"I think that would be a good idea."

Rosalyn lifted an eyebrow. "Mind if I go first?"

He visibly steeled himself. "Go ahead."

With luck he'd understand where she was going with
her request. Only one question remained…how he'd
react to it. "I'd like to renegotiate our agreement, the one
regarding the baby and our marriage."

She'd intrigued him, though he still remained wary.
"Which particular clause?"

"The one that determines where we live."

A muscle leaped in his jaw and his gaze intensified,
filled with desperate hope. "I think I'd be open to a
change in venue. Where do you have in mind?"

"Wherever you're willing to put down roots.
Wherever we can put those roots down together," she
said simply. "If you're willing, that is."

He came for her then, catching her close. "Warn me
if I hurt you."

She shut her eyes and leaned into him. "I've discovered that I can handle a little hurt. I bounce back fast."

"Are you sure, Red? Really sure?"

Her head jerked up and she regarded him with un-flinching certainty. "Absolutely. It doesn't matter if MacKenzie owns Longhorn now. It's dirt, remember? Nothing more than acres of dirt."

He stilled against her and his breath escaped in a long sigh. "I seem to remember saying those words to you when we were on Deseos." A hint of regret drifted across his face. "They were wrong then and they're wrong now."

She pulled back. "What do you mean?"

"I mean I plan to fix it."

She shook her head. "No, you don't need to do that. It doesn't matter where we live." Didn't he get it? She took his hand in hers and placed it low on her abdomen. "Nothing matters except us and our child. We're Texans. They don't grow them any tougher. We can plant our roots anywhere."

"And we will. We'll plant them on Oakley land."

Rosalyn stared in disbelief. "MacKenzie changed her mind?"

"She will."

He swung her into his arms, and with the utmost caution, carried her to the leather couch on the far side of his study. "I don't dare take you upstairs," he said with clear regret. "I'm not sure I could keep my hands off you and you need time to heal."

"Fortunately for us both, I'm a fast healer."

As though unable to help himself he kissed her, his mouth brushing hers with the lightest of touches. It wasn't enough—nowhere near enough. She lifted her mouth for another. With a husky groan he kissed her again, sealing her mouth with his. He delved gently inward, slow and careful and infinitely tender.

"More," she demanded the minute he lifted his head.

"Your bruises…"

"You can kiss them better." She shot him a humorous glance. "It'll be good practice for when the baby's born."

He didn't need any further prompting. He settled back against the cushions and with exquisite sensitivity, helped her stretch out on top of him. "Are you all right?"

"Perfect."

The next several minutes passed in a delicious haze. Her enjoyment of being in his arms again overrode any discomfort she might have experienced from her injuries. His kisses were sweeter than any that had come before, telling her without words all that lay within his heart. Every touch felt soft and slow and keenly aware of how they might impact her injuries. Desire rose like a tide, threatening to spiral out of control. Suddenly he pulled back.

"No more," he insisted, the breath heaving from his lungs. "Not until your doctor gives us the okay."

Realizing that she didn't have a hope of changing his mind, she raised her head and regarded him with undisguised curiosity. "Explain it to me, Joc. Why will MacKenzie sell Longhorn to you? What's changed over the past few days?"

"Meredith happened."

"The promise?" At his nod, she asked, "What promise did you make to her?"

"That I'd never tell anyone why she sold her home to me. And that I'd never sell it without her permission."

"I don't understand," she said in bewilderment.

"Meredith approached me not long after I made my first million—maybe a decade ago. She begged me to buy the property."

She stared, dumbfounded. "Why would she do that?"

"Because she was on the verge of bankruptcy. Between Boss's legal fees and the taxes and fines that resulted from his illegal activities, there was nothing left."

The pieces started to fall into place. "MacKenzie doesn't know any of this, does she?"

Joc shook his head. "No. Nor do her brothers. Meredith didn't want them to know. Pride, I suspect. She split the money among them and claimed it was their inheritance from their father."

"Why did she want you to hold on to the property?"

"I think she has mixed feelings about it. Part of her hates the place because of Boss. Part of her is torn because the homestead has been in Hollister hands for so many years. She felt that as long as I held on to it, she had time to come to terms with her feelings and to decide what she wanted done with it."

Rosalyn blinked in surprise. "I don't get it. Why would you let her make that decision?"

"It was part of our agreement. Since I didn't care what happened to the place, the stipulation didn't bother me. The one thing Meredith has remained adamant about is not passing the homestead on to her children. She didn't want them continuing a legacy that brought them nothing but pain."

"Which is why she didn't want you selling it to Mac-Kenzie, even a decade later." Rosalyn frowned. "Why did she want it after all this time?"

"MacKenzie found out a year ago that I—or rather, one of my corporations—owns the property. She can't stand it and has been after me ever since to sell out to her."

Rosalyn needed to put another issue to rest. "Are you positive you don't want it for yourself?"

Bone-deep anger burned in his eyes. "I've never set foot on Boss's land and I never will."

"What do you think Meredith will do with it?"

"We've discussed turning it into a camp for children suffering from life-threatening diseases, or perhaps a rehabilitation center for troubled teens."

"Are you going to tell MacKenzie the truth?"

He nodded. "I'll arrange a meeting with her and Meredith and see if she won't come on board with her mother's plans. I have a feeling she will, and that once she understands why I refused to sell it to her, she'll allow me to purchase Longhorn." His mouth twisted. "Knowing her, it'll be for a hefty price."

"Why, Joc?" she asked softly. "Why would you do that for your mother's nemesis?"

"Because she saved my life."

Rosalyn lifted onto one elbow. *"What?"*

"It was during that time when I was trying to change

my life around. When I put an end to my more questionable business enterprises—"

"That's a tactful way of putting it."

"I thought so." His smile held a hint of pain. "There wasn't any money coming in once I parted ways with Mick and the others. And I still had the responsibility for Ana."

The penny dropped. "Harvard. Meredith paid for you to go to Harvard, didn't she?"

He shook his head. "Money was tight for her, too. No, she didn't pay for it. But she found people who could. At Meredith's urging, they took a chance on me. They supported me while I got my education and during the years I was getting my business off the ground."

"For which they've since been richly rewarded," Rosalyn guessed shrewdly.

He shrugged. "I've been in a position to help a few of them," he admitted. "Meredith also arranged for references from people who had an in at Harvard. And she arranged for housing, housing that enabled me to keep Ana with me during those early years."

"So much," Rosalyn marveled. "Why would she do all that?"

"Because she understood that Ana and I were the innocent ones, the ones who suffered the most, even more than her own children. Meredith is…she's quite a lady. After what she did for me, how could I refuse her request when she was in trouble?"

"You couldn't."

"She even tried to reconcile the differences between her children, and Ana and me."

"Without success."

He grimaced. "Her attempts only made matters worse. MacKenzie, in particular, resented her mother's interference. She's always thought I had some hold over Meredith, that I put pressure on her. It never occurred to her that it was the other way around."

They lay in silent accord for a long time after that while Rosalyn worked up the nerve to ask her final question. Unable to stand it any longer, she cleared her throat. "Meredith told me something else."

"Meredith's been busy," Joc said drily. "What else did she say?"

"She claimed you loved me." Rosalyn peeked up at him. "Was she right, Joc? Do you love me?"

The tenderness in his expression said it all. "How can you doubt it?" He slid his fingers deep into her hair and tugged her down until their mouths collided. And then he removed all doubts, giving of himself without holding anything back. When she'd melted into a helpless puddle, he released her with a slow grin. "I love you with every fiber of my being, and I always will. Any other questions?"

"Just one. What happens if MacKenzie sells you Longhorn?"

His brows tugged together. "We move in, of course. That's what we agreed, isn't it?"

"But your complex…"

Understanding dawned. "Ah. You're wondering if I won't decide to build my office complex if I end up owning Longhorn."

"It's just that there are a lot of roots on my ranch." She hastened to correct herself. "Your ranch."

"*Our* ranch, Red."

"Our ranch," she repeated. A gentle unloosening swept over her at the word, even as she issued a warning. "You might find those roots trip you up, if you're not careful."

"They can't trip you if your own roots are tangled up there, too. And they are. They're tangled so tightly with yours that they'll never pull loose. And with all those roots cluttering up the place it certainly makes the property inappropriate for anything other than ranching." He kissed away her tears of joy before sliding his hand across her belly in a gesture that had become heartwarmingly familiar. "I have some suggestions for names."

She laughed through her tears. "Already?"

"I had a lot of time to think over the past couple days." He hesitated, revealing an uncertainty that sat oddly on his face. "If it's a boy, how does the name Joshua appeal to you?"

The tears intensified and she had trouble responding. "That—that was the name of my brother."

"Yes, I know. I saw it at the cemetery."

"Thank you. It would mean a lot to name our son after my brother." It took her a moment to regain her control. "Joc?"

"Yes, Red?"

"I love you."

"That's all that's important." He lowered his head, and with infinite care, kissed her.

As Rosalyn surrendered to Joc's embrace, she knew deep in her heart that their child would be a boy. A boy named Joshua with hair as black as ebony and eyes the exact same shade as Texas Bluebonnets. A boy who'd grow tall and strong and broad. A boy who would provide the trunk for a tree that would send out endless branches, each growing large and full, nourished by the roots from which he sprang.

Roots that ran deep into Texan soil.

* * * * *

THE PRINCE'S
ULTIMATE DECEPTION

by
Emilie Rose

Dear Reader,

Like many American girls, I grew up hearing fairy tales and dreaming of my own prince. In my teens I switched to reading Mills & Boon novels, and just like the fairy tales of my childhood, those stories carried me away, filled me with hope and instilled in me a belief in happily ever after.

I hope you enjoy *The Prince's Ultimate Deception*, my modern-day version of Cinderella, as much as I enjoyed creating a magical kingdom and a prince worthy of his princess.

Happy reading,

Emilie Rose

PS Stop by my website at www.EmilieRose.com for updates on my books!

EMILIE ROSE

lives in North Carolina with her college sweetheart husband and four sons. Writing is Emilie's third (and hopefully her last) career. She's managed a medical office and run a home day care, neither of which offers half as much satisfaction as plotting happy endings. Her hobbies include quilting, gardening and cooking – especially cheesecake. Her favourite TV shows include *ER, CSI* and Discovery Channel's medical programmes. Emilie's a country music fan, because she can find an entire book in almost any song.

Letters can be mailed to:

Emilie Rose
PO Box 20145
Raleigh, NC 27619, USA
E-mail: EmilieRoseC@aol.com

To Christine Hyatt for sharing your wisdom
and showing me the path.
You helped me make my dreams come true.

One

"Please. You *have* to help me."

A woman's desperate plea caught Prince Dominic Andreas Rossi de Montagnarde's attention as he and his bodyguard Ian waited for the elevator inside Monaco's luxurious Hôtel Reynard. He observed the reflected exchange between a long-haired brunette and the concierge through the gilt-framed mirror hanging on the wall beside the polished brass elevator doors.

"Mr. Gustavo, if I don't get away from all this prewedding euphoria I am going to lose my mind. Don't get me wrong. I am happy for my friend, but I just can't stomach this much romance without getting nauseous."

Her statement piqued Dominic's curiosity. What had soured her on the fairy-tale fantasy so many others harbored? He had never met a woman who didn't wallow in wedding preparations. Each of his three sisters had dragged out the planning of their weddings for more than a year, as had his beloved Giselle.

"I need a tour guide who can work around my brides-maid's duties for the next month," she continued. "One who knows the best places for day trips and impromptu getaways because I don't know when I'll need to escape from all this—" she shuddered dramatically "—happiness."

American, he judged by her accent, and possibly from one of the Southern states given her slight drawl.

The concierge gave her a sympathetic smile. "I'm sorry, Mademoiselle Spencer, but it is nearly midnight. At this hour I cannot contact our guides to make those arrangements. If you will return in the morning I am sure we can find some-one suitable."

She shoved her fingers into the mass of her thick, shiny curls, tugged as if she were at her wit's end and then shifted to reveal an exquisite face with a classical profile. Her bare arms were slender, but toned, and she had a body to match beneath the floor-length green gown subtly draping her curves. Nice curves deserving of a second glance which Dom-inic willingly took. Too bad he couldn't see if her legs were as superb as the rest of her.

His gaze slowly backtracked to the reflection of her lovely face and slammed into mocking and amused emerald eyes the same shade as her dress. She'd caught his appraisal and repaid him in kind with a leisurely inspection of her own. Her gaze descended from his shoulders to his butt and legs. One arched eyebrow clearly stated she intended putting him in his place. He fought a smile over her boldness, but he couldn't prevent a quickening of his pulse. When her eyes found his once more he saw appreciation but no sign of recognition.

Interesting.

She returned her attention to the concierge. "In the morning I have to ruin two years' worth of dieting and exercise by stuffing myself with wedding cake samples. Please, I'm begging you, Mr. Gustavo, give me a guide's name tonight so I'll at least have the promise of escape tomorrow."

Escape. The word echoed in Dominic's head as he pondered the elevator's unusual slowness. He needed time to come to terms with his future, to marrying and having children with a woman he didn't love and might not even like, without the paparazzi shoving cameras in his face. In a word, he needed to escape—hence the lack of his usual entourage, dying his blond hair brown and shaving the mustache and beard he'd worn since he'd first sprouted whiskers.

This would in all likelihood be his last month of peace before all hell broke loose. Once the paparazzi caught wind of the proceedings at the palace they would descend on him like a plague of locusts, and his life would no longer be his own. He could see the headlines now. Widowed Prince Seeks Bride.

Apparently the American needed to escape, as well. Why not do so together? Looking at her would in no way be a hardship, and discovering how she'd willingly divorced herself from romance would be an added bonus.

He glanced at Ian. The bodyguard had been with him since Dominic's college days and sometimes Dominic swore the older man could read his mind. Sure enough, warning flashed in Ian's brown eyes and his burly body stiffened.

The elevator chimed and opened, but instead of stepping inside the cubicle Dominic pivoted toward the concierge stand. Ian hovered in the background, silently swearing, Dominic was sure. "Perhaps I could be of assistance, Gustavo."

Gustavo's eyebrows shot up, not surprising since the man often arranged Dominic's entertainment.

"Pardon me for eavesdropping, mademoiselle. I could not help but overhear your request. I would be happy to act as your guide if that meets with your approval?" Dominic waited for recognition to dawn in her eyes. Instead a frown pleated the area above her slim nose. From her smooth porcelain skin he guessed her to be in her late twenties or early thirties—far too young to have forsaken love. As was he. But what choice did he have when duty called?

Her gaze traveled over his white silk shirt and black trousers and then returned to his face. "You work here?"

Surprise shot through him. Was his simple disguise so effective? He had hoped to throw off the paparazzi from a distance, but he hadn't expected to fool anyone up close, and yet she apparently didn't know who he was. Admittedly, he'd lived as low profile a life as any royal could in the past few years, and he avoided the press more often than not, but still… Was this possible?

Dominic made a split-second decision not to enlighten her. He'd had a lifetime of cloying, obsequious women due to his lineage. Why not enjoy being a normal man for as long as it lasted? "I don't work for the hotel, but I am here as often as I can be. Hôtel Reynard is my favorite establishment."

She looked at Gustavo. "Can I trust him?"

Gustavo seemed taken aback by the question. As he should be. Dominic, as next in line to the throne of Montagnarde, a small three-island country four hundred miles east of New Zealand, wasn't accustomed to having his integrity questioned.

"*Certainement,* mademoiselle."

Her thickly lashed emerald gaze narrowed on Dominic's. "Are you familiar with Southern France and Northern Italy?"

His favorite playgrounds, and in recent years, prime examples of the types of tourist meccas he intended to develop in his homeland. "I am."

"Do you speak any languages other than English, because

I barely scraped by in my college Latin class, and I only know health-care Spanish."

"I am fluent in English, French, Italian and Spanish. I can get by in Greek and German."

Her perfectly arched eyebrows rose. Amusement twinkled in her eyes and curved her lips, rousing something which had lain dormant inside him for many years. "Now you're just bragging, but it sounds like you're just the man I need, Mr....?"

He hesitated. To continue the masquerade he'd have to lie openly not just by omission and he detested liars. But he wanted to spend time with this lovely woman as a man instead of a monarch before fulfilling his duty and marrying whichever woman the royal council deemed a suitable broodmare to his stud service. What could it hurt? He and the American were but ships passing in the night. Or in this case, one small corner of Europe.

"Rossi. Damon Rossi." He ignored Gustavo's shocked expression and Ian's rigid disapproving presence behind him and extended his hand. Dominic hoped neither man would correct the hastily concocted variation of his name or his failure to mention his title.

"Madeline Spencer." The brunette's fingers curled around his. Her handshake was firm and strong and her gaze direct instead of deferential. When had a woman last looked him in the eye and treated him as an equal? Not since Giselle. Unexpected desire hit him hard and fast and with stunning potency.

A similar awareness flickered on Madeline's face, expanding her pupils, flushing her cheeks and parting her lips. "I guess that only leaves one question. Can I afford you?"

Caught off guard by her breathless query and by his body's impassioned response, Dominic glanced at Gustavo who rushed to respond for him. "I am sure Monsieur Reynard will cover your expenses, mademoiselle, since you are an *honored* guest of the family and a *dear friend* to his fiancée. Hi— Monsieur Rossi should not accept any money from you."

Dominic didn't miss the warning in Gustavo's statement.

Madeline's smile widened, trapping the air in Dominic's chest. "When can we get together to set up a schedule?"

If he weren't expecting a conference call from the palace with an update on the bridal selection process momentarily he would definitely prolong this encounter. "Perhaps tomorrow morning after your cake sampling?"

He realized he hadn't released her hand, and he was reluctant to do so. Arousal pumped pleasantly through his veins— a nice distraction from the disagreeable dilemma which had driven him into temporary exile.

Madeline was apparently in no rush, either, as she didn't pull away or break his gaze. "That'd be great, Damon. Where shall I meet you?"

Dominic searched his mental map for a meeting place not haunted by the paparazzi. The only option his testosterone-flooded brain presented was his suite, but the tour guide he'd implied himself to be could hardly afford penthouse accommodations. Already his lie complicated the situation.

Gustavo cleared his throat, jerking Dominic back to the present. "Perhaps *le café* located in the lower terrace gardens, Your—Monsieur Rossi?"

Dominic nodded his thanks—for the recommendation and for the conspiracy. He was used to being a leader and making decisions, but even a future king knew when to accept wise council. "A very good suggestion, Gustavo. What time will you finish, mademoiselle?"

Straight, white teeth bit into her plump bottom lip and Dominic struggled with a sudden urge to sample her soft pink flesh. "Elevenish?"

"I shall count the hours." He bent over her hand and kissed her knuckles. Her fragrance, a light floral mingled with the tart tang of lemon, filled his lungs, and his libido roared to life like the mythical dragon island folklore decreed lived beneath Montagnarde's hot springs.

Dominic had not come to Monaco with the intention of having a last dalliance before beginning what would in all likelihood be a passionless marriage. But he was tempted. Extremely tempted. However the lie, combined with his duty to his country meant he had nothing to offer this beautiful woman except his services as a guide. He would have to keep his newly awakened libido on a short leash.

It wouldn't be easy.

Madeline Spencer's fingers squeezed his one more time and then she released him with a slow drag of her fingertips across his palm. A sassy smile slanted her lips. "Until tomorrow then, Damon."

With a flutter of her ringless fingers she entered the penthouse elevator—the one he'd just abandoned. The doors slid closed.

Dominic inhaled deeply. For the first time in months the sword of doom hanging over his head lifted. He had a short reprieve, but a reprieve nonetheless.

"Oh. My. God." Madeline sagged against the inside of the penthouse suite door and pressed a hand over her racing heart. "I think I'm in lust."

Candace and Amelia, two of Madeline's three suite mates, straightened from their reclining positions on the sofas of the sitting room. They'd already changed from the evening gowns they'd worn to the casino earlier into sleepwear.

"With whom?" Amelia, wearing a ruffled nightgown, asked.

"I have just hired the most gorgeous man on the planet to be my tour guide."

"Tell all," Candace ordered. The bride-to-be was the reason Madeline, Amelia and Stacy, her bridesmaids, were sharing a luxurious suite in the five-star Hôtel Reynard. The quartet had been granted an all-expenses-paid month in Monaco compliments of Candace's fiancé, Vincent Reynard, to plan the couple's wedding, which would take place here in Monaco in four weeks.

"His name's Damon and he has the most amazing blue eyes, thick tobacco-brown hair and a body that won't quit. He's tall—six-three, I'd guess. It was nice to have to look up at a guy even when I was wearing my heels."

"Are you sure it's not *love* at first sight?" Amelia asked with a dreamy look on her face.

Madeline sighed over her coworker's die-hard romantic notions. "You know better. Love is not a fall I intend to take ever again."

Thanks to her lying, cheating ex-fiancé.

"Not all men are like Mike," Candace said as she stacked the tourist pamphlets she'd been perusing neatly on the table.

For Candace's sake Madeline hoped not. Vincent seemed like a nice guy and he truly doted on Candace. But Mike had done the same for Madeline in the early days, and therefore Madeline no longer trusted anyone carrying the Y chromosome.

"No, thank goodness, but my jerk detector is apparently broken, and there are enough guys out there like Mike that I've decided to focus on my career and avoid anything except brief, shallow relationships from now on. Men do it. Why can't I?"

Not that she'd had time for any kind of relationship lately, meaningless or otherwise, given the extra shifts she'd volunteered for at the hospital and the rigorous exercise program she'd adopted during the two years since Mike split.

"Sounds like you're hoping for more than guided tours from this guy," Candace guessed.

Was she? She couldn't deny the electricity crackling between her and Damon when they'd shaken hands, and when he'd kissed her knuckles her knees had nearly buckled. The man might be a tour guide, but he had class and charisma out the wazoo. She'd bet he could turn a shallow affair into a momentous occasion.

"Maybe I am. Maybe I want to have a wildly passionate vacation fling with a sexy foreigner. If he's not married, that is. He wasn't wearing a ring, but—" Their pitying expressions raised her defenses. "What?"

Amelia frowned. "This is about Mike showing up at the hospital last month with his child and pregnant wife in tow, isn't it?"

"It's not." *Liar.* But hey, a girl had her pride and Madeline planned to cling tightly to the ragged remnants of hers.

Mike had made a fool of her. He'd led her on with a six-year engagement, and then he'd dumped her on her thirtieth birthday when she'd jokingly suggested they set a wedding date or call it quits. As soon as he'd moved out of her town house and left his job as a radiologist at the hospital where they both worked, coworkers she'd barely known had rushed to inform her that while she'd been planning her dream wedding he'd been sharing his excellent bedside manner with other women. And judging by the family he'd brought by the E.R. last month, he'd married someone else and started pumping out babies as soon as he'd dumped her.

The lying, conniving rat.

Love? Uh-uh. Not for her. Never again. And she hoped reality didn't slap Candace in the face. But if that happened Madeline would be there to help her friend pick up the pieces—the way Candace and Amelia had been there for her.

Candace rose and crossed the room to wrap Madeline in a hug. "Just be careful."

Madeline snorted. "Please, I am a medical professional. You don't have to lecture me about safe sex. Besides, I'm on the Pill."

"I wasn't referring only to pregnancy or communicable diseases. Don't let that dickhead Mike make you do anything reckless you'll regret."

Candace and Amelia had never liked Mike. Maybe Madeline should have listened to her friends. But not this time. This time she wouldn't be blinded by love. This time she was looking out for number one. "That's the beauty of it. Assuming Damon is interested in a temporary relationship, he can't lead me on, dump me or break my heart because I'll be leaving right after the wedding. I mean, what can happen in four weeks?"

Amelia winced. "Don't tempt fate like that."

Candace sighed. "I know each of us has different things we want to see and do in Monaco, but don't spend all of your time with him. We want to see some of you, too."

Madeline bit her lip and studied her friend. How could she explain that being immersed in all the wedding hoopla brought back too many painful memories—memories of planning her own aborted wedding and wallowing in every intricate detail to make the day perfect? All for naught. She couldn't, without hurting Candace's feelings.

"I promise I won't abandon my friends or my brides-maid's duties—no matter how good Damon is at guiding or anything else."

She looped an arm around each woman's waist. "Friends are forever and lovers—" she shrugged "—are not."

Good grief, she was as nervous as a virgin on prom night, and at thirty-two Madeline hadn't seen either virginity or prom night in a *long* time.

Her heart beat at double time and it had nothing to do with the sugar rush from sampling too many wedding cakes this morning.

Was her hair right? Her dress? And wasn't that just plain ridiculous? Nonetheless vanity had caused her to pull on a dress with a deep V neckline in the front and back and to don the outrageously sexy shoes she'd bought at the designer outlet down the street. She'd even French braided her unruly hair and added her favorite silver clip.

She scanned the partially open-air café for Damon. He rose from a table in the shadowy back corner, looking absolutely delicious in dark glasses, a casual, short-sleeved white cotton shirt and jeans. Wide shoulders. Thick biceps. Flat abs and narrow hips. Yum.

The glasses were a tad affected given he wasn't seated in the sunny section of the café, but so many people in Monaco sported the same look that he didn't seem out of place. Still— she tipped back her head and looked up at his handsome face—she'd rather stare into his pale blue eyes than at her own reflection.

"*Bonjour,* Mademoiselle Spencer." He pulled out her chair.

She tried to place his accent and couldn't, which was pretty odd since her job exposed her to an assortment of nationalities on a daily basis. And then there was the intriguing way he occasionally slipped into more formal speech….

"Good morning, Damon, and please call me Madeline." His knuckles brushed the bare skin between her shoulder blades as he seated her. Awareness skipped down her spine, startling a flock of butterflies in her stomach. *Ooh* yeah. Definitely a prime candidate for her first string-free fling.

She tugged a pen and pad of paper from her straw purse. "I thought we'd discuss possible outings today. Perhaps you could give me a list of suggestions, and I'll tell you which ones interest me."

"You will not trust my judgment to choose for you?"

As she'd done with Mike?

"No. I'd prefer to be consulted. I'm not sure how much you overheard last night, but I'm here with a friend to help plan her wedding. I'll have to be available for her morning meetings Monday through Friday and whenever else she or the other bridesmaids need me. So you and I will have to snatch hours here and there and not every day. Are you okay with that?"

"I am." He leaned back in his chair and steepled his fingers beneath his square jaw. He really had wonderful bone structure. His blade-straight nose had probably never been broken, and his high zygomatic arches allowed for nice hollows in his lean, smooth-shaven cheeks. Straight, thick, dark hair flopped over his forehead, making him look boyish, but the fine lines beside his eyes and mouth said he had to be in his thirties.

"Last night you said romance made you nauseous. I have yet to meet a woman who did not revel in romance. What happen—"

"Now you have," she interrupted.

His lips firmed and his eyebrows lowered as if her interruption annoyed him, but her sorry love life was not up for discussion.

The last thing she wanted to tell a prospective lover was that she'd been an idiot. She'd been so enthralled with the idea of love and being part of a couple that she'd given in to whatever Mike wanted, and in the process she'd surrendered part of her identity. What ticked her off the most was that even though she'd been trained to assess symptoms and make diagnoses, she'd missed the obvious signs that her relationship was in trouble. Not even the twenty pounds she'd gained over six years while "eating her stress" had clued her in to her subconscious's warnings.

"What happened to make you so wary?" he asked in a firm voice that made it clear he wasn't going to drop it.

She stared hard at him for several moments, trying to make him back down, but he held her gaze without wavering. "Let's just say I learned from experience that planning a perfect wedding doesn't always result in happily ever after."

"You are divorced?"

"Never made it to the altar. Now, about our excursions… Despite what Mr. Gustavo said about Vincent Reynard picking up your tab, I don't want to go overboard with expenses."

"I will keep that in mind. Are you more of an outdoor person or the museum type?"

She said a silent thank-you that he accepted her change of subject. "I prefer to be outside since I spend most of my waking hours inside."

"Doing…?"

Who was interviewing whom here? He didn't act like any potential employee she'd ever questioned. He was a little too arrogant, a little too confident, a little too in charge. But that only made him more attractive. "I'm a physician's assistant in a metropolitan hospital. What kinds of outings do you suggest?"

"There are numerous outdoor activities within a short distance that would cost little or nothing. Sunbathing, snorkeling, sailing, windsurfing, hiking, biking, fishing and rock climbing."

He ticked off the items on long ringless fingers bearing neatly trimmed, clean nails. She had a thing about hands, and his were great, the kind she'd love to have gliding over her skin.

"If you have more than a few hours we can go river rafting or spelunking in the Alpes-Maritimes or drive across the border into Italy or France to explore some of the more interesting villages."

"I'm not a sun lizard. Isn't that what they call the people who lay on the rocks of the jetty? I prefer action to lazing about, and cold, dark places give me the creeps, so let's skip the sunbathing and the spelunking and go with everything else. You'll arrange the tours and any equipment rental and provide me with the details?"

"It will be my pleasure."

She'd bet he knew a thing or two about pleasure, and if she was lucky, he'd share that knowledge. She slid a piece of paper across the table. "Here's my tentative schedule for the next month. I've blacked out the times when I'm unavailable. That's my suite number in the top corner. You'll have to call me there or leave a message for me at the front desk since my cell phone doesn't work in Europe."

She couldn't remember the last time she'd gone somewhere without a pager or cell phone, usually both, clipped to her clothing, and she couldn't decide whether she felt free or naked without the familiar weight bumping her hip.

A breeze swept into the open-air café, catching and ruffling the paper. She flattened her hand over it to keep it from blowing away. Damon's covered hers a split second later as he did the same. The heat of his palm warmed her skin. Electricity arced up her arm. Judging by the quick flare of his nostrils, she wasn't the only one feeling the sparks, but she couldn't see his eyes to be sure and that frustrated her.

She tilted her head, but didn't withdraw her hand. He didn't smile as he slowly eased his away, dragging his fingers the length of hers and igniting embers inside her.

"You know, Damon, if you're going to flirt with me it would be much more effective without the glasses. Hot glances don't penetrate polarized lenses."

He stilled and then deliberately reached up to remove his sunglasses with his free hand. "Are you interested in a flirtation, Madeline?"

The one-two punch of his accented voice huskily murmuring her name combined with the desire heating his eyes quickened her pulse and shortened her breath. "That depends. Are you married?"

"No."

"Engaged?"

"I am not committed to anyone at this time."

"Gay?"

He choked a laugh. "Definitely not."

"Healthy?"

His pupils dilated. He knew what she meant. "I have recently received a clean bill of health."

Excitement danced within her. "Then, Damon, we'll see if you have what it takes to tempt me."

Two

"This is a mistake, if I may say so, Dominic." Only in the privacy of their suite did Ian dare use Dominic's given name. Seventeen years together had built not only familiarity, but friendship.

"Damon. Damon Rossi," Dominic corrected as he packed for his first outing with Madeline Spencer.

"How am I to remember that?"

"D.A. Rossi is the name I sign on official documents, including the hotel registration. Damon is but a combination of my initials and an abbreviation of our country."

"Clever. But if the paparazzi catch you with a woman on the eve of your engagement…"

"As of this morning there is no engagement. A woman has not been selected, and if the council continues to argue as they have done for the past four months over birthing hips, pedigrees and whatever other absurd qualities they deem necessary for a princess, they will never come to an agreement, and I will not be forced to propose to a woman I know or care nothing about."

The council members had dehumanized the entire process. Not once had they asked Dominic's preferences. They might as well be choosing animals to breed from a bloodline chart.

Dominic had been nineteen when the council had chosen Giselle as his future bride, and he had not objected for he'd known her since they were children. His parents and hers had been friends for decades. He had convinced their families to postpone the marriage until after he obtained his university degree, and in those intervening years he and Giselle had become friends and then lovers before becoming husband and wife.

In the nine years since her death he had not met one single woman who made an effort to see the man behind the title and fortune.

And now once again the council would decide his fate as the traditions of his country decreed, a circumstance which did not please him, but one he was duty-bound to accept. But this time the idea of the group of predominantly old men choosing a stranger to be his wife did not sit well.

Dominic threw a change of clothing on top of the towels, masks and fins already in his dive bag. "Mademoiselle Spencer wishes to see Monaco. I wish to explore the tourist venues as a vacationer instead of as a visiting prince. Perhaps I will see a different side to the enterprises than I have seen before. The knowledge will benefit Montagnarde's tourist development plan which, as you know, I will present to the economic board again in two months. This time I will not accept defeat. They will back my development plan."

He had spent the years since he'd left university studying successful tourist destinations and laying the groundwork to replicate similar enterprises in his homeland. He wanted to model Montagnarde's travel industry after Monaco's, but the older members of the board refused to accept that the country had to grow its economic base or continue to lose its youth to jobs overseas. His father had sworn to lend his support in return for Dominic agreeing to marry before the end of his thirty-fifth year. With sovereign backing Dominic's plan would be passed.

"You know nothing about this woman," Ian insisted.

"A circumstance I am sure you have already begun to rectify." Any acquaintance with whom Dominic spent more than a passing amount of time was thoroughly investigated.

"I have initiated an inquiry, yes. Nevertheless, an affair would not be wise."

"Not an affair, Ian. A harmless flirtation. I cannot have sex with a woman to whom I am lying."

We'll see if you have what it takes to tempt me.

His heart rate quickened at the memory of Madeline's enticing banter and vibrant eyes. He would very much like to be her lover, but for the first time in years he found himself savoring the idea of being merely a man whom a beautiful woman found attractive. He didn't want to ruin that unique experience by revealing his identity, but he couldn't sleep with Madeline until he did. "I am aware of the risks."

"How will you explain my presence?"

Dominic zipped the bag and faced Ian, knowing his decision would not be a popular one. "The Larvotto underwater reserve is well patrolled by the Monaco police. No other boats or watercraft are allowed in the area. You can rest easy knowing the only dangers I face while snorkeling are that of the fish and the artificial reef. You will wait on the shore and keep your distance."

"I am charged with your well-being. If something should happen—"

"Ian, I have not given you reason to worry about my safety in years, and I won't now. I am a skilled diver. I have tracking devices in my watch and my swim trunks, and no one knows our plan. I will be fine." He hefted the bag. "Now come. I wish to see if Mademoiselle Spencer looks as good in a swimsuit as I anticipate."

Getting practically naked with a guy on your first date certainly moved things right along, Madeline decided as she removed the lemon-yellow sundress she'd worn as a cover-up over her swimsuit and placed it on the lounge chair beside her sandals and sunglasses.

Her black bikini wasn't nearly as skimpy as the thong suits so popular on the public beach around them. She scanned the sunbathers, shook her head and smothered a smile. The women here thought nothing of dropping their tops on the beach, but they didn't dare lie in the sun without their jewels. *Bet that makes for some interesting tan lines.*

To give him credit, Damon had stalked right past the bare breasts on display without pause. When his attention turned to her, raking her from braid to garnet-red toenail polish, she said a silent thank-you for the discounted gym membership the hospital offered its employees and the sweat and weight she'd shed over the past two years. Her body was tight and toned. It hadn't always been. But she wished Damon would lose the sunglasses. The thinning of his lips and the flare of his nostrils could signify anything from disgust to desire. She needed to see his eyes.

In the meantime, she did a little inspecting of her own as he untied the drawstring waist of the white linen pants he'd worn over his swimsuit due to Monaco's strict rules about no beachwear, bare chests or bare feet on the streets.

Damon's white T-shirt hugged well-developed pectorals and a flat abdomen. And then he dropped his pants. *Nice.* His long legs were deeply tanned, muscular and dusted with burnished blond hair beneath his brief trunks. "You must spend a lot of time outdoors."

He paused and gave her a puzzled look.

"The sun has bleached your body hair and the tips of your lashes," she explained.

"I enjoy water sports." He handed her a snorkel, mask and fins that looked new. "You have snorkeled before?"

"Yes, off the coast back home."

"And where is home?"

"North Carolina. On the eastern coast of the U.S. I live hours from the beach, but I used to vacation there every summer." She missed those boisterous vacations with Mike's family more than she missed Mike. The devious, dishonest rat. How could such a great family spawn a complete schmuck?

She dug her toes into the fine grains beneath her feet. "Is it true that all this white sand is brought in by barge?"

"Yes. That is the case for many of the Riviera beaches. Of the nations bordering the Mediterranean Sea, Monaco has the cleanest and safest beaches because the government is the most eco-conscious. Thanks to the Grimaldi family, the country is almost pollution free. In recent years the government has expanded its territory by reclaiming land from the sea. The underwater reserve we are about to explore was built in the seventies to repair the damage of overfishing and excessive coral gathering. The reefs are home to many fish species and red coral." He indicated the water with a nod. "Shall we?"

He'd certainly studied his guidebook. "Don't you want to take off your T-shirt?"

He tossed his shades on the chair beside hers. "No."

"Do you burn easily? I could put sunscreen on your back." Her palms tingled in anticipation of touching him.

"I prefer to wear a shirt, thank you."

Did he have scars or something? "Damon, I see shirtless men at work every day. If you're worried that I can't control myself…"

His chest expanded, and this time she received the full effect of those hot blue eyes. Arousal made her suck in her breath and her stomach. "It is not your control I question, Madeline. Come, the reef waits."

She'd never get used to the way he said her name with a hint of that unidentifiable accent. It gave her goose bumps every time. And speaking of control, where was hers? She wanted to jump him. Here. Now. "Where did you say you were from?"

"I did not say." He flashed a tight white smile and strode toward the water, where he dunked his fins and mask before donning both.

She mimicked his actions and then stared at him through the wet glass of her mask. "You like being a man of mystery, eh?"

He straightened and held her gaze. "I like being a man. The mystery is all in here." He gently tapped her temple. "Stay close to me. Watch for jellyfish and sea urchins. Avoid both."

Admiring the view of his taut buttocks and well-muscled legs, she followed him deeper into the water. For the next hour she swam and enjoyed the sea life. Each time Damon touched her to draw her attention to another sight she nearly sucked the briny water down her snorkel. Miraculously, she managed not to drown herself. By the time he led her back to shore her nerves were as tightly wound as the rubber band ball the emergency room staff tossed around on slow nights.

"That was great. Thanks." And then she got a good look at the shirt adhered like shrink-wrap to his amazing chest, the tiny buttons of his nipples and his six-pack abs. An even better sight and definitely one she'd like to explore.

"I'm glad you enjoyed it." He dropped his mask and fins on the chair, donned his sunglasses and ruffled his hair to shake off the excess water and then finger-combed the dark strands over his forehead.

"What made you decide to become a tour guide?" She dried off as he bagged their diving gear.

"When a country has few natural resources and limited territory, its people and the tourism industry become its greatest assets."

Surprised by his answer, she blinked. She'd expected a simple response such as he enjoyed meeting new people or the flexible hours, not something so deep. "Studied that, have you?"

"Yes."

She dragged her knit sundress over her head. "Where? I mean, are there tourism schools or what?"

Holding her gaze—or at least she thought he was, beneath those dark lenses—he hesitated so long she didn't think he'd answer. "I have a Travel Industry Management degree from the University of Hawaii at Mānoa."

He seemed tense, as if he expected her to question his statement, and she should. If he had a college degree and spoke four languages fluently then why was he acting as a tour guide? It didn't make sense. She reminded herself that not everyone was as career driven as she was, but Damon didn't seem the type to kick back and let the fates determine his future. She'd seen enough type A guys to recognize the signs and he waved them all like flags. But that was his business. A string-free affair—if they had one—didn't give her the right to interfere.

"The States? No kidding. What brings you to Monaco?"

"I am studying their tourism industry."

"And then what?"

"I'll apply what I've learned to my future endeavors." He zipped the dive bag and grabbed the handles. Eager to go, was he? Before she could ask what kinds of endeavors, he said, "If we leave now we'll have time to stop at the hotel café for a snack before I leave you. You have missed lunch."

"I'm in no rush. I had hoped we could spend the rest of the afternoon together. Maybe play some beach volleyball or jump on the trampoline at the far end of the beach? And this place is surrounded by restaurants. We could grab a bite here."

"I have another appointment."

She tried to hide her disappointment. While she had enjoyed the day, it hadn't gone quite as she'd hoped. Admittedly, she wasn't a practiced seductress, but if she wanted a vacation romance it looked as though she'd have to work harder for it.

Time to initiate Plan B. First she freed and finger-combed her hair while trying to build up her courage, and then she reached beneath her dress, untied her damp bikini top and pulled it through the scooped neckline.

A muscle at the corner of Damon's mouth ticked and his throat worked as he swallowed.

"You may change in one of the dressing rooms, as I will," he said hoarsely. His Adam's apple bobbed as he swallowed.

"No need. Besides, I didn't bring a change of clothing." Her nipples tightened when he didn't look away. Well, *hallelujah*. He'd been so professional and distant she'd begun to think she'd imagined the sparks between them.

And then in an act more brazen than anything she'd ever dared, she reached beneath her dress and shucked her bikini bottom. She twirled the wet black fabric once around her finger before tucking it along with her top in her tote. *Take that, big guy.* If Damon insisted on hustling her back to the hotel and dumping her, then he'd have to do so knowing she was naked except for a thin knit sheath.

Never let it be said that Madeline Spencer wouldn't fight for what she wanted, and in her opinion, Damon Rossi was the perfect prescription to mend her bruised ego and heart. A few weeks with him and she'd return home whole and healed.

"I wonder what all the commotion's about?"

Madeline's question pulled Dominic from his complicated calculations of hotel occupancy rates as the taxi approached Hôtel Reynard. He'd been attempting to distract himself from the knowledge that she was completely nude beneath her dress and failing miserably.

A camera-carrying group of a dozen or so paparazzi stood sentry across the street from the hotel with their zoom lenses trained on the limo parked by the entrance. Dominic silently swore. His escape route had been sealed. He leaned forward to speak to the driver. "Rue Langlé, *s'il vous plaît.*"

Madeline's eyebrows rose in surprise. "Where are we going?"

"I do not wish to fight the crowd. We'll dine in a quiet café instead of the hotel." Ian would not like the unplanned detour, and Makos, the second bodyguard who kept in such deep cover that Dominic rarely spotted him, would like it even less.

"I thought you were in a hurry to get to another appointment."

"It can wait." There was no other appointment. He merely needed time away from the tempting woman beside him before he grabbed her and kissed that teasing smile from her lips. Even in the cool water, touching the wet silkiness of her skin had heated his blood. He'd wanted to flatten his palms over her waist, tangle his legs with her sleek limbs and pull her flush against him. A maneuver that probably would have drowned them both, he acknowledged wryly.

Dominic faced a conundrum. With each passing moment his desire for Madeline increased, and yet his lie stood between them. He ached for her, but he was reluctant to lose the unique relationship they had established. She looked at *him*, flirted with *him*, desired *him*. Not Prince Dominic. He was selfish enough to want to enjoy her attentions a while longer.

She twisted in her seat to stare out the taxi's back window at the paparazzi as the driver took the roundabout away from the hotel. The shift slid her hem to the top of her thighs. A few more inches and he'd see what her bikini bottom should be covering. He gritted his teeth and fisted his hands against the urge to smooth his palm up her sleek thighs and over her bare buttocks.

"It's probably just another celebrity," she said. "Amelia says the hotel is crawling with them."

"Who is Amelia?"

"My friend and one of the other bridesmaids. She's a huge fan of entertainment magazines and shows. She claims the security inside the hotel makes it a celebrity hot spot. Supposedly paparazzi aren't even allowed on the grounds, which would explain why they're staked out across the street."

He'd have to avoid her friend. "You are not interested in star gazing?"

She settled back in the seat and faced him. "No. I don't have time to watch much TV or read gossip rags. I work four or five twelve-hour shifts each week, depending on how much overtime the hospital will allow me, and I usually go to the gym for another hour after work."

That could explain why not even a flicker of recognition entered her eyes when she looked at him—not that he was a household name, but he was known unfortunately, thanks to a couple of wild years after Giselle's death when he'd tried to smother his grief with women and parties. "Your diligence at the gym shows."

She tilted her head, revealing the long line of her throat and the pulse fluttering rapidly at the base. "Is that a compliment, Damon?"

"I am sure you are aware of your incredible figure, Madeline. You do not need my accolades." The words came out stiffly.

Her eyebrows dipped. "Are you okay?"

"Shouldn't I be?"

"You seem a little...tense."

His gaze dropped pointedly to her hiked hem.

She glanced down and her eyes widened. A peachy glow darkened her cheeks, making him question whether the siren role was a new one for her. And then the hint of a smile curved her lips as she wiggled the fabric down to a more respectable level. The woman was driving him insane and relishing every moment of his discomfort.

"Monaco is small enough that we could have walked to the café, you know," she said.

"You have had enough sun." And he was less likely to be recognized in an anonymous taxi. The driver pulled over in the street and stopped. Dominic paid him and opened the door. He noted Ian climbing from a taxi a half a block away. Dominic subtly angled his head toward the Italian café as a signal.

Madeline curled her fingers around Dominic's and allowed him to assist her from the car. She joined him on the sidewalk, but didn't release his hand. The small gesture tightened something inside him. When had he last held hands with a woman? Such a simple pleasure. One he hadn't realized he'd missed.

She tipped back her head. "Monaco has strict protocol. Are you sure we're dressed appropriately?"

One of us is. He had pulled on trousers and a polo shirt before leaving the beach. His attire was acceptable, as was Madeline's if one was unaware she wore nothing beneath the thin yellow sundress. The driver retrieved the dive bag from the trunk. Dominic took it from him. "The café is casual. I recommend the prosciutto and melon or the bruschetta."

He'd prefer to feast on her, on her rosy lips, on her soft, supple skin, on the tight nipples pushing against her dress.

Wondering when his intelligence had deserted him, Dominic led her inside and requested a table in the back. Madeline didn't release his hand until he seated her. He chose a chair facing away from the door. The fewer people who saw his face the better and Ian would cover his back.

The entire afternoon had been an exercise in restraint and a reminder that he was not an accomplished liar. He had been so distracted by his unexpected attraction to Madeline that he had almost blown his cover. Had she not commented on his blond body hair he would have removed his shirt and his secret would be out.

Your secret is keeping her out of your bed.

Without a doubt, he desired Madeline Spencer, but getting women to share his bed had never been difficult. Getting one to see him as a mere man, however, was nearly impossible. He would have to reveal his identity soon for he did not think his control would last much longer, and then if he could be certain Madeline could be happy with a short-term affair, he would explore every inch of her. Repeatedly.

But before he revealed *his* secret he needed to discover *hers*. Why had she renounced love?

After placing their orders Dominic asked, "Did you love him?"

Her smile wobbled and then faded. Her fingers found and tugged one dark coil of hair. He wanted to wind the spirals around his fingers, around his—

"Who?"

Her pretended ignorance didn't fool him. The shadows darkening her eyes gave her discomfort away. He removed his sunglasses and looked into her eyes. "The man who disappointed you."

She fussed with her cutlery. "*Pfft*. What makes you so sure there is one?" When he held her gaze without replying she bristled. "Is this twenty questions? Because if it is, you'll have to give an answer for every one you get."

Risky, but doable if he chose his words carefully. He nodded acceptance of her terms. "Did you love him?" he repeated.

"I thought I did."

"You don't know?"

She shifted in her seat, reminding him of her nakedness beneath the T-shirt thin layer of cotton. "Why don't you tell me what you have planned for our next outing?"

"Because you are a far more interesting topic." His voice came out in a lower pitch than normal as if he were dredging it up from the bottom of the sea. "Why do you question your feelings?"

She sighed. Resignation settled over her features. "My mother was forty-six when I was born and my father fifty

They were too old to keep up with a rambunctious child. I wanted to do things differently when I had children, so I made a plan to get married and start my family before I turned thirty. I met Mike right after college. He seemed like the perfect candidate and we got engaged. But it didn't work out."

"One failed relationship soured you?"

Another squirm of her naked bottom made him wish he could take the place of her chair. "My parents divorced. It wasn't pretty. Have you ever been in a long-term relationship?"

"Yes."

Her arched brows rose. "And?"

"My turn. Why did your relationship end?"

She frowned. "Lots of reasons. First, I spent too much time trying to be the woman I thought he and society expected me to be instead of the one I wanted to be. Second, he found someone else."

"He is a fool."

A smile twitched her lips. "Don't expect me to argue with that brilliantly insightful conclusion."

The waitress placed their meals on the table and departed.

"Have you ever been married?" Madeline asked before biting into her bruschetta.

"Yes."

Her body stilled and her emerald gaze locked with his. She chewed quickly and then swallowed. "What happened?"

"She died." The words came out without inflection. He'd learned long ago to keep the pain locked away behind a wall of numbness.

Sympathy darkened her eyes. "I'm sorry. How?"

"Ectopic pregnancy."

She reached across the table and covered his hand. Her touch warmed him and surprisingly, soothed him. "That must have been hard, losing your wife and child at the same time. Did you even know she was pregnant?"

How could this virtual stranger understand what those closest to him had not?

"Yes, it was hard, and no, we didn't know about the baby." It had infuriated him at the time that many had been more concerned with the loss of a potential heir to the throne than the loss of his wife, his friend, his gentle Giselle. Only recently had his anger subsided enough for him to agree to another marriage. If his sisters had produced sons instead of daughters, he probably never would have.

They finished the meal in silence. He waited until Madeline pushed her plate aside before asking, "You do not wish for another *affaire de coeur* or the American dream of a house with a white picket fence and two-point-something children?"

She straightened and put her hands in her lap. "No. I'm over my urge to procreate. It's time to focus on me. My wants. My needs. My career. I don't need a man to complete me. And I don't need marriage to find passion."

Passion. Arousal pulsed through him. "You can be happy with brief liaisons? Without love?"

"Absolutely. In fact, I prefer it that way. If I want to take a promotion, a trip or stay out late with my friends, then I don't have to worry about anyone's ego getting bent. So, Damon…" Her fingertips touched his on the table. "What you said on the beach about your control…? Losing it with me would not be a problem."

He inhaled sharply. Her meaning couldn't be clearer. She wanted a lover. And he would be more than happy to oblige. The question was should he reveal his identity beforehand, or since she wanted nothing more than a brief affair, did he have to reveal anything at all? Did he have to ruin this camaraderie? For he knew with absolute certainty that the knowledge would change their relationship.

He stood and dropped a handful of bills on the table.

Her hand caught his and the need to yank her into his arms surged through him. "You paid for the taxi. Shouldn't I get this?"

"No." He pulled back her chair. She rose and turned, but Dominic didn't back away. Her breasts brushed his chest. His palm curved over her waist. "I know of a back entrance to the hotel."

Her quick gasp filled his ears and temptation expanded her pupils. "What about your other appointment?"

His gaze dropped from her emerald eyes to her mouth. "Nothing is more important at the moment than tasting you."

Her tongue swiped quickly over her bottom lip and he barely contained a groan. "We could go to your place."

Again the lie complicated matters. He shook his head. "I share with another man."

She grimaced. "And I'm sharing a suite with the bride-to-be and two other bridesmaids. I have my own bedroom, but I wouldn't feel right taking a man to my room."

And he had to avoid her celebrity-watching friend. He clenched his teeth to dam a frustrated growl and laced his fingers through hers. He led her outside the restaurant, passing by Ian on a nearby bench. Dominic scanned the area, for there was one thing that couldn't wait. A narrow flower-lined alleyway beckoned. Dominic ducked in, pulled Madeline behind a potted olive tree and into his arms.

"Wha—"

His mouth stole the word from her soft lips. Desire, instantaneous and incendiary, raced through his bloodstream at the first taste of her mouth. He sought her tongue, stroked, entwined and suckled. Madeline's arms encircled his waist, pressing her lithe body flush against his.

Her flowers and lemon scent filled his nostrils and her warmth seeped deep inside him. He tangled the fingers of one hand in her silky curls, caressed the curve of her hips with the other and pressed the driving need in his groin against her stomach.

A horn sounded in the street, reminding him of where they were and the omnipresent possibility of paparazzi. Except for a few insane months, he'd spent a lifetime carefully avoiding the press, and yet Madeline made him forget. Reluctantly, he lifted his head.

Madeline opened dazed eyes and blinked her long, dark lashes. Her lips gleamed damp and inviting as she gazed up at him. "That was worth waiting for."

For the first time in ages Dominic felt like a man instead of a dynasty on legs or an animal expected to breed on command. "I will arrange privacy for our next outing."

Three

Pain burned Madeline's throat Thursday morning, but she'd be damned if she'd let Candace know it. She gritted her teeth into a bright smile.

Watching the *couturière* fuss and flutter around her petite blond friend reminded Madeline of the wedding dress her mother and aunts had sewn for her. The trio had dedicated a year to creating a gorgeous gown and veil with intricate seed pearl beading and hand-tatted lace. Neither would ever be worn.

It should have been a clue that Madeline's engagement was doomed when her dream dress included a full cathedral train, and yet Mike had claimed he wanted an informal backyard wedding, or better yet, a Vegas quickie—if she'd pay for the trip. Her fiancé had been loaded, and yet he'd been a total miser.

She shook off the memories and widened her smile. "You look gorgeous, Candace. That dress couldn't be more perfect if it had been custom-made for you."

"You think?" Her friend smoothed her hands over the silk douppioni skirt beneath a hand-beaded bodice and twisted this way and that to see her reflection in the three-way mirror. "I'm not showing?"

Another twinge of regret pinched Madeline's heart. If she'd stuck with her plan, she probably would have had several babies by now. But since Mike couldn't keep his pants zipped most likely they would have been divorced and playing tug-of-war with innocent children. Not a pretty picture. She ought to know. Her parents' divorce when Madeline was ten had been rough.

Breaking up with Mike had been for the best, and luckily his paranoia over the two percent failure rate of the Pill had led him to use condoms as a backup every single time. Otherwise, there was no telling what the two-timing louse would have brought home from his extramural adventures.

Candace's expectant expression dragged Madeline back to the present. "Candace, no one will know you're pregnant unless you tell them. The empire waist covers everything—not that there's anything to hide yet. You're only eight weeks along."

Candace had confided her pregnancy to Madeline and sworn her to secrecy before they'd left North Carolina. She'd wanted Madeline's medical assurance in addition to her obstetrician's that traveling in her first trimester wouldn't endanger the baby.

"Okay, this is the dress. *Je voudrais acheter cette robe,*" Candace told the seamstress.

The seamstress rattled off a quick stream of French while she unfastened the long line of silk-covered buttons down Candace's spine, and Candace replied in the same language. Madeline didn't have a clue what either of them said. She should have borrowed those French lesson CDs her suite-mate Stacy had used.

The heavy fabric swished over her friend's head. With the dress draped over her arms, the seamstress departed. Candace quickly pulled on her street clothes, crossed the dressing room to Madeline's side and took her hands. "You had a lucky escape. You know that, right?"

Madeline winced. She should have known her friend would see through her fake merriment. They'd been through a lot together in the past twelve years: college, their engagements to Mike and Vincent and the deaths of Madeline's father and Candace's brother. "I know, and trust me, I am not missing that two-timing dud."

"But the wedding preparations are hard for you." It was a statement, not a question. "I'm sorry. But I couldn't do this without you, Madeline."

"I love seeing you this happy."

"Your turn will come." Candace squeezed her fingers and released her.

Not as long as I have a functioning brain cell. God forbid I ever go through that again. "This month is all about you."

"When will the rest of us get to meet your gorgeous guide?"

"I'm not sure. I'll have to ask. I won't see him again until Saturday." Two days. It seemed like an aeon.

After kissing her into a stupor yesterday Damon had put her in a cab with the promise of passion to come. If that kiss was a sample of what she could expect, then it would be passion unlike any she'd ever experienced. She couldn't remember Mike's embrace ever making her forget where she was.

Last night after dinner with Candace at the world-renowned Hôtel Hermitage she'd returned to the suite and found a message from Damon telling her he had arranged a sailboat for the weekend. He'd found a place for them to be alone. Her mouth dried, her palms moistened and her pulse bounded like a jackrabbit. She felt wild, reckless and free. A first for her.

"Maybe Damon will sweep you off your feet, and we'll have a double wedding in three weeks," Candace interrupted Madeline's illicit thoughts.

Madeline groaned. "Don't start your matchmaking here. It's bad enough that I suffer through your blind date matchups at home. Besides, I'd never be stupid enough to marry a guy I'd known such a short time."

She hitched her purse over her shoulder and opened the door, hoping Candace would leave the topic behind in the dressing room of the chic boutique.

Candace followed her out. "That's just it. When you love someone you don't want to wait. The only reason I waited to marry Vincent was because he insisted on being able to put the wedding ring on my finger himself. The day he reached that point in his physical therapy we set the date."

Which reminded Madeline of the crazy year her friend had had. Vincent had been severely burned along the right side of his body just over a year ago in a freak pit accident at the local race track. Madeline had treated him in the E.R. when he'd first arrived at the hospital and then Candace had been his nurse throughout his months-long stay in the burn unit. Before he'd been released the two had fallen head over heels in love.

Madeline had to give Vincent credit. He'd tried to convince Candace she deserved a man who wouldn't be scarred for life, but Candace didn't care about his scars. Love truly was blind.

A fact you know all too well.

Candace handed her credit card to the clerk and then turned back to Madeline. "The fact that you dated Mike for almost a year before you became engaged and you didn't push him to set a date for six years tells me you weren't in a rush to tie yourself to him till death do you part."

Good point. She hated it when others saw something that should have been obvious to her. "When did you become a shrink? I thought you were a nurse."

Candace shrugged. "Nurse. Shrink. Most days they're one and the same in the burn unit. But I don't need to be a psychiatrist to know that Mike didn't treat you well. You deserve a guy who will, Madeline."

"I'm strictly a love 'em and leave 'em gal from now on."

"That's a knee-jerk reaction to the dickhead's lies. You'll get over it, Ms. Monogamy. You're the one whose only lover was a man you thought you were going to marry."

Madeline's cheeks flashed hot. She glanced at the *couturière*. If the woman understood English—and most people in Monaco did apparently—she gave no sign of being interested in their exchange.

Having older parents meant Madeline's values were from a bygone era, and she'd waited to fall in love before falling into bed. But that was because her father had been a tough, no-nonsense vice squad detective with a habit of scaring off his teenage daughter's potential suitors and later she'd been too busy with school and a part-time job to have the energy to date.

But she had every intention of sowing the wild oats she'd been hoarding—starting with Damon Rossi. "My inexperience is a circumstance I intend to remedy as soon as possible."

"I still think there's more to your instant attraction to Damon than lust. I've never known you to get gaga so fast."

Madeline didn't reply until the shop door closed behind them. She faced her friend on the sunny sidewalk lined with designer shops and wrought iron lampposts. "Candace, I'm not gaga. I'm horny. And that's all it is. I have a two-year itch to scratch. Nothing more. Nothing less."

"Right. It took you ten months to sleep with Mike. You wanted to jump Damon after ten minutes. Listen to your subconscious, Madeline. It's trying to tell you something."

"You're wrong. Completely. Totally. Unequivocally wrong. And I'll prove it. Just watch."

She'd live it up in Monaco and then leave in three weeks' time with her sexual urges satisfied and her heart intact.

This had to be a mistake.

Madeline stopped on a long stretch of sunbaked dock in the Port de Monaco. Over a hundred boats bobbed and swayed around her in neat rows, and because it was Saturday, a number of other boaters were out and about, chatting in a musical chorus of foreign languages. The boats in this line were big. None resembled the small craft she'd expected Damon to rent. She double-checked the slip number on the note the hotel desk attendant had given her. Whoever had taken the message must have misunderstood.

No problem. She slung the strap of her beach bag over her shoulder and started walking. She'd check out slip one-eighteen just in case there was a smaller sailboat tucked behind the big ones. If there wasn't, she'd return to the hotel and wait for Damon to call with the correct instructions. Surely he'd guess something had gone awry when she didn't arrive on time?

Sun warmed her skin. Boat parts clanged and creaked beside her and birds cried overhead. A breeze teased tendrils from her braid and molded her skirt and cropped sleeveless top to her body. She'd only made it past a half-dozen yachts when a familiar dark-haired figure in white pants, a loose white shirt and sunglasses stepped onto the planks from a boat about five car lengths long. Her heart and steps faltered. The hotel hadn't made a mistake. Damon had rented a boat with a cabin. Make that a *yacht* with a cabin.

And because Candace didn't have a morning meeting tomorrow, Madeline was free to spend the night if she chose. She moved forward, one step at a time. Her lungs labored as if she'd sprinted from the hotel instead of ridden in the cushy hired car Damon had arranged for her. She'd never had a wildly passionate no-strings-attached affair, but if she boarded the boat, there would be no turning back.

This is what you wanted.

Maybe so, but that didn't keep her from being nervous. The distance between them seemed to stretch endlessly.

Damon didn't smile, didn't move toward her. Hands by his side and legs braced slightly apart, he waited, looking as if he belonged at a yacht club. But then she supposed a good tour guide should fit into his surroundings. He'd said he enjoyed water sports so he probably had the sea legs to handle a gently undulating dock and a boat that probably cost more than her condo.

She reached his side, shoved her sunglasses up onto her head and waited, poised on a knife edge between tension and anticipation. Her reflection in his dark lenses looked back at her, and his cedar and sage scent teased her nose.

She bit her lip and eyed the yacht. "I'm going to hate billing Vincent for this rental. I'll cover it. If I can afford it."

"The boat is borrowed. There is no charge." Damon took her bag. Their fingers touched and sparks swirled up her arm and settled in a smoldering pile in her stomach. His palm spread across the base of her spine, upping her body temperature by what felt like a dozen degrees. "Come aboard, Madeline."

Still, she balked. "It's only fair to warn you that I've never been on a sailboat. I don't know the bow from the stern."

A hint of a smile flickered on his lips. "You have nothing to fear. I won't ask anything of you that you're not willing to give. Our only task is to enjoy the sail and each other."

Her breath shuddered in and then out. He'd read her pretty easily. It wasn't the sail making her jittery. It was the prospect of being alone with him, of giving in to these foreign and over-whelming feelings and embarking on an uncharted sensual journey. "Okay."

He guided her onto the boat's back deck. A hip-high wall surrounded an area about ten feet square. He descended through a door into the cabin below and then turned and offered his hand. "Watch your step and your head."

Her fingers entwined with his and the heat of his palm spread through her making her knees shaky. At the base of the stairs she paused and blinked, allowing her eyes to adjust to the dimmer interior. Once she could focus, what she saw dazzled her. The luxury of stained wood cabinetry and bisque leather upholstery surpassed anything she'd ever seen—even her plush hotel suite.

Without releasing her hand Damon led her through a sitting area and a kitchen. He stepped through another door and moved aside for her to enter. A bed dominated the spacious stateroom—a bed she'd soon be sharing with him. Her heart thumped harder. The room seemed to shrink in size and the oxygen thinned. Her skin dampened, but her mouth dried.

Long, narrow horizontal windows let in sunlight, warming the cabin. Or maybe it was the knowledge of what lay ahead making her hot. She plucked at her suddenly clingy shirt.

"You may change in here or in the head." He dropped her bag on a bed and indicated a bathroom by tilting his head, and then he removed his sunglasses and tossed them on the mattress. Holding her gaze with desire-laden eyes, he cupped her shoulders. "Need help changing?"

"I, um…no." She swallowed the lump in her throat. She'd wanted adventure and she'd found it. Nerves, excitement and expectation vied for dominance inside her. Nerves won.

His hands coasted down her arms in a featherlight caress and then encircled her waist. He edged his fingers beneath the hem of her top and found the sensitive skin above her skirt. A shiver worked its way outward from the circles he drew on her abdomen with his thumbs. Mike's touch had never affected her this way— not even in the early days when the sex had been good.

"I have been waiting for this." He lowered his head and briefly sipped from her lips.

She didn't want to talk, didn't want to do anything to lessen the intoxicating effect of his lips and hands on her. She wound her arms around his neck and sifted his soft hair through her fingertips. "Me, too."

With a groan he pulled her closer, fusing the length of his body to hers and kissing her hungrily. His torso was hot and hard against hers, his tongue slick and skilled. A gentle tug on her braid tipped her head back, allowing him to delve deeper, kiss harder. Madeline held him close, savoring the sensations whirling through her. She clenched and unclenched her fingers in his hair and then swept her palms over his broad shoulders and down his back.

Footsteps above her startled her into jerking out of his embrace. "What's that?"

"Our crew is casting off. We'll stay below deck until we clear the harbor."

There were strangers on board? She'd thought they'd be alone. Uneasiness prickled her spine. "Why?"

"To stay out of their way while they navigate the channel."

"No, I mean why do we have a crew?"

"Because my attention will be focused on you and not on sailing. Change into your swimsuit and then join me in the galley." He swept his thumb over her bottom lip, grabbed his sunglasses and then left the room, closing the door behind him.

Madeline stared at the wooden panel. Her father had been overprotective—a hazard of his occupation dealing with the seamier side of life. Were his frequent warnings the cause of her uneasiness?

Lose the paranoia. Enjoy your weekend. It makes sense to have a crew on a boat this large, especially since you know nothing about sailing.

Tamping down her misgivings, she reached for her bag.

Seduction on the Mediterranean Sea. Damon had delivered nothing less in the hours since they'd left Monaco behind.

Madeline stood beside him on the front—*bow*—of the anchored sailboat with the deck rocking gently beneath her feet. She sipped her wine and feigned calm when every cell in her body quivered with eagerness for the night ahead. Lights on shore flickered on the ink-dark horizon. She didn't know from which city or even which country.

She turned her head and found Damon's blue gaze locked on her face in the pale moonlight. Sexual energy radiated from him. The entire day had been one long session of foreplay. She'd been wined and dined and tantalized from the moment she'd joined him in the kitch—*galley*. He'd massaged sunscreen into her skin and painted erotic designs on her body with the end of her braid. But he hadn't allowed her to return the favor. He'd kept his shirt on and insisted she keep her hands to herself. Whatever blemishes he was hiding beneath that fabric, she'd prove to him that they didn't matter.

Damon opened his mouth and took a breath as if preparing to speak, but closed it again as he'd done a few times today. He stared at the wine he swirled in his glass, finished it in one gulp and looked at her again.

He wasn't getting shy on her, was he? She never would have pegged him as the reticent type. But then what did she know about him except that he was drop-dead sexy, could drive her to the brink of orgasm without touching the usual parts and that the concierge trusted him?

She slipped an arm around his waist, rose on tiptoe and kissed his chin because she couldn't reach his lips. Damon dipped his head and covered her mouth, parted her lips and swept inside. He tasted like wine, sunshine and the promise of passion. And then he pulled away, cupped her face and pressed it to his shoulder. "Not here. Let's go below."

He laced his fingers with hers and quickly led her inside. There was no sign of Ian and Makos, the crew, in the sitting area or galley. The men must be in their cabin at the rear of the boat. Her worries about them had been unfounded. They'd efficiently done their jobs without encroaching on her and Damon's privacy although she'd been aware of their presence. How could she not be when both men were built like football defensive linemen?

Damon deposited their wineglasses on the counter before leading her into the bedroom at the front of the craft and closing the door behind them. Moonlight seeped through the narrow windows, bathing the room in silvery light. He didn't turn on the lamp and she wondered if that was because of the scars or whatever he hid under his shirt. She could scarcely hear the smack of the waves against the hull over her thundering heart.

Damon's expression turned serious and he seemed a little uneasy. He cupped her shoulders. "Madeline—"

She pressed her fingers to his lips. "It's okay. I'm nervous, too."

He opened his mouth to speak again, but she shook her head and traced his soft bottom lip with her fingertip. "Would you believe I am thirty-two years old and I've only had one lover?" His eyes widened and she cringed. "I'm not telling you that because I want a proposal or anything. I don't. This affair is about here and now and that's all. I just want you to know I might be…limited skillwise. But I'm a fast learner. Now please, kiss me. You've driven me insane all day. I want to do the same for you and I can't wait another second."

But he made her wait ten seconds before banding his arms around her and hauling her close. He took her mouth in a hard, hungry kiss, shifted his head and stole another and another until she clung to him because her legs no longer felt steady. She broke the connection to gasp for air. Their gazes locked and panted breaths mingled.

After a day of not being allowed to touch him, Madeline seized the opportunity to run her hands over him. His shoulder and arm muscles flexed beneath her fingers, and then she shaped his broad back, his narrow waist and finally, his tush. His groan vibrated over her like thunder. He splayed his hands over her bottom and yanked her against the ridge of his erection. Whatever deficiencies he thought he had, that wasn't one of them.

He shoved off the jacket she'd put on after dinner and then bunched the fabric of her top in his hands and whisked it over her head. Her white lace bra glistened in the moonlight and then with a flick of his fingers that, too, was gone and his warm hands shaped her breasts. With a whimper of delight, she closed her eyes and let her head fall back. Pleasure radiated from the nipples he buffed with his thumbs and coalesced into a tight, achy knot of need beneath her navel.

He dipped his head and circled her aureole with his tongue. Hot. Wet. Her knees weakened. She fisted her hands in his shirt and held on. And then he suckled and she whimpered as currents of desire swirled wildly inside her.

"Hurry. Please." She'd never been so aroused in all her life, and he'd barely touched her. She blamed it on the drawn-out foreplay of the day, his scent, his heat, his unique flavor. Her fingers fumbled on the buttons of his shirt, and then finally the last one separated and she pushed the shirt out of her way. The room was too dim to see more than a shadow of chest hair, but his muscles were taut and tight and rippled beneath her questing fingers. No raised or puckered scar tissue marred his supple skin. Nothing to be ashamed of. She found the fastening on his waistband.

He captured her other nipple with gentle teeth, hastily unzipped her skirt and pushed it to the floor. Frantic with need, she sent his shorts and briefs on the same path. She wanted him naked and inside her before she came without him. She'd never been a multiple-o's girl, and she wasn't wasting her one and only on a solo trip. His hand covered the satin front of her panties, stroked, teased. She clenched every muscle and fought off climax, but she was close, too close.

Slapping her hand over his to still him, she gasped, "Condoms. In my beach bag. Now."

His smile gleamed white in the near darkness. "Impatient?"

"Yes."

"I want to taste you."

"Next time. Please, Damon. I'm about to come unglued."

His smile vanished. He hesitated a second before reaching

for her beach bag and handing it to her. She dug until she found the new box of condoms, dropped her bag on the floor and ripped the box open. He reached to take the packet from her.

"No. My turn." She tore the wrapper and reached for him, encircling his thick erection with her fingers and stroking his hard, satiny length. A deep growl rumbled from him.

Mike, the twit, would have a serious case of penis envy if he knew how much better endowed Damon was.

But then Damon tweaked her nipples and thoughts of Mike evaporated in a hot rush of desire. She applied the protection, yanked the covers from the bed and scooted backward toward the headboard. Damon followed, crawling across the mattress like a stalking panther. Impatient for him to pounce, she shimmied her panties over her hips. Damon hooked them with his fingers and tugged them the rest of the way down her legs and tossed them over his shoulder.

"Loosen your braid." His raspy voice against the inside of her knee gave her goose bumps.

She did as he ordered. The moment she finished he plowed his fingers into her hair, cradled her head and devoured her mouth, demanding a response which she was more than happy to give. His body lowered over hers, and hot skin melded to hotter skin from her ankles to her nose. The sheer eroticism of his hair-spattered flesh against hers sent a shiver of delight over her. His masculine scent filled her nostrils, his taste made her crave more. She hooked a leg behind his hip. "Please."

He angled to the side. His fingers parted her curls, found her wetness. And then he did the unforgivable. With only three strokes he made her come. *Without him.* Damn it, she railed even as ecstasy convulsed her body and emptied her lungs.

Before she could protest he filled her with one deep thrust. She'd scarcely caught her breath before he withdrew and returned. Harder. Deeper. Again and again he pounded into her. Instead of relaxing and cooling down the way she usually did after climax, her heart continued to race and her muscles coiled tight again.

She couldn't. Could she?

Not believing what her body was telling her, she dug her nails into his hips and her heels into the mattress and urged him to go faster. And then it happened. Orgasm broke over her like the waves that had crashed over the bow this afternoon, sprinkling sensation on her skin like droplets of seawater.

Smiling with surprise and delight, she buried her face in his neck and then nipped his earlobe. Damon groaned against her temple. His back bowed and he thrust deeper as his climax shook him. And then he collapsed on top of her.

She savored his weight, his warmth, his sweat-slickened skin against her chest and beneath her palms. The sound of water smacking the hull slowly replaced the roar of her pulse.

"Wow," she whispered. "Thank you."

Damon braced himself on his elbows and lifted, his satisfied gaze locking with hers. "Good?"

"Oh yeah." Had her responsiveness been a fluke? She couldn't wait to find out. "Wanna do it again?"

Life didn't get any better than this.

With anticipation dancing across her skin Madeline opened the bathroom door and eased into the bedroom. She lifted a hand to shield her eyes from the blinding sunlight flooding through the cabin windows.

Damon rolled over looking smug, sexy and disheveled beneath the rumpled covers. He'd earned the right. They'd made love three times last night, and he'd made a multiple-o's girl out of her each time. In fact, he'd made her wish for a few fleeting moments that this could be more than just a vacation fling. She liked him, and the man was divine in bed.

His hungry gaze raked her nakedness, inflaming her and making her feel sexy, desired and special. He flipped back the sheet and patted the mattress. "Come here."

Something wasn't right. Madeline's steps faltered. The hair on Damon's head was a rich tobacco-brown, but the curls on his chest and surrounding his impressive erection were dark golden blond.

Like the beard stubble on his chin.

Like the hair on his arms and legs.

Not sun bleached.

Huh?

"You're a natural blond?"

Guilt flashed in his eyes. "Yes."

"Damon, why would you—"

He grimaced and shook his head. "Dominic. My name is Dominic. Not Damon."

Warning prickles danced along her spine. She wrapped her arms around her naked middle. "Your— What?"

"I can explain." He swung his long legs over the side of the bed, stood and stepped toward her.

She held up a hand to halt him and backed away from his rampant masculinity while she struggled with the facts. One corner of her mind registered that he had a body worthy of the cover of a fitness magazine or a centerfold, but the other…

"You lied to me?"

"Other than my name, everything I've told you is true."

The man who'd given her the most incredible night of her life was a liar?

Shades of Mike.

"You expect me to believe that?"

"Yes." He exhaled. "Madeline, I am sorry for the deception, but I wanted a chance to be with you as a man instead of—" his chin shifted, his shoulders squared and resignation settled over his face "—instead of a monarch."

Confused, she blinked. "As in 'butterfly?'"

A smile twitched his lips. "As in Prince Dominic Andreas Rossi de Montagnarde at your service." He bowed slightly.

"Huh?" What in the hell did that mean? He thought he was a prince? Was he certifiable?

His eyes narrowed as he straightened. "The name means nothing to you?"

"Should it?"

"My father is the King Alfredo of Montagnarde, a three-island nation in the South Pacific. I am next in line to the throne."

Fear slithered through her, making her heart blip faster. She was somewhere in the Mediterranean Sea at least a mile off-shore with a delusional guy. "Sure you are. A prince, I mean."

Where were the survival instincts her father had drilled into her from an early age? Why had she ignored the warning prickles when she found out there were strangers on board? And why had she ignored the voice that said Damon was too good to be true?

Adrenaline flooded her veins, making her extremities tingle and her heart pound. Medical professionals called it the fight-or-flight response. Her father had called it live-or-die instinct, and he'd credited it with saving his life on more than one occasion. She'd put herself in danger, but she was going to get out of it. There was no other option.

Without taking her eyes off Damon, she reached for the skirt she'd discarded last night, yanked it on and zipped it. "Take me to shore."

"Madeline—"

"Now." She fumbled on her bra and then her shirt. Where had he thrown her panties? She couldn't afford to be vulnerable in any way, shape or form. She located the scrap of lace and donned it.

"I can't do that. Not yet."

She stilled and alarm raced through her. "Why not?"

"You must listen to me first. I wish to explain."

She didn't know why Damon had lured her onto a yacht, but she wished like the devil she'd paid more attention to the grim warnings of white slave trade and crime outside Monaco that Candace's future sister-in-law had shared along with etiquette lessons, but Madeline had written the woman off as an obsessed alarmist.

Wrong.

Inhaling deeply, she tried to recall what she'd been taught about handling unbalanced people and hazardous situations in the E.R. It didn't happen often, but there had been a few times when she'd had to protect herself and the other patients until security arrived.

Rule one: be aware of your surroundings. "Where are we exactly?"

"Off the coast of France."

Rule two: don't alarm the suspect. Keep him calm.

She forced a smile, but it wobbled. "Damon, I'd really like to go ashore."

"That's impossible. You don't have your passport."

Good point. But wouldn't the authorities understand just this once?

He moved closer. "Madeline—"

"Stop. Stop right there."

Rule three: when all else fails use the weapons at hand. There were knives in the kitchen. She'd seen them last night when she and Damon had prepared dinner together. Damon had cooked. What prince cooked? Royalty had servants for that kind of thing. Therefore, he was no prince.

She shoved her feet in her shoes, jerked open the cabin door and scanned the kitchen—*galley. Dammit, who cares what it's called?* She had to get off this boat. Ian and Makos sat at the table. Would they help her? Or were they in on this, too? She could take one guy. But three would be tricky.

She opened drawers until she found the one containing a razor-sharp filet knife with a nine-inch blade. And then Damon—Dominic…whatever the hell his name was—entered the small kitchen and reached for her. Using one of the self-defense moves her father had taught her she grabbed his right arm, ducked and turned and twisted his wrist up behind his back. She pressed the knife to his throat.

"Tell your friends to take me to shore. Now."

She heard an ominous sound and looked up to see two handguns pointed at her from across the room. Big, black ugly weapons. The crew members were in on this and armed.

My God. She was being kidnapped.

Four

"Ian, Makos, lower your weapons," Dominic stated calmly. Neither man complied. "That is an order."

"But Your Highness—" Ian protested.

"Do it. Madeline isn't going to hurt me." Dominic honestly believed it. He could feel the frightened quiver of her tense body pressed against his bare back and see the fine tremor of the hand at his jaw—the same hand that had brought him indescribable pleasure last night.

"That's what you think, buster. I'm a trained medical professional. I know where to cut to take you down instantly." The hand clamped around his wrist might not be completely steady, but her grip and voice were strong. She honestly believed her life was in danger—a circumstance he deeply regretted.

His bodyguards had lowered their guns, but raised them again upon hearing her threat.

Dominic subtly shifted a couple of inches to his right to

prevent the men from getting a clear shot at her. "Perhaps I should mention that Ian and Makos are my bodyguards. It is not wise to provoke them."

A slight shake of his head had the guards returning the weapons to the holsters concealed by their jackets with obvious reluctance.

He didn't doubt Madeline had the skill to kill him, but he doubted she had the nerve, and he wouldn't give her reason to find it. "If you incapacitate me, you will lose not only your human shield, but also your bargaining power. As a medical professional you took an oath to do no harm. Release me before someone gets hurt."

"Right." Disbelief colored the word. "And then what? You and your goons sell me? Ransom me? What?"

"I have no intention of ransoming or selling you. We'll return to port. Ian, give Madeline your phone so that she may call the hotel. Gustavo will vouch for me."

Her breasts nudged his back and her breath puffed against his nape as she snorted. "The concierge is probably in on this…this kidnap attempt. He told me I could trust you. If I call anyone, it'll be the police."

"You haven't been kidnapped. You boarded this yacht of your own free will as any of the other marina patrons will attest. And you will be returned unharmed. Call the authorities if you must, but doing so will be time consuming and embarrassing once the press gets involved."

"What press?"

"The ones I had hoped to avoid with my disguise. I colored my hair and shaved my beard because I wished to vacation without being hunted by the paparazzi. That's why I avoided the hotel after our swim at Larvotto. I did not wish to be recognized by predators with telephoto lenses."

A half minute passed. Although he'd never needed to use his skills, he'd been trained from an early age for situations like this. If he weren't concerned about hurting Madeline, he could escape her hold. An elbow here. A head slam there. He could easily hook one of her legs out from under her with his and send her tumbling to the floor. But she might impale herself as she fell. So he wouldn't. He'd already violated her trust by deceiving her. He wouldn't add physical injury to his crimes.

"Put the guns on the counter and slide them this way. Grips first," she demanded. "The phone, too."

He signaled with his free hand for Ian and Makos to do as she ordered. Both men looked at him as if he'd lost his mind but after a tense silence complied.

She edged closer to the weapons, towing him along with the knife still at his throat. The sad truth was her strength and bravery impressed him and turned him on. Luckily, he'd donned his pants before coming after her or she and his crew would see exactly how strongly she affected him.

He'd never met a woman like Madeline Spencer. Each time he thought he had her figured out she threw a new and intriguing puzzle piece at him—one that didn't fit his image of her.

Who was this woman who didn't hesitate to defend herself? And what had her ex-fiancé done to disillusion her so about love and to make her so distrustful? It had to be more than merely ending the relationship or finding someone new. And why did the knowledge fill Dominic with rage and a thirst for revenge on her behalf?

She halted a yard from the counter. To use the cell phone she'd have to have at least one hand free. He waited for her to choose between releasing him and putting down the knife, but evidently she came to the same conclusion. "I want to go ashore."

"Then you must allow Ian and Makos to go on deck. We can

be back in Monaco in an hour." That would give him time to convince her to trust and forgive him. He'd had every intention of telling her the truth before making love to her. Each time he'd opened his mouth to do so he had looked into her eyes and considered what he stood to lose. Her sassy, confident smile. Her relaxed yet seductive grace. The easy flow of conversation between a man and a woman who were equals. He'd lived with stiff formality for too many years. She'd given him a taste of what he'd been missing, of what a relationship should be, but what his future marriage would very likely not entail.

Last night when she'd stopped his words with gentle fingers on his lips he'd been weak enough to let desire overrule his conscience, but this morning he hadn't been able to stomach having her call him by the fictitious name. He wanted her crying out his name next time she climaxed.

And there would be a next time. He was more determined than ever to enjoy his last days of freedom in Madeline's company and in her bed. Whatever experience she might believe she lacked as a lover she more than made up for with an earthy sensuality that had brought him pleasure more intense than any he'd ever experienced. He wasn't ready to let her go. Not yet. But soon, unfortunately, he would have to.

She jerked his wrist upward with enough force to get his attention, but not enough to do permanent damage. "How stupid do you think I am? They could sail anywhere."

"You can see the GPS screen from here and know if they sail away from port. You'll have the phone, a pair of handguns and me as your hostage if they head in the wrong direction. And Madeline, my passport is in the cabin. Check it."

Another snort. Another brush of her breasts against his back. Another spark of arousal below his belt. "As if you couldn't fake that."

"Then pull me up on the Internet."

"Gee whiz. I forgot to pack my computer in my beach bag," she drawled sarcastically.

"When we get back to Hôtel Reynard then. I have a laptop in my suite."

"Do you think I'll follow you anywhere after this? And what do you mean 'your suite?' You're staying at Hôtel Reynard?"

"Yes. On the same floor as you, but at the opposite end of the hall in the Royal Suite. We are temporary neighbors. Why else do you think I was waiting for the penthouse elevator the night we met?"

She frowned as she considered that and then growled in anger and shifted on her feet behind him. Each movement rubbed her breasts against his naked back, a distraction he didn't need if he wished to avert disaster.

"Your henchmen can go on deck, but we're locking the door behind them and if they try to come through, I'll shoot because I think you're full of sh—"

"You know how to handle a gun?" Most shooting accidents happened at the hands of the inexperienced and he would prefer to avoid bloodshed. Particularly his.

"My father was a vice cop. I can not only handle a gun, I'm a damned good marksman. He made sure of it."

Ian caught Dominic's attention and tapped his thigh, indicating the smaller weapon Ian kept strapped above his ankle. Dominic signaled the negative and maintained eye contact long enough for the man to understand Dominic would handle the situation. Ian clearly didn't like it, but he accepted Dominic's silent command with a slight nod.

"Pull up anchor and return to port." Dominic's order contradicted every oath his bodyguards had taken. Members of the royal guard had to be willing to die for their country. That meant not leaving one of their leaders with a knife at his throat. But Ian and Makos did as he requested, climbing the ladder and closing the cabin door behind them.

Madeline pulled him toward the hatch and latched it.

"Sit." She shoved him toward the sofa.

Flexing his shoulder, Dominic sat because not fighting would serve his purpose better than asserting his authority or his physical dominance.

Poised on the balls of her feet, Madeline kept the knife at the ready and her eyes fixed on him as she quickly closed the blinds on each window. Smart move. Being unable to see inside the cabin would prevent Ian from trying anything heroic.

To make her feel less threatened Dominic propped his feet on the coffee table, crossed his ankles and leaned back, linking his fingers over his belly. As soon as he did Madeline backed toward the galley and collected the guns.

She handled the firearms comfortably, competently, checking the safeties and the clips of each weapon before shoving the knife back into the drawer. His respect for her climbed another notch. She was smart, resourceful, strong and calm in a crisis. Not to mention sexy as hell.

If a little misguided.

"My passport is in my bag. I'm blond and have a beard in the photo, but you've known me for a week and spent the night in my bed. You should be able to see past facial hair and a temporary dye job."

She kept the width of the room between them. "I don't care about your stupid and probably forged passport. You're still a liar."

Guilty as charged. "I didn't originally intend to conceal my identity, but Madeline, when you looked at me that night by the elevator I saw a woman who desired *me,* not a woman who wanted to land a prince. Do you have any idea how rare that is? It has only happened one other time. With Giselle, my wife."

"Spare me the sob story. I'm sure that was fiction, too."

"Sadly, it is not. I had known Giselle since we were children. We became engaged when I was nineteen and she sixteen."

Her nose wrinkled in distaste. "That's positively feudal."

He shrugged, but didn't waste time trying to explain a bridal selection process he knew she would neither like nor understand. "I agree. She was too young. That is why I insisted we postpone the marriage until I graduated from the university. And then as I told you in the café, she died two years into our marriage along with our first child."

"I don't want to hear it."

He ignored her words and kept talking to keep her calm and to get her to let down her guard. "My country is raw and largely untamed due to the royal advisory council's fear of change."

She rolled her eyes. "Uh-huh."

"It is believed that Montagnarde was once a massive volcano, but sixty million years ago the ocean breached the walls and extinguished the fire. There are three islands now surrounding an inland sea of crystal clear water."

"What a great imagination. You should write a book."

He smiled at her acid tone. She didn't believe him. Would she, like so many others, become deferential, obsequious and more interested in what his wealth and power could do for her once she accepted his identity? Undoubtedly. And when she did he was certain his fascination with her would end. "My youngest sister is writing a history of the islands. I have three sisters. Danielle, Yvette and Brigitte.

"Each generation of monarchs must have an agenda. My great-grandfather's was to protect our borders from outsiders and pests which might devastate our crops or wildlife. My grandfather focused on building a first-class transportation system within and around the islands, and my father on exporting our products. I am determined to introduce the world to the beauty of Montagnarde. Like Monaco, we should maximize our tourist potential. That is why I focused my degree and the past ten years' study on tourism. I intend to implement change and put my country on the map."

"So you admit 'your country' isn't on the map." More sarcasm.

"In terms of global recognition, not yet. But our wines, olive oils and organic produce are beginning to find success in foreign markets. As for our tourism development potential, we have mountains suited to skiing or climbing, depending on the season, blue seas perfect for sailing, sport fishing or surfing, underwater caverns to explore and hot mineral springs for rejuvenation. The natural reefs off our shores put the man-made ones in Monaco to shame and the species of fish and marine life are incredible."

The urgency to share the beauty of his country with her was unexpected and unwelcome, not to mention impossible. "The emeralds mined in Montagnarde are almost as lovely as your eyes, Madeline."

She snorted. "Save your breath. I am *so* over your flattery and so over you."

Frustration rose within him. He had power and wealth at his fingertips and yet the one thing he wished for he couldn't have. He wished for more time with Madeline. But time was a luxury he did not have….

Unless he could turn this disaster to his advantage.

A gurgle of disgust erupted from Madeline's throat. "You are really something."

"So you told me last night. I believe *magnificent* is the word you used."

She wanted to smack that confident smirk off Damon's face. A shocking fact, since she'd never been one prone to violence. Her cheeks burned hot. She'd been a fool for swallowing his garbage the way she had Mike's. Just how stupid was she to let two handsome faces override her common sense?

"Keep it up, bucko, and I might just shoot you for the fun of it. I don't like being made a fool of."

"Is that what your ex did? Made you look foolish?"

She very deliberately released the safety on the gun. "It's not smart to piss off an armed lady."

Damon held up his hands as if in surrender. "Then I will tell you more about my homeland instead." He lowered his arms and linked his fingers over his navel. She could not believe she had nibbled her way down that lying rat's goodie trail last night.

Worse, the proof of Damon's deceit had been right in front of her. Only she'd failed to see the signs because the lights had been out. Sort of like her relationship with Mike. She'd only seen what she wanted to see until he'd forced her to acknowledge the truth.

She hated feeling stupid. Clueless. Duped.

"Each of the islands of Montagnarde has one or more glacial lakes with water pure enough to bottle. The streams and rivers are a fisherman's paradise. Like New Zealand, we have no poisonous snakes or spiders."

Blah. Blah. Blah. She focused on the GPS screen and tried to tune out his words. Whatever he said would be more lies anyway. She could hear the men above them moving about and raising the sails.

Trapped on a yacht with a trio of lunatics. What had she done to deserve this? And would she live to tell the tale?

Yes, dammit, you will. Your mother's depending on you.

"My country was discovered in the 1700s by the Comte de Rossi, a Frenchman searching for a shorter route to the spices of India," he continued. "His ships veered off course in a storm. He landed on the main island searching for food and to make repairs. He decided to stay and explore."

"Right. And the natives just let the French drop anchor and take over?"

"Initially, the islands' inhabitants were bribed with the luxuries on board the ships, but sadly, within the first year the majority of them were decimated by European diseases—also on board de Rossi's ships. The Comte, owner of the fleet, declared himself king and named the islands Montagnarde for the peaks that pierced the clouds. During his lifetime he selectively allowed his countrymen and the finest craftsmen to immigrate, and it is said his advisors kidnapped the most beautiful woman in all of France to be his bride and queen."

Until he uttered the last part his tall tale had *almost* sounded plausible. Her mouth dried. "You'd better not be thinking along the same lines."

"I regret that our affair must end when I leave Monaco."

"In case you missed the bulletin, our affair is already over." Her stomach growled. She glanced at the coffeepot and inhaled the aroma of the strong brew. Her racing heart didn't need the caffeine jolt, but she did need something in her empty stomach to counteract the light-headedness caused by an adrenaline rush combined with not replacing the large number of calories she'd burned off in the past twelve hours.

Naked and entwined with the dishonest snake.

With a gun in her right hand she found a mug with her left and mounded a diet-wrecking amount of sugar inside, and then she poured a stream of coffee on top and swished it around to mix it. She didn't risk taking her eyes off Dominic long enough to search for a spoon or cream. She sipped the syrupy brew. *Eeew.*

"There are pastries in the cabinet to your left and eggs, sausage, fruit and cheese in the refrigerator."

His words made her salivate, but blocking her view of her captive to search the fridge was out of the question. "You'd love it if I'd drop my guard, wouldn't you?"

"I would enjoy breakfast more. We worked up quite an appetite last night."

Her body flushed all over. "Jerk."

She opened the cabinet, found the croissants and hurled one at him with enough force to break a window had it been a rock.

He snagged it out of the air. "Thank you. I am fond of Ian's coffee, as well."

She almost flung her mug at him. Instead she extracted another from the cabinet, filled it and shoved it to the far end of the bar. He was out of luck if he wanted cream or sugar.

He rose and slowly approached. "You don't need the gun, Madeline."

She cursed him, using the one four-letter word she *never* used and he grinned.

"I believe you did that last night. Three times. And with extremely satisfying results."

She gaped. Did the man have an ounce of sense? She had a loaded gun in her hand and he insisted on provoking her.

He moved around the end of the bar. Good God, she didn't want to shoot him. She didn't take lives. She saved them. And until he'd betrayed her she'd liked him. Maybe she could just maim him. But where? She considered her artery-avoiding options. "Don't even think about it."

He stopped his advance and leaned his hip against the counter.

"I can think of nothing but the softness of your skin. Your scent. Your taste. That voracious mouth. The slick clench of your body as you drove me out of my mind. I have never desired a woman as I do you, Madeline. And we could be rediscovering that passion at this moment if you would put the gun down."

Damn him and his low-pitched seductive voice. Arousal tumbled through her. How was that possible in this situation? She briefly closed her eyes—no more than a blink—as the images of last night inundated her, and in that split second Damon lunged forward. His long fingers latched around her wrist. He shoved her gun hand toward the ceiling and slammed his body into hers, backing her against the refrigerator door and forcing the breath from her lungs. The gun exploded with a deafening sound and bits of ceiling rained down.

She struggled, but Damon had her pinned like an insect on a collector's board with his broad chest, his muscular hips and rock-hard thighs grinding against hers.

"Release the gun, Madeline," he ordered calmly.

The hatch door rattled viciously.

"Release the gun," he repeated this time with his warm breath and prickly morning stubble against her jaw. "I promise you are in no danger."

There was nothing remotely sexy about wrestling for a gun, and yet there wasn't an inch of him she couldn't feel imprinted on her skin. Her traitorous brain remembered being this close to him just hours ago with nothing but a thin sheen of sweat between them. How dare her body betray her at this moment. She stiffened her softening muscles.

"As if I'd believe anything you say," she muttered and tried to bow her spine to earn some breathing room.

"You have no choice." There was a hard, commanding edge to his voice that hadn't been there before.

Her hand started to go numb from the pressure he exerted on her radial nerve. Her grip loosened at the same time as the hatch splintered open. Over Damon's shoulder she saw Ian charge in, leading with a small pistol.

"Stand down," Damon called out. His big body blocked hers from his henchmen. He held up his hand, displaying the weapon he'd taken from her.

The other gun lay on the counter out of reach.

Damn. Damn. Damn. She'd let her guard down. Had her father been alive he would have been disappointed in her. Determined she would never be a victim of the kind of crimes he investigated, he'd drilled self-defense techniques into her once a week from the day he'd moved out.

"Ian, Makos, retrieve your weapons. Mademoiselle Spencer will be joining me in the captain's cabin."

"In your dreams, *prince.*" She practically spat his fake title.

"Give us a few moments and then we would like breakfast." He grasped each of her arms and then lifted his weight and yanked her forward before transferring her wrists to one big hand behind her back. His long fingers compressed like a vise.

"Don't make me tie you up," he murmured in her ear. "Although we might enjoy that another time."

"Bite me."

"I would be more than happy to in the privacy of our cabin." He turned her and steered her toward the cabin. Try as she might she could not wriggle free. Man, the guy was strong. And then he closed the door and locked it behind them. Damon released her.

She hustled to the far side of the room, scanning the surfaces for weapons and finding none. Not even a vase to crack over his head. But even if she incapacitated him she'd still have to deal with the two armed thugs in the other room.

He reached into his luggage, withdrew something and tossed it onto the bed. His passport fell open to the picture and her breath caught. As handsome as Damon was as a brunette, he was drop-dead gorgeous as a blond with his hair slicked back to reveal his amazing bone structure and those pale blue eyes.

She inched closer and snatched up the booklet. It named him as Prince Dominic Andreas Rossi de Montagnarde. Hair: blond. Eyes: blue. Height: six feet three inches. She did the math and came up with his age: thirty-five. She flipped through the pages and read stamped ports of entry from across the globe.

But the "passport" was a fake. It had to be. Princes didn't pretend to be tour guides. They traveled with an entourage of toadying staff, and they didn't hang out with commoners like her. She knew that much from *CNN*.

Was Damon some sort of charlatan who connived his way around the globe with a false title? With his looks, charm and sexual prowess he could swindle big-time. But he should focus on women with money. Maybe he thought she was loaded because she'd told him she'd be in Monaco an entire month.

"Recognize me now?" he asked.

"No. And it doesn't matter anyway because once we dock I don't ever want to see you again unless it's to ID you in a police lineup." She flung the documentation back onto the tangled sheets and tried not to recall how the linens had become so mussed.

"I am very sorry to hear that. Because I have not had my fill of you, Madeline. I find your company quite refreshing."

"Too bad." She paced the length of the cabin. "Okay, here's the deal. Put me ashore and I'll forget this ever happened. I won't report you or your thugs."

Not exactly the truth, but—

"Good try, but no." Damon sat on the bed, stretched his legs out before him and leaned back against the headboard, looking as comfortable as he had in the middle of last night when he'd sat in the same spot and watched her shower through the open bathroom door. The memory of how he'd taken the towel from her and lapped the water from her skin afterward shortened her breath and tightened her nipples. She turned her back and stared out the narrow window. Better that than look at his naked chest and remember what an idiot she'd been last night and what an idiot she was being right now by getting distracted by sex.

Wasn't it just her luck that the best lover she'd ever had was a step lower on the slug meter than Mike? Her ex might have been a liar and a cheat, but as far as she knew he'd never broken the law or stooped to kidnapping.

Twenty tense, silent minutes later a knock on the door brought Damon to his feet. He let Ian and breakfast in and then relocked the door after the man left. Food was the last thing she wanted, but if she had to swim or run for it then she'd need whatever fuel she could get. She inched toward the tray while Damon pulled on a blue shirt with a gold crest on the pocket and traded his wrinkled pants for clean briefs and a pressed pair of khakis. He buttoned the shirt and tucked it in, adding a leather belt, and then he stepped into rubber-soled boat shoes. As a final touch he raked his hair back off his forehead with his fingers, exposing his aristocratic bone structure. In that getup he looked like one of the rich and famous. Very "yacht club" and a far cry from her tour guide-lover-kidnapper.

"You realize you have threatened the life of a monarch?" Damon asked casually as he spread cherry preserves on a croissant.

How long was he going to persist in that fairy-tale garbage? Grabbing a pastry with one hand, she flipped him a rude gesture with the other. She bit through the flaky crust and into the moist croissant, chewed, swallowed with inelegant haste until she'd consumed most of her breakfast-fuel supply.

He finished his with less speed, poured a cup of coffee and sipped. "The offense is punishable by imprisonment or death in my country."

She nearly choked on her last bite of pastry and then gulped down the formerly butter-rich now tasteless wad. It hit her stomach like lead. His threat wasn't funny. She'd been worried before, but this ratcheted up the tension in her muscles another ten notches. What exactly was she dealing with here? Because she didn't believe for one second that he actually was royalty.

She eyed the coffee carafe and considered whacking him with it. Did it have enough weight to knock him out? And then what would she do? "We're not in your country."

"The Monaco authorities will be even less lenient."

Other than a sick churning in her stomach she had no answer for that. She wished she'd used Ian's cell phone to call Candace and Amelia and ask them to send the harbor police or whatever they were called.

Who would look after her mother if Madeline ended up not making it back to Charlotte? May Spencer wasn't in fragile health yet, but she was seventy-eight. She didn't travel well and flying made her seriously ill. Would she be able to handle a trip overseas to search for her missing daughter?

Don't think like that. Damon hasn't hurt you. In fact, he stepped between you and the goons' guns twice. Surely if he intended to harm you he wouldn't have?

Or maybe she was worth more alive than dead.

"What do you want from me? I don't have any money. My father is dead and my mother lives on a cop's and a retired teacher's pensions. Trust me, that's a pittance. And I hear the U.S. doesn't negotiate with terrorists."

"I am neither a terrorist nor a kidnapper. I merely wish to continue our…assignations."

Her mouth dropped open. Was he nuts? *Of course he is. He thinks he's a freaking prince.* "You want to remain my tour guide?"

"I would prefer to be your companion and your lover for the remainder of your vacation and mine."

The man had balls of steel and a pea-size brain. "I don't do forced sex."

His bearing snapped military straight and his aristocratic nose lifted. He had the arrogance thing down pat, and he even looked like royalty for a minute there. "I am neither a rapist nor an extortionist. When you return to my bed, Madeline, it will be because you desire me as much as you did last night."

How ungentlemanly of him to mention her enthusiasm. "Not going to happen."

"Would you care to place a wager on that?" One corner of his mouth slanted upward.

Foot stomping overhead followed by the boat's engine rumbling to life preempted her scathing reply—which was a good thing since she couldn't think of one. She moved back to the window and saw the port of Monaco in the distance—swimmable distance if she could get out of this cabin and past the thugs who sounded like elephants overhead. She eyed the skylight in the ceiling, but there was no way she could reach it let alone get through it before Damon could grab her legs.

"We have reached the marina," Damon stated.

Fifteen minutes later the sound of voices—more than had occupied the dock when they'd left—filtered through the closed windows. Damon looked outside and cursed. "Paparazzi. Along with the Sûreté Publique. Ian must have called for assistance."

The police? Thank God. She pressed a palm to her chest.

He caught her shoulders and her gaze. "You will do exactly as I say when we disembark. I would not like to see you inadvertently injured."

"And if I don't?"

"I will press charges."

Jeez, how long was he going to play this gig?

All she had to do was agree. She'd be screaming for help the second she got outside, but he didn't need to know that. She'd report him to the authorities, and she'd tell Vincent Reynard and have the imposter kicked out of the hotel—maybe even banned from all of Reynard's hotels worldwide. Maybe the Monaco Sûreté Publique would haul Damon off in handcuffs. After the scare he'd given her she'd enjoy watching that.

"Okay. I'll do what you say." The lie didn't even make her twitch.

The boat bumped against the dock. Heavy footsteps immediately boarded, rocking the craft.

"Follow my lead and do not say anything to incriminate yourself."

Incriminate herself? That was a riot coming from a con man.

Keeping her behind him Damon opened the cabin door and rattled off something in French. Madeline ducked under his arm, intending to sprint for the hatch, but she skidded to a halt at the sight of the overcrowded galley.

Police. Six of them. With weapons drawn. They fired off commands—commands she couldn't understand and moved toward her in a threatening manner. She backed into Damon.

"English please." Damon's hands encircled her waist and

then he shifted her to his side and draped an arm across her shoulders as if they were friends. Or lovers. "Mademoiselle Spencer does not speak French. And the weapons are unnecessary. She is unarmed."

"You are under arrest, mademoiselle, for assaulting Prince Dominic," one of the officers said.

She gaped. "Me? What about him and his henchmen? They kidnapped me!"

Two of the men reached for her but Damon stopped them with an outstretched and upraised hand. "I apologize for wasting your time, officers. My bodyguards misunderstood the nature of our—" he paused to stare intently into Madeline's eyes "—love play."

He compounded that lie by kissing the tip of her nose.

Her cheeks caught fire over the insinuation while confusion tumbled through her brain. "That's not what hap—"

"*Madeline.*" Damon cupped her shoulders and gave her a gentle shake. "The game is over. You do not want the police to arrest you. Do you?"

She looked from the officers to Damon and back again. The cops had handcuffs, guns and attitude. Enough testosterone crackled in the air to fill a Super Bowl team's locker room. She had encountered hundreds of law enforcement officers through her father and in the E.R.—enough to recognize the real deal when she saw it. These guys weren't pretending. And apparently Damon—*Dominic*—whatever he called himself, wasn't, either.

Her stomach lurched. She gulped back the breakfast rising in her throat and turned to the nearest uniformed man, a fox-faced guy about her age. "He's really a prince?"

The man blinked in surprise. "*Oui,* mademoiselle. Prince Dominic is a frequent and welcome visitor to Monaco."

Uh-oh.

"If you would give us a moment to gather our belongings," Damon said in more of an order than request, "I would be most grateful if you could assist us through the paparazzi outside."

A man whose name tag read Inspector Rousseau said, "*Certainement,* Your Highness. We are happy to be of service."

Numbly, Madeline allowed Damon to steer her back into the cabin. She closed her eyes and locked her jaws on a groan.

Oh, spit. She really had assaulted a member of royalty.

This was *so* not how she'd planned to spend her vacation.

Five

"I guess 'Oops, I'm sorry' won't cut it?" Madeline asked Dam—Prince Dominic in a barely audible voice. She glanced over her shoulder at the officers watching diligently from outside the open door.

"That depends on whether or not you agree to my terms," he replied as quietly.

Her stomach knotted. "Continue the, uh…relationship?"

Dominic nodded once—sharply—with his gaze drilling into hers. Funny how regal he looked all of a sudden. "And you will keep details of our affair private. I have no wish to read about my Monaco mistress in the tabloids."

The Prince's Monaco Mistress. She could see the headlines now. Ugh. She'd never wanted to be famous—certainly not famous for stupidity. Being humiliated by Mike in her small corner of the world had been more than enough exposure, thanks very much.

Spending time with a man who'd lied to her and tricked her into bed under false pretenses ranked low on her to-do list. But it beat incarceration. She knew nothing about Monaco law except the country had an extremely low tolerance for crime. There were cameras on every street corner as a deterrent. Even if she could convince a judge or whoever was in charge of the legal system here to understand her side, she couldn't afford to worry her mother, and she'd prefer not to ruin Candace's wedding with a scandal. And then there was the likelihood that getting arrested would probably jeopardize her job.

"Fine," she bit out ungraciously. "But remember, you are not the prince of me. I'm not doing anything illegal, immoral or disgusting no matter what you threaten."

His lips twitched. "Duly noted. You have two minutes to make whatever adjustments you wish to your appearance before we face the paparazzi."

She ducked into the bathroom and quickly cleaned up, then returned to the bedroom.

"Put on your hat and sunglasses," Da—Dominic ordered. The new name would take some getting used to.

Madeline complied. The last thing she wanted her mother or her coworkers at the hospital to see was her face on *CNN* or *Entertainment Tonight*.

"Your hair is easily recognizable. You might wish to conceal it beneath your hat."

She twisted it into a rope and shoved it beneath the cap.

"Once we exit the yacht keep your head down and do not answer any questions no matter how provocative."

Once they had their bags packed he took hers from her and turned back to address the police through the open door. "Officers, once again I apologize for the misunderstanding.

Should you require it, I will be more than happy to come down to the station and make an official report after I return Mademoiselle Spencer to the hotel."

"That will not be necessary, Your Highness," Rousseau said.

The youngest officer offered to carry their bags. Dominic handed them off and strode toward the hatch.

Where had her sexy, laid-back tour guide gone? The man in front of her stood straight, tall and regal as he followed half of the officers from the cabin.

How could he follow and still give the impression of leading?

He paused at the top of the ladder and turned to help Madeline ascend. The wall of voices and the whir of cameras slammed her as soon as her head cleared the cabin. She pulled down the bill of her cap. From the dock, dozens of camera-toting reporters shouted questions in a variety of languages. Dominic ignored them.

No, *ignore* wasn't quite the correct word. He acted as if he didn't see or hear them, as if they didn't exist.

"Head down. Let's go," he said into her ear and then he grabbed her elbow and half led, half dragged her over the planks in the wake of three officers who cleared a path. Ian and Makos followed with two other officers behind them. One remained on the boat—to guard it, she presumed. Or to write up a damage report. She winced. No telling how much paying for those repairs was going to set her back.

The crush of sweaty, smelly bodies jostling to get a picture of Dominic nearly overwhelmed her. The only other time she'd seen something even remotely close to this was when Vincent, Candace's fiancé, had been brought to the E.R. after being badly burned last year at a NASCAR race. The press had crowded into the lobby of the E.R. and security had struggled to keep them out.

A white Mercedes limo waited by the curb. An attendant opened the door as they approached. Dominic urged her to enter first. He quickly followed, choosing the seat directly across from hers. The door closed and silence and blessedly cool air-conditioned air enfolded them. The trunk thumped shut, presumably on their bags.

She looked at the milling crowd outside the tinted windows. The police kept them away from the car. "You live like this?"

"Yes. Now do you understand the need for a disguise?"

She could see how it might appeal, but still— "You should have told me who you were before we slept together."

He nodded acknowledgment. "Agreed."

She waited for him to make excuses. He didn't.

The driver climbed in. Ian joined him in the front seat. Their doors shut with a quiet *thunk* that shouted expensive car.

"The hotel, Your Highness?" the driver asked through an open black glass panel between the front and back seats.

"Yes." The glass rose and the car moved forward.

Angry and confused, Madeline shifted uneasily on the leather seat and then ripped off her sunglasses. "What game were you playing? Slumming with the commoner who didn't have the sense to know who you were? Were you laughing at my ignorance the entire time?"

"I have never considered you ignorant. Nor did I laugh at you. I enjoyed your lack of pretense. Revealing my identity would have changed that."

"You think I'm going to suck up to you now?"

He studied her appraisingly from behind dark lenses. "In my experience I find it likely."

"In your dreams, bucko." And then she recalled the protocol lessons from Candace's future sister-in-law. *Never address royalty by their first names.* "Do you expect me to call you 'Your Highness?' Because I have kissed your butt—literally. I'll be damned if I'll start bowing and scraping—"

His low chuckle winded her. "I would prefer you did not."

"Okay then. Now what? I can't imagine our outings will be any fun if we have to contend with that." She nodded toward the crowd they'd left behind—the one now scurrying along the sidewalk like a fat millipede trying to keep up with them. She couldn't imagine the dates would be fun period since she'd be participating under duress.

"We will have to be more resourceful."

"Where's your entourage? Every bigwig I've seen on TV has one."

"I left them behind. This was supposed to be a quiet, in-cognito vacation. Ian will arrange for additional security."

At least with security men around there wouldn't be any more intimate encounters. "How long before you accept my apology and let me off the hook?"

"Not until I tire of your company." He leaned forward and splayed his palms across her knees and lower thighs. Heat shot upward from the points of contact. "And, Madeline, I don't think that will happen anytime soon."

The sensual promise in his voice and his touch melted her anger frighteningly fast. She abruptly shifted her legs out of reach and struggled to rally her flagging ire. "Just don't expect me to sleep with you again."

He sat back and looked down his aristocratic nose at her. "You have issued that challenge once already. Repeating it only makes me more determined to prove you wrong."

"We will have lunch in my suite," Dominic announced as they exited the elevator on the hotel's penthouse floor.

"I don't think so." Eager to escape, Madeline turned in the opposite direction and marched toward her suite.

He followed, along with his bodyguards. "I insist."

She stopped outside her door and glared at him. "Insist all you want. But the answer's still no. You don't own every minute of my time. That wasn't part of our deal. I want a shower and a few hours away from you. In case you haven't noticed, I'm still ticked off."

She swiped her electronic key card. The latch whirred and the green light winked. She extended her hand. "Give me my bag."

"Give me your passport."

"Are you nuts?" *Isn't that becoming a familiar refrain?*

"I will not allow you to flee Monaco and escape fulfilling your end of our bargain."

The idea appealed. Immensely. "I can't leave. I have a friend's wedding to help plan and to be in. *I* would never screw someone who trusted me."

From the tightening of his lips she guessed he hadn't missed her implication that he had. "Regardless, I will take your passport as insurance."

The door opened and Amelia stood in the threshold, her hazel eyes cautious as she took in the foursome in the hall. "Is everything okay?"

"No, everything is not okay," Madeline informed her.

Dominic bowed slightly, turning on the charm and flashing a high wattage smile. The action made Amelia's cheeks flush and Madeline seethe. "*Bonjour,* mademoiselle."

"Um, hi." Amelia's gaze flicked back and forth between the men and Madeline.

Madeline grimaced. She'd have to make introductions even though she'd prefer to keep starry-eyed Amelia away from His

Royal Pain in the Butt. Amelia was waiting for a prince to sweep her off her feet. But not this prince.

"Amelia Lambert, my friend, suitemate and coworker. This is Da—Dominic— How in the hell am I supposed to introduce you?"

Dominic's eyes twinkled as if she'd asked a loaded question, and Madeline's pulse tripped.

Stop that. You are immune to him now.

He offered his hand to Amelia. "Dominic Rossi."

Madeline waited, but he didn't offer his title. "He's a freaking prince. And my former tour guide."

Amelia snatched her hand from Dominic's. "Excuse me?"

"The lying snake in the grass omitted telling me he's royalty. The big guys are his bodyguards, Ian and Makos." She jerked a thumb toward the lurking men.

Amelia blinked uncertainly. "Um, nice to meet you?"

"I'll explain later. Just let me in."

Amelia stepped back, opening the door wider. Madeline jerked her bag from Dominic's hand and squeezed past her friend. Dominic, damn him, followed. Ian and Makos remained in the hall like big totem poles flanking the door.

"Your passport, Madeline," Dominic reminded her. "Or I can call the Sûreté Publique."

"Go to he—"

"Why does he need to call the police?" Amelia interrupted. "Did something happen?"

Madeline fought the urge to squirm and glared at Dominic. "We had a misunderstanding, which, of course, was entirely *his* fault."

"It is hardly my fault you chose not to believe the truth," he replied in an infuriatingly calm voice.

"Since you'd been so honest up until that point?" she drawled sarcastically.

He had the decency to flush.

"The prince of what?" Amelia, bless her peacemaking heart, interrupted again.

"Montagnarde," Dominic replied, directing another one of his ligament-loosening smiles her friend's way.

"Really?" she whispered in an awestruck voice.

Surprised, Madeline stared. "You've heard of the place?"

"Absolutely. It's southwest of Hawaii. All the burn unit nurses want to go there—if we ever win the lottery, that is. The queen's books about an adventurous dragon are immensely popular with the children on the floor."

Madeline's gaze bounced from Dominic to Amelia and back. Was she the only one without a clue about him or his homeland? "You said your sister was the author."

"Brigitte is writing a history of the islands, but my mother writes children's books. They're the stories she told my sisters and me when we were young."

She did not want to picture him as a boy curled up in his mother's lap for a bedtime story. He'd probably been disgustingly cute then, too.

Amelia frowned and narrowed her eyes on Dominic. "Forgive my impertinence, Your uh, Highness? But I thought you were a blond and you…" She pointed at her jawline.

"Dominic, please." He pulled out his wallet, extracted a business card and offered it to Amelia. "I was incognito until Madeline broke my cover. E-mail the hospital address to me and I will have Mama send a box of autographed books to your hospital. If you would like, you may include the first names of the children currently residing on the floor so she can personalize them."

Wide-eyed, Amelia clutched the card to her chest. "I'll do that as soon as I get back to Charlotte. Thank you."

Madeline clenched her teeth. She did not want him doing nice stuff. She'd rather remember him as the sneaky, lying bastard forcing his company on her.

And he hadn't given *her* a card. Not that she wanted one. Nope. She'd be happy if she never laid eyes on him, his card or his henchmen ever again.

His blue gaze caught Madeline's. "Perhaps Mademoiselle Lambert would like to join us for lunch in my suite."

The moment she saw the pleasure bloom in Amelia's face, Madeline knew she should have killed Da—Dominic while she had the chance. The conniving opportunist had set the trap so smoothly she hadn't seen it and she'd stepped right into it. If she refused to eat with him now Amelia would be crushed.

Madeline flipped him a rude hand gesture behind her friend's back.

His smile turned wicked. "I'll take that as a yes."

Grrr. "May I see you in my room for a moment?"

"My pleasure."

"You wish." She turned her back on Amelia's dreamy sigh, stomped into her bedroom, tapped her toe impatiently until he crossed the threshold and then shut the door behind him with a restrained click. Slamming it would have been much more satisfying. She settled for heaving her overnight bag onto the bed and then planting her fists on her hips.

"Leave Amelia out of this."

"Your friend is charming."

"And off-limits to you." If the lift of his eyebrow was any indication, her tone had sounded a tad too possessive. Or protective. Or bitchy. Probably all three. "Should I expect more underhanded maneuvering from you?"

"Only if you make it necessary. I am usually quite straight-forward in my desires. And at the moment I desire your company…and you, Madeline."

Her pulse tripped over the raspy edge of his voice and her body heated at the memory of exactly what fulfilling his desires had entailed. He hadn't neglected one single inch of *her* body last night while taking care of *his* needs.

"Can't say the same about yours and you," she lied with only a pinch of discomfort.

His smile turned predatory. "Another challenge?"

She almost snarled, but settled for a glare.

He extended his hand. "Your passport, please."

"What if I want to cross the border on a sightseeing trip?"

"You will be with me, and I will have your passport. Tomorrow morning we'll go to the Rainier III Shooting Range. I wish to see how good you are with a weapon."

She ungraciously dug her passport out of the dresser drawer, slapped it into his hand and then studied her nails. "I might be busy."

"You're afraid I'm a better marksman?" He slipped the booklet into his pants pocket.

"Don't try reverse psychology on me. It won't work."

He moved closer. The dresser behind her prevented her escape. He lifted his hand and dragged a fingertip along the skin fluttering wildly over her carotid artery. "Would you prefer I stroke your erogenous zones instead? As I recall, that made you quite amenable last night."

She cursed her weakening knees and the revealing goose bumps marching across her skin. Last night his caresses had turned her mind and body to mush. She would have agreed to practically anything he asked.

But that was then. Now she knew he was the kind of guy

who'd lie his way into a woman's bed. She clenched her teeth, jerked her head out of reach and folded her arms across her tattletale breasts. She ought to plant a knee in his crotch.

He must have read her mind because he lowered his hand and stepped back. "I will expect you and Mademoiselle Lambert in my suite in an hour. And Madeline, do not disappoint me."

A stranger opened the door. A gorgeous, blond-haired, blue-eyed, freshly shaven stranger expensively attired in a dove-gray suit and a stark white open-collared shirt.

Dominic. Madeline's mouth dried and her heart stuttered. She'd recognize that incredible bone structure anywhere. He'd been handsome as a brunette, but now… *Wow.* He'd brushed his hair back from his forehead, setting off his pale blue eyes and tanned skin.

But his phenomenal looks didn't matter. She had a zero tolerance policy for liars. "You have a hairdresser at your beck and call?"

Her waspish question didn't faze him. "Hôtel Reynard is quite accommodating. Come in, mesdemoiselles."

The layout and opulence of his suite resembled the one she shared with Amelia, Candace and Stacy, but whereas theirs was light and airy, his was decorated in jewel-tone fabrics and darker woods. The dining room table had been set with enough silver, crystal and china to buckle the legs of a less substantial piece of furniture. Afternoon sunlight streamed through the floor-to-ceiling windows overlooking the Mediterranean, making the wine and water goblets sparkle like diamonds scattered across the ivory linen tablecloth.

Rich. Formal. Elegant. Dominic's world. She was only a visitor—and a reluctant one at that. Better not forget it.

She felt the weight of Dominic's gaze on her as she studied

the setup. He believed his having loads of money would impress her. But he was wrong. She worked with dozens of consulting doctors and surgeons through the E.R. Some were incredibly wealthy, certainly not in Dominic's heir-to-the-kingdom league, but a money surplus didn't keep them from being jackasses. A seven- or eight-figure net worth meant nothing if no one liked, respected or trusted you.

Self-satisfaction was more important than mucho bucks any day. She wanted to work where she could help the largest number of people and maybe even catch a few lost souls before they slipped through the bureaucratic health-care cracks. A county hospital provided the best venue. And when her head hit the pillow each night she could rest easy knowing she'd made a difference that day. The way her father had as a cop. The way her mother had as an inner-city schoolteacher.

She glanced at her friend. Amelia seemed a little ill at ease around *Prince* Dominic. Or maybe it was the four waiters lined up like a firing squad on the far wall or the stone-faced Ian over in the corner making her uneasy.

"He doesn't like me much, does he?" Madeline asked sotto voce so the bodyguard in question wouldn't overhear.

"Would you expect otherwise? You threatened to slit my throat," Dominic replied in an equally quiet tone—but not so quiet she missed the amusement tingeing his voice.

"Madeline!" Amelia squeaked.

Madeline winced. She'd escaped telling Amelia what happened by ducking into the shower and dawdling over dressing for lunch. The extra care she'd taken with her appearance had absolutely nothing to do with impressing Dominic. She didn't care if he liked her slim-fitting lime-green sundress or her strappy sandals. She'd chosen this outfit because it complemented her eyes and showed off her hard-earned shape.

Right now she needed the confidence booster of looking good because she felt stupid. Not an emotion she enjoyed or one she experienced often, thank goodness. She had a reputation at work for thinking fast on her feet and being good in a crisis. That would be worthless if this debacle slipped out. Talk about jumping to erroneous conclusions… She'd taken a dive into the Mariana Trench.

"Rest assured, Mademoiselle Lambert, Madeline had reason to question her safety. But that is something we shall not discuss around outsiders." Dominic indicated the waiters with a slight inclination of his head.

His defense surprised Madeline as did the reminder that others would be interested in his life.

"Please be seated." He touched his hand to the base of Madeline's spine and sparks skipped up her vertebrae like stones skimming across a pond's surface. Her breath hitched. She didn't look at him as she crossed the long room to the lavishly laid table.

Frankly, the entire episode, or rather her lack of perception, was embarrassing. How could she have believed him to be a simple tour guide? From his fluency with languages to his expensive clothing, his regal bearing and complete acceptance of the waiters rushing forward to pull back their chairs, everything about Dominic screamed wealth and privilege.

Dominic stood behind the seat at the head of the table, waiting for the staff to seat Madeline on his right and Amelia on his left. Once the women were settled he sat and commenced a wine tasting ritual that launched a meal more elaborate than any Madeline had ever experienced. Each mouthwatering course arrived hot and fresh from the kitchen, and then finally, what seemed like forever later, the waiters placed dessert in front of them. Dominic dismissed the servers. Only Ian remained in watchful silence.

Madeline stared at the confection in front of her. She didn't even want to think about how many calories she'd consumed or how many extra hours she'd have to spend in the hotel gym to make up for this meal. But that didn't stop her from sampling the warm chocolate tart topped with Bavarian cream mousse. She'd never tasted anything as rich, decadent and delicious. Her mouth practically had an orgasm. Her eyes closed and a moan sneaked past her lips.

Embarrassed, she pressed her napkin to her lips and peeked at Dominic only to find his attention riveted on her face. His pupils dilated and his intense gaze shifted to her mouth. His lips parted slightly and he moistened them with his tongue. A slowly indrawn breath expanded his chest.

The raw passion in his eyes torched her body like dry kindling. Memories of his lovemaking licked through her. His touch. His taste. His incredible heat. The powerful surge of his body into hers.

Her skin flushed and dampened. The fabric of her dress abraded her suddenly sensitive breasts and desire pooled and pulsed in her pelvis.

So much for pretending indifference or forgetting even one second of last night. If a single desire-laden glance from his bedroom blue eyes could bring it all rushing back, then staying out of his bed wasn't going to be nearly as easy as she'd hoped.

Well, dammit, she'd just have to try harder. Failure wasn't an option.

She makes the same sound when she climaxes.

Madeline's moan hit Dominic like a sucker punch. Memories of their passionate night erupted inside him with the force of a volcano. Desire coursed through his veins like streams of molten lava. He instantly recalled the slick, tight heat of her body, the scrape of her nails on his back as she arched beneath him and the band of her legs around his hips urging him deeper.

She scowled at him and flicked back her hair. Remembering the sweep of her soft curls across his belly as she took him into her hot, wet mouth made him shudder. From the toes curled in his shoes to his clenched jaw, each of his muscles contracted. Sweat beaded on his upper lip.

He had spent the past two hours waiting for Madeline to become cloying, obsequious and more interested in what his wealth and power could do for her. As soon as she did he was certain his fascination with her would end.

The elaborate luncheon had been but a small sample of the luxuries he could shower upon her now that his identity had been revealed. But instead of using her position as his lover as leverage, other than an occasional unsuccessful attempt to derail the conversational path he'd chosen, she'd been unusually reticent.

She'd barely contributed to the discussion about the sights and clubs she and her suitemates had already visited or the upcoming wedding—the reason for her presence in Monaco. Her friend had been more forthcoming, but Amelia's comments had only led to more questions about the puzzling Madeline Spencer.

Finally, Amelia pushed her dessert plate away.

"You enjoyed lunch?" He hoped his impatience didn't show.

"Yes. Thank you so much for including me, Your Highness."

"Dominic. And it was my pleasure."

Her cheeks flushed. "Dominic."

He should be polite and linger over coffee, but he had lost

ground to recover and a limited time in which to do so. He stood. "Ian, please escort Mademoiselle Lambert to her suite."

Madeline shoved back her chair and rose. "I'm going, too."

Dominic caught her wrist and held firmly when she tried to pull away. Her pulse quickened beneath his fingers. "You and I have unfinished business to discuss."

She made no attempt to conceal her displeasure as she plopped back into her chair, forcing him to release her. She picked up her fork and stabbed it viciously into her dessert. No doubt she'd rather plant the tines in him.

Looking between him, Madeline and Ian, Amelia hesitated. Dominic suspected she'd stay with the slightest encouragement from her friend, but Madeline waved her away. "It's okay. I'll be right there."

Moments later the door closed behind Ian and Amelia. Dominic refilled Madeline's wineglass and then his own. "How long did your engagement last?"

"None of your business." She shoved a bite of confection between her lips and the urge to taste it on her tongue swelled within him. Normally he didn't care for sweets, but licking the rich cream from Madeline's skin appealed. Immeasurably.

"Shall I call back your friend? She seemed quite willing to provide information."

"And you were not in the least bit subtle in prying my personal data out of her."

He couldn't stop a smile. "I don't think she noticed."

"*I* noticed."

"How long?"

She huffed out a breath and pushed away her plate. "Six years."

"Six *years?*" What man could possibly allow such an eternity to pass without claiming Madeline as his own? He and Giselle had waited three years, but that was because Giselle had been too young when their engagement began. "Your fiancé had commitment issues?"

"Aren't you a smart guy to figure that out so quickly. It took me a lot longer."

"So you once believed in love? And now you don't."

"Nice analysis, Dr. Freud. Can I go now?"

"How did you make the transition?"

She blinked. "Huh?"

"How did you make yourself accept the idea of a life without a connection or bond with someone who actually gives a damn about you?"

Her lips parted and her eyes widened. "Holy moly. You're a romantic."

He debated telling her about the sterile selection process underway at home, but what point would that serve? It certainly wouldn't aid his cause in getting Madeline back into his bed and stockpiling his need for passion before he commenced a life without it. And since their relationship was temporary, what happened in Montagnarde would not affect her.

"I am tired of one-night stands. I wish to have someone share my bed for reasons other than duty, greed or fleeting attraction."

"Why bother? You'll just get disappointed in the end."

"My parents have been married for almost forty years and each of my sisters for nearly a decade. Their marriages are strong and happy."

"For now." She grabbed her wine and took a healthy sip. "My parents were married for thirty-five years before my father walked out."

The pain and sadness in her eyes tightened his chest. "Why did he leave?"

She rose. "Does it matter?"

"Apparently it matters to you. I've heard children often blame themselves for their parents' divorce."

"There you go again. Practicing psychology without a license. Don't they have laws against that in Monaco?"

But the sudden rigidity of her posture told him he'd hit a nerve. "Do you blame yourself?"

"Of course not," she replied too quickly. "I was only ten."

He captured her chin, lifted her face until she met his gaze, and repeated, "Do you blame yourself?"

She glared at him for a full thirty seconds before her lids lowered and her shoulders sagged on a sigh. "They were married twenty-five years before I came along. A menopause surprise baby. So yes, for most of my life I wondered if my arrival had upset the balance."

She shook off his hand, and hugging herself, moved to the window. "After my father died I finally found the courage to ask my mother what really happened. According to her they split because of indifference. They just fell out of love. Neither cared enough about the other to fight for their marriage, but they fought about anything and everything else. I was actually relieved when Daddy moved out and the shouting stopped."

She was tough, a fighter, and yet at the moment she seemed fragile and lost. Struggling with the urge to take her in his arms, for he doubted she would welcome his comforting embrace, Dominic joined her by the glass.

"Did you feel the same indifference for your lover?"

"What!" She pivoted to face him with her mouth agape.

"You did not love him enough to push forward with your wedding plans, and yet you did not dislike him enough to end your engagement. It appears he suffered the same indifference." He shrugged. "I would not wish for such a passionless relationship."

"It wasn't passionless," she said through clenched teeth.

"No? Did you not say last night that you had never had so many orgasms in one night nor found such pleasure? Tell me, Madeline, did you hunger for his touch the way you do for mine?"

A white line formed around her flattened lips and her face turned red. "My relationship with Mike is none of your business."

"I have heard most women choose men like their fathers."

The color drained from her cheeks and she actually staggered back a step. "What does that have to do with us? Because you sure as heck aren't looking for anything long-term with me."

He'd be damned if he knew why understanding Madeline Spencer was so important when she would be gone from his life in a matter of days. "No. As I have said before, I regret that here and now is all I can offer you."

And for some reason that left him feeling more dissatisfied and trapped by his life than he had in a very long time.

Six

Madeline stumbled midjog Tuesday morning when she saw her face on the cover of a tabloid paper.

She jerked to a halt on the cushioned running track along Boulevard du Larvotto and stared in dismay at the newsstand rack. Not one, but two papers carried photos of her and Dominic on their covers. She moved closer to examine the pictures of the two of them leaving the boat. With her hair tucked beneath her hat, her sunglasses covering part of her face and her profile angled away from the cameras, only her mother and closest friends would recognize her beside Dominic, who looked tall and commanding and royal.

Boy, had she misread him.

The captions were in French...or maybe Italian. She had no idea what they said. She reached into her shorts pocket for the euros she'd brought along to buy a bottle of water at the end of her run and picked up a copy of each paper. Her hands shook as she paid the man at the newsstand and accepted her change.

Hopefully Candace or Stacy would be able to translate. But were they awake yet? Despite their late nights here in Monaco, Madeline couldn't seem to break her wake-at-dawn habit.

With her plan to burn off the surplus of calories she'd consumed recently with a long morning run derailed, she rolled the papers into a baton and jogged back to the hotel. She let herself into the suite. Silence greeted her. None of her suite-mates were awake. But she couldn't wait. She had to know what the articles said now.

So much for avoiding His Royal Hemorrhoid today by ducking out of the hotel early.

Returning to the hall she marched the length of the plushly carpeted corridor to Dominic's door and mashed the doorbell long and hard. He'd gotten her into this mess. It would serve him right if she woke him.

The door opened. "Good morning, Ian. Where is he?"

She tried to enter, but Ian's bulk blocked her way. "Prince Dominic is unavailable."

"Make him available."

The burly chest swelled. "Mademoiselle—"

"Let her in," Dominic's deep voice called from inside.

Five heartbeats later Ian stepped aside. Could he be a little more obvious that he didn't want her here? Madeline plowed past him only to jerk to a halt at the sight of a black-robe-clad Dominic sitting at the table with coffee and a newspaper. The silky fabric gaped as he rose, revealing a wedge of tanned chest dusted in golden curls. Below the loosely tied belt his legs and feet were bare.

Was he naked under there?

Get over it. You've already seen him naked and you see naked men at work every day.

With no small effort she pried her gaze upward. Burnished stubble covered the lower half of his face. His hair was mussed and his pale eyes curious. Her mouth dried and her pulse quickened. Clearly her body had not received the message from her brain that she was totally and completely over him and that there would be no more nookie.

"Good morning, Madeline. You are eager for my company today. That bodes well for our time together."

The devil it did. Her hands fisted. Paper crinkled, reminding her why she'd come. *The tabloids.* She crossed the room, thrust them at him and then after he took them, she retreated to the opposite end of the table.

His gaze traveled from her hastily braided hair to her chest in a snug tank top and breast-flattening jog bra and then down her bare legs to her running shoes. She'd dressed the way she always did for a workout, but suddenly she became uncomfortable with her skimpy attire and lack of makeup. Maybe she should have changed before coming here.

No. You are not trying to attract him anymore.

Tugging at the hem of her very short shorts, she cleared her throat. "What do they say?"

He unrolled the papers, scanned one and then the other, his lips compressing more with each passing second, and then his gaze returned to hers. "Our affair has become public knowledge. The good news is they haven't printed your name which means they don't know it yet. There is only speculation as to whom I'm seeing."

"But what do they say *exactly?*"

His frown deepened. He gestured to first one tabloid and

then the other. "The Prince's Paramour and The Prince's Playmate. Shall I translate the articles for you?"

"No." Her stomach churned. Why had she insisted on knowing what the tabloids said? Because she'd never bought into the ignorance is bliss theory—especially since Mike. But suddenly she wished she did. Gulping down rising panic she asked, "Why would anyone care about me? I'm a nobody."

"When you became a prince's lover you became a person of interest."

She felt as if she'd swallowed a gallon of seawater. A little queasy. A *lot* uncomfortable. "I did not sign on for that."

"Would you like coffee?" He gestured to the tray on the table. A second cup already had coffee in it. A third remained empty. She glanced at the frowning, dark-suited Ian. Was he more than an employee? And what about the missing Makos? Was the third cup for him?

Who cares? This is all about you, remember? Your mistake. Your humiliation. Your fraying credibility.

She turned back to Dominic. "I don't want coffee. I want to be left alone. By the paparazzi. And by you. I have things to do and places to see and a reputation to protect."

"Too late, I'm afraid. I will arrange for someone to guard you, but until he is in place you might wish to avoid crowded tourist attractions or risk being cornered by the paparazzi."

Guard her? Oh, please. "*Hello.* I am a tourist. I want to see the sights. I still haven't found a gift for my mother, so I *will* see them. And I don't want anyone shadowing me." She tugged at her braid. "What can we do?"

One shoulder lifted in a shrug. "Ride it out."

How could he be so laid-back? "I don't want to be branded as your mistress in the papers."

"I would have preferred to avoid it, as well, but what's done is done."

"Fix it, Dominic. Make them print a retraction or something."

"Demanding a retraction would only draw more interest. I am sorry, Madeline. We will do what we can to conceal your identity from the press so you will not be bothered once you return home, but I can offer no guarantees."

She groaned and a heavy weight settled on her chest. This could *not* follow her back to Charlotte. The whispers, abruptly stalled conversations and questions about her judgment had barely stopped from the Mike debacle.

"Your Highness, we could return to Montagnarde," Ian suggested.

Madeline's muscles tensed. Why? She wanted to be rid of Dominic. Didn't she?

She turned on Ian. "You called him Damon on the boat. Why get prissy now?"

When Ian remained silent Dominic explained, "That was before you knew my identity. Ian is a stickler for protocol in public."

"One, I have slept with you, so I'm not 'the public.'" She marked the words with quotation marks in the air. "Two, if he hadn't called the cops then we would not be having this conversation."

Dominic flung the papers on the table and closed the gap between them in three long strides, stopping so close she could smell his unique scent, feel the heat radiating from his body and see each individual blade of morning beard on his jaw and upper lip.

"Three," he continued, "if I had not misled you then four, you would not have threatened me, and Ian would not have called the police. We come full circle. Protecting me is his job.

We all share the blame, but the lion's share is mine because I am the one who began the masquerade."

Good point. And as much as she hated to admit it, Dominic's willingness to accept part of the blame surprised and impressed her. She was used to guys who shucked responsibility for their mistakes whenever possible. For example, the way Mike had blamed her for his cheating.

She pressed her fingertips to her temple. This was not turning out to be a good day. "What are our options?"

He caught her hand and carried her fingers to his lips. A shock wave of awareness swept over her before she snatched her hand away. "We could remain sequestered in my suite for the remainder of your stay in Monaco."

Temptation swamped her. It took a second to force her lungs to fill and oxygenate her brain enough for reason to return. "Not going to happen. I didn't come to Monaco to hide out in a hotel. And since I may never get back to Europe I plan to see some of it—which is why I wanted a tour guide."

"Then we will keep as low a profile as possible and continue as we had originally planned once additional staff is in place."

"Is that doable?"

"It is the way I live my life. Being watched or followed is unavoidable. In the future you might wish to consider that before venturing out alone, and I would suggest you not sunbathe topless unless you want the paparazzi to enjoy your beautiful breasts as much as I do."

His compliment was lost in a tidal wave of heart-sinking, skin-prickling panic. She hugged her arms across her chest. Had anyone been watching her this morning? What about yesterday when she'd sneaked out of the hotel at the crack of dawn and hidden out in a cybercafe until she could tour the

Monaco Porcelain Factory? Had someone been watching last night when she'd returned to the hotel and been immediately whisked up to Dominic's suite by Makos? The thought gave her the creeps.

"Join me for breakfast, Madeline."

The way he voiced the invitation, low and husky and intimate, caused her pulse to spike despite her concerns.

Good grief. Haven't you learned anything?

"I have to get back for Candace's morning meeting and to get the details of some ball thing from Stacy."

The doorbell chimed. His long fingers curled around her upper arm, infusing heat into her chilled muscles. "Come into my bedroom."

She tried and failed to yank free. "Have I been too subtle? I'm. Not. Interested."

"Breakfast has arrived. Would you prefer the server report that you were in my suite when I was not dressed?"

Ugh. "That kind of thing happens?"

"Yes. Hôtel Reynard is one of the best chains in the world for screening employees, but it is wise to be cautious."

"You mean paranoid." She shook off his hand and reluctantly accompanied him to the adjoining room. A king-size bed covered in tangled tan sheets dominated the space. The burgundy-and-gold paisley spread lay crumpled at the foot. They'd left the bed on the boat in a similar condition. Her body flushed hot and her clothing clung to her dampening skin.

Excuse me. You're over him. Remember?

He closed the door, leaned one shoulder against it and folded his arms over his chest. The move separated the fabric of his robe. "Tell me about the ball."

She forced her eyes away from the triangle of skin and the barely tied knot at his waist. "Not much to tell. I found a note from Stacy this morning saying there's going to be a ball Saturday night and that Franco is buying our gowns. That's all I know."

"Le Bal de L'Eté, a charity event which opens the season at the Monaco Sporting Club, is this weekend. Who is Franco?"

"Stacy's…friend." Her suitemate was having a passionate vacation fling, the kind Madeline had hoped to have, but—

"I don't like another man buying your dress."

"Tough." Through the door she heard the sounds of the room service cart being rolled into the dining area, the rattle of dishes and the low hum of voices, and then the cart leaving.

"I'll purchase your gown."

"And won't that look great in the tabloids? I'm no man's kept woman."

"And yet you would let this Franco pay for your dress."

She'd only met the sexy French chocolatier a couple of times, and normally she wouldn't let a stranger buy her clothing, but Franco only had eyes for Stacy. "He doesn't expect anything in return."

"You believe I would buy gifts for you to coerce you back into my bed?"

"We both know you want me there." And she was just as determined not to return. If he'd lied about one thing, he'd lie about another.

"Yes, I do. What's more, you want it, too."

Right.

Wrong! "That's quite a large ego you have there. Does Ian help you lug it around?"

Dominic's lips twitched and humor sparkled in his eyes. "I'll escort you to the ball."

"Oh yeah. That's being discreet. Forget it. I'm going with my suitemates. A girls' night out. And I plan to dance with every handsome man there." She cringed inwardly. That had sounded childish. But Dominic didn't own her and he'd better stop acting as if he did.

His nostrils flared and frustration thinned his lips. "You cannot evade me or the passion between us, Madeline."

"Watch me." Intent on a quick escape, she turned and reached for the doorknob.

In a flash his palm splayed on the door above her head, holding it shut. He leaned closer until the warmth of his chest against her back sandwiched her against the wooden panel. His breath stirred her hair seconds before his lips brushed her nape. Her lungs stalled and a shudder racked her. His morning beard rasped the juncture of her neck and shoulder, and then he traced a spine-tingling line down her backbone with one finger. Her senses rioted.

How can you still want him?

"You can't forget that night any more than I can," he whispered against her jaw.

The words scraped over her raw nerves and she swallowed hard. Almost every part of her being urged her to turn, wrap her arms around him, drag him to that rumpled bed and revel in the passion he offered. All she'd have to do is turn her head and their lips would touch.

The man's kisses could cause a nuclear meltdown.

But a lone brain cell reminded her of the hell she'd already lived through, of being made to look foolish and losing the respect of her coworkers and the uphill battle to regain it.

She squared her shoulders and tightened her fingers on the cool knob. "I might not have forgotten, but neither am I willing to become a topic of gossip again."

She yanked on the door. This time he let her go. "Be ready to leave for the shooting range as soon as your meeting ends."

She stopped halfway across the sitting room and pivoted to face him. "And if I'm not?"

"Have I ever mentioned Albert and I are well acquainted?"

Albert. Prince of Monaco. And he and Dominic were apparently on a first-name basis.

She was sunk.

"Hey, this isn't the way to the hotel," Madeline protested later Tuesday morning.

On the seat beside her in the hired car driven by Ian, Dominic angled to face her. His thigh touched hers. Touching meant sparks and sparks meant instant heat which she couldn't seem to control no matter how hard she tried. She inched away.

"You wished to purchase a gift for your mother."

Darn him for remembering that. "You could have asked if I wanted to go shopping."

He captured a dark curl, wound it around his index finger and tugged gently. She felt the pull deep inside. "You would have refused."

He had her there. But she'd just spent an hour matching him shot-for-shot at the shooting range and having more fun with their competition than she should have in the she'd-decided-to-hate-him circumstances. The man had a competitive streak that rivaled her own and a willpower-melting grin whenever he bested her. She needed a break from his magnetism.

"I also told you I'm having dinner with Candace at Maxim's tonight. So whatever you have planned had better be short and sweet."

"That's why we're taking a helicopter to Biot instead of driving."

A helicopter. She swallowed.

EMILIE ROSE 107

"I'm not crazy about helicopters." Not since a turbulent toss-her-cookies ride on a Life Flight chopper. Sure, she'd taken the helicopter taxi to Monaco from the Nice airport, but she'd been overexcited about being on foreign soil for the first time in her life and she'd had Dramamine in her system.

"I will be more than happy to distract you during the flight." His gaze dropped to her lips and her abdominal muscles contracted. She'd bet he would. She could guess how. But she wasn't kissing him again. Ever. Because his kisses sent her self-control AWOL.

"Would saying no make any difference?"

A smile teased his lips. "No. We'll land in time for lunch and then tour and shop. I'll have you back before dinner."

She sighed. It would serve him right if she barfed all over him. "Okay, you win."

"Always."

He really should try to rein in that cocky attitude. But darned if that smug smile didn't look good on him.

"What's so special about Biot?" she asked to distract herself as she reclaimed her hair. Each time he twined a curl around his finger she remembered the other things he liked to wrap it around and that wasn't good for her willpower.

"It's a small French village known for its pottery and hand-blown glass. Their earthenware production dates back to the Phoenicians, but since the 1960s Biot's bubble glass has gained international acclaim. My mother collects it. I thought yours might like it."

His mother. She didn't want to think about someone somewhere loving him. And she didn't want him to be thoughtful. He was a lot easier to dislike when he was arrogant, dictatorial and throwing his royal weight around. "You can force me to go with you, but you can't make me enjoy it."

"Have I mentioned how much I delight in your challenges?"

Five hours later Madeline stood in the shadows beneath a pointed archway of Biot's Place des Arcades and admitted she'd have to eat her words. Pleasantly tired and carrying a bag containing several carefully wrapped brightly colored pieces of bubble glass, she leaned against a sun-warmed stone wall and reluctantly looked up at Dominic.

He'd been an intelligent and amusing companion during this unwanted outing, and he'd taken her not to tourist traps, but to authentic out-of-the-way shops and a restaurant frequented by locals. His language and bargaining skills had been invaluable, and he wasn't exactly hard on the eyes. What more could a woman ask for in a date? If it hadn't been for his fib and his princeliness she could almost wish this idyllic period didn't have to end so soon.

"At the risk of inflating your already gargantuan ego, I have to confess, I enjoyed today. Lunch, the galleries, the museum...all of it."

"I'm glad." Dominic braced his shoulder on the wall beside her. He stood too close, but she couldn't seem to muster the energy to widen the gap between them.

He won points for not gloating.

They hadn't been bothered by paparazzi, and she'd only spotted Ian and Makos skulking in the background a few times. She hadn't even become ill on the helicopter flight because Dominic had applied acupressure to the inside of her wrist. A secret from the Montagnarde natives, he'd told her. Well, she'd studied acupressure, too, but she must have missed that chapter. Or maybe Dominic's touch had worked magic.

He slowly reached up and removed his sunglasses and then hers. Their gazes locked and held. The smile in his eyes faded and his pupils dilated with desire. Her pulse quickened and her mouth dried. After warning her to be on the lookout for paparazzi, surely he wouldn't—

His mouth covered hers. Tenderly. Briefly. Before she could react he swooped in again, cradling her jaw in his palm and settling in for a deeper taste. His tongue parted her lips and tangled with hers.

Need coiled tightly inside her, sending heat spiraling from her core to her limbs. She shouldn't be kissing him, shouldn't be savoring the hint of coffee on his tongue or the scent of his cologne. She shouldn't be curling her fingers into the rigid muscles of his waist or leaning into the warmth of his chest.

You definitely shouldn't be considering dragging him to the nearest inn.

Where was her remarkable willpower, her vow to keep their lips forever separate? Turning her head aside, she broke the kiss and gasped for air. She craved the man more than she did carbohydrates when PMSing. And that was saying something.

She gathered her tattered resistance and backed away. "We should go. I have to get ready for tonight."

And she had to brace herself for their next encounter, because she couldn't afford to let Dominic Rossi slip beneath her guard again.

Even if she could overlook his fib, a prince and a commoner had no future.

Not that she wanted one.

Seven

Time was running out.

Dominic snapped his cell phone closed Saturday night, shoved it in his tux pocket and inhaled deeply, but the constriction of his chest tightened instead of loosening.

"News?" Ian asked from beside him on the limo seat.

"The list of bridal candidates has been narrowed to three." Which meant Dominic's days of passion and freedom were numbered. He had to get Madeline back into his bed.

"This is not unexpected, Dominic."

That didn't mean he had to like it. "No."

"Perhaps your outings with Miss Spencer have spurred the council to make a decision."

"We have been discreet." As much as he hated sneaking in and out of back doors and service entrances, he'd willingly done so to spend time with Madeline. But this week she'd avoided all but the most casual of touches.

"The council won't give you the women's names?" Ian asked.

"No. They don't want me to interfere with the selection process." The council would make the decision, negotiate the diplomatic agreements, and then he would meet the woman and propose for formality's sake. The way it had been done for three centuries.

The car stopped in front of the Monaco Sporting Club. Ian climbed out first. Dominic remained seated. He didn't want to waste an evening rehashing the same shallow conversations or battling the predatory females whom he could not afford to offend. He would prefer to be alone in his suite—in his bed—with Madeline. But Madeline would be here, and her vow to dance with every male present chafed like an over-starched shirt. Absurd since once his bride-to-be was chosen he would have no claim on Madeline. He would tell her goodbye and immediately fly off to fulfill his duty to his country and his promise to his father to continue the tradition and the monarchy of Montagnarde.

The weight of his obligations had never weighed as heavily on his shoulders as it did now.

Ian's face appeared in the open door. "Your Highness?"

Dominic climbed from the car and entered the gala. The upper echelons of European society were out in full force at the charity ball. These were the very people he needed to court and attract to Montagnarde. At the moment he couldn't care less. He scanned the crowd, searching for Madeline, but didn't see her. An acquaintance greeted him. Dominic forced a smile and commenced his job as businessman and ambassador for his country.

But as he worked the room, politely fending off unwanted advances, some subtle, some not, he wondered if his future bride was among the women in attendance tonight, for this was very likely the pool from which she would be chosen. He found the prospect unappealing since none of the women attending the ball attracted him in the least.

Three-quarters of an hour later movement at the entrance drew his attention. Madeline and her suitemates had arrived. Urgency made his heart pump harder.

Madeline had pulled her dark hair up, leaving her shoulders bare. Her drop-dead sexy black dress molded itself to the curves of her exquisite figure. When she stepped forward a slit opened almost to the curls concealing her sex to reveal one sleek, tanned leg. She turned as a dark-haired man claimed the woman beside her, and Dominic stifled a groan. Other than straps encircling her shoulders in a figure eight, the back of her dress left the smooth line of her spine completely bare to just above the crease of her bottom.

Beautiful, seductive Madeline. He had to have her. Tonight.

"Prince Dominic," a high-pitched voice said nearby.

He blinked and looked back at the woman whose red talons gripped the sleeve of his tuxedo jacket. He couldn't recall her name. "Yes?"

"I asked if you'd like to see me home tonight." She followed the words with an inviting pout and a flutter of false eyelashes which did nothing for him.

"I am honored, mademoiselle, but I must decline. I have a previous engagement. Excuse me." He bowed and made his way toward Madeline only to be delayed again and again. His frustration grew. He had to reach Madeline before another man claimed her.

She was his.

For now. And he would have his fill of her before his desolate future consumed him.

* * *

How hard could it be to *not* kiss a guy? Madeline silently fumed as she stood near the entrance of the exclusive La Salle Des Étoiles.

She "not kissed" guys every day. Dozens of them. Coworkers, patients, paramedics, her letter carrier, for Pete's sake. So what was the big deal about not kissing one more? But that was her goal.

She'd succeeded Monday night, thanks to dinner with Dominic being interrupted by an urgent call from the palace which he'd had to take.

She'd blown it Tuesday in Biot, but she'd managed to keep her lips from straying on Wednesday when he'd surprised her with a behind-the-scenes tour of the Prince's Palace, including rooms not open to the general public. She'd stuck to her guns again on Thursday because Candace and Amelia—bless 'em—had run interference by accompanying her on the visit Dominic had arranged to Princess Grace Hospital. Afterward, her suitemates had dragged her out for a night at the theater sans Dominic.

But resisting him hadn't been easy. Each day his hungry gaze had gobbled her up bite by bite, leaving her more than a little ravenous and close to bingeing on the taste, scent and feel of him.

Thank God for Friday when she'd had the good fortune to avoid Dominic completely. She hadn't been hiding *exactly*. She'd kept herself busy away from the hotel by shopping and doing wedding minutiae with her suitemates from breakfast until bedtime.

She'd been so happy to evade temptation that she hadn't even minded the reminders of her own aborted engagement. In fact, she'd barely thought of Mike, the mistake. But that was because another man had planted his flag in her subconscious and claimed her thoughts. Damn Dominic Rossi for that.

Her gaze collided with Dominic's across the haute couture and jewel-encrusted crowd of Le Bal de L'Eté and her breath caught. Speak of the devil. Her luck had apparently run out.

With his regal bearing, aristocratic bone structure and wealth of confidence, no one looking at him now would ever doubt his royal lineage. The man commanded attention without even trying, and he turned wearing a tux into an art form.

A blonde so thin the wind could blow her away stood beside him with a rapt expression on her immobile Botox-filled face. He flashed a smile at her, said a few words then broke free and headed in Madeline's direction only to be side-lined by a squinty redhead and then a big-toothed brunette whose invitation to dance horizontally as well as vertically was obvious from clear across the room.

Madeline gritted her teeth and turned her back on the prince and his fawning females. She was not jealous. Nope. Not her. He could do the mattress merengue with every other woman in the room for all she cared.

"See anybody you recognize?" she asked wide-eyed Amelia. If there was a celebrity or royal in attendance, Amelia would be able to name him or her.

"Are you kidding? This place is a who's who smorgasbord. And I'm sorry to say, that includes Toby Haynes. I cannot believe Vincent sent that race car Casanova to babysit us."

"Vincent meant well, and Toby is his best man." Vincent had been working overseas, but moments ago he'd surprised Candace by arriving at the ball unexpectedly. He'd quickly swept his bride-to-be onto the dance floor where the two gazed at each other with so much love in their eyes it made Madeline uneasy. She'd once believed herself that much in love, and how she'd survived the aftermath was still a mystery. She could guarantee she'd never let herself care like that again.

"He should know we're old enough to stay out of trouble."

Amelia's comment made Madeline shift guiltily in her stiletto heels. The edges of her heavy black sequined dress abraded her skin. She hadn't managed to stay out of trouble, but she'd neglected to fill her suitemates in on the embarrassing details. Amelia knew nothing more than what Dominic had told her—that Madeline had threatened him. Her friend didn't know the threat involved an actual knife against his princely throat or firing a gun over his royal head.

Madeline followed Amelia's disgusted gaze toward the NASCAR driver who'd been a thorn in her friend's side since their first day in Monaco. Thanks to Candace's misguided matchmaking attempts, Madeline had dated Toby a couple of times back in Charlotte. She'd quickly labeled him a player and lost interest. The attraction—or lack thereof—was mutual.

Toby was a nice enough guy and definitely good-looking, but as far as she could tell he was serious about racing and little else. Amelia, on the other hand, had taken an intense dislike to Toby during Vincent's hospital stay last year when Toby had been a frequent visitor to the burn unit. No amount of prying—subtle or otherwise—on Madeline's part had uncovered the reason for the tension between those two.

"Do you see those women drooling over him?" Amelia grumbled. Amelia was the most easygoing woman Madeline had ever met, and seeing her friend bristle and hiss like an angry cat was totally out of character. There had to be a reason.

The back of Madeline's neck prickled, and it had nothing to do with Toby spotting them and extracting himself from the women clustered around him to head in their direction. "What is it with these chicks and their sycophantic admiration? Do they have no pride? And don't even get me started on how these guys are sucking up the adulation as if it's their due."

"Good evening, Amelia, Madeline." Dominic's baritone behind her confirmed the reason for her uneasiness. Her bones turned soupy. She cursed her wilting willpower. So much for her plan to avoid the man who had the power to kiss her right out of her clothes.

"Dominic, Amelia would like to dance," she said as she turned. She tried to keep her gaze on his blue eyes, but she couldn't help soaking up the breadth of his shoulders.

"Madeline!" Amelia protested.

"It's either Dominic or Toby. Take your pick." Madeline indicated the approaching driver with a tilt of her head.

Amelia's eyes widened with panic. She looked beseechingly at Dominic and even curtsied. "I would love to dance, Your Highness."

With a polite smile Dominic inclined his head and offered Amelia his arm. "Dominic, please. I would be delighted, Amelia."

But his eyes promised Madeline retribution as he led her friend away.

Ha! He couldn't get even if he couldn't catch her. She'd make a point of dancing in the arms of other men all night—even if she had to ask them herself. She'd chosen a dress which guaranteed their answers would always be yes.

Toby reached Madeline's side moments later. His appreciative gaze zipped from her upswept hair down her black form-fitting dress to her silver sandals before he met her gaze. "If your goal is to bring these European guys to their knees, I'll bet my new engine you'll succeed. You look good enough to make me reconsider making a run for you myself, Madeline."

A girl—this one anyway—liked to have her ego stroked even

if she suspected the compliment generated from habit rather than genuine interest. "Thanks, Toby. You look sharp, too."

Toby Haynes might be blond-haired and blue-eyed and of a similar height and athletic build to Dominic, but that's where the likeness ended. Even though both men wore what were probably custom-tailored tuxes, Toby had rough edges aplenty whereas Dominic was smooth, polished perfection. But Toby didn't trip her hormonal switches. Dominic, regrettably, did.

"Who's the stiff?"

She didn't pretend not to understand Toby's question. How could she, since his eyes practically shot fire toward the man in question? "Prince Dominic Rossi of Montagnarde."

"Montag—what? Never heard of the place. Must not have a race track."

Nice to know she wasn't the only geographically challenged one present. "Montagnarde. It's a country somewhere between Hawaii and New Zealand."

"Wanna dance?"

Not the smoothest invitation she'd ever had, but it beat standing near the entrance like a wallflower. "Sure. Why not?"

Toby led her onto the floor and swept her into the flow of other dancers with skill she wouldn't have expected from a car jockey. "You're pretty light on your feet."

He grimaced. "Comes with the territory. For the most part NASCAR drivers only drive two days a week. Qualifying and race day. The rest of the time we're on the road schmoozing for the sponsors. Reynard Hotels loves swanky parties like this."

And Vincent Reynard's hotel chain sponsored Toby's racing team. "You don't?"

"Depends on the reason I'm there." He drew alongside Amelia and Dominic. "Hey, buddy, switch?"

Madeline's insides snarled. She should have known a competitive guy like Toby would have an agenda. But it was too late to escape the man she'd hoped to avoid.

Dominic stopped and released Amelia. "Certainly. Thank you for the dance, Amelia."

He bowed slightly.

Darn, she liked that stupid little bow.

Toby whisked her none-too-happy friend away.

Madeline stood in the middle of the floor and met Dominic's gaze while the other guests drifted past them. "I don't want to dance with you."

"The floor is the best place for us unless you are ready to leave." Dominic's hand captured hers. The only way to escape his unbreakable grip was to cause a scene—not part of the plan if she wanted to avoid more publicity.

"Are you kidding me? I just got here."

He pulled her into the circle of his arms and spread his palm on her naked back just above her buttocks. Her pulse tripped. She hoped her feet wouldn't embarrass her by doing likewise.

She searched for a distraction from the heat of his hand on her skin and tried to ignore the slide of his thighs against hers as he guided her across the floor. "Where's the towering twosome? Did you check your bodyguards at the door?"

"Ian and Makos remained outside as did Fernand."

"Who is Fernand?"

"Your protection."

She stumbled then and fell into his broad chest. His arm banded around her waist, welding her to the hot, hard length of his torso and keeping her there. He continued dancing without missing an orchestral beat. "My what?"

"You have had security since Wednesday."

"You've had someone following me?" The erotic rasp of

his tuxedo jacket sleeve against her back tightened her throat, making her words come out in a husky whisper.

"I told you I would."

"Yes, but…" She rewound the reel of events in her head. Had she done anything she wouldn't want reported back to Dominic? Because she'd bet his spy guy was doing exactly that. "I haven't seen him."

"You weren't supposed to." His smooth-shaven chin brushed her temple as he executed a series of quick turns that required her to cling to him or fall on her face. Ballroom dancing had never been her thing, but she had to admit following his lead was easier than expected. Good thing, since sprawling on the floor given her attire, or lack thereof, would be humiliating.

"Why do I need a shadow?"

"There are those who might believe that because you're my lover—"

Stumble. "I'm not anymore."

"—you might be a valuable negotiating piece," he continued as if she hadn't interrupted.

Fear crept up her spine like a big, hairy spider. She leaned back to look into his eyes. Unfortunately, that pressed their hips together. "I'm in danger because I slept with you?"

"Probably not. As you pointed out, Montagnarde is off the radar for most, but I prefer to be proactive rather than reactive. And while you are mine I will protect you."

The possessive words made her skin tingle. And then she remembered to object. "I. Am. Not. Yours."

The hand on her back lifted, giving her a momentary reprieve and an opportunity to fill her wheezy lungs, but then Dominic traced the edge of her dress from her shoulder to the base of her spine. The tips of his fingers slid just beneath the fabric and his short nails raked lightly across the top of her cheeks. She shivered, cursed her traitorous hormones and sent out a mental SOS to her willpower. Wherever it might be.

"You look lovely tonight. Very sexy. Come back to my suite with me, Madeline," his deep voice rumbled in her ear.

Stumble. He caught her even closer—something she would not have believed physically possible five seconds ago. Even through the heavy chain mail weight of her dress she could feel his thickening arousal against her belly. Flames of desire flickered through her and her resistance softened like warm candle wax. She was so close to melting it wasn't even funny.

But the man had broken rule number one. He'd lied to her.

And still…she wanted him. Shamelessly.

Girl, you are absolutely pitiful.

But she couldn't help remembering how good it had been between them, how amazingly wonderful he'd made her feel or how he listened to every word as if she were going to utter the secret to world peace in her next sentence.

You are in serious trouble.

"Get me off this floor," she said through clenched teeth.

"Or else what?" A smile played on his lips as he pulled her into another series of complicated make-her-cling-to-him steps. "You'll pull a weapon? Because I don't see where you could possibly conceal one beneath that dress. It caresses your curves the way I want to."

Stumble. Help. She could not argue and concentrate on fancy footwork at the same time. She planted her feet, shoved his rock-hard chest and yanked free of his hold. "Do you really want to test me here and now, Dominic?"

Ignoring the curious stares of those around her, he held her gaze as if considering calling her bluff, but then inclined his head and led her toward the edge of the floor. They had barely stepped out of the crowd when a woman wearing a take-me-I'm-yours smile appeared in front of him.

"Bonsoir, Your Highness. Remember me?"

Dominic made introductions, but Madeline only half listened to the simpering blonde's chatter about past parties and people Madeline knew nothing about. She scanned the well-heeled guests looking for her suitemates and a possible rescue. She spotted Stacy and Franco and Vincent and Candace, but both couples were totally wrapped up in each other. There was no sign of Amelia and/or Toby.

"…come by my apartment later?" the blonde said.

Huh? Madeline blinked in disbelief and tuned back into the conversation. Had that she-cat just propositioned Dominic despite his hand planted firmly on Madeline's waist?

Hello! What am I? Invisible?

"Excuse us, Dominic was about to get me a glass of champagne." She grabbed his arm and urged him toward the bar and then jerked to a stop. *Argh. Is your brain on hiatus?* She'd wanted to escape him, and she'd just wasted a perfect opportunity. She should have let the she-cat have him.

So why didn't you?

She had a feeling she wouldn't like the answer.

"Thank you," he said.

Before she could tell him to take his gratitude and shove it, the catty incident replayed itself again and again and again. Different woman. Same pounce. Every three yards. Jeez, fighting off the felines was exhausting. Forget champagne. At the rate they were going she'd need an entire bottle of gin to wash down the fur balls by the time they reached the bar.

Patience deserted her and she yearned to scratch a few

overly made-up eyes out. While Dominic clearly did not enjoy or encourage the attention, he remained unfailingly polite each time. Most men would have been ecstatic to hear so many come-ons in a single evening, but not him. Why was that? Was his little black book already full? Or did he consider Madeline a sure thing?

She found the encounters pretty darn insulting since it meant these pedigreed felines didn't consider her competition, and she'd had enough.

"Excuse me. I guess you missed the fact that he's with me," she interrupted a woman about to spill from her rhinestone-studded collar—um, dress.

"Dominic, *dahling*," Madeline purred in a throaty voice similar to the ones his accosters had used, "I could use that double martini you promised me right about now."

Laughter lurked in his eyes as they said their goodbyes, and then Madeline nudged him not toward the bar but toward a quiet corner. "Is there some kind of contest to see who carries home the richest prize at the end of the evening?"

The first genuine smile she'd seen in an hour curved his lips. "You have discovered the secret."

"Is that why you wanted to stay on the dance floor? To avoid the stalking women?"

"An apt description."

"Why don't you just tell them to get lost?"

He glanced toward the gathering and then back at her. "I can't."

"Some princely code or something?" But she didn't wait for his answer. "If it's always like this, then why do you come to these things?"

"Usually I come because I want to entice their business to Montagnarde." His blue gaze held hers as he lifted her hand to his lips. "Tonight I came because I wanted to hold you in my arms."

Her knees weakened and the bottom dropped out of her stomach. The room seemed to fade until all that remained was him and the desire burning in his eyes. For her. In this room full of beautiful, elegant, worldly, predatory women, he wanted her.

"Good answer," she wheezed.

And why are you resisting?

She mentally smacked a palm against her forehead. She'd wanted a man to help her heal her fractured ego and rebuild her confidence. Dominic did that. He made her feel feminine and desirable. He gave her multiple-o's.

He'd reminded her more times than she could count that here and now was all they'd have. But that was okay. More than okay. A brief vacation fling was exactly what she wanted.

It wasn't as if she'd let herself fall in love or imagine marrying him. Just as well since Dominic, like Prince Charles, probably had to marry a virgin. And she wasn't one. Not even close.

Between tonight, the incident with the paparazzi and having to sneak in and out back doors all week she could even understand Dominic's motivation for concealing his identity. But he was selling himself short if he truly believed these women wanted him only for his title and fortune. Dominic Rossi, Prince of Montagnarde, was a gorgeous piece of work, and every time she looked at him she recalled the perfection of his naked body and the way he made her body sing.

She'd bet the drooling females wanted a chance to do the same. Knowing she knew something the other more sophisticated women didn't made her feel just a teensy bit superior.

And you're wasting time here when you could be getting your hands on all that perfection.

Her pulse quickened and her mouth dried. She tightened her fingers around his. "Get me out of here, Prince, and you can hold me in your arms without a ten-pound dress between us."

The flash of heat in his eyes nearly consumed her on the spot. "As you wish."

Eight

Apparently the wealthy didn't wait for cabs or even valet service.

Within seconds of her shameless declaration Dominic had hustled her out of the gala and into a waiting limo which he'd summoned with one touch on his cell phone. She chose the bench seat facing the limo's rear window.

Dominic joined her instead of sitting across from her. From shoulder to knee the hot length of his body pressed her side as hot and hard as an iron. The door closed, sealing them in darkness and near silence, and then the car pulled away from the club.

She risked a glance at him and found his jaw muscles knotted and his gaze burning into hers. Hunger stiffened every line of his body, inspiring a similar tension in hers.

She'd never wanted anyone this badly. Digging her fingers into her tiny beaded purse and hoping to slow her racing pulse, she focused on the passing lights of Monte Carlo outside the window as the driver carried them toward the hotel. No luck.

She squirmed impatiently, but the only thing her wiggling accomplished was to make the slit in her dress part, revealing her leg from ankle to hip. Before she could adjust the gaping skirt she heard Dominic's sharply indrawn breath, and then his hand covered her knee. Ever so slowly his warm palm glided upward, his fingertips slipping beneath the edge of the heavy, sequined fabric. Her insides clenched. She'd very likely leave a puddle of desire on the seat if she didn't stop him.

She slapped a hand over his and leaned toward him to whisper in his ear. "What are you doing? Ian and the driver are right behind us."

"The privacy screen is closed and the speaker turned off. They can see and hear nothing." His fingers inched higher and his masculine scent filled her lungs with each shaky breath. "You wish me to stop?"

"Yes. No. Yes. I…don't know." She struggled to bring order to her scrambled thoughts. "Do you, um…do this often?"

A short nail scraped back and forth along the top of her thigh, each pass drawing closer to the spot aching for his touch. "I have never made love in a limo."

"Me, neither." But she was tempted. Seriously tempted. She forced her heavy lids to remain open. "We're almost at the hotel."

"Then I'd better hurry." His hand rose another inch and he found her wetness with the tip of his finger. Their groans mingled. "You're not wearing panties."

"Dress. Too. Tight," she whispered brokenly as he circled her center bringing her closer and closer to the brink. How did he do that so quickly? Arousal made it difficult to think and tension made her tremble. She covered his hand with hers, intent on stopping his audacious behavior…in a minute. "Dominic—"

"Shh. Come for me, Madeline," he whispered hoarsely.

"H-here?" Their hotel was less than a block away and privacy screen or not, Ian and the driver were only inches away.

"Now. I want you so wet that I can be inside you the moment we reach the suite."

His throaty words and talented fingers sent her flying. Her back bowed and her tush lifted off the seat as wave after wave washed over her. She bit hard on her bottom lip and fought to remain silent as her pleasure went on and on and on. When it finally ended she leaned heavily against his side.

His breathing sounded as harsh as hers in the insulated passenger compartment and she hadn't even touched him. To anyone who happened to glance in the rearview mirror or through the tinted windows, they probably looked like any other couple riding home from a ritzy party. No one would guess she'd just crash-landed from a trip to the stars.

"Your turn." She spread her palm on his thigh, but he stopped her wandering hand by lacing his fingers through hers and carrying her hand to his lips.

"Hold that thought." The limo stopped outside Hôtel Reynard's back entrance. Her body seemed heavy, melded to the upholstery. Dominic released her hand and straightened the folds of her dress. He squeezed her thigh and then released her. "Ready?"

"Are you kidding me? I don't think I can walk."

His low chuckle aroused her all over again. His breath teased her bare shoulder a second before his teeth lightly grazed her skin. In her hypersensitive state the brief contact sent a bolt of lightning straight to her womb. "If I carry you inside we'll definitely draw unwanted attention. Shall I ask the driver to circle the block?"

She sucked air into her deprived lungs and grappled for sanity. "No. I can't wait that long to have you inside me."

Dominic's breath whistled through clenched teeth. "Nor I."

Dominic had had sex before. Hot, sweaty, animalistic sex. He'd even had sex with Madeline. But he'd never been as close to saying to hell with propriety and taking a woman regardless of their location. The limo. The elevator. The carpeted hallway outside his suite. He shook with need, and he couldn't remember the last time that had happened. Only Ian's scowling presence prevented him from taking action. Here. Now.

Madeline stood beside him in the hotel hallway without touching him. But her scent filled his lungs with every breath. Flowers. Lemon. *Sex.* He waited impatiently for Makos to do a security sweep of the suite. The moment the man gave the all's clear signal Dominic grabbed Madeline's hand and dragged her over the threshold, through the sitting room and into his bedroom. He shut the door in his bodyguards' faces, backed Madeline against the panel and slammed his mouth over hers.

She opened for him instantly, suckling his tongue and curling her fingers into his shoulders. She shoved at his tuxedo jacket and then tore at his tie and the buttons of his shirt without breaking the kiss. The garments landed on the floor behind him. With their lips still fused he raked his hands over the cool sequins of her dress searching feverishly but fruitlessly for the zipper. He gave up and tried to lift her skirt, but the fitted fabric clung stubbornly to her hips. He considered ripping it—this dress another man had bought—from her.

He wanted skin. Her skin. Against his. Now.

Madeline's nails scraped over him, drawing a line from his

Adam's apple to his navel, and then she palmed his erection through the fabric of his pants. Arousal detonated inside him. He released her mouth long enough to gasp, swear and demand, "Zipper."

"Here." She carried his hand across her breasts to her underarm. His fingers fumbled, found the tab, and tugged it to her hip. At a loss as to how to remove the seductive dress, he stepped back.

"Over my head."

He fisted the fabric, uncaring if he damaged it. He'd buy her another. A dozen. The weight of the garment surprised him. The moment the hem cleared her head he twisted and tossed it on a nearby chair. And then he turned back to Madeline and his heart slammed into his ribs like an airplane hitting a mountainside. He staggered back a step, two. His jaw went slack.

Naked, save a pair of silver high heels sharp enough to be classified as lethal weapons, she lifted her arms to pull pins from her hair. His lungs seized. He'd never seen a more seductive sight than Madeline, with her back arched and her breasts offered like a banquet. She stood with her long, lean legs slightly parted. Moisture glistened in the dark curls between her legs—moisture he'd created.

And he was about to lose it like a teenage boy.

He snapped his jaw closed and swallowed once, twice. But it did nothing to ease the constriction in his throat or the tightness in his chest. Need, painful in its intensity, clawed through him. One by one, long, dark ringlets fell over her shoulders as she released her hair, concealing her tightened nipples from his view. A criminal offense.

He captured a silky coil and painted a pattern over her puckered flesh and then brushed her hair aside to cup and caress her warm, satiny skin. Her breasts filled his hands, the nipples prodding his palms. He rolled the tips between his fingers until she whimpered and leaned against the door.

"Please, Dominic, don't make me wait." She reached for the waistband of his trousers.

He kissed her again, relishing the sharp bite of desire and the hunger fisting in his gut beneath her tormenting fingers. The moment she shoved his pants over his hips and curled her fingers around him he lifted her leg to his waist with one hand, cupped her bottom with the other and drove into her welcoming wetness. Her body clenched around him and her cries of pleasure filled his ears. He thrust again and again and again. More. Deeper. Harder. Faster. The heel of her shoe stabbed his buttocks. That little jab had to be the most erotic thing he'd ever felt.

Pressure built. He fought to hold on until her nails bit into his shoulders and she tore her mouth away from his to gasp his name. She shuddered in his arms and her internal muscles contracted. He could no more stop his own release than he could dam a volcano. His passion erupted, pulsing through him in mind-melting bursts. He muffled his groans against her warm, fragrant throat, and then sapped and sated, he fell against her.

When he recovered an ounce of strength, he braced his forearms on the door beside her head and lifted his sweat-dampened body scant inches from her torso. The arms she'd looped around his neck kept him close—not that he intended going anywhere. He stared into her beautiful face. A smile curved her moist, swollen lips, and her lashes cast dark crescents on her flushed cheeks. He absorbed the image, imprinting it on his brain to drag out during the long barren years ahead.

Two more weeks won't be enough.

It must be.

Madeline deserved more than to be a prince's paramour. She deserved a man who would look past her prickly exterior to the soft heart she fought so hard to protect. She'd once believed in love, and the right man would make her believe again. But that man wasn't him, for no matter how empty his marriage might be he would abide by his vows and his duty to his country.

Chilling arrows of regret pierced him. Madeline deserved to be happy. Even if he couldn't be.

"Wow." Her lids fluttered open and her satisfied gaze met his. And then noting his expression, she stiffened and pleasure drained from her face. She pushed against his chest and uncoiled her leg from his hip. "What's wrong?"

He slipped from her body and then it hit him. "We didn't use protection."

His pulse kicked erratically. With hope? Of course not. His fate was sealed and he'd accepted it.

But what if he, like Albert of Monaco, fathered a child out of wedlock? Would paternity and a potential heir excuse him from an arranged marriage? No. Tradition and the council demanded a bride of royal lineage. A pedigreed princess.

But a child would tie him to Madeline and give him an excuse to see her in the future even if he could not continue the affair.

She averted her face and wrapped her arms around her waist. "I'm on the Pill. So we're in the clear unless you lied about your health."

Why didn't that revelation fill him with relief? And why did the reminder of his dishonesty still sting? He'd had good reason for his deception, hadn't he?

No. If he'd learned anything from this it was that there was never a good reason for deceit. He would have to tell Madeline about his impending marriage. She deserved to know why he must let her go—this woman who'd brightened his days. But not now. When he said goodbye would be soon enough.

"I'm clean." He'd been poked and prodded, examined from top to bottom, inside and out, by the royal physicians. His health records would be provided for perusal to the family of the woman the council chose as his bride.

They could examine his vital statistics as they would a prize stallion. And like a stud for hire, he'd have no say over his mate. His obligation to provide heirs to the throne was a burden. Or was it a curse?

Madeline Spencer, jet-setter. Who would have believed it?

Madeline stared at the man standing beside her in the noonday sun in the tiny seaside town of Ventimiglia, Italy. She tried not to drool as sexy Italian words rolled off his tongue. Her tour guide extraordinaire and lover *magnifique*. Dominic.

He switched languages as easily as blinking whereas she'd struggled to pick up the necessary French phrases he'd taught her. He was probably discussing something as mundane as the weather with the merchant, but whatever he said made her want to jump him despite having left his bed just hours earlier.

She hated creeping from his suite every morning at sunup to sneak back to her room, but that was a small price to pay to keep their affair private and her name out of the tabloids. Thus far it had worked. Beyond those first couple of pictures there hadn't been more.

Curling her fingers against the urge to trace the veins on the thickly muscled arm closest to her, she focused her attention on the gold jewelry for sale. She'd already bought necklaces for her mother and Amelia and earrings for Candace and

Stacy from another vendor. Dominic, bless him, had handled the haggling and she'd ended up paying far less than she would have in the States.

An intricately engraved wide cuff bracelet caught her eye. She picked it up, saw the price and quickly put it down.

"You like it?" he asked.

"It's beautiful, but even if you talked him down to a fraction of what he's asking it would still be too expensive."

"I'll buy it for you."

She caught his hand as he reached for his wallet and stared at her floppy-hat-wearing reflection in his dark lenses. "It's bad enough that you won't let me split expenses for our outings. I'm not letting you spend more."

His jaw set in the stubborn line she'd come to recognize whenever she tried to insist on paying her way. She hadn't won a single one of those arguments, and she knew better than to expect to win this one, so she changed the subject. "What were you and the vendor discussing?"

His lips compressed, letting her know he hadn't missed her attempt at distraction. He said a few more words to the merchant and then placed his palm against Madeline's spine and guided her away from the table. He glanced over his shoulder—checking to see if Ian and Fernand followed, she suspected. It would be easy to lose them in the market-day crowd—even with her brightly colored hat, which had been chosen specifically to make her easy to track.

"I asked about market conditions. What improvements could be made and which features were absolute requirements. Montagnarde has many craftsmen. A marketplace like this would be a desirable asset to my tourism plans."

"But first you have to get the rich to visit Montagnarde and hemorrhage money." Normal people plotted to buy or pay off their homes. Princes, apparently, dreamed on a bigger scale. One night as they'd lain in the dark after making love, Dominic had told her about his development plan and his determination to move forward despite the elder council's refusal to support him.

"What did your American movie say? 'If you build it they will come?' It's the trickle-down theory. Each tourist generates income for the working class by creating multiple service jobs. Attract the big spenders and everyone will benefit. My investors and I are already constructing luxury hotels on two of the three islands. I would be interested in speaking with Derek Reynard about his family's chain constructing a third."

"I can probably arrange a meeting with Mr. Reynard, but Vincent, his son, is the director of new business development. And since I'm one of Vincent's wedding party, I know I can hook you up with him."

"I accept your offer and promise to reward you handsomely." His wicked grin sent a heat wave tumbling through her.

Dominic would make a great king one day. It made no sense for her to be proud of him and his forward-thinking agenda to bring tourists and jobs to his country. What he did once he left Monaco *and her* behind was none of her business. But there was no denying the pride swelling in her chest.

A gentle sea breeze caressed her skin as they walked hand in hand along the narrow street. She scanned the postcard view of red-roofed homes clinging to the hillside like pastel-colored building blocks. Ventimiglia was a combination of ancient history and New World charm, and she would have missed it without Dominic.

She'd never been happier than she had in the week since the ball. She'd spent the greater part of each day with Dominic. He'd taught her to windsurf and shown her bits of France: the carnival atmosphere of the summer jazz festival in Juan Les Pins; Grasse, the perfume capital of the world; and the blooming lavender fields and craft galleries in Moustiers Ste. Marie. Today when she'd only had a few hours to spare between brides-maid's duties he'd surprised her with this jaunt to the Friday open-air market only twenty minutes from Monaco.

He thought nothing of day trips via helicopter or private jet, claiming the impromptu excursions to out-of-the-way places kept the paparazzi off their tails. She didn't want to tell him that she no longer needed to escape the wedding hoopla. Funny how the preparations didn't hurt anymore.

The only bacteria growing in the petri dish of Madeline's life was not knowing when Dominic would have to return to Montagnarde and when her time with him would end. He'd promised to show her Venice and Paris in the coming week— if he was still here. And that "if" kept her on a knife edge. Apparently, there was something pending in his country which required a nightly call from home—a call that left him increasingly tight-lipped and broodingly silent.

Madeline had learned a few techniques guaranteed to erase the frown from his face like the one currently deepening the worry lines on his forehead. She smiled and considered dragging him into an alley to distract him with one of those methods now, but a quick glance behind her revealed their bodyguards shadowing them.

Dominic lowered his sunglasses. His gaze found hers and the passion gleaming in his bedroom blue eyes made her steps falter. His fingers tightened around hers. "Do we need to take a siesta?"

Her heart skipped a beat. He read her so easily.

I could get used to this.

No, you can't. This is temporary and don't you forget it.

But there'd been a few times this week when a hint of yearning for more time with Dominic had slipped through her defenses. On each occasion she reminded herself that she no longer wanted forever with anyone. No more laying her heart on the line for some guy to trample. She'd abandoned dreams of children and a home in the suburbs the day Mike walked out.

Besides, Dominic was a prince, and even if she wanted more with him she couldn't have it.

"No can do. I have to get back for that thing with Candace's future in-laws."

His fingers stroked the inside of her wrist and her pulse quickened. "Too bad."

She didn't want to go to the dinner or the engagement party that followed and couldn't care less that the festivities would take place on the largest privately owned yacht in the world, which just happened to be docked in Monaco's harbor. Her reluctance had nothing to do with avoiding the reminders of her own aborted wedding and everything to do with not wanting to waste one moment of her remaining time with Dominic. "I could probably finagle an invitation for you."

He shook his head, adjusted the bill of his baseball cap and steered her away from a group of tourists studying him a little too intently. "The bride and groom should be the center of attention. You've seen what happens when I make an appearance."

She had and the surplus of kiss-up attitude nauseated her. But still, she didn't want to go without him.

Alarm skittered through her. Was she getting in too deep?

No. Dominic made her head spin in bed and out, but her growing attachment to him over the past three weeks could be blamed on the surreal circumstances of living the lifestyle of the rich and famous. Here she was a fish out of water. She clung to him because he made her feel as if she fit in and he smoothed her language difficulties. Once she was back in Charlotte and on familiar ground she wouldn't need him as a crutch or interpreter.

But she'd miss him.

Her heart beat faster and a peculiar emptiness spread through her like chilling fog. She was greedy for his company and she resented the interruptions. That's all it was.

She nibbled her lip as they approached the lot where they'd left the car. Maybe she should start weaning herself from him.

He leaned closer to murmur in her ear. "Come to my room after the party. Call my cell. No matter how late. I'll let you in."

Her mouth dried. "I was supposed to spend the night on the boat. Promise to make leaving worth my while?"

The glasses came off and his hungry gaze locked on hers. "I will make you beg for mercy."

And he could do it. Her breaths shortened and her skin dampened. The area between her legs tingled. "Deal."

Best-case scenario she had one more week with Dominic and wise or not, she intended to enjoy every second of it. Next Friday Candace and Vincent would have their civil ceremony followed by the church service on Saturday. Her friend would marry Vincent in the same church where Prince Rainier had shocked the world by marrying his commoner bride, Grace Kelly.

So royalty marrying a nobody could happen. It just wasn't going to happen to Madeline. And she was okay with that. Really.

She glanced at the man beside her and hoped she wasn't fooling herself, because on Sunday—only eight short days away—Madeline, Amelia and Stacy would fly back to the States. Madeline's days of living like a princess would be over, and soon all she'd have left were her memories of *Once upon a time in Monaco*.

Nine

"I thought you were known for speed," Madeline complained to Toby as she tried in vain to hurry him away from the yacht.

He'd graciously offered to walk her back to the hotel. No doubt when he'd made the suggestion he'd believed Amelia would be leaving with her. There was definitely something going on with those two, but her friend wasn't talking.

"I knew there was a reason we never slept together. You insult a guy's car before he even pulls it out of the garage," he replied in a teasing tone. He gripped her elbow and slowed her to his own leisurely pace. "Sweetheart, I always take it slow when it counts."

She snorted and rolled her eyes. "Oh please. Save the car jockey chatter for someone dumb enough to fall for it. You're lagging behind now, Haynes. Get the lead out."

He ignored her. She could have covered the next twenty yards of the jetty faster on her hands and knees. He must have sensed her impatience. "You have a hot date at midnight?"

Thinking of the night ahead, of hot embraces and even hotter kisses, Madeline's body heated. "I don't kiss and tell."

"Do your friends?"

The edge in his voice stopped her. "Should they? Because I swear, Toby, if you hurt Amelia—"

A darkly dressed figure separated itself from the shadows at the end of the jetty. Madeline's fight-or-flight response kicked in. She turned, ready to defend herself, but before she could act Toby hooked an arm around her waist and shoved her behind him so fast she almost fell off her four-inch heels. Her heart skipped for an altogether different reason when she recognized their "assailant."

Tension drained from her muscles. "Dominic. What are you doing here?"

"Waiting for you." Dominic's hair was slightly mussed and beard stubble shadowed his jaw. His gaze took in Toby's protective stance and his eyes narrowed.

Was that a possessive glint in his eyes? Darn the darkness. She couldn't tell. And it didn't matter anyway. Never in her life had she been more conscious of the countdown on her days with Dominic.

She stepped around Toby. "I don't think you two were introduced the night of the ball. Dominic, this is Toby Haynes, an American NASCAR car driver and team owner. Toby, Dominic Rossi, Prince of Montagnarde."

After a moment's hesitation, Dominic offered his hand. Madeline glanced from Dominic to Toby and back as the men shook hands. Had the testosterone tide swept in? And then with a sharp nod each man released simultaneously. Had she missed something?

Madeline touched Toby's forearm and Dominic stiffened beside her. For Pete's sake, he couldn't be jealous? Could he?

She knew Dominic cared about her. No man could be as passionate and unselfish a lover without some feelings for his partner, but love? Of course not. They both knew this was a dead-end relationship.

So why did a thrill race through her? She blinked away her irrational thoughts and blamed them on that last glass of champagne—the one she'd had to try because someone told her a single bottle of Krug Clos du Mesnil cost more than her monthly mortgage payment.

"Toby, I'm going to take a rain check on your offer of an escort back to the hotel."

"You're sure?"

"Absolutely. Good night and thanks. See you tomorrow."

After a moment's hesitation, Toby pivoted and headed back toward the yacht.

"Why will you see him tomorrow?"

"A wedding thing. Why are you really here, Dominic?"

"I was impatient for your company."

"Good answer."

His gaze caressed the deep décolletage of her halter-neck gown. "You look lovely. Very sexy. Very beddable."

Her nipples tightened in response to the desire in his eyes and his voice. "Thank you."

She glanced around. "I don't see Ian. Usually, I can spot him."

Was that a guilty flush on his cheekbones? "He's not here."

Surprise and concern rippled over her. "Voluntarily? Because the guy hates to let you out of his sight. I swear he'd be in the bedroom with us if given a choice. He still doesn't trust me."

Dominic's teeth flashed white in the moonlight, but his tight smile didn't completely erase the strain deepening the lines on his face. "He feels he failed me where you're concerned and it disturbs him."

He took her hand in his and guided her away from the harbor. "I used to be very good at giving Ian the slip. I decided to see if I still could."

"Hmm. So you have a few drops of rebel in your blue blood. I like that. And Fernand?"

"I informed him you'd been invited to spend the night on the yacht."

"I was. But I declined. As you well know." Amelia, Candace and Stacy had accepted. She glanced up and down the uncrowded area. Parts of Monaco rocked late into the night. This wasn't one of them. "Is it safe—for you, I mean—to wander the streets alone?"

Dominic shrugged. "Monaco is the safest country in the world. And I'm wearing tracking devices and carrying a panic button."

"So what's the plan? I'm guessing you didn't sneak out just to sneak back in again."

"Have I mentioned that I find your intelligence a turn-on?"

Her pulse spiked. "At least a dozen times. So what gives?"

"I'd like to walk through Monaco-Ville and enjoy the musicians and magicians of the Midsummer Night's Festival." He studied her shoes. "Or should we find a piano bar and sit?"

"Lucky for you, my shoes are not the kamikaze kind despite the stiletto heels." What had he told her? He wanted to feel like a man instead of a monarch? There weren't many gifts she could give a prince, but she could handle that request. She looped her arm through his. "Let's walk—if you're sure it's safe."

His hand covered hers on his forearm. He held her gaze. "I would never do anything to endanger you, Madeline."

"I know. You're a prince of a guy," she replied tongue in cheek. "Besides, you know you'll get lucky if you get me back to the hotel safely."

Dominic choked a laugh, dragged her into a shadowy alcove and covered her mouth with his. She *mmmphed* a protest through smiling lips, but dug her fingers into his waist and pulled him closer. Her smile faded as the heat of his body seeped into hers and hunger for Dominic took control of her brain. His lips were firm and his kisses hard and desperate with a dangerous edge that stopped just shy of being too rough.

The unusual aggression turned her on like nobody's business. By the time he lifted his head her heart raced and her legs quivered like a marathon runner's after crossing the finish line.

He leaned his forehead against hers and sucked in deep breaths. "Your puns are terrible. Stick to medicine."

"Your wish is my command, Your Royal Buffness," she replied with a wink and curtsied as she often had during the past five days. She only did it because she'd discovered how much kowtowing irritated him. As usual her smart-aleck quip made him chuckle. Good. She wanted to ease whatever somber mood had taken hold of him.

They strolled through the streets of Monaco-Ville for over an hour enjoying music, magic and sharing vendor foods like any other couple. But that was the catch. They weren't like any other couple and never could be. Tonight was a stolen moment—one they'd never repeat. The realization saddened Madeline enough to make her eyes burn and her chest hurt.

Dominic must have misinterpreted her silence as tiredness, for he waved down a taxi to carry them back to the hotel. When they arrived he silently escorted her inside, and then backed her against the wainscoted elevator wall, cradled her face in his hands and looked deep into her eyes.

"I will never forget our time together." The gravity of his voice made the fine hairs on her body rise.

"Neither will I."

And then he kissed her. She knew she was in trouble because she couldn't hold him tight enough, couldn't burrow close enough. And she didn't want to let him go.

Oh, my God. I'm falling for him.

Her stomach plunged as if the elevator had dropped to the basement. She gasped and broke the kiss.

The doors opened on the penthouse floor. Dominic threaded his fingers through hers and stepped toward the doors, but Madeline's muscles refused to engage. Had she been fooling herself by believing she could have an affair without her heart getting involved?

No. No. It's not love. It's only a crush. A crush due to circumstances, romantic settings, a man larger than life and a surplus of sexual satisfaction.

"Madeline?"

She blinked and swallowed. She wasn't dumb enough to fall for a prince. Was she?

Nope. Not love. Her rapid pulse, quickening breaths and the tension swirling in her belly were by-products of sexual arousal. Nothing more. And her chest ached only because Dominic had become a friend—a friend she'd soon have to say goodbye to.

Mentally kick-starting her muscles into motion, she traveled down the corridor beside him, tiptoed into the suite and then his bedroom. The covers looked rumpled, as if Dominic had been in bed but unable to sleep before coming after her. The bedside lamp cast a dim glow over the room. The digital clock read 2:00 a.m. She'd been up since 5:00 a.m. and should be exhausted, but energy hummed through her veins.

Behind her, the door lock clicked. She turned her head.

Dominic leaned against the panel with his hands behind his back. "Undress for me."

"Is that a royal command?"

"Need it be?"

"You first."

His lips twitched. He shook his head, but kicked off his shoes and reached for his belt. "Some man needs to tame you."

"*Pfft.* That'll never happen."

"I know. It's part of your charm." The belt slid free. He tossed it aside. "Your turn."

The longer this took the more time she'd have with him. Tomorrow—today—was Saturday. Candace didn't have a meeting and Madeline didn't have to be anywhere until noon. She and Dominic could sleep the morning away if they wanted. She kicked off her shoes and removed the silver clip from her hair.

Dominic removed his watch. She mirrored the action.

Without a word Dominic fisted his shirt, yanked the tails free and then reached beneath the fabric to unfasten his pants. His trousers slid to the floor. He kicked them aside.

All she could see was his great legs beneath the shirttail hem. "Tease. Two can play that game."

She reached beneath her dress and removed her panties. She shot them toward him like a rubber band. He caught the scrap of black lace, crushed it in his hand and stroked it across his cheek. He dropped her panties and shoved his briefs to the floor. A kick piled them on top of his discarded pants.

She released the button fastening the halter top of her dress at her nape and squared her shoulders. The black satin fabric fell to her waist, revealing her breasts.

Dominic's sharply indrawn breath broke the silence of the

room. He swiftly unbuttoned his shirt, fumbling with a few
of the buttons as if his fingers refused to cooperate, and then
ripped it off and flung it aside, leaving him naked. His thick
arousal rose from a tangle of dark golden curls. A bead of
moisture glistened on the tip.

She wet her lips, curled her fingers against the need to
stroke him and turned her back. "Zip?"

She didn't hear him approach. Her first inkling that he had
was the touch of his lips on her shoulder, and then his hands
spanned her waist and slid up to cup her breasts. He rolled
the tightened tips in his fingers. Desire coiled tightly between
her legs. She leaned against him. His hard, hot erection
pressed against her spine and his beard stubble erotically
rasped her neck as he sipped a string of kisses on her skin. He
murmured something in a language she couldn't understand.

She lifted a hand to cradle his face, stroke his bristly jaw
and trace his soft, parted lips. She turned her head and whispered against his lips, "No fair. Speak English."

He ignored her request, lowered her zipper and pushed her
dress from her hips. And then he pulled her flush against him
and bound her close with his strong arms.

She'd miss this. His strength. His gentleness. His passion.
The radiator-hot warmth of his hard body against her, surrounding her.

He stroked and caressed her, her breasts, her belly, her
bottom and finally, the knot of need between her legs. Her
muscles quivered with each deft stroke. She could barely
stand. And then he scooped her into his arms and carried her
to the bed. Madeline gasped. She'd never had a man literally
sweep her off her feet. And she liked it.

She roped her arms around his neck and pulled him down
with her. His thigh parted hers, but instead of taking her he

lay beside her, burying his erection against her hip instead of inside her where she wanted it, needed it, craved it. She wanted him to hurry, but his hands mapped her body with slow precision, tracing each curve and indention, circling her aureole, her navel, her sex. She arched against him. He released her and twisted toward the nightstand.

Finally.

She expected to see a condom in his hand. Instead, the bracelet she'd admired at the market rested on his palm. Her heart clenched. "Dominic, you shouldn't have. But how did you...?"

"Ian purchased it for me. Accept this as a reminder of our time together."

How could she refuse? "Thank you."

She lifted her wrist. He slipped it on and then kissed each of her knuckles.

This feels like goodbye.

A knot formed in her throat and her pulse skipped with alarm. "Dominic, are you leaving tomorrow?"

"No departure date has been set." He sipped his way to her elbow, her shoulder, her neck. Madeline shoved aside her disquiet and lost herself in his passionate possession of her mouth. His hands seemed to be everywhere, arousing her, coaxing her, stroking her. She returned his embrace, sculpting the muscles of his shoulders, his back, his buttocks. His soft lips traveled over skin made more sensitive by the rasp of his evening beard.

Need spiraled inside her, coiling tighter and tighter until she squirmed beneath him. "Please."

He rose over her and eased inside her one tantalizing inch at a time. No condom, a corner of her mind insisted. But condoms didn't matter. She was protected. And she wanted to be as close to Dominic tonight as she possibly could be.

He withdrew and thrust deep. She countered his every move again and again until the tingles of orgasm, headier than that glass of expensive champagne, bubbled through her, racking her body with pleasure.

Dominic groaned her name against her neck and then crashed in her arms.

She held him tight.

And wasn't sure she ever wanted to let him go.

Madeline jolted upright in the bed.

Dominic's bed.

She shoved her tangled hair out of her face and blinked, trying to clear her groggy mind and her vision. What had woken her? She looked around. No clue.

Dominic's side. Empty. She smoothed a hand over the pillow. Cool. Checked the clock—11:00 a.m. She'd overslept. Oops.

A smile flitted across her lips. She'd had good reason for snoozing late. But now she'd have to hurry. Candace had a noon appointment with the bishop at St. Nicholas Cathedral and she wanted her wedding party to be there. That included Madeline.

Why hadn't Dominic woken her as he'd done every other morning? With kisses and caresses and slow and easy lovemaking? Because she'd forgotten to tell him about the church thing and it wasn't on the calendar she'd given him.

Unfamiliar masculine voices penetrated the closed bedroom door. She snatched the covers up to cover her nakedness.

Dominic had company. She had to get dressed.

Her dress lay draped across the back of the chair instead of puddled on the floor where he'd dropped it. Her panties, hair clip, purse and shoes sat in the chair. She tossed back the covers, raced toward her clothing, scooped up the bundle and ducked into the lavish bathroom only to skid to a halt.

Eeek. Her hair resembled a frizzy string mop and the remnants of her makeup looked hideous. She dumped her stuff on the counter, quickly braided her hair and then bent to wash her face. She brushed her teeth with her finger and a dab of Dominic's toothpaste. Better. Not great. Will have to do.

The bathroom light glinted on the bracelet. Her quick smile turned into a frown. Should she hide in here or leave?

Leave unless you want to arrive at the church looking like last night's leftovers.

She tugged on her clothing and stepped into her heels. The ensemble might have been fabulous last night, but at eleven in the morning it looked exactly like what it was—the outfit of a woman who'd spent the night.

"So," Madeline mumbled to herself, "how are you going to get out of the suite?"

The only entrance lay through the sitting room. Past Dominic and his visitors. In last night's wrinkled dress. Ugh.

She returned to the bedroom. She could still hear the voices, but it sounded as if the men had moved to the balcony—the balcony spanning the entire suite, including the bedroom. Her gaze darted to the window. Curtains closed. Whew.

The balcony. That could be good. She could slip out the front door while they were outside and maybe they wouldn't see her. Still, she listened at the bedroom door for a few seconds before daring to slowly twist the knob and ease the panel open a couple of cautious inches.

"Wedding preparations will begin at once," a male voice pronounced.

Wedding? Madeline peeked out the door. Dominic and two older men stood on the balcony. One, of perhaps sixty, had a thick head of silvered blond hair, Dominic's erect posture and bone structure. The other was older, more wizened looking. A little bent. Bald.

She scanned the rest of the room and slammed into Ian's dark stare. Her heart stuttered. He stood stiffly on the far side of the room. Uh-oh. Unless Dominic had told him, Ian hadn't known she was here. She put a finger to her lips in the universal "be quiet" symbol. He didn't respond with as much as a blink.

"And if I'm not ready to return?" Dominic asked. He wore last night's clothing, but his black shirt and pants didn't look as out of place as her cocktail dress. He hadn't shaved and his hair looked as if it had only been finger-combed.

"You knew that as soon as your bride was chosen you would have to return home," the thick-haired one replied.

Bride?

Madeline's world slowed to a standstill.

Bride? Her heart bolted into a racing rhythm. Dominic was getting married? To whom? Warmth—*hope*—filled her chest before she could stymie it.

Whoa. Where had that come from?

"I'm not ready. I need more time." Dominic again.

"Why? So you can play here with your paramour? I have seen the papers and heard the reports. Do you think I don't know where you were last night and with whom?" the regal guy asked.

Paramour. Madeline's brain snagged on the word and her stomach plunged.

Paramour. *Her.*

Not the bride in question. The strength seeped from her limbs. She leaned weakly against the doorjamb and closed her eyes. The tremor started deep inside and worked its way to her extremities.

What is your problem? You knew he wasn't going to marry you.

"I have promised to do as you wish, Father. I will take a bride. One of the council's choosing. But I need more time."

A bride of the council's choosing? Her confused brain couldn't make sense of that.

"Her family awaits your arrival," baldy said. "Promises have been made and agreements signed. The jet will fly you to Luxembourg this afternoon. Your father has brought your grandmother's engagement ring. You will propose tomorrow. A gala to announce and celebrate the engagement will take place next Saturday evening."

Nausea. Dizziness. Rapid heart rate. Cold, clammy hands. Shock, Madeline diagnosed. She struggled to inhale, but it hurt too much. Pain sliced through her like an explosion of surgical blades.

What had Dominic said that day in the café? He wasn't *committed to anyone at this time?* She remembered the exact words because she'd thought it an odd answer. As odd as him saying he wanted to share a bed for reasons other than duty, greed or fleeting attraction. She hadn't understood then. She did now.

He'd been planning to marry all along. A woman of some mysterious council's choosing.

She'd never been more to him than a way to pass the time while awaiting the name of his bride.

God, she hurt. Which made absolutely no sense.

Why? Why does it hurt so much?

Because, fool, you fell in love with him.

You knew this was temporary and that he was out of your reach. And you fell for him anyway.

She bit her lip to stop a whimper of pain. She loved him.

Did you expect him to marry a commoner like Prince Rainier did?

And what about virgins? Did you conveniently forget that Dominic, like Prince Charles, might have to marry a virgin?

Her hands fisted and her nails dug into her palms. At some point her subconscious must have started believing in fairy tales. Otherwise she wouldn't be feeling as if she'd been shoved off the deck of an ocean liner. Adrift. Drowning. Lost.

Ian. She suddenly remembered the unfriendly bodyguard. Her gaze found his. How often had he witnessed the crash of a woman's world? A woman who'd fallen in love with his unattainable boss.

Hurt and humiliated, she silently closed the door, staggered back into the bedroom and braced her arms on the desk. How could she sneak out when she could barely walk?

She couldn't face Dominic. Couldn't look into his eyes and know that the man she loved was destined to marry someone else.

One more pertinent fact he'd neglected to mention.

She'd been nothing more to him than a vacation fling. A no-strings-attached affair.

A half laugh, half sob burst from her lips. She shoved her fist against her mouth to stifle the pitiful sound. He'd given her *exactly* what she asked for. And it was breaking her heart.

He may have avoided full disclosure, but she was the one who'd set up the parameters and then screwed up and broken the rules by falling in love. Sucking in a fortifying breath, she squared her shoulders. She would never let him know how badly he'd hurt her.

She sank into the chair, yanked open the desk drawer and extracted a piece of hotel stationery and a pen. The pen slipped from her fingers. Twice. Her hands shook so badly she could barely put the tip to the page.

Pull it together before Dominic comes in here and finds you wrecked.

Gulping deep, painful breaths, she struggled for calm, the way she did when a heinous accident landed in her E.R.

She would not act like those shameless women who'd flung themselves at him at the ball. She wouldn't beg for crumbs of his attention. She had too much pride for that. And she would cling to what was left of her tattered pride until her last breath.

What she needed was a cool, emotionless, nonnegotiable goodbye. A final goodbye. Because she didn't want him to come looking for her. She couldn't bear a face-to-face encounter because she didn't think she could hide her feelings, and he would pity her if he figured out her secret. Or worse, he'd be patient and polite and detached—the way he'd been with the other women who'd made their availability so obvious.

Gritting her teeth, she formed each letter, each word, each painful phrase until she had nothing left to say. At least nothing she could or would print. And then she folded the stationery and rested her head on the desk.

Empty. She felt completely drained and empty inside.

As far as Dear Johns went, hers sucked. But she didn't have time for another draft. She straightened and shoved the note into an envelope. Her mouth was too dry to lick the seal, so she tucked in the flap and earned herself a paper cut for her trouble. She sucked the stinging wound.

How fitting that her goodbye left her cut and bleeding. Dominic had cut out her heart without even trying.

She stared at the bracelet. Should she leave it with the note? No. She wanted something to remind her not to put her trust in men. Each time she'd done so she'd been hurt.

The bedroom door opened. Startled, she sprang to her feet and spun around, clutching the letter to her chest.

Ian stepped inside and closed the door. His face showed no emotions. "I will show you out."

How many times had he said those words? "Do you always clean up his messes?"

"Dominic doesn't make messes."

She blinked in surprise. The man rarely spoke to her. She hadn't expected an answer. And Ian had used Dominic's name instead of his title. Progress. But too late.

He noted her cut, opened a dresser drawer, withdrew a white handkerchief and offered it to her.

Dominic's handkerchief. She carried it to her nose and inhaled a faint trace of his cologne and then wrapped it around her finger in a compression bandage. "How are you going to get me past Dominic's guests?"

"The Royal Suite has a hidden escape exit. Come with me." He stalked into the walk-in closet, bypassed Dominic's neatly hanging clothing and perfectly aligned shoes and twisted a fleur-de-lis at the base of the sconce light on the far wall. A panel slid sideways to reveal a dimly lit space beyond.

She edged forward, leaned in and looked at the shadowy area. "Where will this take me?"

"Follow the hall to the fire stairs."

So this was it. She was being shuffled out the back door like…a mistress. She gulped down tears of shame and loss and looked at the note in her hand. She should have left it on the desk.

"Would you give this to him?" She stabbed it toward Ian. After a moment's hesitation he accepted it. The guy didn't like her. Would he deliver her message?

Madeline cupped his hand with hers and looked into his dark eyes. "And, Ian, please, *please,* keep him safe."

Ten

"She's a child." Dominic stared at the photograph in dismay. "What will I have in common with such a baby?"

"She is nineteen. The same age as your first wife when you married," Ricardo, the Minister of State and senior council member said as he laid three more photographs of the pale blonde on the glass-topped balcony table. "Young enough to bear many heirs."

Disgust rolled through Dominic. It wasn't the girl's fault. She was attractive enough, but far too young for his tastes. He preferred mature women. Women who weren't too shy, insecure or inexperienced to speak their minds. Women like Madeline.

He looked over his shoulder at the closed bedroom door. Time had run out. He'd have to tell Madeline the truth and then say goodbye. He wouldn't get to show her Paris or Venice as planned. An odd sensation of panic bound his chest, making it difficult to breath.

His gaze returned to the picture in his hand. He'd always known his obligations to Montagnarde took precedence over his personal wishes. He led a privileged life, but those privileges came at a price. "Have I ever met her?"

"Twice, she says."

He had no recollection of either occasion. This young woman had made no impression on him whatsoever. That did not bode well for their future. And yet he was expected to marry her, bed her, impregnate her. The sooner the better.

His father placed a hand on his shoulder. "Love will come, Dominic. It did for your mother and I and for each of your sisters. It did with Giselle." His fingers tightened, released. "Ricardo and I are in need of sustenance. We will adjourn to the dining room downstairs. Clean up and join us."

The pair left, the suite door clicking shut behind them. Their bodyguards would be waiting outside. Only Dominic's insistence had kept Ian present for this confidential meeting. Matters such as this required the utmost discretion.

Dominic faced the bedroom door with a growing sense of dread. When Ian's knock had awoken him this morning, Dominic had not suspected the upheaval about to take place. And then Ian had informed him that his father was in the elevator and on the way upstairs. The weight of Dominic's responsibilities had crashed down on him. His father's arrival had been a surprise—an unpleasant one. For the king's arrival could only indicate two things. The end of Dominic's freedom. The end of his days with Madeline.

He glanced at his wrist and realized he'd failed to don his watch in his haste to dress and get out of his room before his father entered. Since Giselle's death his father had adopted the habit of sitting in Dominic's room at the palace and discussing the upcoming day's events while Dominic dressed.

Dominic hadn't wanted to expose Madeline to the embarrassment of his father barging into the room.

He shoved a hand through his hair. He wouldn't be able to wake Madeline with leisurely lovemaking this morning as he had each day for the past week. And once he told her the truth the best interlude of his life would be over.

Over.

His future committed to someone else.

The choking sensation intensified. He tugged at his already loose collar to no avail. Loss mired his steps as he approached the bedroom. He braced himself, turned the knob, pushed open the door.

The bed was empty, the bathroom dark. He entered, searching for her hiding place. "Madeline? You can come out. They're gone."

"She is not here, Dominic," Ian said behind him.

Dominic glanced at the digital clock on the nightstand and exhaled. She usually sneaked out at dawn, but not this morning. He smiled, but the smile vanished when he realized there would be no more sunrises with Madeline.

"She's gone."

The finality of Ian's words made the back of Dominic's neck prickle and his stomach tense. "How?"

"There is an emergency exit. I showed her the way."

"Why have I never been told of this exit?"

"I feared what you would do with the knowledge." Ian offered him an envelope bearing the Hôtel Reynard insignia in the upper left corner. "She overheard your conversation with your father and the Minister of State."

Dominic closed his eyes, clenched his teeth and let his head fall back. She should have heard the words from him. Exhaling a pent-up breath, he extracted the letter and read.

Dominic

Thank you for making my vacation memorable.

I'll be swamped with wedding duties over the next week. No time for fun and games or distractions.

You were great. Just what the doctor ordered. But like any prescription, this one has run its course.

I hate goodbyes, so this is the only one you'll get.

Goodbye.

I wish you the best.

Madeline

Pain swamped him like a tsunami. He called on numbness, his familiar companion in years past, but it refused to come. He swallowed once and then again. His hands fisted, the letter crumpling in his grip.

Madeline deserved the truth. The whole truth. She needed to know how important she was to him. How magnificent a lover. How good a friend. And he had to explain why he must say goodbye. She would understand. He would make her understand. "Where is she?"

"I don't know."

"What do you mean you don't know?"

"Fernand was excused from his duty while Mademoiselle Spencer *supposedly* spent the night on the yacht. In my urgency to remove her from the suite this morning I did not call him to track her when she left this room. I assumed she would return to her suite. She did not."

"She can't have gone far. I have her passport."

"It appears both of you went missing last night which proves my point about the secret exit. I am too old for shenanigans like this, Dominic."

Censure tainted Ian's voice. Censure Dominic deserved. "She treats me like a man, Ian. Not a future king."

Ian nodded sympathetically. "I know, but you have your destiny. And if you insist on putting yourself in danger I will not be able to do what Mademoiselle Spencer asked of me. Keep you safe."

Dominic's head jerked up. He searched Ian's eyes. "She didn't leave cursing me for my deception?"

"I cannot read the woman's mind. But she was not swearing or throwing things."

"Find her."

"Dominic, perhaps it is best to let things be."

"Find her." And when Ian didn't move, Dominic added, "That is a royal command."

Ian snapped to attention, pivoted sharply and headed toward the door. Dominic had never spoken to him as harshly.

"She ran," Dominic called after him. Ian stopped without turning. "Why did she run, Ian? Madeline Spencer is no coward. She is courageous and mouthy and she fights back. The Madeline I've come to love would have been in my face and reprimanding me for another lie of omission."

His heart slammed against his ribs like a ship against an iceberg, winding him, chilling him. *Love.*

He loved her.

He loved her sassy mouth. Her earthy sensuality. Her refusal to kowtow. He loved the way she listened to his plans for Montagnarde and added her own suggestions.

He loved her. And he couldn't have her. Agreements had been signed. Promises made. Breaking them could cause an international incident.

Ian slowly turned, looking as if he, too, were shocked by Dominic's discovery.

"Why would she run?" he repeated.

"Perhaps she does not wish to engage in a losing battle, Your Highness."

Dominic didn't believe that. There had to be more. But what? He straightened the crumpled page and studied it more closely. What wasn't she saying? Despite the bland note, he knew she had feelings for him. She'd shown it in countless ways in bed and out. She'd ended things far too easily.

Dominic rubbed a hand over his bristly jaw and tried to decipher the puzzle of Madeline Spencer. Too courageous to run, replayed in his head. And then the pieces of the puzzle slid into place.

She'd only had one other lover. A man she'd believed she loved. Could she possibly love him, Dominic wondered? He could not leave Monaco without finding out.

"She would only run if it hurt too much to say goodbye," he told Ian. He ripped off his shirt. "I must shower and join my father. I want Mademoiselle Spencer found and in my suite when I return. If she wants to say goodbye, then she'll have to say it to my face."

"I need you to hide me," Madeline said as soon as she, Candace and Vincent reached the shadowy alcove of the cathedral.

"What?" Candace asked.

"Just for the rest of the day." She fussed with the buttons on the dress she'd bought in a nearby boutique rather than risk returning to her suite.

"Come again?" Vincent stood to her right presenting her with his unscarred left side. Candace said the wounds he'd sustained in the pit fire still bothered him despite the numerous plastic surgeries which had reduced the severity of his scars.

"I need to hide from Prince Dominic of Montagnarde and his henchmen," she whispered.

Candace straightened to her full five feet three inches. "Did that jerk hurt you because if he did, I'll—"

"Have you done something illegal?" Vincent interrupted.

How like a man to cut to the chase, dealing with the facts rather than the emotions. "I haven't broken any laws, and Dominic didn't hurt me. He did exactly what I asked him to do. He gave me great sex and a memorable vacation."

"But?" Candace prompted.

Madeline scrunched her eyes. Candace possessed the stubbornness of a mule. If Madeline wanted her cooperation it would cost her. The truth.

"I fell in love with him."

Candace squealed and bounced in her sandals.

"Keep it down, for crying out loud. We're in a church," Madeline whispered. "And do not say 'I told you so.' I'm a little too raw for that right now."

"But this is great!"

Vincent shifted on his feet and looked back toward the others gathered in the cathedral as if he'd rather be anywhere except the middle of a girlie tête-à-tête.

"No, it's not great. He's flying off to meet his fiancée this afternoon."

Candace's smile morphed into a fierce scowl. "He's engaged? The lying two-timing royal rat."

"He wasn't committed to anyone else until today." Madeline honestly believed that. "From what I overheard I gather some committee or other has been searching for an acceptable princess-to-be. Now they've found her. And he's going to marry her." Just saying the words made her throat feel as raw as if she had a full-blown case of strep.

She grabbed Candace's and Vincent's hands. "I won't let
you down with my wedding duties, but until Dominic is gone
I need to stay out of sight. And I can't do that by myself. I
don't know the language and I don't know the country."

"I'll handle it," Vincent said without hesitation.

"Thank you." Madeline's eyes burned, but she blinked back
the tears. If one seeped through she feared a torrent would follow.

One day. She only had to get through one more day. And
then Dominic would be gone and she could lose herself in
Candace's wedding preparations until she returned home.

She would have laughed if she weren't afraid it would turn
into hysteria. She'd come to Monaco wanting to avoid the
wedding preparations. Now she wanted to bury herself in
them and occupy her every thought with marriage minutiae
so she wouldn't have time to think of what she'd never have
with Dominic or anyone else. Because this time her heart had
sustained too much damage to ever recover.

The dining room was crowded. Too crowded for what
Dominic had to say.

He stopped beside his father's table, but waved away the
waiter who rushed forward to pull back his chair. Instead he
slipped him a large tip and asked him, "Would you please have
our luncheon served in the suite?"

"Certainly, Your Highness." The man hustled toward the
kitchen.

"Dominic, what is the meaning of this?" his father asked.

"I have something to say and you don't want me to say it
here."

"Your Highness," Ricardo began, but Dominic silenced him
with a frown. The councilman, who'd risen at Dominic's
approach, shifted on his feet and looked to his king for guidance.

Dominic's father rose. "Very well, son. If we must."

The return to the suite passed in tense silence due to the presence of other hotel guests in the elevator. Dominic recognized Derek Reynard, the owner and CEO of the world-renowned Reynard Hotel chain, and his wife. It was the perfect opportunity for Dominic to introduce himself and ask for a meeting to discuss the construction of a Hôtel Reynard in Montagnarde, but he had more important matters to deal with at the moment. The couple turned toward Madeline's suite. He wanted to follow, but first he had to deal with more critical issues.

The moment Ian closed the suite door behind them, Dominic faced his father. "I cannot marry the girl the council has chosen."

The minister sputtered. Dominic feared the septuagenarian might have a heart attack.

Dominic's father tensed, but otherwise showed no reaction. "Why not?"

"Because the woman I love is here in Monaco."

"And what of your duty to the crown?"

"I willingly serve my country, but I should not be cursed with an indifferent marriage due to a three-hundred-year-old custom. That custom, like our economy, needs modernizing."

"What of the agreements, Your Highness?" Ricardo asked. "The negotiations?"

"I'll renounce my title, if my decision causes difficulties for Montagnarde, but I will not marry that child or any other the council selects. I would rather live in exile than spend my life with a woman I care nothing about. I'm not a stud whose sole purpose is to service a mare."

"You would leave your family and your country for this woman you've been consorting with during your stay in Monaco?" his father asked.

"Yes, sir. I prefer to live happily elsewhere with Madeline than miserably at home without her."

"Doing what, Dominic? How will you support yourself and your wife if you leave your title and fortune behind?"

"I have the qualifications and connections to find work in the hotel industry."

His father's eyebrows rose. "You would work as a commoner? Draw a salary. Pay a mortgage?"

"Yes."

"What of your plans to develop Montagnarde's tourist potential?"

"I would mourn the loss of my dream, but not as much I would regret losing Madeline. I have dedicated the past fifteen years of my life to the betterment of Montagnarde. My plan is a sound one, and with or without me you should pursue it. But I would walk away from it all in an instant for her."

"What makes you think she's worthy of becoming a queen?"

"She's intelligent and courageous and doesn't have an obsequious bone in her body. She doesn't care about my title or wealth, and she fights me for the check after dinner. She calls me the most hideous names." Your Royal Beefcake, His Serene Sexiness and Sir Lickalot were but a few. The memories brought a smile to his lips.

His father's eyes narrowed speculatively. "She's never married?"

Dominic sucked a surprised breath at the question which cracked open the door to possibility.

Ian cleared his throat, drawing the king's attention. "Your Majesty, if I may speak?" He waited for acknowledgment. "I have the full report on Mademoiselle Spencer if you wish to peruse it."

The king made a go-ahead motion with his hand and Ian

left the room and returned with a folder. He opened it and read, "Madeline Marie Spencer, thirty-two, has never married although she has had one long engagement. She has no children, graduated near the top of her university class and is currently employed as a physician's assistant in a trauma center in Charlotte, North Carolina, U.S.A., where she is well-respected by her peers. Her credit rating is excellent, her personal debt minimal, and she has no criminal record. Not even a parking ticket. Her father, a policeman, is deceased and her mother is a retired schoolteacher."

"Where is she, this paragon?" Dominic's father asked.

"She has not been located, Your Majesty, since she left the hotel this morning. At Prince Dominic's request, we are searching."

Dominic's frustration level rose. He had to find her.

"I would like to meet this woman who has mesmerized my son in such a short time. When she's found bring her here." His attention returned to Dominic. "This will not be without complications, you understand?"

Adrenaline pulsed through Dominic's system at his father's acceptance. "I do."

"She has accepted your suit?"

"I have not been free to state my intentions."

"But, Your Majesty, the agreements… This could cause a diplomatic scandal," Ricardo protested.

Dominic's father held up a hand to silence him. "My son has had enough unhappiness in his life, Ricardo. Dominic and I will deal with the agreements. We will fly to Luxembourg this afternoon to personally make our apologies and any reparations required." He turned back to Dominic. "You're sure she's the one?"

"I've never been more certain of anything in my life."

"And do you believe she will accept your proposal?"

Tension invaded his limbs. "I don't know, Papa. But if I can't have Madeline I don't want anyone else."

"I don't know why you couldn't just use your passkey and take Madeline's passport from Dominic's room safe," Candace whispered to Vincent in the hallway of the American Consulate on Tuesday afternoon.

"Because it's stealing," Vincent replied patiently for the third time. "The hotel cannot afford the reputation of violating its guests."

"But it's *hers*."

"Stop," Madeline interjected. "As much as I love you, Candace, Vincent's right. We can't go digging around the safe just because we *think* my passport might be there. I've reported it lost and the consulate guys have promised to put a rush on it. I should have a replacement before I fly home on Sunday."

Madeline leaned against the wall beside the exit while Vincent stepped outside and signaled the waiting car. She slid on her new oversize Jackie-O sunglasses and covered her hair with a silk scarf. Disguised like a fugitive and her only crime was falling for the wrong guy.

She grimaced. "I can't believe Dominic didn't check out of the hotel. Why is he keeping the suite? Is he coming back? I can't go on riding in the floorboard of Vincent's car and hiding at his apartment."

Candace squeezed her hand. "You have no choice. Dominic had that Fernand guy following you. You had to disappear. You'll only be riding in floorboards and sneaking up service elevators for a few more days."

"But you had to reschedule everything except the wedding and rehearsal party because Dominic had my schedule."

"Like that's the worst catastrophe to ever befall a bride. Jeez, get over it, Madeline. I've said it's not a big deal."

But it was a big deal. Candace had enough stress dealing with planning a wedding in a foreign country. She didn't need the additional pressure of shuffling times and meeting places at the last minute because of Madeline's mistake.

"Maybe I should just see him and get it over with when he returns. *If* he returns."

She hoped it wouldn't kill her. God knows, losing Mike had never hurt like this. But then she'd realized in the three days since her affair with Dominic had ended that Mike's defection had hurt her pride not her heart. She'd been more concerned with what her coworkers thought of her for being so easily duped than with Mike's leaving.

She hadn't loved Mike. Not the way she loved Dominic.

Not once had she pictured herself growing old with Mike. She'd focused more on the house and children they'd have and thought more about being a mother than a wife. Not so with Dominic. She'd miss waking up beside him, making love with him and listening to his aspirations in the darkness. She'd miss his stupid little bows, the way he could melt her with his smile and his loyalty to the hulking Ian. Children? Oh yeah, a few little princes and princesses would have been nice, too, but Dominic was the main attraction.

"No, you won't confront him," Candace interrupted her pity party. "There's no reason to put yourself through that. And he might have *her* with him."

Madeline flinched. Good point. She didn't really want to come face-to-face with the woman who would be living *her* dream.

"Your Dear John generously gave him an easy out—which is more than he deserved, if you ask me. I think you should have skewered his nuts and roasted them over the barbecue." Candace held up her hands. "I know. I know. He made no promises. I got the stringless affair part the first time you explained it. And even though I thought it was a dumb idea, I really thought he was the right guy for you, Madeline. I've never seen you as happy. And I'm seriously peeved over being wrong."

At Vincent's signal Madeline and Candace raced to the car stopped by the curb and scooted in, and then Vincent turned around and looked at Madeline over the back of the seat. Her stomach sank at his serious expression.

"The hotel called. Rossi's back."

Eleven

Twenty-four more hours and she'd be gone.

Madeline kept to the outer fringes of the large private garden housing the wedding reception. An hour ago she'd completed her bridesmaid duties. The happy couple had danced their first dance and cut the cake. By this time tomorrow Madeline would be winging her way back to the States.

She didn't understand why Dominic was still looking for her unless it was to return her passport—an item he could easily leave at the hotel's front desk. Last night he'd shown up uninvited at the posh Italian Restaurant where the dinner following Candace and Vincent's civil service had been held and demanded to speak to her. Luckily, Madeline had spotted him before he'd seen her, and she'd been able to make a hasty exit out a side door through the kitchens and into the back alley.

Today she'd been so tense during the religious ceremony

at the cathedral that she'd barely heard the service. She'd kept expecting Dominic to burst through the doors, and she'd startled at every sound. She felt guilty as hell for tainting her friend's special event with unpleasant thoughts, but Candace, bless her, was taking Madeline's distraction in stride.

During the past week Madeline had adopted Amelia's habit of watching entertainment TV and reading the English tabloid papers. She kept waiting for news of Dominic's engagement to break.

Wait a minute.

Madeline dropped the leaf she'd been folding like sloppy origami. According to what she'd overheard in Dominic's suite last Saturday, the official announcement of his engagement would be made tonight at a gala in Luxembourg. Loss weighted her stomach and goose bumps crept over her skin despite the sunny day and comfortable temperatures. She hugged her silk stole around her bare shoulders.

If Dominic was there, he couldn't be here. Right?

Right.

So she didn't need to hide out here in the dappled shade of the lemon trees. She could rejoin the party and celebrate her friend's happiness.

She could even find it in her battered heart to be happy for Mike because he'd deserved more than the indifferent emotion—Dominic had diagnosed her failed engagement well—Madeline had offered. And her feelings for Mike had been indifferent, she admitted, because she'd held back and never fully committed her heart. He was still a jerk for cheating, but part of the failure of their relationship rested squarely on her shoulders.

Picking up her discarded bouquet from the stone bench, she made her way back across the flagstones to the center of the patio and stopped by Candace's side. Her friend's radiant smile faded and a worried look took its place.

Madeline hugged her. "Don't look like that. I am happy for you. Both of you."

And she meant it. Just because her dreams hadn't come true didn't mean she couldn't be thrilled her friends' had.

Candace took her hand. "You know I love you, right?"

Madeline stiffened. The back of her neck prickled. Why did that sound ominous? "Candace…?"

Madeline shot an anxious glance toward the château and spotted Makos. Her breath left in a whoosh. She turned toward the back corner of the garden where she'd been hiding, and saw Fernand yards away from her hiding spot. She then saw Ian in the opposite corner. Panic fluttered in her belly and squeezed her lungs. She spun left, right, searching for an exit, but every escape route had been blocked by a bodyguard. Members of the royal security team wore blank faces and had stiff bearings. Her years of exposure to law enforcement officers made them easy for her to pick out of the crowd.

Gulp.

"Dominic's here," she croaked.

Candace's fingers tightened. "Yes."

Bewildered, Madeline stared at her friend and tried to comprehend the betrayal.

She had to get out of here.

Toby blocked her path, parked a big paw on her shoulder. "Hear him out, Madeline. And then if you still want me to, I'll beat the crap out of him."

Madeline scanned the faces around her. Amelia and Toby, Candace and Vincent, Stacy and Franco. Were they all in on this? She clenched her teeth on a panicked, furious cry.

The bodyguards closed in until she was surrounded by a circle of dark-suited men. Three she could handle. A dozen? Probably not. Her heart raced, her mouth dried and adrenaline flooded her bloodstream.

Run, her conscience screamed.

No, dammit, I am no coward. I am through running.

But I can't let him know how much he's hurt me.

Madeline closed her eyes, inhaled deeply and exhaled slowly, fighting to still the tremors racking her. When she lifted her lids Dominic stood inside the circle and only two yards away. He wore a black suit with what she now recognized as Montagnarde's gold crest on the breast and a white open-collared shirt. His brushed-back hair accentuated his smooth-shaven jaw, but beneath his tan his face looked pale. A thin, white line rimmed his mouth and his blue eyes stared somberly into hers.

The silver-haired man, Dominic's father, stood to Dominic's right, the bald guy to his left.

"Why aren't you in Luxembourg?" she choked out.

"Father, this is the woman who held a knife to my throat and threatened my life," Dominic announced clearly, distinctly and loud enough for the crowd surrounding them to hear.

The guests' gasps barely registered. Why would he cause a scene? He knew how much she hated publicity. Madeline lifted her chin. "Tattletale. You asked for it."

Dominic's father stepped forward. "Mademoiselle, in Montagnarde threatening the life of a monarch is a serious offense."

That wasn't news. She narrowed her eyes. She looked from one man to the other. Why were they replaying this?

"There is only one way to commute the sentence," the bald guy said. "The accused must look the victim in the eye and swear she doesn't love him."

Her heart stopped. In a second someone was going to have to start CPR. But then her heart spontaneously jolted back into rhythm which meant she had to live through this instead of conveniently dying of mortification.

She sought Dominic's gaze. How could he ask that of her? How could he publicly humiliate her this way? "And if I refuse to participate in this ridiculous charade?"

Posture erect and looking totally regal, he closed the gap between them, stopping a foot away. "You stole from me, Madeline Spencer."

Confused, she blinked and shook her head. "Ian gave me that handkerchief and you bought me this bracelet. I never took anything else."

"You took the most important thing." His eyes and mouth softened. "You took my heart."

She gasped and struggled to make sense of his words. Was this a cruel joke? Was he going to marry his princess and ask Madeline to be his mistress or something? She glanced at Candace and saw tears streaming down her friend's smiling face.

She turned back to Dominic. "What about your bride-to-be? The one the council chose? The one who's supposed to wear your grandmother's ring? The one you're supposed to get engaged to tonight, for Pete's sake?"

Dominic's gaze didn't waver. "I agreed to marry without love because I never believed I would find it again."

A smile lifted one corner of his mouth. He lifted a hand and cradled her face. She wanted so badly to lean into his touch that it took all her strength to jerk away.

"When you held that knife to my throat you changed my life, Madeline. I have never known a woman with your courage. No other woman treats me like a man instead of a monarch. And no other woman loves me as completely and unselfishly as you do."

She flinched. *He knew.* A lie of denial sprang to her lips, but the intense emotion in his eyes made her forget the words.

"Tell me I'm wrong, Madeline. Tell me you don't love me, and I'll walk away."

She wanted to believe. God, she wanted to believe what she thought he was saying. Her breath shuddered in and then out.

"I'm not a virgin. And you know it," she whispered.

His eyes twinkled with laughter. "Good thing that's not a requirement."

Her eyes and chest burned. She blinked rapidly to keep the tears—happy, hopeful tears—at bay and extended her arms, wrists together. "I guess you're going to have to cuff me and take me into custody. Because I can't lie."

Dominic's eyes widened. Surprise and happiness filled their depths and a brief smile flashed across his lips before he once more donned the serious mask. "Then I hereby sentence you to life, Madeline Spencer. Life with me."

He dropped to his knee and bowed his head. For a moment it looked as if he said a silent prayer. Then Dominic's gold-tipped lashes lifted and his bedroom blue eyes found hers. "Marry me, Madeline. Be my friend. My lover. My wife. And one day, my queen."

He reached into his pocket and withdrew an exquisite emerald ring in an antique-looking gold setting.

She pressed her trembling fingers to her lips. A warm tear slid over her fingertip. "You forgot your handcuffs?"

He grinned. "I promise I'll find them later if you say yes."

She looked at Dominic's father and found acceptance and even approval in his face. "You're okay with this? Clearly, I'm not princess material."

"I beg to differ, mademoiselle. Now give my son the answer he desires."

She stared into the face of the man she loved, the man who'd stolen her heart in a matter of moments. "I always thought I wanted an on-your-knees proposal. But I was wrong."

Uncertainty flickered in Dominic's eyes.

"It's not how the proposal is delivered that matters. It's who's asking the question." She caressed his cheek, cupped his smooth jaw and stroked a finger over his lips. "Get up, Dominic. I refuse to have this discussion unless we're eye-to-eye, face-to-face and heart-to-heart."

He slowly rose.

"You are such a romantic. I love it. And I love you." She rose on her tiptoes and brushed her lips to his. She tasted tears. "Yes, Dominic, I'll marry you."

His arms banded around her with crushing force and he lifted her off the ground. The crowd surrounding them let out a deafening cheer.

Dominic set her down and kissed her so gently her heart swelled to squeeze the air from her lungs. He pulled back a fraction and braced his forehead against hers. "I love you, Madeline."

He cradled her face, brushing her tears away with his thumbs. "I hope you know what you're getting into. Royal weddings are extravagant affairs."

Madeline laughed. She never thought she'd be grateful for those six wasted years. "I have a little wedding planning experience. As long as I have you, I can handle it."

* * * * *

Look for
The Playboy's Passionate Pursuit,
the next book by Emilie Rose

Coming in July 2008
from Desire™

Two men have vowed to protect the women they love...

New York Times bestselling author
DIANA PALMER

Hard to Handle

Hunter

On a top secret operation in the desert, chief of
security Hunter knew Jennifer Marist needed his
protection. Soon he discovered the lure of Jenny's
wild, sweet passion – and a love he'd never
dreamed possible.

Man in Control

Eight years after DEA agent Alexander Cobb had
turned Jodie Clayburn down, Alexander could
hardly believe the beauty that Jodie had become...
or that she'd helped him crack a dangerous
drug-smuggling case. Would the man in control
finally surrender to his desires?

Available 20th June 2008

2 Books
and a surprise gift!

We would like to take this opportunity to thank you for reading this Mills & Boon® book by offering you the chance to take TWO more specially selected titles from the Desire™ series absolutely FREE! We're also making this offer to introduce you to the benefits of the Mills & Boon® Reader Service™—

- ★ FREE home delivery
- ★ FREE gifts and competitions
- ★ FREE monthly Newsletter
- ★ Exclusive Reader Service offers
- ★ Books available before they're in the shops

Accepting these FREE books and gift places you under no obligation to buy, you may cancel at any time, even after receiving your free shipment. Simply complete your details below and return the entire page to the address below. You don't even need a stamp!

YES! Please send me 2 free Desire books and a surprise gift. I understand that unless you hear from me, I will receive 3 superb new titles every month for just £4.99 each, postage and packing free. I am under no obligation to purchase any books and may cancel my subscription at any time. The free books and gift will be mine to keep in any case.

D8ZEF

Ms/Mrs/Miss/Mr ....Initials ....

Surname .... **BLOCK CAPITALS PLEASE**

Address..

....

....Postcode ....

Send this whole page to:
UK: FREEPOST CN81, Croydon, CR9 3WZ